Alex Kava dedicated herself to writing in 1996, having had a successful career in PR and advertising. Praised by critics and fans alike, Alex Kava's Maggie O'Dell novels, *A Perfect Evil*, *Split Second*, *The Soul Catcher* and *A Necessary Evil*, have all been *New York Times* bestsellers as well as appearing on bestseller lists around the world.

Alex
KAVA

The Soul
Catcher

HARLEQUIN® MIRA®

First published in Great Britain 2002. This edition 2016.
Harlequin MIRA, an imprint of Harlequin (UK) Limited,
Eton House, 18-24 Paradise Road,
Richmond, Surrey, TW9 1SR

© S.M. Kava 2002

ISBN 978 1 848 45127 8

60-0312

This book is dedicated to two amazing women—
fellow authors, wise mentors, treasured friends.

For
Patricia Sierra
who insisted I stay grounded, focused and
on track, then nagged me until I did.

And for
Laura Van Wormer
who insisted I could soar, then gave me a gentle
shove in the right direction.

In a year that asked more questions than provided
answers, just having the two of you believe in me
has meant more than I can ever express in words.

ACKNOWLEDGEMENTS

I'm a firm believer in sharing credit and giving thanks, so please be patient, as the list seems to grow with each book. Many thanks to all the professionals who so generously gave of their time and expertise. If I've gotten any of the facts wrong or have creatively manipulated a fact or two, blame me, not them. My appreciation and respect go to the following experts.

Amy Moore-Benson, my editor, my crusader, my creative partner and my common sense—you are truly the best.

Dianne Moggy for your patience, your focus and your wise counsel—you are a class act.

The entire crew at MIRA Books for their enthusiasm and dedication, especially Tania Charzewski, Krystyna de Duleba and Craig Swinwood. Special thanks to Alex Osuszek and an incredible sales force that continues to surpass goals and records I never dreamed to be reaching, let alone surpassing. Thanks to all of you for allowing me to be part of the team and not just the product.

Megan Underwood and the experts at Goldberg McDuffie Communications, Inc., once again, for your unflinching dedication and unquestionable expertise.

Philip Spitzer, my agent—I will forever be grateful for you taking a chance on me.

Darcy Lindner, funeral director, for answering all my morbid questions with professional grace, charm, directness and enough details to give me a tremendous respect for your profession.

Omaha police officer Tony Friend for an image of cockroaches that I'm not likely to forget.

Special Agents Jeffrey John, Art Westveer and Harry Kern for taking time out of your busy schedules at

Quantico's FBI Academy to show me around and give me some idea of what it's like to be a 'real' FBI agent and profiler. And also, thanks to Special Agent Steve Frank.

Dr Gene Egnoski, psychologist and cousin extraordinaire, for taking time to help me psychoanalyse my killers and not thinking it strange to do so. And special thanks to Mary Egnoski for listening patiently and encouraging us.

John Philpin, author and retired forensic psychologist, for generously answering without hesitation every question I've ever thrown at you.

Beth Black and your wonderful staff for your energy, your unwavering support and your friendship.

Sandy Montang and the Omaha Chapter of Sisters in Crime for your inspiration.

And once again, to all the book buyers, booksellers and book readers for making room on your lists, your shelves and in your homes for a new voice.

Special thanks to all my friends and family for their love and support, especially the following:

Patti El-Kachouti, Jeanie Shoemaker Mezger and John Mezger, LaDonna Tworek, Kenny and Connie Kava, Nicole Friend, Annie Belatti, Ellen Jacobs, Natalie Cummings and Lilyan Wilder for sticking by me during the dark days of this past year as well as celebrating the bright ones.

Marlene Haney for helping me keep things in perspective and then, of course, helping me 'deal with it.'

Sandy Rockwood for insisting you can't wait for the finished product, which in itself is always a much-appreciated pat on the back.

Mary Means for taking such loving care of my kids while I'm on the road. I couldn't do what I do without the peace of mind you provide.

Rich Kava, retired firefighter and paramedic as well as cousin and friend, for listening, encouraging, sharing your stories and always making me laugh.

Sharon Car, fellow writer and friend, for letting me vent despite my good fortune.

Richard Evnen for witty repartee, kind and genuine words of encouragement and a friendship that includes pretending I know what I'm doing, even though we both know otherwise.

Father Dave Korth for making me realise what a rare gift it is to be a 'co-creator.'

Patricia Kava, my mother, whose undeniable strength is a true inspiration.

Edward Kava, my father, who passed away October 17, 2001, and who was surely a co-creator in his own right.

And last but certainly never least, a 'from the heart' thank-you to Debbie Carlin. Your spirit and energy, your generosity, your friendship and love have made an amazing difference in my life. I will always feel blessed that our paths have crossed.

Beware the soul catcher
Who comes in a flash of light.

Trust not a word.

Meet not his eye.

Lest he catch your soul,
Trapping it for all eternity
In his little black box.

—Anonymous

CHAPTER 1

WEDNESDAY
November 20
Suffolk County, Massachusetts,
on the Neponset River

Eric Pratt leaned his head against the cabin wall. Plaster crumbled. It trickled down his shirt collar, sticking to the sweat on the back of his neck like tiny insects attempting to crawl beneath his skin. Outside it had gotten quiet—too quiet—the silence grinding seconds into minutes and minutes into eternity. What the hell were they up to?

With the floodlights no longer blasting through the dirty windows, Eric had to squint to make out the hunched shadows of his comrades. They were scattered throughout the cabin. They were exhausted and tense but ready and waiting. In the twilight, he could barely see them, but he could smell them: the pungent odor of sweat mixed with what he had come to recognize as the scent of fear.

Freedom of speech. Freedom from fear.

Where was that freedom now? Bullshit! It was all bullshit! Why hadn't he seen that long ago?

He relaxed his grip on the AR-15 assault rifle. In the last hour, the gun had grown heavier, yet, it remained the only thing that brought him a sense of security. He was embarrassed to admit that the gun gave him more comfort than any of David's mumblings of prayer or Father's radioed words of encouragement, both of which had stopped hours before.

What good were words, anyway, at a time like this? What power could they wield now as the six of them remained trapped in this one-room cabin? Now that they were surrounded by woods filled with FBI and ATF agents? With Satan's warriors descending upon them, what words could protect them from the anticipated explosion of bullets? The enemy had come. It was just as Father had predicted, but they'd need more than words to stop them. Words were just plain bullshit! He didn't care if God heard his thoughts. What more could God do to him now?

Eric brought the barrel of the gun to rest against his cheek, its cool metal soothing and reassuring.

Kill or be killed.

Yes, those were words he understood. Those words he could still believe in. He leaned his head back and let the plaster crumble into his hair, the pieces reminding him again of insects, of head lice burrowing into his greasy scalp. He closed his eyes and wished he could shut off his mind. Why was it so damned quiet? What the hell were they doing out there? He held his breath and listened.

Water dripped from the pump in the corner. Somewhere a clock ticked off the seconds. Outside a branch scraped against the roof. Above his head, a crisp fall breeze streamed in through the cracked window, bringing with it the scent of pine needles and the sound of dry leaves skittering across the ground like the rattle of bones in a cardboard box.

It's all that's left. Just a box of bones.

Bones and an old gray T-shirt, Justin's T-shirt. That was all that was left of his brother. Father had given him the box and told him Justin hadn't been strong enough. That his faith hadn't been strong enough. That this is what happened when you didn't believe.

Eric couldn't shake the image of those white bones, picked clean by wild animals. He couldn't stand the thought of it, bears or coyotes—or maybe both—growling and fighting over the ripped flesh. How could he endure the guilt? Why had he allowed it? Justin had come to the compound, attempting to save him, to convince him to leave, and what had Eric done in return? He should have never allowed Father's initiation ritual to take place. He should have escaped while he and Justin had a chance. Now what chance was there? And all he had of his younger brother was a cardboard box of bones. The memory brought a shiver down his back. He jerked it off, opening his eyes to see if anyone had noticed, but found only darkness swallowing the insides of the cabin.

"What's happening?" a voice screeched out.

Eric jumped to his feet, crouching low, swinging the rifle into position. In the shadows he could see the robotic jerks of the others, the panic clicking out in a metallic rhythm as they swung their own weapons into place.

"David, what's going on?" the voice asked again, this time softer and accompanied by a crackle of static.

Eric allowed himself to breathe and slid back down the wall, while he watched David crawl to the two-way radio across the room.

"We're still here," David whispered. "They've got us—"

"No wait," the voice interrupted. "Mary should be joining you in fifteen minutes."

There was a pause. Eric wondered if any of the others found Father's code words as absurd. Or for that matter, wouldn't anyone listening in find the words strange and outrageous? Yet without hesitation, he heard David turn the knobs, changing the radio's frequency to channel 15.

The room grew silent again. Eric could see the others positioning themselves closer to the radio, anxiously awaiting instructions or perhaps some divine intervention. David seemed to be waiting, too. Eric wished he could see David's face. Was he as frightened as the rest of them? Or would he continue to play out his part as the brave leader of this botched mission?

"David," the radio voice crackled, channel 15's frequency not as clear.

"We're here, Father," David answered, the quiver unmistakable, and Eric's stomach took a dive. If David was afraid, then things were worse than any of them realized.

"What's the situation?"

"We're surrounded. No gunfire has been exchanged yet." David paused to cough as if to dislodge the fear. "I'm afraid there's no choice but to surrender."

Eric felt the relief wash over him. Then quickly he glanced around the cabin, grateful for the mask of darkness, grateful the others couldn't witness his relief, his betrayal. He set the rifle aside. He let his muscles relax. Surrender, yes of course. It was their only choice. This nightmare would soon be over.

He couldn't even remember how long it had been. For hours, the loudspeaker had blared outside. The floodlights had sprayed the cabin with blinding light. While inside the radio had screeched on and on with Father reminding them to be brave. Now Eric wondered if perhaps it was a thin line that separated the brave and the foolish.

Suddenly, he realized Father was taking a long time to respond. His muscles tensed. He held his breath and listened. Outside, leaves rustled. There was movement. Or was it his imagination playing tricks on him? Had exhaustion given way to paranoia?

Then Father's voice whispered, "If you surrender, they'll

torture you." The words were cryptic, but the tone soothing and calm. "They have no intention of allowing you to live. Remember Waco. Remember Ruby Ridge." And then he went silent, while everyone waited as if hanging by a thread, hoping for instruction or, at least, some words of encouragement. Where were those powerful words that could heal and protect?

Eric heard branches snap. He grabbed his rifle. The others had also heard and were crawling and sliding across the wooden floor to get back to their posts.

Eric listened, despite the annoying banging of his heart. Sweat trickled down his back. His fingers shook so violently he kept them off the trigger. Had snipers moved into position? Or worse, were agents getting ready to torch the cabin, just as they had done in Waco? Father had warned them about the flames of Satan. With all the explosive ammo in the storage bunker beneath the floorboards, the place would be a fiery inferno within seconds. There would be no escape.

The floodlights blasted the cabin, again.

All of them scurried like rats, pressing themselves into the shadows. Eric banged his rifle against his knee and slid down against the wall. His skin bristled into goose bumps. The exhaustion had rubbed his nerves raw. His heart slammed against his rib cage, making it difficult to breathe.

"Here we go again," he muttered just as a voice bellowed over the loudspeaker.

"Hold your fire. This is Special Agent Richard Delaney with the FBI. I just want to talk to you. See if we can resolve this misunderstanding with words instead of bullets."

Eric wanted to laugh. More bullshit. But laughter would require movement, and right now his body stayed paralyzed against the wall. The only movement was that of his trembling hands as he gripped the rifle tighter. He would place his bet on bullets. Not words. Not anymore.

David moved away from the radio. He walked toward the

front window, his rifle limp at his side. What the hell was he doing? In the floodlight, Eric could see David's face, and his peaceful expression sent a new wave of fear through Eric's veins.

"Don't let them take you alive," Father's voice screeched over the static. "You're all heroes, brave warriors. You know what must be done now."

David kept walking to the window as though he didn't hear, couldn't hear. Hypnotized by the blinding light, he stood there, his tall, lean figure wrapped in a halo, reminding Eric of pictures he had seen of saints in his catechism books.

"Give us a minute," David yelled out to the agent. "Then we'll come out, Mr. Delaney, and we'll talk. But just to you. No one else."

He saw the lie. Even before David pulled the plastic bag from his jacket pocket, Eric knew there would be no meeting, no words exchanged. The sight of the red-and-white capsules made him light-headed and dizzy. No, this couldn't be happening. There had to be another way. He didn't want to die. Not here. Not this way.

"Remember there is honor in death," Father's voice came smooth and clear, the static gone now, almost as if he were standing in the room with them. Almost as though he were answering Eric's thoughts. "You are heroes, each and every one of you. Satan will not destroy you."

The others lined up like sheep to the slaughter, each taking a death pill, reverently handling it like hosts at communion. No one objected. The looks on their faces were of relief, exhaustion and fear having driven them to this.

But Eric couldn't move. The convulsions of panic had immobilized him. His knees were too weak to stand. He clutched his rifle, hanging on to it as though it were his final lifeline. David, zeroing in on Eric's reluctance, brought the last capsule to him and held it out in the palm of his hand.

"It's okay, Eric. Just swallow it. You won't feel a thing."

David's voice was as calm and expressionless as his face. His eyes were blank, the life already gone.

Eric just sat there, staring at the small capsule, unable to move. His clothes stuck to his body, drenched in sweat. Across the room the voice droned on over the two-way radio. "A better place awaits all of you. Don't be afraid. You are all brave warriors who have made us proud. Your sacrifice will save hundreds."

Eric took the capsule with shaking fingers and enough hesitation to make David stand over him. David popped his own pill into his mouth and swallowed hard. Then he waited for the others and for Eric to do the same. The calm was unraveling in their leader. Eric could see it in David's pinched face, or was it the cyanide already eating its way out of his stomach lining?

"Do it!" David said through clenched teeth. Everyone obeyed, including Eric.

Satisfied, David returned to the window and called out, "We're ready, Mr. Delaney. We're ready to talk to you." Then he raised his rifle to his shoulder, taking aim and waiting.

From the position of the rifle, Eric knew without seeing that it would be a perfect head shot, without risk of wasting any ammo on a bullet-proof vest. The agent would be dead before he hit the ground. Just as all of them would be dead before David's rifle ran out of ammunition and the mass of Satan's warriors crashed through the cabin's doors.

Before the first shot, Eric lay down like the others around him, allowing for the cyanide to work its way through their empty stomachs and into their bloodstreams. It would take only a matter of minutes. Hopefully they would pass out before their respiratory systems shut down.

The gunfire started. Eric laid his cheek against the cold wooden floor, feeling the vibrations and shattered glass, listening to the screams of disbelief outside. And as the others closed their eyes and waited for death, Eric Pratt quietly spit

out the red-and-white capsule he had carefully concealed inside his mouth. Unlike his little brother, Eric would not become a box of bones. Instead, he would take his chances with
Satan.

CHAPTER 2

Washington, D.C.

Maggie O'Dell's heels clicked on the cheap linoleum, announcing her arrival. But the brightly lit hallway—more a whitewashed, concrete tunnel than a hallway—appeared to be empty. There were no voices, no noises coming from behind the closed doors she passed. The security guard on the main floor had recognized her before she displayed her badge. He had waved her through and smiled when she said "Thanks, Joe," not noticing that she had to glance at his name tag to do so.

She slowed to check her watch. Still another two hours before sunrise. Her boss, Assistant Director Kyle Cunningham, had gotten her out of bed with his phone call. Nothing unusual about that. As an FBI agent she was used to phones ringing in the middle of the night. And there was nothing unusual about the fact that he hadn't awakened her with his call. All he had interrupted was her routine tossing and turning. She'd been awakened once again by nightmares. There were enough bloodied images, enough gut-wrenching experiences in her memory bank to haunt her subconscious for years. Just the thought clenched her teeth, and only now did she realize she had developed a walk that included hands fisted at her sides. She shook the fists open, flexing her fingers as if scolding them for betraying her.

What had been unusual about Cunningham's phone call was his strained and distressed voice. Just one of the reasons for Maggie's tension. The man defined the term *cool and collected.* She had worked with him for almost nine years, and couldn't remember ever hearing his voice being anything other than level, calm, clipped and to the point. Even when he had reprimanded her. However, this morning Maggie could swear she had heard a quiver, a twinge of emotion too close to the surface, obstructing his throat. It was enough to unnerve her. If Cunningham was upset about this case, then it had to be bad. Really bad.

He had filled her in on the few details he knew, still too early for specifics. There had been a standoff between the ATF and FBI and a group of men holed up in a cabin somewhere in Massachusetts on the Neponset River. Three agents had been wounded, one fatally. Five suspects in the cabin were dead. One lone survivor had been taken into federal custody and sent to Boston. Intelligence had not nailed down, yet, who the young men were, what group they belonged to or why they had stockpiled an arsenal of weapons, fired on agents and then taken their own lives.

While dozens of agents and Justice Department officials combed the woods and the cabin for answers to those questions, Cunningham had been asked to start a criminal analysis of the suspects. He had sent Maggie's partner, Special Agent R.J. Tully, to the scene and Maggie—because of her forensics and premed background—had been sent here into the city morgue where the dead—five young men and one agent—were waiting to tell their tale.

As she came to the open door at the end of the hall, she could see them. The black body bags lined up on steel tables one after another, looking like a macabre art exhibit. It almost looked too strange to be real, but then, wasn't that the way so many recent events in her life had been? Some days it was difficult to distinguish what was real and what was simply one of those routine nightmares.

Maggie was surprised to find Stan Wenhoff gowned up and waiting for her. Usually Stan left the early morning call-ins to his competent and able assistants.

"Good morning, Stan."

"Humph." He grunted his familiar greeting as he kept his back to her and held up slides to the fluorescent light.

He would pretend the urgency and stature of this case weren't the reason he had crawled out of bed to be here, when his normal method would have been to call one of his assistants. It wasn't that Stan would want to make certain everything was carried out by the book as much as he wouldn't want to miss an opportunity to be the point man for the media. Most pathologists and medical examiners Maggie knew were quiet, solemn, sometimes reclusive. However, Stan Wenhoff, the chief medical examiner for the District, loved being in the limelight and in front of a TV camera.

"You're late," he grumbled, this time glancing over at her.

"I got here as quickly as I could."

"Humph," he repeated, his fat, stubby fingers rattling the slides back into their container to signal his discontent.

Maggie ignored him, took off her jacket and helped herself to the linen closet, knowing there would be no invitation issued. She wanted to tell Stan that he wasn't the only one who didn't want to be here.

Maggie looped the plastic apron's strings around her waist. She found herself wondering how much of her life had been dictated by killers, getting her out of bed in the middle of the night to hunt them down in moonlit woods, along churning black rivers, through pastures of sandburs or fields of corn? She realized that this time, she might actually be the lucky one. Unlike Agent Tully's, at least this morning her feet would be warm and dry.

By the time she returned from the linen closet, Stan had unzipped their first customer and was peeling back the bag, careful that any contents—including liquid contents—didn't fall or run out. Maggie was startled by how young the boy looked, his gray face smooth, having never yet experienced a razor. He couldn't be more than fifteen or sixteen years old. Certainly not old enough to drink or vote. Probably not old enough to own a car or even have a driver's license. But old enough to know how to obtain and use a semiautomatic rifle.

He looked peaceful. No blood, no gashes, no abrasions— not a single mark that explained his death.

"I thought Cunningham told me they committed suicide? I don't see any gunshot wounds."

Stan grabbed a plastic bag off the counter behind him. He handed it to her across the boy's body.

"The one who survived spit his out. I'm guessing arsenic or cyanide. Probably cyanide. Seventy-five milligrams of potassium cyanide would do the trick. Eat through the stomach lining in no time."

The bag held one ordinary red-and-white capsule. Maggie could easily see the manufacturer's name stamped on the side. Though intended to be an over-the-counter headache medication, someone had replaced the contents, using the capsule as a convenient container.

"So they were well prepared for suicide."

"Yeah, I'd say so. Where the hell do kids come up with these ideas today?"

But Maggie had a feeling it hadn't been the boys' idea. Someone else had convinced them they could not be taken alive. Someone who amassed arsenals, concocted homemade death pills and didn't hesitate to sacrifice young lives. Someone much more dangerous than these boys.

"Can we check the others before you start the autopsies?"

Maggie made it sound like a casual request. She wanted to see if all the boys were Caucasian, supporting her initial hunch that they might belong to a white supremacist group. Stan didn't seem to mind her request. Maybe he was curious to get a look himself.

He started unzipping the next bag and pointed a stubby finger at Maggie.

"Please put your goggles down first. They're not doing you any good on top of your head."

She hated the suffocating things, but she knew Stan was a stickler for rules. She obeyed and pulled on a pair of latex gloves. She glanced at the bag Stan had opened as she unzipped the one in front of her. Another blond-haired Caucasian boy slept peacefully as Stan pushed the black nylon material down around his face. Then she looked at the bag her fingers were peeling open. She didn't get very far when she stopped. She snapped back her hands as though she had been stung.

"Oh Jesus!" Maggie stared at the man's gray face. The perfectly round bullet hole was small and black against his white forehead. She could hear the sloshing of liquid behind his head; liquid that she had disturbed but that still remained captured inside the bag.

"What?" Stan's voice startled her as he leaned over the body, trying to see what had upset her. "It must be the agent. They said there was one dead." He sounded impatient.

Maggie stepped back. A cold sweat washed over her body. Suddenly she grabbed onto the counter, unsure of her knees. Now Stan was staring at her, concern replacing impatience.

"I know him" was the only explanation she could manage before she took off for the sink.

CHAPTER 3

Suffolk County, Massachusetts

R.J. Tully hated the *whop-whop* of the helicopter blades. It wasn't that he was afraid of flying, but helicopters made him aware that he was riding hundreds of feet above ground in nothing more than a bubble with an engine. And something this noisy couldn't possibly be safe. Yet he was grateful the noise prevented any conversation. Assistant Director Cunningham had appeared agitated and visibly shaken the entire trip. It unnerved Tully, who had known his boss for less than a year. He had never seen Cunningham reveal much emotion other than a frown. The man didn't even swear.

Cunningham had been fidgeting with the helicopter's two-way radio, trying to get updated information from the ground crew investigating the scene. All they had been told so far was that the bodies had been airlifted to the District. Since the standoff had been a federal matter, the investigation—including the autopsies—would be handled under federal jurisdiction instead of county or state. And Director Mueller had personally insisted that the bodies be brought to the District, especially the one dead agent.

There were still no IDs being issued. Tully knew it was the identity of the fallen agent that had Cunningham jerking around in his seat, looking for things to occupy his hands and readjusting his headset every few seconds as if a new radio frequency would bring him new information. Tully wished his boss would sit still. He could feel the extra motion shake the helicopter, even though he realized it was probably scientifically impossible to do so. Or was it?

As the pilot skimmed the treetops looking for a clearing to land, Tully tried not to think of the rattle under his seat. It sounded suspiciously like loose nuts and bolts. Instead, he tried to remember if he had left enough cash on the kitchen table for Emma. Was today her school field trip? Or was it this weekend? Why didn't he write these things down? Although shouldn't she be old enough and responsible enough to remember on her own? And why didn't this get any easier?

Lately, it seemed as though all his parenting had been learned the hard way. Well, if the field trip was today maybe it wouldn't hurt for Emma to learn a few lessons. If he shortchanged her, maybe it would finally convince her to look for a part-time job. After all, she was fifteen years old. When Tully was fifteen he was working after school and in the summers, pumping gas at Ozzie's 66 for two dollars an hour. Had things changed that drastically since he was a teenager? Then he stopped himself. That was thirty years ago, a lifetime ago. How could it be thirty years?

The helicopter began its descent and Tully's stomach flipped up into his chest, bringing him back to the present. The pilot had decided to take them down on a patch of grass no bigger than a doormat. Tully wanted to close his eyes. He stared at a rip in the back of the pilot's leather seat. It didn't help. The sight of stuffing and springs only reminded Tully of the nuts and bolts rolling loose underneath him, probably disconnecting the landing gear.

For all his anxiety, the helicopter was grounded in seconds with a bounce, a thump and one last flip of Tully's stomach. He thought about Agent O'Dell and wondered if he would rather have traded places with her. Then he thought about watching Wenhoff slicing into dead bodies. Easy answer. No contest. He'd still take the helicopter ride, loose screws and all.

A uniformed soldier had come out of the woods to meet them. Tully hadn't thought about it, but it made sense that the Massachusetts National Guard would be brought in to secure the expansive wooded area. The soldier waited in military stance, while Tully and Cunningham pulled their belongings off the helicopter—an assortment of rain gear, a Coleman thermos and two briefcases—all the while trying to keep their heads down and their necks from being whiplashed by the powerful blades. When they were clear, Cunningham waved to the pilot, and the helicopter didn't hesitate, taking off and scattering leaves, a sudden downpour of crackling red and gold.

"Sirs, if you follow me, I'll take you to the site." He reached for Cunningham's briefcase, knowing immediately which of them to suck up to. Tully was impressed. Cunningham, however, wouldn't be rushed, holding up a hand.

"I need to know names," Cunningham said. It wasn't a question. It was a demand.

"I'm not authorized to—"

"I understand that," Cunningham interrupted. "I promise you won't get in trouble, but if you know, you need to tell me. I need to know now."

The soldier took up his military stance again, not flinching and holding Cunningham's gaze. He seemed determined to not divulge any secrets. Cunningham must have realized what he was up against, because Tully couldn't believe what he heard his boss say next.

"Please, tell me," Cunningham said in a quiet, almost conciliatory tone.

Without knowing the assistant director, the soldier must have recognized what it had taken for him to say this. The man relaxed his stance and his face softened.

"I honestly can't tell you all their names, but the one who was killed was a Special Agent Delaney."

"Richard Delaney?"

"Yes, sir. I believe so, sir. He was the HRT—the Hostage Rescue Team—negotiator. From what I heard, he had them ready to talk. They invited him into the cabin, then opened fire. The bastards. Sorry, sir."

"No, don't apologize. And thank you for telling me."

The soldier turned to lead them through the trees, but Tully wondered if Cunningham would manage the trek. His face had gone white; his usual straight-backed walk seemed a bit wobbly.

With only a quick glance at Tully, he said, "I fucked up big time. I just sent Agent O'Dell to autopsy a friend of hers."

Tully knew this case would be different. Just the idea that Cunningham would use the words *please* and *fucked* in the same day, let alone the same hour, was not a good sign.

CHAPTER 4

Maggie accepted the cool, damp towel from Stan and avoided his eyes. With only a quick glance, she could see his concern. He *had* to be concerned. Judging from the towel's softness, she could tell it had come from Stan's own privately laundered stash, unlike the institutional stiff ones that smelled like Clorox. The man had a cleaning obsession, a fetish that seemed contradictory to his profession; a profession that included a weekly, if not daily, dose of blood and body parts. She didn't question his kindness, however, and without a single word, took the towel and rested her face in its cool, plush texture, waiting for the nausea to pass.

She hadn't thrown up at the sight of a dead body since her initiation into the Behavioral Science Unit. She still remembered her first crime scene: spaghetti streaks of blood on the walls of a hot, fly-infested double-wide trailer. The blood's owner had been decapitated and hanging by a dislocated ankle from a hook in the ceiling like a butchered chicken left to jerk and drain out, which explained the blood-streaked walls. Since then, she had seen comparable, if not worse—body parts in take-out containers and mutilated little boys. But one thing she had never seen, one thing she had never had to do, was look down into a body bag soaked with the blood, cerebral spinal fluid and the brain matter of a friend.

"Cunningham should have told you," Stan said, now watching her from across the room, keeping his distance as if her condition might be contagious.

"I'm sure he didn't know. He and Agent Tully were just leaving for the scene when he called me."

"Well, he'll certainly understand you not assisting me." He sounded relieved—no, pleased—with the prospect of not having her shadow him all morning. Maggie smiled into the towel. Good ol' Stan was back to his normal self.

"I can have a couple autopsy reports ready for you by noon." He was washing his hands again, as if preparing the damp towel for her had somehow contaminated his precious hands.

The urge to escape was overwhelming. Her empty but churning stomach was reason enough to do just that. Yet there was something that nagged at her. She remembered an early morning less than a year ago in a Kansas City hotel room. Special Agent Richard Delaney had been concerned about her mental stability, so much so that he had risked their friendship to make sure she was safe. After almost five months of him and Agent Preston Turner playing her bodyguards, protecting her from a serial killer named Albert Stucky, it had come down to that early morning confrontation, Delaney pitting his stubbornness against hers all because he wanted to protect her.

However, at the time, she had refused to see it as protection. She had refused to simply see it as his attempt to, once again, play the role of her surrogate big brother. No, at the time, she had been mad as hell at him. In fact, that was the last time she had spoken to him. Now here he lay in a black nylon body bag, unable to accept her apology for being so pigheaded. Perhaps the least she could do was to make certain he received the respect he deserved. Nausea or not, she owed him that.

"I'll be okay," she said.

Stan glanced at her over his shoulder as he prepared his shiny instruments for the first boy's autopsy. "Of course you will be."

"No, I mean I'm staying."

This time he scowled at her over his protective goggles, and she knew she had made the right decision. Now, if only her stomach would agree.

"Did they find the spent cartridge?" she asked as she put on a fresh pair of gloves.

"Yes. It's over on the counter in one of the evidence bags. Looks like a high-powered rifle. I haven't taken a close look yet."

"So we know cause of death beyond a doubt?"

"Oh, you betcha. No need for a second shot."

"And there's no mistaking the entrance wound or the exit wound?"

"No. I imagine it won't be difficult to figure out."

"Good. Then we won't need to cut him. We can make our report from an external examination."

This time Stan stopped and turned to stare at her, then said, "Margaret, I hope you're not suggesting that I stop short of doing a full autopsy?"

"No, I'm not suggesting that."

He relaxed and picked up his instruments before she added, "I'm not suggesting it, Stan. I'm insisting you don't do a full autopsy. And believe me, you don't want to fight me on this one."

She ignored his glare and unzipped the rest of Agent Delaney's body bag, praying her knees would hold her up. She needed to think of his wife, Karen, who had always hated Delaney being an FBI agent almost as much as Maggie's soon-to-be ex-husband, Greg, hated her being one. It was time to think of Karen and the two little girls who would grow up without a daddy. If Maggie could do nothing else, she'd make certain they didn't have to see him mutilated any more than necessary.

The thought brought back memories of Maggie's own father, the image of him lying in the huge mahogany casket, wearing a brown suit Maggie had never seen him in before. And his hair—it had been all wrong—combed in a way he would never have worn it. The mortician had tried to paint over the burned flesh and salvage what pieces of skin were still there, but it wasn't enough. As a twelve-year-old girl, Maggie had been horrified by the sight and nauseated by the smell of some sort of perfume that couldn't mask that over-powering odor of ashes and burned flesh. That smell. There was nothing close nor worse than the smell of burned flesh. God! She could smell it now. And the priest's words hadn't helped: *You are dust and unto dust you shall return, ashes to ashes.*

That smell, those words and the sight of her father's body had haunted her childhood dreams for weeks as she tried to remember what he looked like before he lay in that casket, before those images of him turned to dust in her memories.

She remembered how terribly frightened she had been seeing him like that. She remembered the crinkle of plastic under his clothes, his mummy-wrapped hands tucked down at his sides. She remembered being concerned about the blisters on his cheek.

"Did it hurt, Daddy?" she had whispered to him.

She had waited until her mother and the others weren't looking. Then Maggie had gathered all of her child-size

strength and courage and reached her small hand over the edge
of the smooth, shiny wood and the satin bedding. With her fingertips she had brushed her father's hair back off his forehead,
trying to ignore the plastic feel of his skin and that hideous
Frankenstein scar at his scalp. But despite her fear, she had
to rearrange his hair. She had to put it back to the way he always liked to wear it, to the way she remembered it. She
needed her last image of him to be one she recognized. It was
a small, silly thing, but it had made her feel better.

Now, looking down at Delaney's peaceful gray face, Maggie knew she needed to do whatever she could, so that two
more little girls wouldn't be horrified to look at their daddy's
face one last time.

CHAPTER 5

Suffolk County, Massachusetts

Eric Pratt stared at the two men, wondering which of them would be the one to kill him. They were seated facing him, so close their knees brushed against his. So close he could see the older man's jaw muscles clench every time he stopped chewing. Spearmint. It was definitely spearmint gum he was grinding his teeth into.

Neither looked like Satan. They had introduced themselves as Tully and Cunningham. Eric had been able to hear that much through the fog. Both men looked clean-cut—close-cropped hair, no dirt beneath their fingernails. The older one even wore nerdy wire-rimmed glasses. No, they looked nothing like Eric had expected Satan to look. And just like the others now crawling around the cabin floor and combing the woods outside, these guys wore the navy-blue windbreakers with the yellow letters, FBI.

The younger one had on a blue tie, pulled loose, his shirt collar unbuttoned. The other wore a red tie, cinched tight at the buttoned collar of a brilliant white shirt. Red, white and blue, with those government letters emblazoned across their backs. Why hadn't he thought of it before? Of course Satan would come disguised, wrapped in symbolic colors. Father was right. Yes, of course, he was always right. Why had he doubted Father? He should have obeyed, not doubted, not taken his chances with the enemy. What a fool he had been.

Eric scratched at the lice still digging into his scalp, digging deeper and deeper. Could Satan's soldiers hear the scratching sounds? Or perhaps they were the ones making the imaginary lice dig into his skull. Satan had powers, after all. Incredible powers he could transmit through his soldiers. Powers that Eric knew could easily inflict pain without so much as a touch.

The one called Tully was saying something to him, lips moving, eyes burrowing into Eric's, but Eric had turned down the volume hours ago. Or was it days ago? He couldn't remember how much time had passed. He couldn't remember how long he had been in this cabin, how long he had sat in this straight-backed chair with his wrists handcuffed and his feet in shackles, waiting for the inevitable torture to begin. He had no sense of time, but he did know the exact moment his system had begun to shut down. The exact second his mind had gone numb. It was the instant that David dropped to the floor, the thud of his body forcing Eric to risk opening his eyes. That was when he found himself staring directly into David's eyes, their faces only inches apart.

Eric had seen his friend's mouth open. Thought he heard a faint whisper, three words, no more. Maybe it had been Eric's imagination, because David's eyes were already empty when the words "He tricked us" left his lips. He must have heard his friend wrong. Satan hadn't tricked them at all. They had tricked him, instead. Hadn't they?

Suddenly, the men were scrambling to their feet. Eric braced himself as best he could, closed fists, shoulders hunched, head down. Only there were no blows, no bullets, no wounds inflicted of any kind. And their voices melted together, the hysteria in them breaking through Eric's self-imposed barrier.

"We need to get out of the cabin. Now."

Eric twisted around in the chair, just as one of the men pulled him to his feet and started to shove him toward the door. He saw another man, with some weird contraption mounted on top of his head, come up out of the floorboards. Of course, they had found the hidden arsenal. Father would be disappointed. They had needed that stockpile of weapons to fight Satan. Their mission had failed before they could deliver them back to their home camp. Yes, Father would be very disappointed. They had let everyone down. Maybe more lives would be lost, because all the weapons that had taken months to amass would now be confiscated and put under Satan's control. Precious lives might be lost because they had failed their mission. How could Father protect any of them without these weapons?

The men shoved and pulled at him, hurrying out the cabin door and down into the woods. Eric didn't understand. What were they running from? He tried to listen, tried to hear. He wanted to know what could possibly frighten Satan's soldiers.

They gathered around the man with the strange headgear, who brought out a metal box with blinking lights and odd wires. Eric had no idea what it was, but it sounded like the man had found it down with the weapons.

"There's an arsenal underneath large enough to blow this place to kingdom come."

Eric couldn't help but smile and immediately felt a jab to his kidneys. He wanted to tell Mr. Tully, the owner of the elbow in his back, that he wasn't smiling about them being blown up, but rather at the idea that any of them believed they would ever be allowed into the Kingdom of God.

No one else noticed his smile. They focused on the dark-haired man with the crazy gogglelike contraption now pushed up on top of his head, reminding Eric of some life-size insect.

"Tell us something we don't already know," one of the men challenged.

"Okay. How about this. The entire cabin is wired," the insect man told them.

"Shit!"

"It gets even better. This is only a secondary switch." He showed them the metal box he held. "The real detonator's off-site." Then he pointed to the blinking red button and flipped a switch. The light shut off. Within seconds it snapped back on, blinking again like a pulsing red eye.

The men turned and twisted, craning their necks and looking around them. Some of them had their guns drawn. Even Eric's head pivoted, his eyes suddenly clear and squinting into the shadows of the woods. He didn't understand. He wondered if David had known about the metal box.

"Where is it?" demanded the big guy with no neck, the one everyone seemed to treat as being in charge, the only one dressed in a navy blazer instead of a windbreaker. "Where's the goddamn detonator?"

It took Eric a minute to realize the man was asking him. He met his eyes and stared like he had been taught, looking directly into the black pupils and not blinking, not flinching, not letting the enemy win even one word.

"Hold on a minute," the one named Cunningham said. "Why wouldn't they want the detonator inside the cabin, so they could control when and how to blow it up? We already know they were willing to take their own lives. So why not do it by blowing themselves and the arsenal up?"

"Maybe they still intend to blow us up." And there was more shuffling, more worried heads pivoting.

Eric wanted to tell them Father would never blow up the cabin. He couldn't sacrifice the weapons. Father needed them to fight, to continue to fight. Instead, he simply transferred his stare to Cunningham, who not only held his gaze but bore into him as if his powers could wrench out the truth with only a look. A knot in Eric's stomach twisted, but he didn't blink. He couldn't show weakness.

"No, if they wanted to blow us up, we'd already be dead," Cunningham continued without looking away. "I think the real targets are already dead. I think their leader just wanted to make sure they did the right thing."

Eric listened. It was a trick. Satan was testing him. Seeing if he would flinch. Father wanted to save them from being taken alive and tortured. This was simply the beginning of that torture, and Satan's soldier, this Cunningham, knew his job well. His eyes wouldn't let Eric go, but he wouldn't blink. He couldn't look away. He had to ignore the thunder of his heart in his ears, and the knot tightening in his gut.

"The detonator," Cunningham said without a single blink of his own eyes, "may have been a backup plan. If they didn't swallow their death pills, he was prepared to blow them to pieces. Some leader you have, kid."

Eric wouldn't take the bait. Father would never do such a thing. They had voluntarily given up their lives. No one had forced them. Eric simply hadn't been strong enough to join them. He was weak. He was a coward. For a moment he had dared to lose faith. He had not been a brave, loyal warrior like the others, but he wouldn't show weakness now. He wouldn't give in.

Then suddenly, Eric remembered David's last words. "He tricked us." Eric thought David had meant Satan. But what if he meant…? It wasn't possible. Father had only wanted to save them from being tortured. Hadn't he? Father wouldn't trick them. Would he?

Cunningham waited, watching and catching Eric as he

blinked. That's when he said, "I wonder if your precious leader knows you're still alive? Do you suppose he'll come to your rescue, just like he did last night?"

But Eric was no longer sure of anything as he stared at the metal box flashing its strange lights, red and green, stop and go, life and death, heaven and hell. Maybe David and the others were not only the brave ones; now Eric wondered if perhaps they were also the lucky ones.

CHAPTER 6

SATURDAY
November 23
Arlington National Cemetery

Maggie O'Dell gripped the lapels of her jacket into a fist, bracing herself for another gust of wind. She regretted leaving her trench coat in the car. She'd ripped it off in the church, blaming the stupid coat for her feeling of suffocation. Now, here in the cemetery, amid the black-clad mourners and stone tombstones, she wished she had something, anything, from which she could draw warmth.

She stood back and watched the group huddle together, surrounding the family under the canopy, intent on protecting them from the wind, as though compensating for the mistakes that had brought them all here today. She recognized many of them in their standard dark suits and their trained solemn faces. Except in the middle of this graveyard, even those bulges under their jackets couldn't prevent them from looking vulnerable, stripped by the wind of their government-issue, straight-backed posture.

Watching from the fringes, Maggie was grateful for her colleagues' protective instincts. Grateful they prevented her from seeing the faces of Karen and the two little girls who would grow up without their daddy. She didn't want to witness any more of their grief, their pain; a pain so palpable it threatened to demolish years of protective layers she had carefully constructed to hide and stifle her own grief, her own pain. Standing back here, she hoped to stay safe.

Despite the crisp autumn gusts attacking her bare legs and snapping at her skirt, her palms were sweaty. Her knees wavered. Some invisible force knocked at her heart. Jesus! What the hell was wrong with her? Ever since she opened that body bag and saw Delaney's lifeless face, she had been a wreck of nerves, conjuring up ghosts from the past—images and words better left buried. She sucked in deep breaths, despite the cold air stinging her lungs. This sting, this discomfort, was preferable to the sting the memories could bring.

After twenty-one years, it annoyed her that funerals could still reduce her to that twelve-year-old girl. Without will or warning, she remembered it all as though it had happened yesterday. She could see her father's casket lowered into the ground. She could feel her mother tugging at her arm, demanding that Maggie toss a handful of dirt on top of the casket's shiny surface. And now, in a matter of minutes, she knew the lone bugler's version of taps would be enough to knot her stomach.

She wanted to leave. No one would notice, all of them wrapped in their own memories or vulnerabilities. Except that she owed it to Delaney to be here. Their last conversation had been one of anger and betrayal. It was too late for apologies, but perhaps her being here would bring her a sense of resolution, if not absolution.

The wind whipped at her again, swirling dried and crackling leaves like spirits rising up and sailing between the graves. The howl and ghostly moans sent additional chills down Maggie's back. As a child, she had felt the spirits of the dead, surrounding her, taunting her, laughing at her, whispering that they had taken away her father. That was the first time she had felt the incredible aloneness, which continued to stick to her like that handful of wet dirt she had squeezed between her fingers, squeezing tight while her mother insisted she toss it.

"Do it, Maggie," she could still hear her mother say. "Just do it already and get it over with" had been her mother's impatient words, her concern more of embarrassment than of her daughter's grief.

A gloved hand touched Maggie's shoulder. She jumped and resisted the instinct to reach inside her jacket for her gun.

"Sorry, Agent O'Dell. I didn't mean to startle you." Assistant Director Cunningham's hand lingered on her shoulder, his eyes straight ahead, watching.

Maggie thought she was the only one who had not joined the group gathered around the freshly cut grave, the dark hole in the ground that would house Special Agent Richard Delaney's body. Why had he been so cocky, so stupid?

As if reading her mind, Cunningham said, "He was a good man, an excellent negotiator."

Maggie wanted to ask, Why then was he here rather than at home with his wife and girls, preparing for a Saturday afternoon of watching college football with the gang? Instead, she whispered, "He was the best."

Cunningham fidgeted at her side, shoving his hands deep into his trench coat's pockets. She realized that, although he would never embarrass her by offering his coat, he stood in such a way that protected her from the wind. But he hadn't sought her out just to be her windbreak. She could see there was something on his mind. After almost ten years, she recognized the pursed lips and furrowed brow, the agitated shifting from one foot to the other, all subtle but telling signs for a man who normally defined the term *professional.*

Maggie waited, surprised that he, too, appeared to be waiting for some appropriate time.

"Do we know anything more about these men—what group they belonged to?" She tried to coax him, keeping her voice low, but they were far enough back that the wind would never allow them to be overheard.

"Not yet. They weren't much more than boys. Boys with enough guns and ammo to take over a small country. But someone else, someone was definitely behind this. Some fanatical leader who doesn't mind sacrificing his own. We'll find out soon enough. Maybe when we dig up who owns that cabin." He pushed at the bridge of his glasses and immediately replaced his hand into his pocket. "I owe you an apology, Agent O'Dell."

Here it was, yet he hesitated. His uncomfortable behavior surprised and unnerved Maggie. It reminded her of the knot in her stomach and the ache in her chest. She didn't want to talk about this, didn't want the reminder. She wanted to think of something else, anything other than the image of Delaney crumpling to the ground. With little effort, she could still hear the sloshing of his brains and see the pieces of his skull in the body bag.

"You don't owe me an apology, sir. You didn't know," she finally said, letting the pause last too long.

Still keeping his eyes straight ahead and his voice quiet, he said, "I should have checked before I sent you. I know how difficult that must have been for you."

Maggie glanced up at him. Her boss's face remained as stoic as usual, but there was a twitch of emotion at the corner of his mouth. She followed his eyes to the line of military men who were now marching onto the cemetery and into position.

Oh, God. Here we go.

Maggie's knees grew unsteady. Immediately, she broke

into a cold sweat. She wanted to escape, and now she wished Cunningham wasn't right next to her. However, he didn't seem to notice her discomfort. Instead, he stood at attention as the rifles clicked and clacked into position.

Maggie jumped at each gunshot, closing her eyes against the memories and wishing they would stay the hell away. She could still hear her mother warning her, scolding her, "Don't you dare cry, Maggie. It'll only make your face all red and puffy."

She hadn't cried then, and she wouldn't cry now. But when the bugle began its lonesome song, she was shivering and biting her lower lip. Damn you, Delaney, she wanted to curse out loud. She had long ago decided God had a cruel sense of humor—or perhaps He simply wasn't paying attention anymore.

The crowd suddenly opened to release a small girl out from under the tent, a piece of bright blue spilling between the black, like a tiny blue bird in a flock of black crows. Maggie recognized Delaney's younger daughter, Abby, dressed in a royal-blue coat and matching hat and being led by her grandmother, Delaney's mother. They were headed straight for Maggie and Cunningham, and they were about to destroy any hopes Maggie had of trying to isolate herself.

"Miss Abigail insists she cannot wait to use the rest room," Mrs. Delaney said to Maggie as they approached. "Do you have any idea where one might be?"

Cunningham pointed to the main building behind them, hidden by the slope of the hill and the trees surrounding it. Mrs. Delaney took one look and her entire red-blotched face seemed to fall into a frown, as though she faced one more hill than she could possibly endure on this day of endless hills.

"I can take her," Maggie volunteered before realizing she might be the worst possible person to comfort the girl. But surely, bathroom duty was something she could handle.

"Do you mind, Abigail? Would it be okay for Agent O'Dell to take you to the rest room?"

"Agent O'Dell?" The little girl's face scrunched up as she looked around, trying to find the person her grandmother was talking about. Then suddenly, she said, "Oh, you mean Maggie? Her name's Maggie, Grandma."

"Yes, I'm sorry. I mean Maggie. Is it okay if you go with her?"

But Abby had already taken Maggie's hand. "We need to hurry," she told her, without looking up and pulling Maggie in the direction she had seen Cunningham point.

Maggie wondered if the four-year-old had any understanding of what had happened or why they were even at the cemetery. However, Maggie was simply relieved that her only task at the moment was to fight the wind and trek up the hill, leaving behind all those memories and wisps of spirits riding the wind. But as they got to the building that towered over the rows of white crosses and gray tombstones, Abby stopped and turned around to look back. The wind whipped at her blue coat, and Maggie could see her shiver. She felt the small hand squeeze tight the fingers it had managed to wrap around.

"Are you okay, Abby?"

She nodded twice, setting her hat bouncing. Then her chin stayed tucked down. "I hope he doesn't get cold," Abby said. Maggie's heart took a plunge.

What should she say to her? How could she explain something that even she didn't understand? She was thirty-three years old and still missed her own father, still couldn't understand why he had been ripped away from her all those years ago. Years that should have healed the gaping wound that easily became exposed at the sound of a stupid bugle or the sight of a casket being lowered into the ground.

Before Maggie could offer any consolation, the girl looked up at her and said, "I made Mommy put a blanket in there with him." Then, as if satisfied by the memory, she turned back toward the door and pulled Maggie along, ready to continue with the task at hand. "A blanket and a flashlight," she added. "So he'll be warm and not scared of the dark. Just till he gets to God's house."

Maggie couldn't help but smile. Perhaps she could learn a thing or two from this wise four-year-old.

CHAPTER 7

Washington, D.C.

Justin Pratt sat on the steps of the Jefferson Memorial, pretending to rest his feet. Yeah, his feet were sore, but that wasn't why he wanted to escape. For hours they had been walking between the monuments, handing out pamphlets to touring groups of giggling and shouting high school kids. They had hit the city at the right time—fall field trips. There must have been more than fifty groups from across the country. And they were all a fucking pain in the ass. It was hard to believe he was only about a year or two older than some of these idiots.

No, the real reason Justin had excused himself involved much more sinister thoughts than sore feet; illicit thoughts, according to the gospel of Reverend Joseph Everett and his followers. Jesus, would he ever get used to calling himself one of those followers, one of the chosen few? Probably not as long as he took breaks from handing out the word of God, only to sit back and admire Alice Hamlin's breasts.

She looked up and waved at him as if she had read his thoughts. He fidgeted. Maybe he should take off his shoes to play up the sore-feet thing. Or had she already figured him out? She certainly couldn't mind. Why else would she have worn such a tight pink sweater? Especially on a bus trip where they were to spend the day handing out godly propaganda. And then later, in about an hour, they'd be at the fucking prayer rally.

Jesus! He needed to watch his language.

He looked around, checking to see if any of Father's little messengers could hear his thoughts. After all, Father sure as hell made it appear that he could. The man seemed to be telepathic or whatever that term was for reading people's minds. It was downright spooky.

He grabbed one of the pamphlets so Alice would think he took their job seriously and maybe not notice that breast thing. The slick four-color pamphlets were pretty impressive with the word *freedom* in raised letters. What did Alice call it? Embossing? Very professional. It even included a color photograph of Reverend Everett and listed on the back the entire schedule of future prayer rallies, city by city. From the looks of the brochure, you'd think they could afford to eat something better than beans and rice seven days a week.

When he looked back at Alice, a new group of potential recruits had surrounded her. They listened and watched intently as her face and gestures became animated. She was three years older than Justin, an older woman. Just the idea gave him a hard-on. She didn't have much street smarts, but she knew stuff about so many different things. She amazed him. Like all the quotes of Jefferson's she had memorized. She recited them before they got up all the steps to read them off the walls. She kicked ass when it came to that history crap. And she knew that one-two-three thing about Jefferson. That he was the first secretary of something or another, second vice president and third president. How could she even remember that fucking shit?

It was one of the many things Justin admired about her. That had to be a good sign, that he didn't care only about her great pair of tits, which had usually been the case with him and girls in the past. In fact, there was a whole list of things he liked about Alice. For one thing, she could make religion sound almost as exciting as if it were some fucking NASCAR race to heaven. And he liked the way she looked into her listeners' eyes as though they were the only souls on earth for that moment. Alice Hamlin could make a suicidal maniac feel special and forget why he was out teetering on a ledge. Or at least, that's how she made Justin feel. After all, he had been that suicidal maniac just a couple months ago.

Sometimes he still felt it, that restlessness, that urge to just forget about everything and stop trying so hard to make it look like he had his shit together. Especially now that Eric had left him and was off on some mission.

In fact, he had felt the urge as recently as this morning when he found himself wondering how he might take the blades out of his plastic disposable razor. He knew if the veins at the wrists were cut vertically instead of horizontally that a person bled to death much quicker. Most people fucked it up and did the horizontal thing. Cutting himself didn't bother him. Getting his tattoo probably hurt a hell of a lot more than slitting your wrists.

Alice was bringing a group of girls up the stairs toward him. She'd want to introduce him. Earlier she had told him he was cute enough to convince any girl to attend Father's rally. Words didn't usually mean a fucking thing to Justin. Not after a lifetime of people telling him stuff. But when Alice said stuff, it was hard not to believe her. So he didn't mind. Besides, he enjoyed watching girls walk up steps. Of course, he'd much rather be watching from behind, but this view wasn't bad.

It was a chilly day and yet all three wore short-sleeved blouses. One even had on a tight knit top, cut short to show her flat stomach. It was a false indicator of a wanna-be wild side, since even from this distance, Justin could see the belly button was pierce-free. But it was still nice to look at.

Now, if they'd just shut up. Did all high school girls have that same high-pitched giggle? Where the fuck did they learn that squeal? It grated on his nerves, but he smiled, anyway, and offered a cute little tip of his baseball cap that only seemed to set them off again, but an octave higher. Dogs had to be pitching their ears for miles.

"Justin, I want you to meet some of my new friends."

Alice and the three girls stopped in front of him, right at crotch level, and suddenly he forgot about sore feet or even Alice's perfectly shaped tits—for a few minutes, anyway. The tall blonde and her shorter counterpart shielded their eyes from a momentary and rare appearance of the sun. The third one, a short girl with dark eyes, looked older up close. She wasn't afraid to meet his eyes like the blonde and her book-end.

"This is Emma, Lisa and Ginny. Emma and Lisa are best friends from Reston, Virginia. Ginny lives here in the District. They never met each other before today, and see, we're already good friends."

The two blondes giggled and the tall one said, "Actually, her name is Alesha, but she hates that, so we shortened it to Lisa."

"Well, my name is really Virginia," the dark-eyed girl told them, only it came out as though it was a competition, and she needed to outdo her new friends.

"No way," the blondes said in practiced unison.

"My dad thought it would be cute since we're from Virginia. Which, by the way, my dad would kill me if he knew I was attending this sort of thing tonight. He hates this kind of stuff." This she said to Alice, and like the name thing, she made it sound like a challenge instead of a simple statement.

Justin watched for Alice's reaction. This girl wasn't exactly a prize recruit, and Justin wondered why Alice had even invited her to stay for the prayer rally. Already Ms. Ginny-my-name-is-really-Virginia was showing signs of doubt. That was supposed to be a big red flag. Next there would be questions. Father hated questions.

"We can't always rely on our parents to guide us in the correct direction," Alice told her with a smile, sounding like a mother herself, and the girl nodded, pretending to know exactly what Alice meant, because Alice was too cool to disagree with or contradict.

Justin crossed his arms over his chest. It was all he could do to keep from rolling his eyes.

A scuffle at the bottom of the steps made them all jerk around, the girls rocking on ridiculous platform shoes while trying not to fall down the steps. Justin got to his feet, climbing a few more steps to get a better look. Down below, a James Dean look-alike was shoving at an older guy while he tried to yank the man's camera out of his hands.

"Wow! He's really cute," the one called Ginny managed to say without a squeal.

Justin sat back down with a sigh of frustration that no one noticed. Leave it to fuckin' Brandon to steal all the attention.

CHAPTER 8

Ben Garrison knew a thing or two about causing pain. The kid was younger and taller, but Ben knew he was stronger and definitely wiser. This hothead would last about five seconds if Ben shot a hand to his throat and squeezed in just the right place.

"No fucking reporters, Garrison. How many times do we have to tell you that?" the kid screamed at him.

He grabbed at Ben's Leica, managing to yank the strap wrapped around Ben's neck. The 35 mm camera was almost as old as Ben and probably tougher. Hell, it had survived a stampede of caribou in Manitoba and getting dropped in an Egyptian sand dune. It could certainly survive some pissed off religious freak.

"Why no reporters? What is your precious leader afraid of? Huh?" Ben egged him on. He knew this kid from the short visit he had paid to their camp at the foot of the Appalachian Mountains. Hell, he even kind of liked the kid. From what he had seen in the past, this kid, this Brandon, had a lot of passion, a lot of fire in his belly, but he didn't have a clue as to what to do with it.

Brandon swiped at the camera again, and this time Ben gave him a shove that sent him onto his backside. Now the kid's red face almost matched his red, goop-backed hair. He looked up at Ben like a bull, revving up and getting ready to charge. Ben could see his nostrils flaring and his hands balling into fists.

"Give it up, kid." Ben laughed at him and snapped a couple of shots to prove the kid couldn't rattle him. "Reverend Everett may have tossed me out of his hideout, but he isn't gonna get rid of me that easy. Why doesn't he send a real man to do a real man's job?"

Brandon was back on his feet, his jaw and teeth clenched, his hands ready at his sides. Ben imagined little clouds of steam coming out of his ears like in the comic strips. The kid would need more than those accompanying bubbles of "Pow" and "Wham" to scare off Ben Garrison. Hell, he had survived an Aborigine's blow dart and a Tutsi's swipe of a machete. Like the Leica, he had seen a few death battles before, and this wasn't one of them. Not even close. Poor kid. And with all his precious little friends watching. But there was no Reverend Everett to swoop in and save the souls of his little lost fools.

A crowd had gathered, hiking up the Jefferson Memorial steps to get a better look, but they kept their distance. Even the gang of young men, the redhead's gang, circled like dogs in heat, but yellow-bellied dogs that stayed out of the way. Ben scratched his bristled jaw, bored with the whole thing. He had spent the afternoon getting some lame shots of tight-assed, hipless nymphettes. A few he had recognized. One he had even followed for a while, hoping for a risqué *Enquirer* shot, to embarrass her big-shot daddy. He'd stay and get a few of the prayer rally, with the precious, fucking Reverend Joseph Everett in action. This poor excuse of a rebel without a cause wouldn't stop him. They couldn't stop him, especially if they insisted on using public property.

He walked up several steps, leaving the hothead to snort and stomp and pretend to be choosing the godly thing of turning the other cheek. In the distance, Ben could see people starting to flock to the FDR Memorial.

It surprised him that Everett had chosen this spot for his rally in the District, especially over the Jefferson Memorial. Jefferson seemed more in tune with Everett's philosophy of individual freedoms and limited government. Hell, hadn't FDR put into place some of the very government programs Everett abhorred? The good reverend was a complicated piece of shit. But Ben was determined to expose the bastard for what he really was. And it would take more than this hotheaded punk to stop him.

CHAPTER 9

FBI Headquarters
Washington, D.C.

Maggie waited for Keith Ganza to finish the work she had interrupted. He was used to her barging into his lab at FBI headquarters, whether invited or not—usually not. And although he grumbled about it, she knew he didn't mind, even late on a Saturday afternoon when everyone else had already called it a day and left.

As the head of the FBI crime lab, Ganza had seen more in his thirty-plus years than any one person should ever see. Yet he seemed to take it all in stride, unruffled—unlike his outward appearance—by any of it. As Maggie waited and watched his tall, thin frame hunched over a microscope, she wondered if she had ever seen him in anything other than a white lab coat, or rather a yellowed-at-the-collar, wrinkled lab coat with sleeves too short for his long arms.

Maggie knew she shouldn't be here—she should wait for

the official report. But four-year-old Abby's tenacity had only strengthened Maggie's resolve to find out who was responsible for Delaney's murder. Which reminded her—she pulled out a string of red licorice Abby had given her and began unwrapping it. Ganza stopped at the sound of crinkling plastic and glanced up at her over the microscope and over his half glasses that sat at the end of his nose. He looked at her with a familiar frown, one that remained in place, whether he was delivering a joke, talking about evidence or, in this case, staring at her impatiently.

"I haven't eaten today," she offered as an explanation.

"There's half a tuna salad sandwich in the frig."

She knew his offer to be generous and sincere, however, she had never gotten used to eating anything that had spent time on a shelf next to blood and tissue samples.

"No, thanks," she told him. "I'm meeting Gwen in a little while for dinner."

"So you buy licorice to tide you over?" Another frown.

"No. I got this at Agent Delaney's funeral."

"They were handing out red licorice?"

"His daughter was. Are you ready for me to interrupt you yet?"

"You mean you haven't already?"

Her turn to frown. "Very funny."

"I'm getting the file to A.D. Cunningham first thing Monday morning. Can't you wait until then?"

Without answering, she folded the long string of licorice, holding it up in front of her to measure, then pulling it apart at the fold. She handed him one section of candy. He took the bribe without hesitation. Satisfied, he left his microscope, began nibbling at the candy and searched the counter for a file folder.

"It was potassium cyanide in the capsules. About ninety percent with a mixture of potassium hydroxide, some carbonate and a smidge of potassium chloride."

"How difficult is it to get your hands on potassium cyanide these days?"

"Not difficult. It's used in a lot of industries. Usually as a cleaning solution or fixative. It's used in making plastics, some photographic development processes, even in fumigating ships. There was about seventy-five milligrams in the capsule the kid spit out. With little food in the digestive tract, that dose causes almost an instantaneous collapse and cessation of all respiration. Of course, that starts only after the plastic capsule is dissolved, but I'd say within minutes. Absorbs all the oxygen out of the cells. Not a pretty or fun way to die. The victims literally strangle to death from the inside out."

"So why not just stick their guns in their mouths like most teenage boys who commit suicide?" Both images bothered Maggie, and Ganza raised his eyebrows at the impatience and sarcasm in her voice.

"You know the answer to that as well as I do. Psychologically it's much easier to swallow a pill than pull the trigger, especially if you're not so keen on the idea to begin with."

"So you don't think this was their idea?"

"Do you?"

"I wish it were that simple." She ran her fingers through her hair, only now noticing the tangles. "They found a two-way radio inside the cabin, so they were in contact with someone. We just don't know who. And, of course, there was a huge arsenal underneath the cabin."

"Oh, yes, the arsenal." Ganza opened a file folder and shuffled through several pages. "We were able to track the serial numbers on about a dozen of the weapons."

"That was fast. I'm guessing they were stolen instead of bought at some gun show, right?"

"Not exactly." He pulled out several documents. "You're not going to like it."

"Try me."

"They came from a storage facility at Fort Bragg."

"So they *were* stolen."

"I didn't say that."

"Then what exactly did you say?" She came to stand at his side, looking over his arm at the document he had extracted.

"The military never knew they were missing."

"How is that possible?"

"They retired the weapons long ago, sent them to storage. Whoever got ahold of them would have had to have high-level clearance or some type of official access."

"You're kidding!"

"It gets even more interesting." He handed her an envelope stamped Document Department and motioned for her to open it.

Maggie pulled out several sheets of paper, which included a land title from the state of Massachusetts for ten acres of property, as well as for a cabin and docking rights to the Neponset River.

"Great," she said after scanning the copy. "So the land was donated to some nonprofit organization. These guys really know how to hide their tracks."

"Not that unusual," Ganza said. "A lot of these groups filter weapons and money, even property, through bogus NPOs. Saves them from paying taxes and allows them to thumb their noses at the government they profess to hate so much. That's usually all they have the courage to do."

"But this group is into more dangerous stuff than tax evasion. Whoever is behind this, this maniac's willing to sacrifice his own men…boys, really." Maggie flipped through the pages. "So what in the world is the Church of Spiritual Freedom? I've never heard of it before." She looked back up at Ganza, who shrugged his bony shoulders. "What the hell did Delaney get in the middle of?"

CHAPTER 10

Justin wished he didn't have to stay for the prayer rally. After all, they had worked all day to get a good crowd here. Didn't they deserve a break? He was beat and starving. Would Father really be able to tell if he and Alice ducked out? Except he knew Alice would never go for it. She lived for these yawners and really seemed to get into the singing and clapping and hugging. Actually, he had to admit that he did enjoy the hugging. And tonight they had gathered some serious babes.

He watched Brandon talking to the blond bookends. Brandon was pointing at one of the granite walls. The one that had carved: Freedom of Speech, Freedom of Religion, Freedom From Want, Freedom From Fear. Justin had heard Father repeat those same words many times, especially when he got on a roll about the government and its conspiracies to suppress people. In fact, for a while Justin had thought the reverend had been the one who had come up with the words.

Whatever bullshit Brandon was telling them, Justin could tell the girls were eating it up. The tall one, Emma, kept flipping her hair back and tilting her head in that way high school girls must all learn in Flirting 101. Maybe that's where they learned that fucking giggle, too.

"Hey, Justin."

He felt a tap on his shoulder and turned to find Alice and the dark-eyed Ginny. The first thing he noticed was the big pretzel and can of Coke Ginny was holding. The smell of the pretzel made his stomach rattle. Both girls heard and laughed. Ginny handed him the pretzel.

"Want some?"

He glanced at Alice, checking for her disapproval, but she was looking in the other direction, looking for someone, and immediately he wondered if it was Brandon.

"Maybe just a bite," he told Ginny.

He bent down and bit into the doughy pretzel, tugging a piece away while Ginny held it and pulled. It tasted wonderful, and he thought about asking for a second bite, but Ginny was already biting off a piece for herself from the same spot, licking her lips while her eyes met his. Jesus! She was coming on to him. He looked to see if Alice had noticed, but now she was waving to someone. He turned to find Father, flanked by his core group: several older women and one black man. Following close behind were three Arnold Schwarzenegger look-alikes, his bodyguards.

Justin thought Father looked more like a movie actor than a reverend. Earlier on the bus, he had even seen Cassie, Father's beautiful black assistant, applying makeup to the reverend's face. She had probably styled his hair, too. Father went way out for these rallies. Ordinarily, he wore his longish black hair slicked back, but today it stayed in place on its own, tucked neatly over his ears and collar just enough to be stylish and not shaggy. Later during the rally, when the man had what he called one of his "passionate moments," strands of hair would fall onto his forehead, sorta reminding Justin of Elvis Presley when he got all shook up. He wondered if Father would mind the comparison. He certainly wouldn't mind having people refer to him as "the King."

The rest of Father looked like a well-paid business executive. Tonight he wore a charcoal-gray suit, white shirt and red silk tie. The suits always looked expensive. Justin could tell. They looked like something his dad would wear, probably several thousand dollars a pop. And there were the gold cuff links, a Rolex watch and gold tie bar, all gifts from rich donors. Sorta pissed Justin off. Why were there always donors to buy expensive jewelry, but when it came to toilet paper, they had to use old newspapers? And it was shreds of old newspaper, at that—pieces too small to even provide any college football scores.

The sun had just set, only pink-purple stains remaining, yet Father still wore his sunglasses. He took them off now as he approached. He smiled at Alice, reaching both his hands to her, waiting for her to do the same. Justin watched the reverend's hands swallow Alice's, his fingers overlapping onto her wrists and caressing her.

"Alice, my dear, who is your lovely guest?" He was smiling at Ginny, his eyes working their magic.

Ginny seemed flustered by the sudden attention, her hands clumsily trying to dispose of her pretzel and Coke. Justin started to offer to take them when she turned and tossed the precious pretzel into a nearby trash can. He wondered if everyone could hear his sigh of disappointment, but instead they were already mesmerized by Father's charm. Justin moved aside, not wanting to risk being shoved aside by one of the Schwarzenegger triplets. It had happened to him once before.

He sat down on one of the benches. Everyone was watching Father now, including Brandon and the blond bookends. Except that Brandon looked a little pissed. Justin wondered if he hated Father stealing the attention away from him.

Father took each of Ginny's hands, in the same way he had done with Alice, only now, probably because he knew he had everyone's attention, he was making a fucking ceremony out of it. He looked into her eyes, smiling down at her and going on and on about what a beautiful young woman she was. Ginny was even smaller than Alice, so the reverend's large hands practically wrapped around her entire forearms.

The skeptical Ginny, who had told them several times that her father would be so pissed if he knew she had come tonight, appeared to be eating up the attention. Justin had to admit the man was a charmer…a snake charmer. Just then, Father looked over at Justin and frowned.

Jesus! Justin thought. Maybe the guy really could read minds.

CHAPTER 11

Ginny Brier could barely hear the clapping and singing from down below. Dried leaves crackled underneath them and a twig poked into her thigh. But all she paid attention to was Brandon panting in her ear as he fumbled with her blouse buttons.

"Careful, don't rip any," she whispered, which only seemed to make his fingers more urgent and reckless.

The back of his neck was wet, but she continued to caress him there, hoping it would calm him, though she liked how hot and bothered she could make him. She wondered if perhaps he hadn't done it in a long time or something. That would explain his fumbling. Or was he nervous they'd get caught? Did he worry that reverend guy would get mad if he found out? Actually, that was what turned Ginny on even more. She liked that this incredibly cool guy, who had been staring at her all evening, had come up behind her, taken her hand and led her around the back of the monument.

The sharp glare of the monument's lights didn't reach up here in the wooded area just above and behind the granite wall. If she listened closely, she could hear the waterfall below. But instead, she concentrated on Brandon's heavy breathing. He had finally gotten through the button obstacle course and was ready to start on her bra. Suddenly, in one quick and rough motion, he grabbed the bottom of her bra and simply shoved it up over her breasts. She almost protested until his mouth devoured her and made her forget.

She reached down and undid his belt buckle, undoing the snap and his zipper in a smooth, almost expert motion. But he didn't wait for her. He was taking himself out while pushing her back into the leaves. She tried to slow him down, whispering in his ear and rubbing his back and shoulders.

"Slow down, Brandon. Let's enjoy this."

But it was already too late. He hadn't even made it all the way inside her when he exploded. In seconds he lay limp on top of her. More panting while he tried to catch his breath, drowning out Ginny's exaggerated sigh of disappointment. Then he sat up, wiped his wet hair off his forehead and pulled his zipper up, all as casually as if he were getting dressed in the morning. Ginny felt as if she had become invisible. Why were the cute ones always the quick triggers and the insensitive shitheads?

"That's it?" She unleashed her disappointment. She no longer cared if anyone heard her, though her voice couldn't compete with the waterfall, the Reverend Yacky-Yack and the mind-numbing clapping.

He finally looked at her, his brown eyes black and empty in the shadows. It felt worse than being invisible. His look made her feel dirty. She pushed her bra back into place and tried to pull her skirt down, noticing that he had ripped the crotch of her underwear.

"You klutz." She showed him the damage. "Now what am I supposed to do?"

"I don't know. What do whores like you usually do afterward?"

She stared at him, stunned by his words. She needed to hold on to her anger, because without it, she would start to be frightened.

"You really are a bastard, aren't you?" Two could play this word game, only his response this time came without words as his fist slammed into her mouth. Ginny fell into the leaves, grabbing at her jaw, and felt the blood trickling down her chin. She crawled out of his reach. Her anger was quickly replaced by fear.

"Leave me alone, or I swear I'll scream."

He laughed, then threw back his head to the stars and laughed louder, as if to prove no one would hear. And he was right. The singing below only made his laughter sound like a piece of the harmony.

He picked up her purse, wiped his hand over it to clear the debris and tossed it to her.

"Don't forget to button your blouse before you come back down," he told her, his voice suddenly calm and polite, almost solemn but so distant it gave her a chill. How was he able to do that? How could he disconnect like that? And so quickly.

She grabbed her purse and scooted farther away, leaning against a tree as if for protection. Without saying anything more, he turned and left, taking the same path they had used to come up.

Down below, she could hear a woman's voice replace the good reverend's, but Ginny didn't pay attention to the words. Pretty soon there was more singing, even louder now, gaining volume as the night went along. They were singing something about coming home to a better place. What a bunch of losers.

Ginny breathed a sigh of relief. God, how stupid she had been this time. She bet that Justin guy wouldn't treat a girl like this. Why was she always choosing the wrong ones? The bad-boy types? Maybe she did it simply because she knew it pissed off her dad and embarrassed the hell out of her soon-to-be step-mom. Not like they cared about her, only about their public images, their precious reputations. They screamed at each other in private and made cow eyes at each other in public. It was pathetic. At least she acted on her real emotions, her real feelings, wants and needs.

Something rustled in the bushes behind her. Did Brandon have a change of heart? Maybe he was coming back to apologize. Then she realized he had taken the path at the opposite end. She jerked around, scrambling to her feet and squinting into the dark.

Something moved. Something in the shadows. Oh, jeez! It was only a branch.

She needed to get the hell out of here before she scared herself to death. She reached down for her purse. Something whipped in front of her, a glowing cord that looped over her head. It pulled tight against her neck before she could grab at it.

Ginny tried to scream but it came out as a gasp, stuck in her throat. She choked and gulped for air. Her hands and fingers clawed at the cord, then clawed at the hands that held it. She dug her fingernails into skin, ripping at her own flesh, and still couldn't breathe. She couldn't stop it. Couldn't keep it from tightening even more. Already she felt herself slipping to her knees. There were flashes of light behind her eyes. No air. She couldn't breathe. Her feet kicked, then slipped out from under her. Now her neck bore all the weight as her body dangled on a single cord.

She couldn't regain her balance. Couldn't see. Couldn't breathe. Her knees wouldn't work. Her arms flayed. Her fingers dug even deeper into her own skin, but nothing helped. When blackness came, it came as a relief.

CHAPTER 12

Downtown
Washington, D.C.

Gwen Patterson transferred the strap of her briefcase to the other shoulder and waited for Marco. She squinted into the dimly lit pub, the antique gas-flamed lanterns and candelabras preserving the historic atmosphere of the saloon. This late on a Saturday evening Gwen knew Old Ebbitt's Grill would be free of all the politicos who usually hung out there, which would make getting a booth possible and would please her friend, Maggie O'Dell, who seemed to hate the political atmosphere of the District.

Ironically, the very things about the District that Maggie hated, Gwen thrived on. She couldn't imagine living anywhere more exciting and loved her brownstone in Georgetown and her office overlooking the Potomac. She had lived here for more than twenty years, and though she had grown up in New York, the District was her home.

Marco smiled as soon as he saw her and waved her down the aisle to where he was standing.

"She beat you this time," he said, and pointed to the booth at the end of the aisle where Maggie was already seated, a glass of Scotch on the table in front of her.

"Not like this is a first." She winked at Maggie, who was always on time. Gwen was the late one.

Maggie smiled, watching Marco fawn over her, helping her with her coat, even taking the briefcase. He started to hang it from the brass hook beside their table, then thought better of it and leaned it carefully and safely inside their booth.

"What are you carrying around these days?" he complained. "Feels like a load of bricks."

"Close. It's a load of my new book."

"Ah…yes, I forget that you are now a famous author as well as a famous shrink to the pundits and politicos."

"I'm not sure about that famous-author part," she told him as she smoothed her skirt with both hands and scooted into the booth. "I doubt that *Investigating the Criminal Mind of Adolescent Males* will make it onto the *New York Times* bestseller list anytime soon."

Marco's massive eyebrows rose, along with his hands, in mock surprise. "Such a large and weighty subject for such a small and beautiful woman."

"Now, Marco, every time you flatter me like that I end up ordering the cheesecake."

"Sweets for the sweet. Seems appropriate."

This time Gwen rolled her eyes at him. He patted her shoulder and headed off to greet a pair of Japanese men waiting at the door.

"Sorry," she said to Maggie. "We go through this every time."

"It must pay off. He gave us the best booth in the place."

Gwen sat back and took a long look at her friend. Maggie seemed pleasantly amused by the whole charade. Maybe it was simply the effects of the Scotch, because when Maggie had called earlier, she had sounded depressed, almost pained and stricken. She had told Gwen she was in the city and wanted to know if she had time for dinner. Gwen knew her friend had to be working. Maggie lived in Virginia, almost an hour away, in one of the District's ritzy suburbs. She seldom drove into the city for recreation, least of all on the spur of the moment.

"How did the book signing go?" Maggie sipped her Scotch, and Gwen caught herself wondering if this was her first. Maggie noticed. "Don't worry. This is my one and only. I need to drive home later."

"The signing went well," she said, deciding to bypass an opportunity to lecture Maggie about her newly acquired habit. The fact was, she worried about Maggie. She rarely saw her anymore without an accompanying glass of Scotch. "I'm always surprised how many people are interested in the strange and twisted minds of criminals." She waved down a waiter and ordered a glass of chardonnay. Then to Maggie, she said, "I've been cabbing it all day, so I get more than one."

"Cheater."

Gwen was relieved that Maggie could still joke about it, especially after their last dinner together when Gwen had suggested Maggie needed the Scotch more than she wanted it. Gwen had gotten off with only a glare that told her to butt out. Useless, really. Maggie was stuck with her friendship, and with it—whether she liked it or not—came a buttinsky maternal instinct that Gwen couldn't even explain to herself.

Gwen was fifteen years older than Maggie, and ever since the two met, back when Maggie was a forensic intern at Quantico and Gwen a consulting psychologist, Gwen had felt a protectiveness toward Maggie that she had never experienced before. She had always believed she didn't have a maternal bone in her body. But for some reason she became the proverbial mama bear, ready to claw the eyes out of anyone who threatened to hurt Maggie.

Now Gwen shoved her menu aside, ready to play psychologist, friend and mother. She hadn't learned how to separate those roles. So what if she never did. Maggie could use someone to look after her, whether she believed it or not.

"What brought you to the city? Something at headquarters?"

Maggie worked out of Quantico in the Behavioral Science Unit and rarely made it to FBI headquarters at Ninth and Pennsylvania Avenue.

Maggie nodded. "Just got back from visiting Ganza. But I was out at Arlington before that. Today was Agent Delaney's funeral."

"Oh, Maggie. I didn't realize." Gwen watched her friend, who was doing an excellent job of avoiding Gwen's eyes, sipping her Scotch, rearranging the cloth napkin on her lap. "Are you okay?"

"Sure."

It came too quickly and too easily, which for Maggie meant "No, of course not." Gwen waited out the silence, hoping for more. Maggie opened her menu. Okay, so this was going to take some pulling and prodding. Not a problem. Gwen had a Ph.D. in pulling and prodding, though officially her certificate called it a Ph.D. in psychology. Same difference.

"On the phone, you sounded like you needed to talk."

"Actually, I'm working a case and could use your professional insight."

Gwen checked Maggie's eyes. That's not what she meant earlier on the phone or she would have said so. Okay, so if her friend wanted to talk shop and put off the real stuff, Gwen could be patient. "What's the case?"

"The standoff at the cabin. Cunningham wants a criminal profile of these guys, so that we might connect them to whatever organization they belong to. Because six young men certainly didn't do this on their own."

"Right. Yes, of course. I read something about that in the *Washington Times.*"

"And the criminal psychology of adolescent male minds is your new specialty," Maggie said with a smile that Gwen recognized as pride. "Why would six teenage boys put down their guns, take cyanide capsules and then lie down and wait to die?"

"Without knowing any of the details, my first reaction is that it wasn't their idea. They simply did what they were told or instructed to do by someone they feared."

"Feared?" Maggie looked suddenly interested, leaning in, elbows on the table, her chin on her hands. "Why do you automatically say *feared?* Why not because they believed so strongly in their cause? Isn't that the reasoning behind most of these groups?"

A waiter delivered Gwen's glass of chardonnay and she thanked him. She wrapped her hands around the glass and set the wine swirling. "At that age they don't necessarily know what they believe. Their opinions, their ideas are still easily molded and manipulated. But boys usually have a natural tendency to fight back. There's actually a physiological reason for that."

Gwen sipped her wine. She didn't want to sound like she was lecturing Maggie on something she already knew, but her friend seemed eager to hear more, so she continued, "It's not just their higher levels of testosterone, but boys have lower levels of the neurotransmitter serotonin. And serotonin inhibits aggression and impulsivity. That could explain why more males—especially adolescent males—than females carry through with suicide, become alcoholics or shoot up school yards as a way to solve their problems."

"Also why their first instinct when trapped in a cabin with an arsenal of guns would be to think they could impulsively shoot their way out." Maggie sat back and shrugged. "Which brings me back to the same question, why lie down and die?"

"Which brings me to my same answer." Gwen smiled. "Fear. Someone may have had them convinced they had no alternative." Gwen watched as Maggie cradled the Scotch. "But you already knew most of that, didn't you? Come on, now, I'm not telling you anything new here. Why did you really call me for dinner? What do you really *need* to talk about?"

The silence continued longer than Gwen normally allowed.

"To be honest—" Maggie grabbed the menu again and avoided Gwen's eyes "—I'm really, really hungry." But she glanced over the top and managed a tense smile at Gwen's frown. "And I needed to be with a friend, okay? A living, breathing, wonderful friend whom I absolutely adore."

This time Gwen got a glimpse at Maggie's deep brown eyes. They were serious, even a tad watery, which was why she went back to hiding them behind the menu. Gwen could see she was trying to cover up a vulnerability that had slipped too close to the surface; a vulnerability that the tough Maggie O'Dell worked hard to keep to herself and harder to conceal from others, even from her living, breathing, wonderful friends.

"You should try the hickory burger," Gwen said, pointing to the menu.

"A burger? The gourmet is recommending a burger?"

"Hey! Not just any burger, but the best damn burger in town." She saw Maggie relax. The smile genuine now. Okay, so Gwen would pull and prod next time. Tonight they would eat burgers, have a couple of drinks and simply be living, breathing friends.

CHAPTER 13

He needed to sit. The haze seemed thicker this time. Had he taken too much of his homemade concoction? He needed it only to enhance, only to help him see beyond the dark. He certainly didn't need this. He needed to sit. Yes, sit and wait for the haze to move from back behind his eyes.

He'd sit and concentrate on his breathing, just as he was taught to do. He would ignore the anger. Wait. Was it anger? Frustration, maybe. Disappointment, yes. But not anger. Anger was a negative energy. Beneath him. No, it was simply frustration. And why wouldn't he be frustrated? He honestly thought this one would last longer. She had certainly tried. And he was almost sure that on the third time he had seen it. Yes, he was quite certain he had seen the light behind her eyes, that glimmer, that flash, that moment of life escaping the body, just as she drew her final breath. Yes, he had seen it and he had come so close.

Now it would be days, maybe even a week before he could try again. He was running out of patience. Why the fuck did she have to give in so soon? One more chance was all he needed. He had been so close. So close that he didn't want to wait.

He gripped the book and let the feel of its leather binding soothe him. He sat on a hard bench in a dim corner of the terminal, ignoring the screech of hydraulic brakes, the endless clacking of heels rushing, bodies shoving—all of them in such a fucking hurry to get where they were going.

He closed his eyes against the lifting haze and listened. He hated the noise. Hated the smells even more—diesel fuel and something that smelled like dirty wet socks. And body odor. Yes, body odor from the assholes who abandoned their cardboard homes in the alley to venture in and beg for pocket change. Worthless assholes.

He opened his eyes, pleased that his vision was clearing. No more haze. He watched one of the worthless assholes by the vending machines, checking the return slots for change. Was it a woman? It was difficult to tell. She wore everything she owned, layer after filthy layer, pant cuffs dragging behind her, adding to the slow motion of her absent shuffle. Her ragged and stretched-out stocking cap gave a crooked point to her head and made her dirty blond hair stick out like straw. Such a coward. No survival instinct. No dignity. No soul.

He lay the book in his lap and let it fall open to the page where he had left his homemade bookmark—an unused airline ticket, creased at the corners and long expired. He needed to let the book calm him. It had worked before, the words offering guidance and inspiration, even direction and justification. Already his hands grew steady.

He pulled his shirt cuff down over the caked blood. She had scratched him good. It had hurt like hell, but nothing he couldn't ignore for the time being. He'd wash his hands later. Right now, he needed to feel some sense of completion and validation. He needed to calm the frustration and find some reserve of patience. Yet, all he could think about was having come so close to his goal. He didn't want to wait. If only he could find a way so he didn't need to wait.

Just then the pointy-headed loser stuck her smelly, gloved hand in his face. "Can you spare a dollar or two?"

He looked up into her smudged face and realized she was quite young, maybe even once attractive underneath that dirt and smell of decay, of rotten and sour garbage. He searched her eyes—clear, crystal blue and, yes, there was light behind them. No hollow look of despair. Not yet. Maybe he didn't need to wait, after all.

CHAPTER 14

Newburgh Heights, Virginia

The cold wind pricked at Maggie's skin, but she continued running, welcoming the sensation. Delaney's death had triggered a swell of emotions that she hadn't anticipated, that she wasn't prepared to deal with. And his funeral had released an avalanche of memories from her childhood, memories she had worked long and hard to keep safely behind a barrier. The battle to contain them left her feeling numb one minute and angry the next. Amazing that both emotions could be so exhausting. Or perhaps the exhaustion came from keeping them concealed, shoving them down away from the surface, so that no one could witness how easily she could feel nothing one moment and explode the next. No one, that is, except Gwen.

Maggie knew her friend could sense her vulnerabilities, despite Maggie's effort to hide them. It was one of the curses of their friendship, a comfort as much as an annoyance. Sometimes she wondered why the hell Gwen put up with her, and at the same time, she didn't want to know the answer. Instead, she was simply grateful for this wise, loving mentor who could take one look into her eyes, see all the turmoil, sift through the hidden wreckage and somehow manage to inspire strength and good from some reserve Maggie hadn't even known existed. And tonight Gwen had been able to do all that without a single word. Now, if only Maggie could hold on to that strength.

When she first became a criminal profiler she thought she could learn how to compartmentalize her feelings and emotions, separate the horrors and images she witnessed as part of the job from her personal life. Not that Quantico taught them such a thing. But since she had done it all her life with the unpleasant memories and images of her childhood, why wouldn't she be able to do it with her career? The only problem was that every time she thought she had the technique down pat, one of those damn compartments sprung a leak. It was annoying as hell. Especially annoying that Gwen could see it no matter how hard Maggie tried to hide it from her.

She picked up the pace. Harvey panted alongside her. The big dog wouldn't complain. Ever since she had taken him in, he had become her shadow. The pure white Labrador retriever had become a bit overprotective with her, jumping at sounds that Maggie never heard, barking at footsteps whether they belonged to the mailman or the pizza-delivery person. But then Maggie could hardly blame him.

Last spring the dog had witnessed his owner being violently kidnapped from their home, by a serial killer named Albert Stucky, who Maggie had already put in jail once and who had escaped. And though Harvey had put up a good fight, he hadn't been able to stop the attacker. For months after Maggie had taken him in, he looked out the windows of Maggie's huge Tudor home, looking, waiting for his owner. When he realized she wouldn't return, he attached himself to Maggie with such a protectiveness that she wondered if perhaps the dog was determined not to lose a second owner.

What would Harvey think if he knew, if he could possibly understand, that his previous owner had been taken and killed simply because she had met Maggie? It was Maggie's fault that Albert Stucky had taken Harvey's owner. It was one of the things she had to live with, one of the things that caused her nightmares. And one of the things that was supposed to have its own little compartment.

Her breathing came in rhythmic gasps, timed to the pounding of her feet and the beat of her heart, which filled her ears. For a few minutes her mind cleared, and she concentrated instead on her body's basic responses, its natural rhythms, its force. She pushed it to its limit, and when she felt her legs strain, she pushed harder, faster. Then suddenly, she noticed Harvey favoring his front right paw though he didn't dare slow down, forcing himself to stay alongside her. Maggie came to an abrupt halt, surprising him with a tug of the leash.

"Harvey." She stopped to catch her breath, and he waited, cocking his head. "What's wrong with your paw?"

She pointed to it, and he crouched to the ground as if preparing for a scolding. She gently took the big paw in both her hands. Even before she turned it over she felt a prick. Embedded deep between his pads was a clump of sandburs.

"Harvey." She hadn't meant for it to sound like a scold, but he cowered closer to the ground.

She scratched behind his ears, letting him know he had done nothing wrong. He hated having these things pulled out, preferring to hide and endure the pain. But Maggie had learned how to be quick and efficient. She grabbed the clump between her fingernails, instead of fingertips, and gave one quick yank. Immediately, he rewarded those same fingers with grateful licks.

"Harvey, you need to let me know about these things as

soon as you get them. I thought we agreed that neither of us would play hero anymore."

He listened while he licked, one ear perched higher than the other.

"So do we have a deal?"

He looked up at her and gave one sharp bark. Then he climbed to his feet, ready to run again, his entire hind end wagging.

"How 'bout we take it easy the rest of the way?" She knew she had pushed it a bit too hard. As she stood and stretched, she could feel a cramp threatening her calf. Yes, they'd walk the rest of the way, despite the wind chilling her sweat-drenched body and making her shiver.

A bulging orange moon peeked from behind a line of pine trees and the ridge that separated Maggie's new neighborhood from the rest of the world. The houses were set far back off the street with enough property and landscaping between them to make it difficult to see the next-door neighbors. Maggie loved the seclusion and privacy. Though without any streetlights, darkness came quickly. It still freaked her out a bit to run after dark. There were too many Albert Stuckys out there. And even though she knew *he* was dead—that she'd killed him herself—she still sometimes ran with her Smith & Wesson tucked in her waistband.

Before she got to her long circular driveway, she saw a glimmer of windshield. She recognized the spotless white Mercedes and wanted to turn around. If he hadn't seen her, she might have done just that. But Greg waved from the portico, leaning against its railing as if he owned the house.

"It's a little late to be out running, isn't it?" This was his greeting, which sounded more like a scolding, and she found herself flinching instinctively, just as Harvey had earlier. The gesture represented a microcosm of their relationship, which had been reduced to instinctive survival tactics, and Greg still wondered why she wanted a divorce?

"What do you need, Greg?"

He looked like he had stepped off the pages of *GQ*. He was dressed in a dark suit, with sharp creases she could see even in the moon's dim light, not a wrinkle in sight. His golden hair was moussed and styled, not a strand out of place. Yes, her soon-to-be ex-husband was certainly handsome, no question about that. She knew he must be on his way home from dinner with friends or business associates. Maybe he had a date, and immediately she wondered how she would feel about that. Relieved, was her quick and easy answer.

"I don't need anything." He sounded hurt, and she saw him shift to his defensive stance, another survival tactic in his own arsenal. "I just thought I should check up on you."

As they got closer, Harvey started growling, his signal that warned of any stranger on their property.

"Good Lord!" Greg backed up, only now noticing Harvey. "That's the dog you took in?"

"Why are you checking up on me?"

But Greg was now preoccupied with Harvey. Maggie knew he hated dogs, though while they were together he had made excuses that he was allergic to them. Seemed the only thing he was allergic to was Harvey's growl.

"Greg." She waited until she had his attention. "Why are you here?"

"I heard about Richard."

Maggie stared at him, waiting for more of an explanation. When one didn't come, she said, "It happened days ago." She stopped herself from adding that if he was so concerned, why did he wait until now.

"Yeah, I know. I did hear about it on the news, but the name didn't ring a bell with me right away. Then I talked to Stan Wenhoff this morning about a case I'm representing. He told me about what happened at the morgue."

"He told you about that?" Maggie couldn't believe it. She wondered who else he had told.

"He was just concerned about you, Maggie. He knows we're married."

"We're getting a divorce," she corrected him.

"But we're still married."

"Please, Greg. It's been a long day and a long week. I don't need any lectures. Not tonight, okay?" She marched past him to the front door, letting Harvey lead, so that Greg moved out of the way.

"Maggie, I really did just stop to see if you're okay."

"I'm fine." She unlocked the door and hurried to reset the buzzing alarm system inside the entrance.

"You could be a little more grateful. I did come all this way."

"Next time, perhaps you should call first."

She was ready to close the door on him, when he said, "That could have been you, Maggie."

She stopped and leaned against the doorjamb, looking up at him and into his eyes. His perfect forehead was creased with concern. His eyes startled her with flecks of dampness she didn't recognize.

"When Stan told me about Richard...well, I..." He kept his voice low and quiet, almost a whisper, and there was an emotion in it she hadn't heard for years. "The first thing I thought of was, what if it had been you?"

"I can take care of myself, Greg." Her job had been an ongoing debate in their marriage—no, *argument* was a better word. It had been an ongoing argument between the two of them for the last several years. She wasn't in the mood for any "I told you sos."

"I bet Richard thought he could take care of himself, too." He stepped closer and reached to caress her cheek, but Harvey's growl cut the gesture short. "It made me realize how much I still care about you, Maggie."

She closed her eyes and sighed. Damn it! She didn't want to hear this. When she opened her eyes, he was smiling at her.

"Why don't you come with me. I can wait while you get ready."

"No, Greg."

"I'm meeting my brother, Mel and his new wife. We're gonna have a nightcap at their hotel."

"Greg, don't—"

"Come on, you know Mel adores you. I'm sure he'd love to see you again."

"Greg." She wanted to tell him to stop, that she wouldn't be meeting with him and Mel probably ever again. That their marriage was over. That there was no going back. But those watery gray eyes of his seemed to replace her anger with sadness. She thought of Delaney and of his wife, Karen, who had hated Delaney's career choice as much as Greg hated hers. So instead, she simply said, "Maybe some other time, okay? It's late and I'm really wiped out tonight."

"Okay," he said, hesitating.

For a minute she worried that he might try to kiss her. His eyes strayed from hers to her mouth, and she felt her back tense up against the doorjamb. Yet in that moment of hesitation, she realized she wouldn't resist the gesture, and that revelation surprised her. What the hell was wrong with her? There was no need to worry, however. Harvey's renewed growl cut short any attempt at intimacy, drawing away Greg's attention.

He scowled at Harvey, then smiled back at Maggie. "Hey, at least you don't have to worry about security with him around."

He turned to leave, then spun back around. "Oh, I almost forgot," he said, pulling a clump of torn and wrinkled papers from his jacket's inside breast pocket. "These must have blown out of your garbage can. The wind was nuts today." He handed her what she recognized as several ripped ad inserts, stuffers from her credit card statements and a notice about her *Smart Money* magazine subscription. "Maybe you need tighter lids," he added. Typical Greg, practical Greg, not able to resist the chance to correct or advise her.

"Where did you find these?"

"Just under that bush." He pointed to the bayberry along the side of the house as he headed to his car. "Bye, Maggie."

She watched him wave and waited for him to get inside, predicting his routine of checking his reflection in the rearview mirror, followed by one quick swipe at his already perfect hair. She waited until his car was down the street and out of her sight, then she took Harvey and rounded the garage. Instantly, the lights rigged to the motion detector came on, revealing the two galvanized steel garbage cans, lined up exactly where she kept them, side by side, securely against the garage wall, each can with its lid tightly intact.

She glanced through the pieces of crumpled paper, again. She shredded the important stuff, so she didn't need to worry. She was always careful. Still, it was a bit unnerving to know that someone had bothered to go through her garbage. What in the world had they hoped to find?

CHAPTER 15

Washington, D.C.

Ben Garrison dropped his duffel bag inside the door of his apartment. Something smelled. Had he forgotten to take out the damn garbage again?

He stretched and groaned. His back ached, and his head throbbed. He rubbed the knot at his right temple, surprised to find it still there. Shit! It still hurt like a bitch. At least his hair covered it. Not like he cared. He just hated people asking a lot of goddamn questions that weren't any of their business to begin with. Like that yappy old broad on the Metro, sitting next to him. She smelled like death. It was enough to make him get off early and take a cab the rest of the way home—a luxury he rarely allowed himself. Cabs were for wusses.

Now all he wanted was to crawl into bed, close his eyes and sleep. But he'd never be able to until he knew whether or not he had gotten any decent shots. Oh, hell, sleep was for wusses, too.

He grabbed the duffel bag and spilled its contents onto the kitchen counter, his large hands catching three canisters before they rolled off the edge. Then he began sorting the black film canisters according to the dates and times marked on their lids.

Out of the seven rolls, five were from today. He hadn't realized he had shot so many, though lack of lighting remained his biggest problem. And the lighting around the monuments was often too harsh in places while too dark in certain corners. He usually found himself in the dark corners and shadows where he hated to risk using a flash, but did, anyway. At least the cloud covering from earlier in the day was gone. Maybe his luck was changing.

There was so much left to chance in this business. He constantly tried to eliminate as many obstacles as possible. Unfortunately, dark was dark and sometimes even high-speed film or that new infrared crap couldn't cut through the black.

He gathered the film canisters and headed for the closet he had converted into a darkroom. Suddenly the phone startled him. He hesitated but had no intention of picking it up. He had stopped answering his phone months ago when the crank calls began. Still, he waited and listened while the answering machine clicked on and the machine voice instructed the caller to leave a message after the beep.

Ben braced himself, wondering what absurdity it would be this time. Instead, a familiar man's voice said, "Garrison, it's Ted Curtis. I got your photos. They're good but not much different from my own guys'. I need something different, something nobody else is running. Call when you've got something, okay?"

Ben wanted to throw the canisters across the room. Everybody wanted something different, some fucking exclusive. It had been almost two years since his photos of dead cows outside Manhattan, Kansas, broke the story about a possible anthrax epidemic. Before that, he had been on a roll, as if luck was his middle name. Or at least, that was how he explained being outside that tunnel when Princess Diana's car crashed. Wasn't it also luck that put him in Tulsa the day of the Oklahoma City bombing? Within hours he was there, shooting exclusives and sending photos over the wires to the top bidders.

For several years afterward, everything he shot seemed to be gold, with newspapers and magazines calling him nonstop. Sometimes they were just checking to see what he had available that week. He went anywhere he wanted and shot anything that interested him from warring African tribes to frogs with legs sprouting out of their fucking heads. And everything got snatched up almost as quickly as he could develop the prints. All because they were *his* photographs.

Lately, things were different. Maybe his luck had simply run dry. He was fucking tired of trying to be in the right place at the right time. He was tired of waiting for news to happen. Maybe it was time to make some of his own. He squeezed the canisters in his hands. These had better be good.

Just as he turned for the darkroom again, he noticed the answering machine flashing twice, indicating a message other than Curtis's. Okay, so maybe Parentino or Rubins liked the photos that Curtis didn't want.

Without emptying his hands, he punched the message-play button with his knuckle.

"You have two messages," the mechanical voice recited, grating on his nerves. "First message recorded at 11:45 p.m., today."

Ben glanced at the wall clock. He must have just missed the first call before he came in.

There was a click and a pause, maybe a wrong number. Then a young woman's polite voice said, "Mr. Garrison, this is the customer service office at Yellow Cab. I hope you enjoyed your ride with us this evening."

The film canisters slipped to the floor and scattered in different directions while Ben grabbed the countertop. He stared at the answering machine. No cab company on this planet called its passengers to see if they enjoyed their ride. No, it had to be them. Which meant they had moved from crank calls to watching him. And now they wanted him to know they were watching.

CHAPTER 16

Justin Pratt waited outside the McDonald's rest room. Who'd think the place would be this busy at this time of night? But where else were kids supposed to hang out? Shit! What he wouldn't do for a Big Mac. The smell of French fries made his mouth water and this stomach ache.

He had carelessly suggested to Alice that they grab a bite to eat. Even before her nose crinkled and she gave him that exasperated look, he knew she wouldn't agree. That was one of the things he admired: her unflinching self-discipline. Yet, at the same time, what would it hurt to have one fucking cheeseburger?

He needed to watch his language. He glanced around again. It was becoming a habit for him to check that no one could hear his thoughts. What the hell was wrong with him? He was creeping himself out.

He couldn't believe how jumpy he was. It was as if he had no control over his body or his thoughts. He scratched his jaw and combed his fingers through his greasy hair. He hated taking timed showers. The water never got warm, and this morning his two minutes were up before he could get the shampoo out of his hair.

He leaned against the wall and crossed his arms over his chest to stop his fidgeting. What was taking her so long? He knew part of the jumpiness had to be withdrawal from nicotine and caffeine. No cigarettes, no coffee, no cheeseburgers—Jesus! Was he out of his fucking mind?

Just then, Alice came out of the rest room. She had tied back her long blond hair, revealing more of her smooth white skin and her pouty lips, lips cherry-red without the aid of any cosmetics. When her green eyes met his, they sparkled, and she smiled at him like no one had ever smiled at him before. And once again, none of what he had given up mattered, as long as this beautiful angel continued to smile at him like that.

"Any sign of Brandon?" she asked, and immediately Justin felt wrenched from his temporary fantasy.

"No, not yet." He stared out the window, pretending to watch.

Fact was, he had forgotten about Brandon, and even now, didn't care if he showed up. He couldn't figure out how the hell his brother, Eric, had been such good friends with the guy. Brandon wasn't anything like Eric. In fact, he wished Brandon would just sorta disappear off the face of the earth. He was sick of him and his macho Casanova, oh-look-at-me-I'm-so-cool attitude. He didn't care if he was supposedly some precious Father-in-training.

Justin also couldn't understand why Brandon had to tag along everywhere he and Alice went. The guy could have any girl he wanted. Why couldn't he leave Alice the fuck alone? Except that Justin knew Father insisted members never travel anywhere alone. And since Justin wasn't a full-fledged member yet, anyone with him would still be considered traveling alone.

Eric had attempted to explain all the rules and crap to him, but then Father sent Justin out into the woods for almost a week. Father had called it an initiation ritual, and Eric hadn't argued with the man. Although Justin still wasn't sure what camping out, sleeping on the ground and eating cold canned beans had to do with being initiated into anything.

Luckily, he had wandered into Shenandoah National Park, and some campers ended up taking him in—fed him pretty damn well, too. He worried he had put on weight instead of looking the emaciated, frightened fledgling that Father had hoped would return. Unfortunately, when he got back, Eric was gone, off on some top-secret mission that no one could tell him about. He hated all the cloak-and-dagger shit. It felt as goddamn stupid as it sounded.

Alice scooted into a corner booth to wait. Justin hesitated. He really wanted to sit next to her. He could use the excuse that he needed to watch for Brandon, but Alice was already doing that, watching so intently he found himself hating Brandon for drawing away her attention.

Justin slid into the booth on the opposite side. He surveyed the restaurant, checking to see if anyone cared that they take up a booth when they hadn't ordered anything. The place was filled with late-night customers getting their Saturday-night junk-food fix. It was long past dinnertime. No wonder his stomach ached. The bite of Ginny's pretzel was all he'd had since lunch. And not like that gummy rice and beans they fed him would last, despite it feeling like it stuck to the inside walls of his stomach. How the hell did they eat that crap day after day? And since they were on the road, today's ration had been served cold. Yuck! He could still taste it.

Realizing it might take a while, Alice wiggled out of her jacket. Justin followed her lead, trying not to stare at her incredible tits. Yet, he couldn't stop thinking how hot she looked in that tight pink sweater.

She reached into her jacket pocket and brought out the bulging leather pouch, clumping it down on the table and making the quarters chink against one another. Justin thought about asking if they could, at least, get a couple of Cokes. She had used only one quarter for the phone call that seemed to be a big part of their mission. But then Alice had left just a short message, some weird code about a cab ride.

Justin didn't try to figure it out. Truth was, he didn't much care about the group's politics or religious beliefs. Or even their travel arrangements, for that matter. He simply wanted to be with Alice. Not like he had any place better to be.

He had been gone almost a month, and he doubted that his parents gave a fuck that he wasn't around. Maybe they hadn't even noticed he was gone. They certainly didn't seem to care when Eric left home. All his dad said was that Eric was old enough to screw up his own life, if that's what he wanted to do. But Justin didn't want to think about them. Not now. Not when he was sitting across the table from the only person who had ever made him feel like he was someone special.

Alice smiled at him again, but this time she pointed over his shoulder.

"Here he is."

Brandon slid into the booth next to Alice, taking up too much space and squeezing Alice against the wall. She didn't seem to mind, but Justin felt his hands clenching into fists, so he kept them in his lap under the table.

"Sorry I'm late," Brandon muttered, though Justin knew he didn't mean it. He knew guys like Brandon said "sorry" like some people asked "how are you?"

Justin examined the tall redhead, who reminded him of that dead actor in all those rebel movies—James Dean. Brandon's head pivoted, his eyes looking everywhere except at the two of them. Justin glanced over his shoulder. Was Brandon wor ried someone had followed him? It sure as hell looked like it. His eyes kept darting all over the place. If Justin didn't know better, he'd think Brandon was high on something. Except that was impossible. Brandon pretended to be a rebel, but he wouldn't dare cross Father. And drugs were forbidden.

"We need to get back to the bus," Alice politely and quietly instructed them. "The others will be waiting."

"Give me a chance to catch my breath." Brandon saw the pouch of quarters and reached for it. "I could use something to drink."

Justin waited for Alice to scold Brandon in her soft, strict way. Instead, she stared at his hands. Then Justin noticed what had stopped Alice. Brandon's left knuckle had something caked on it. Something dark and red that looked an awful lot like blood.

CHAPTER 17

Reston, Virginia

R.J. Tully held down the button on the remote and watched the TV's channels flip one after another after another. Nothing on the screen could distract him from the clock on the wall—the clock that now showed twenty minutes after midnight. Emma was late! Another night of breaking curfew. No more Mr. Nice Guy, no matter what her excuse. It was time for RoboDad. If only it were possible to access some mechanical part inside himself and let it take over without emotion getting in the way.

Nights like this made him miss Caroline the most. Probably a sign that parenthood had driven him completely over the edge. After all, shouldn't a red-blooded guy miss his ex-wife's sexy, long legs or even her to-die-for lasagne? There was a whole list of more likely things than missing her ability to sit next to him and reassure him that their daughter was just fine.

Caroline had always been so creative in their plans for punishing Emma, zooming in on the one thing she knew would bug the hell out of their daughter. Simple things like making her sort all the household socks for the entire month. Stuff he'd never dream of in a million years. Sorting socks was fine when Emma was eight or nine and caught riding her bike past the territorial limits they had set. But at fifteen, it was increasingly difficult to get her attention, let alone find meaningful ways of disciplining her.

He scraped a hand over his face, attempting to wipe away the sleep and the brewing anger. He was just tired. That's why he was irritable. He left the TV on Fox News and traded the remote for the bag of corn chips he'd left on the secondhand coffee table. He had to sit up to make the exchange, and only now did he notice the remnants of his previous snack attack crumbling out from the folds of his Cleveland Indians T-shirt. Jeez! What a mess. But he made no effort to clean it up. Instead he sank back into the recliner. How much more pathetic could he get? Sitting here on a Saturday night, eating junk food and watching the late night news?

Most days he didn't have time to feel sorry for himself. However, Caroline's earlier phone call had set him on edge. No, actually, it had pissed him off. She wanted Emma for Thanksgiving, and was sending the airline tickets by FedEx on Monday.

"It's all been worked out and scheduled," she had told him. "Emma's looking forward to it."

All worked out and scheduled before she even checked with him. He had custody of Emma, something Caroline had willingly agreed to when she decided having a teenage daughter had become an inconvenience to her as a CEO and new dating-game member. She knew Tully could say no to a Thanksgiving trip, and she wouldn't have a legal foot to stand on. So, of course, she had planned it beforehand with Emma, getting the girl excited, using her as a pawn. That way Tully had no choice but to agree to the trip. The woman headed an internationally successful advertising agency, why wouldn't she be an expert at manipulation?

Putting his feelings aside, Tully knew Emma needed to spend time with her mother. There were things that only mothers and daughters should discuss, things Tully felt totally inept at, not to mention downright uncomfortable with. Caroline wasn't the most responsible person in the world, but she did love Emma. Maybe Tully was simply feeling sorry for himself, because this would be the first Thanksgiving he would spend alone in more than twenty years.

A car door slammed. Tully sat up, grabbed the remote and turned down the TV's volume. Another car door slammed, and this time he was certain it came from his driveway. Okay, he needed to put on his stern expression, his I'm-so-disappointed-in-you face. But what punishment had he decided on? Oh, crap! He hadn't come up with anything. He slumped into the recliner again, pretending to be caught up in the news as he heard the front door unlock.

There were more than one set of footsteps in his entrance. He twisted around in the recliner and saw Alesha's mother coming in behind Emma. Oh, jeez! What the hell happened this time?

He stood, brushing more crumbs from his T-shirt and jeans, running his fingers through his hair and quickly swiping his mouth. He probably looked like hell. Mrs. Edmund looked impeccable as usual.

"Mr. Tully, sorry to interrupt."

"No, I appreciate you doing the chauffeuring tonight." He watched Emma but couldn't decide if her discomfort was embarrassment or worry. These days anything he said or did in front of her friends or her friends' parents appeared to embarrass her.

"I just wanted to come in and let you know that it's my fault Emma's late *in* getting home tonight."

Tully continued to watch Emma out of the corner of his eyes. The girl was an expert manipulator, just like her mother. Had she put Mrs. Edmund up to this? Finally, he crossed his arms over his chest and gave his full attention to the petite blonde, an older mirror image of her own daughter. If she had hoped to cover for Emma without providing an explanation, she was mistaken.

He waited. Mrs. Edmund fidgeted with her purse strap and pushed back an unruly strand of hair. Usually people didn't act nervous unless they were guilty of something. Tully didn't bother to fill the discomforting silence, despite seeing Emma squirm. He smiled at Mrs. Edmund and waited.

"They wanted to go to a rally at one of the monuments instead of going to a movie. I thought it would be okay. But afterward, traffic was just nuts. I hate driving in the District. I got lost a couple of times. It was just a mess." She stopped and looked up at him as if checking to see if that was sufficient. She continued, "Then I couldn't find them. We crossed wires as to the exact place I'd pick them up. Thank God, it didn't rain. And all that traffic—"

Tully held up a hand to stop her. "I'm just grateful you're all safe and sound. Thanks again, Mrs. Edmund."

"Oh, please, you must start calling me Cynthia."

He could see Emma roll her eyes.

"I'll try to remember that. Thanks so much, Cynthia." He escorted her out the front door, waiting on the steps until she made it safely into her car. Alesha waved at him and her mother joined in, the distraction almost causing the woman to back into his mailbox.

When he stepped back inside, Emma was in his spot, a leg over the recliner arm and channel surfing. He snagged the remote, shut the TV off and stood in front of her.

"You made Mrs. Edmund drive all the way into the District? What happened to going to a movie?"

"We met some kids during our field trip. They invited us to this rally. It sounded fun. Besides, we didn't make Mrs. Edmund drive us. She said it was okay."

"That's almost an hour's drive. And what kind of a rally was this? Were drugs and alcohol being passed around?"

"Dad, chill out. It was some religious revival thing. Lots of singing and clapping."

"Why in the world would you and Alesha even want to go to something like that?"

She sat up and started taking off her shoes, as if suddenly dead tired and in need of getting to bed.

"Like I said, we met some cool kids on our field trip, and they told us we should come. It was sort of a yawner, though. We ended up walking around the monuments and talking to some kids we met."

"Kids? Or boys?"

"Well, there were boys and girls."

"Emma, walking around the monuments at that time of night could be dangerous."

"There were like tons of other people, Dad. Busloads. They have tour groups. Real sight-seeing fanatics, rubbing their little pieces of paper on the wall and taking umpteen pictures with their cheap disposables."

Tully did remember that there were several night tours of the monuments. She was probably right. They were probably just as safe as in the daylight. Besides, didn't the monuments have twenty-four-hour security?

"You were really funny with Mrs. Edmund." She smiled up at him.

"What do you mean?"

"I thought for a minute there you were gonna ground her." She giggled and Tully couldn't help but smile.

The two of them ended up laughing, eating the rest of the corn chips and staying up to watch the last half of Hitchcock's

Rear Window on *American Movie Classics*. Yes, his daughter was a chip off her mother's block, already knowing what buttons to push. And Tully wondered, once again, if he'd ever get this parenting thing right.

CHAPTER 18

Justin pretended to sleep. The converted Greyhound bus was finally quiet, the rumble of the engine and tires a welcome lullaby. Thank God! No more fucking "Kumbaya" songs. Getting through that wacky "praise the Lord" and "Yahweh rules" at the too-long prayer rally had been bad enough. But Justin knew his head would surely explode if he had to listen to that crap for the three-hour bus ride home.

He had reclined his bus seat just far enough back that he could keep a half-closed eye on Brandon and Alice. They were sitting together one row behind him and across the aisle. The interior of the Greyhound bus was dark except for the track lighting on the floor, like little-bitty runway lights. He could barely see Alice's silhouette, her head turned to look out the window. She had kept that same pose since they left D.C. Even when the rest of the bus had been wailing at the top of their lungs, he could see Alice's lips move only when she occasionally looked back. Otherwise she kept staring out the window. Maybe she couldn't stand the sight of Brandon, either. Hey, he could hope, couldn't he?

With the seat reclined, he could watch Brandon a little easier. Justin kept his eyes on Brandon's hands. The guy better keep those fucking hands off Alice. Once in while, in the light of oncoming cars, he caught a glimpse of his face. Contentment. Fucking contentment, like he didn't have a worry in the world. It still pissed Justin off that Brandon had rammed his way into the bus, practically shoving him aside and plopping down in the seat next to Alice as if it were marked his. The bastard took anything and everything he wanted without ever thinking of asking.

Justin heard the whispered murmurs before he twisted around and noticed Father coming from his private compartment in the back of the bus. Rumors were that it included a bathroom and bed for Father to catch up on his rest. Now, as he walked slowly up the aisle, holding on to the backs of seats to keep his balance, Justin couldn't help thinking the man looked pretty ordinary in the shadows of the dark bus. What? The guy walked on water, but he had to hang on for a short trek down a bus aisle?

Justin kept his head pressed to the back of his seat, shifting slightly, so no one would think he was fully awake. He even snorted a little under his breath, a sound he had heard himself make other times in a half-conscious state.

Through the slits of his eyes, he could see Father stop, standing right at Justin's head. His dark features made it impossible for Justin to tell through half-shut eyes whether or not the man was looking down at him.

Then he heard him whisper, "Brandon, go sit with Darren up in front for a few minutes. I need to talk with Alice."

Brandon got up and obeyed without a word. Justin wanted to smile. Good, the bastard won't be bothering Alice for a while. Maybe Father had noticed Brandon's obsession with Alice. After all, he preached about celibacy being necessary in order for all of them to fulfill their mission. It was bullshit, of course, but he had witnessed the punishment imposed for disobeying. A couple who had gotten caught the first week Justin came to the compound were still being ostracized by the others.

"Alice, I wanted to commend you," Justin heard Father say, though his voice was hushed. "You did an excellent job recruiting young people to come to the rally."

"Justin and Brandon helped." Alice's voice was a whisper, but Justin's radar seemed to be picking it up. He loved that soft, tender, sweet voice of hers. It sounded like a bird's song, the words melodic, no matter what she said.

"That's just like you to give some of the credit away."

"But it's true. They did help."

Father gave a laugh that Justin didn't recognize. He tried to remember if he had ever heard the man laugh.

"Do you have any idea how special you are, my dear girl?"

Justin smiled, glad that someone else noticed that important fact. Except Alice didn't seem happy—the look on her face was almost a grimace. Too much modesty? She certainly needed to learn how to take a compliment, especially—what the hell?

Now, he could see what had quieted Alice. In the faint light of oncoming traffic, Justin could just make out Father's right hand on Alice's thigh. Justin kept his head against the seat but opened his eyes for a better look. Yes, the bastard's fingers were sliding in between Alice's thighs, moving their way up to her crotch. Shit! What the hell?

He felt a cold sweat wash over him, and a panic hammered in his chest. He looked back up at Alice's face and this time she noticed him watching. She gave just a slight shake of her head, a definite "no." At first, he thought it was meant for Father, but the man seemed fixated on the route his hand was taking. So the "no" was for Justin.

Fuck! Everything on her pained face told him she didn't want what was happening, and yet she was telling him not to interrupt?

Shit! He had to do something. He couldn't see Father's hand anymore. It was too dark again, the stream of traffic having passed. But from the movement of the man's shoulder, Justin figured he must be digging into her. Maybe by now, he had his goddamn hand down the front of her pants.

Justin laid his head back. He had to do something. Fuck! He needed to think. Suddenly he decided. He jerked and twisted, flaying his body back and forth in the seat, faking a nightmare as best he could. Then he slammed his body forward and yelled, "Stop it! Don't do it!"

It was enough to wake everyone, and several people hung over or around their seats to look. Justin shook his head and rubbed his eyes and face.

"Sorry, everybody. Bad dream, I guess. I'm okay."

He glanced at Father. The man was staring at him, the anger easily visible in the dim light. As he stood, he scowled down at Justin, holding that pose as if wanting everyone to witness his disapproval. How could he justify being angry about a nightmare? Of course, no one else would know the real reason for his anger. But Justin didn't care if anyone else knew. He was just glad the pervert had stopped. He simply shrugged at Father. Then he shifted in his seat away from that piercing and condemning stare, mumbling an apology to the zit-faced dittohead sitting next to him.

Finally, he heard Father turn, but Justin waited until he heard the click of the back compartment's door before he looked over at Alice. Her face was turned to the window again, but, almost as if reading his mind, she glanced at him over her shoulder and again slowly shook her head, only this time she didn't look pained. This time, she looked worried, and he knew he was probably in a whole lot of trouble with their leader, their so-called fucking soul caretaker. How could he take care of their souls when he couldn't even keep his fucking hands to himself?

CHAPTER 19

SUNDAY
November 24
The Hyatt Regency Crystal City
Arlington, Virginia

Maggie checked her watch again. Her mother was fifteen minutes late. Okay, some things never changed. Quickly, she chastised herself for the thought. After all, her mother was trying to change. Her new friends seemed to have had a positive influence on her. There had been no drunken bouts or botched suicide attempts in more than six months. That had to be a record, yet Maggie remained skeptical.

Her mother rarely left Richmond, but lately she was traveling some place new every other week. Maggie had been surprised to get the phone call last night and even more surprised to find her mother had been calling from the Crystal City Hyatt. She couldn't remember the last time her mother had been to the District. She had told Maggie she'd come for a prayer meeting or some such thing, and for a brief moment Maggie had panicked that it was the prayer thing she was being invited to. Now Maggie wondered why she thought having breakfast with her mother would be any less awkward. Why hadn't she just said no?

She sipped her water, wishing it were Scotch. The waiter smiled at her again from across the restaurant, one of those sympathy smiles that said, "I'm sorry you've been stood up." She decided if her mother didn't show, she'd order bacon, scrambled eggs and toast with a tumbler of Scotch instead of orange juice.

She refolded her napkin for the third time when all she wanted to do was dig the exhaustion from her eyes. She had only gotten about two hours of sleep, fighting images of Delaney's head exploding over and over again. God, she hated funerals! Even Abby's innocent acceptance of her father's death hadn't stopped Maggie's memories from leaking into and invading her sleep. The nightmare that finally convinced her to stay awake was one of herself, tossing handful after handful of dirt into a dark hole. The process seemed endless and exhausting. When she finally looked over the edge, she saw the dirt quickly turning to maggots scattering and crawling across her father's face, his wide eyes staring up at her. And he was wearing that stupid brown suit with his hair still combed the wrong way.

Maggie blinked and shook her head, willing the image out of her mind. She looked for the waiter. There was no sense in putting off the Scotch. Just then she saw her mother come in the restaurant door. At first, Maggie glanced right by her, not recognizing the attractive brunette dressed in a navy coatdress and bright red scarf. The woman waved at Maggie, and Maggie did a double take. Her mother usually wore absurd combinations that confirmed how little she cared about her appearance. But the woman approaching the table looked like a sophisticated socialite.

"Hi, sweetie," the imposter said in a sugary tone that Maggie also didn't recognize, though there was a familiar raspiness, a leftover from a two-pack-a-day habit. "You should see my room," she added with an enthusiasm that continued the charade. "It's huge! Reverend Everett was so kind to let us stay here last night. He's just been so good to Emily, Stephen and me."

Maggie barely managed to utter a stunned greeting before her mother sat down and the waiter was at their table.

"Would you ladies like to start off the morning with some juice and coffee or perhaps a mamosa?"

"The water's fine for now," Maggie said, watching her mother, waiting to see if she would take the waiter up on his invitation to drink before noon. Time of day had never stopped her in the past.

"Is this tap water?" Kathleen O'Dell pointed to the glass in front of her.

"I think so. I guess I'm not sure."

"Could you please fetch me a bottled water? Spring water from Colorado would be good."

"Colorado?"

"Yes, well…bottled spring water. Preferably from Colorado."

"Yes, ma'am. I'll see what I can do."

She waited until the waiter was out of sight, then she leaned across the table and whispered to Maggie, "They put all kinds of chemicals in tap water. Nasty stuff that causes cancer."

"They?"

"The government."

"Mom, I am the government."

"Of course you're not, sweetie." She sat back and smiled, smoothing the cloth napkin into her lap.

"Mom, the FBI is a government agency."

"But you don't think like them, Maggie. You're not part of…" She lowered her voice and whispered, "The conspiracy."

"Here you are, ma'am." The waiter presented a beautiful,

crystal stemmed water glass filled to the brim and garnished with a wedge of lemon. His efforts were only met with a frown.

"Oh, now, how do I know this is bottled spring water if you bring it to me already in a glass?"

He looked at Maggie as if for help. Instead, she said, "Could you bring me a Scotch? Neat."

"Of course. One Scotch, neat, and one bottled spring water in the bottle."

"Preferably from Colorado."

The waiter gave Maggie an exasperated glance, as if checking for any other demands. She relieved him with, "My Scotch can be from anywhere."

"Of course." He managed a smile and was off again.

The waiter barely left before her mother leaned over the table again to whisper, "It's awfully early in the day to be drinking, Maggie."

Maggie resisted the urge to remind her mother that perhaps this was a tendency she had picked up from her. Her jaw clenched and her fingers twisted the napkin in her lap.

"I didn't get much sleep last night," she offered as an explanation.

"Well, then some coffee might be more appropriate. I'll call him back." She started looking for the waiter.

"No, Mom. Stop."

"Some caffeine is just what you need. Reverend Everett says caffeine can be medicinal if not abused. Just a little will help. You'll see."

"It's okay. I don't want any coffee. I don't really even like coffee."

"Oh, now, where did he run off to?"

"Mom, don't."

"He's over at that table. I'll just—"

"Mom, stop it. I want the goddamn Scotch."

Her mother's hand stopped in midair. "Well…okay." She tucked the hand into her lap as if Maggie had slapped it.

Maggie had never spoken to her mother like that before. Where the hell did that come from? And now, as her mother's face turned red, Maggie tried to remember if she had ever seen her mother embarrassed, though there had been plenty of times in the past that would have justified such a response. Like making her daughter drag her half-conscious body up three flights of stairs or waking up in a pool of vomit.

Maggie looked away, watching for the waiter, wondering how she'd get through an entire meal with this woman. She'd rather be anywhere else.

"I suppose that dog kept you awake," her mother said as if there were no dark cloud of the past hanging over their table.

"No, actually it was my government job."

She looked up at Maggie. There was yet another smile. "You know what I was thinking, sweetie?" As usual she conveniently changed the subject, a tactical expert at avoiding confrontation. "I was thinking we should do a big Thanksgiving dinner."

Maggie stared at her. Surely, she must be joking.

"I'll cook a turkey with all the trimmings. It'll be just like the good ole days."

The good ole days? That must be the punch line, but from what Maggie could tell, her mother was serious. The idea that the woman even knew which end of the turkey to baste seemed incomprehensible.

"I'll invite Stephen and Emily. It's about time you met them. And you can bring Greg."

Ah, no punch line. But definitely an ulterior motive. Of course, why hadn't she seen that one coming?

"Mom, you know that's not going to happen."

"How is Greg? I miss seeing him." Again, Kathleen O'Dell continued the charade as if Maggie hadn't spoken.

"I suppose he's fine."

"Well, the two of you still talk, right?"

"Only about the division of our mutually accumulated assets."

"Oh, sweetie. You should simply apologize. I'm sure Greg would take you back."

"Excuse me? What exactly should I apologize for?"

"You know."

"No, I don't know."

"For cheating on him with that cowboy in Nebraska."

Maggie restrained her anger by strangling the cloth napkin in her lap.

"Nick Morrelli is not a cowboy. And I did not cheat on Greg."

"Maybe not physically."

This time her mother's eyes caught hers, and Maggie couldn't look away. She had never told her mother about Nick Morrelli, but obviously Greg had. She had met Nick last year. At the time he had been a county sheriff in a small Nebraska town. The two of them had spent a week together chasing a child killer. Ever since then she hadn't been able to get him out of her mind for very long, a task made more difficult now that he was living in Boston, an A.D.A. for Suffolk County. But she was not even seeing Nick, had insisted, in fact, that they have little contact until her divorce was final. And, despite her feelings, she had not slept with Nick. She had never cheated on Greg, or at least not in a legal sense. Maybe she was guilty of cheating on him in her heart.

Never mind. It wasn't any of her mother's business. How dare she claim that she had some secret access to Maggie's heart. She had no right. Not after all the damage she had done to it herself.

"The divorce papers have already been drawn up," Maggie finally said with what she hoped was enough finality to close the subject.

"But you haven't signed them yet?"

She continued to stare at her mother's concerned look, puzzled by it as much as she was uncomfortable with it. Was her mother sincerely trying to change? Was she genuinely concerned? Or had she talked to Greg, discovered he was having second thoughts and agreed to some secret alliance? Was that the real reason behind this good ole Thanksgiving plan?

"Whether we sign the divorce papers or not, nothing will change between Greg and me."

"No, of course not. Not as long as you insist on keeping that government job of yours."

There it was. The subtle but oh-so-effective jab to the heart. Much more effective than a slap to the face. Of course, Maggie was the bad guy, and the divorce was all her fault. And, according to her mother, everything could be fixed if only Maggie apologized and swept all the messy problems out of sight. No need to solve anything. Just get them the hell out of sight. After all, wasn't that Kathleen O'Dell's specialty? What you don't acknowledge can't possibly exist.

Maggie shook her head and smiled up at the waiter who had returned and deposited in front of her a tumbler of amber, liquid salvation. She picked up the glass and sipped, ignoring the frown on her mother's new and carefully made-up face. Indeed, some things never changed.

Her cellular phone began ringing, and Maggie twisted around to pull it out of her jacket, which hung on the back of her chair. Only two rings and the entire restaurant was now joining her mother to frown at her.

"Maggie O'Dell."

"Agent O'Dell, it's Cunningham. Sorry to interrupt your Sunday morning."

"That's fine, sir." This new apologetic Cunningham could easily start to grate on her nerves. She wanted her old boss back.

"A body's been found on federal property. District PD's on the scene, but I've gotten a request for BSU to take a look."

"I'm already at the Crystal City Hyatt. Just tell me where you need me to be." She could feel her mother scowling at her. She wanted another sip of Scotch, but set it aside.

"Meet Agent Tully at the FDR Memorial."

"The monument?"

"Yes. The fourth gallery. The District's lead on the scene is…" She could hear him flipping pages. "Lead is a Detective Racine."

"Racine? Julia Racine?"

"Yes, I believe so. Is there a problem, Agent O'Dell?"

"No, sir. Not at all."

"Okay then." He hung up without a goodbye, a sign the old Cunningham was still in charge.

Maggie looked at her mother as she wrestled into her jacket and peeled out a twenty dollar bill to leave for the breakfast she hadn't yet ordered.

"Sorry. I need to leave."

"Yes, I know. Your job. It tends to ruin quite a few things, doesn't it?"

Rather than even try to find the correct answer, Maggie grabbed the tumbler of Scotch and drained it in one gulp. She mumbled a goodbye and left.

CHAPTER 20

Everett's Compound
at the foot of the Appalachian Mountains

Justin Pratt jerked awake at the sudden blast of music, almost falling off the narrow army cot. Had he done so, he would have crashed on top of several members stretched out in sleeping bags. He knew he should be grateful to have a cot in the cramped sleeping quarters that housed almost two dozen men. After his probationary period—whenever the hell that ended—he was certain he would be on the floor with the rest of them.

It wouldn't matter, with the little sleep they were allowed. And then to wake up to that god-awful music over the loudspeakers. It sounded like an old scratched LP of "Onward, Christian Soldiers." No, he shouldn't complain. He needed to remember to be grateful. At least, until Eric got back. Then they could figure out what to do together. Maybe they could hitchhike to the West Coast. Although he wasn't sure how they'd survive without a fucking dime. Maybe they could go back home. If only he could convince Eric. He wouldn't leave without Eric.

He rubbed the blur from his eyes. Shit! It felt like he hadn't even slept. Out of habit, he looked at his wrist before he remembered that the expensive Seiko watch his grandfather had given him was gone. It had been just one of the hedonistic material things confiscated for his own good. Like knowing what time it was would fucking send him straight to hell.

Now Justin wondered if perhaps the real reason Father didn't allow them to keep anything of value was to make them dependent on him. And they were. For everything. Everything from that buggy rice to the scraps of newspaper they used as toilet paper.

"Get up, Pratt." Someone shoved his shoulder from behind.

Justin felt his hands ball up into fists. Without looking, he knew it was Brandon. Just once he'd like to slam a fist into that smug, arrogant face. Instead, he pulled a clean pair of underwear and socks from the clothesline in the corner. Brandon had been good enough to share it with him, because it seemed that even something like a cheap piece of fucking clothesline was a rare commodity around this place. The socks were still damp, which meant that once again his feet would be cold all day.

He took his time dressing while the others scurried to get in line for the showers. From the small, single-paned window, Justin could see the line forming. It curved all the way around the concrete building's corner. He combed his fingers through his greasy hair. Fuck it! Maybe he could sneak in a shower later. He was tired of waiting in line after line. Besides, he was starving, and his stomach reminded him with a rumble that he hadn't eaten since yesterday's lunch.

Justin headed for the cafeteria, looking around as he walked across the compound. That's what they called it, a fucking compound. The only other time he had heard someone refer to a place as a compound was on a cable special about the Kennedy family and their estate; an estate that they called a compound. So, of course, when Eric had told him about the compound, Justin had imagined something similar with servant cottages and horse stables and a huge mansion. But this place looked like army barracks—stark, metal and concrete buildings surrounded by trees and more trees, secluded in the Shenandoah Valley.

Piles of brush and uprooted trees were stacked on the south side where they had bulldozed and cleared just enough land to set up their compound. It didn't seem very organized, either. Wells hadn't been dug deep enough and many of the buildings didn't have plumbing. There certainly was never enough warm water. And hot water? Forget about it.

The whole place looked temporary, and Justin had heard rumors about Father building a new compound somewhere else, some paradise he was promising everyone. But after last night, Justin wasn't about to trust the asshole or anything he said. The pervert was a fucking hypocrite. Not like he had trusted him much before. Trust was a rare commodity with Justin. He should have known from his first week that the guy was nothing but a fraud.

That first week, Eric had taken him to what Father called a cleansing ritual. All of those who attended had to write down their most embarrassing moment, as well as one of their deepest fears. They were supposed to sign the papers, too.

"No one else will see these confessions," Father had assured them in his smooth, hypnotic manner. "The signatures are strictly an exercise for you to own up to your past and face your fears."

The folded papers were then collected in a black, square metal box. Justin had been asked to collect them and told where to set the dented box, back behind Father's huge wooden chair. A chair that looked more like a throne and was flanked by his Cro-Magnon bodyguards. At the end of the evening, Father brought out the black box with all those confidential secrets. He threw a single lit match into the metal container, setting the confessions on fire. There had been sighs of relief, but Justin couldn't help noticing that the black box no longer had a dent in it.

Later, when Justin told Eric about the miracle of the disappearing dent, his brother had practically snapped his head off.

"Some things require faith and trust. If you can't accept that, you don't belong here," his brother had told him in a pissed-off tone he had never used with him before that night. Justin remembered thinking that Eric sounded like he wasn't just trying to convince him. That maybe he was trying to convince himself, too.

Justin took a shortcut to the cafeteria, hopping over some sawhorses and wandering through a maze of stacked lumber and archaic construction equipment. He couldn't help thinking that a couple of pairs of Father's solid-gold cuff links could probably buy a small new forklift that would put the old John Deere tractor with the front loader and rusted plow hitched behind out of its misery.

He could smell the garbage dump and decided his shortcut wasn't such a hot idea. No wonder everyone avoided this area. Just as he was weaving his way back to the main path, he saw several men digging behind the piles of garbage. Maybe they were finally burying the smelly mess. But as he stopped, he saw that they had several strongboxes they were lowering into the ground.

"Hey, Justin."

He turned to find Alice waving at him over the stacks of lumber. She was making her way through the maze. Her silky hair glistened in the morning sun, and her clothes were crisp and fresh. No way were *her* socks still damp. Suddenly, he wished he had taken the time for that cold two-minute shower.

When she looked up at him, her face immediately scrunched into that cute little worried expression.

"What are you doing, Justin? No one's allowed back here."

"I was just taking a shortcut."

"Come on, let's get out of here before someone notices." She took his hand to lead him away, but he stayed put.

"What are those guys doing over there?"

She frowned at him, but put a hand to her forehead and squinted into the morning sun, taking a look at where he was pointing.

"It's none of your concern."

"So, you don't know?"

"It doesn't matter, Justin. Please, you don't want to get caught back here."

"Or what? No one will talk to me for weeks? Or no, maybe I won't get my week's ration of gummy rice and beans."

"Justin, stop it."

"Come on, Alice. Just tell me what those guys are burying, and I'll go nice and quiet like."

She dropped his hand, practically shoving it away, and suddenly he realized how stupid he was being. She was the only person he cared about, and now he was pissing her off, just like he seemed to piss off everyone else.

"They're burying the money we collected at the rally last night."

At the end of each rally, about a half-dozen wicker baskets were passed around for what Father called a "gratitude offering" to God. Those baskets usually ended up overflowing.

"Whaddya mean, they're burying it?"

"They bury all the cash we take in."

"They're putting it in the ground?"

"It's okay. They put mothballs in the boxes, so the bills don't get all moldy."

"But why bury it?"

"Where else would they put it, Justin? You can't trust

banks. They're all controlled by the government. ATMs and electronic transfers—all of that stuff is just so the government can monitor and take your money whenever it wants."

"Okay, so why not at least invest some of it, like in the stock market?"

"Oh, Justin, what am I going to do with you?" Alice smiled and patted his arm as though he had made a joke. "The stock market is controlled by the government, too. Remember reading in your history classes about the Great Depression?" She was using her calm teacher voice with him. At least the worry lines had left her face for the time being. "Anytime the stock market takes a plunge, it's the government causing the decline, stealing people's hard-earned money and making them start all over again."

Justin hadn't really thought about it before. He knew his dad got really pissed when he lost money in the market. Alice knew so much more about this stuff than he did. History had never been one of his strongest subjects. He shrugged, pretending it didn't matter to him. This time when she took his hand to lead him away, he let her and enjoyed the feel of her soft skin. He wanted to ask her about last night, about Father and the perverted moves he had made on her. Yet, at the same time, he didn't want to talk about it. He just wanted to forget it had ever happened. Maybe it was best that they both did.

As they walked to the cafeteria, Justin decided instead to think about how much money must be buried in that hole. He couldn't help wondering how many others knew about it. When they decided to leave maybe he and Eric wouldn't need to hitchhike, after all.

CHAPTER 21

FDR Memorial
Washington, D.C.

Ben Garrison put his gloves back on and slapped the back of his camera shut on a fresh roll of film. He certainly didn't want to waste any time or give Detective Racine a chance to change her mind. He stepped in closer, focusing on the woman's face. She looked so peaceful, almost as if she were simply sleeping, despite being set up against a tree. Ben was fascinated by the blue tint of her skin. Had it been caused by the cold last night or a delayed reaction to the strangulation?

Even more fascinating were the flies, hundreds of them, persistent despite the activity of officers and detectives examining the area around them. They were huge and black, not your ordinary houseflies, and they seemed to be taking up residence in every one of the body's orifices, especially the warmer, moist areas like her eyes and ears. Her dark pubic hair looked alive with them. Already Ben could see what had to be milky gray eggs nestled in the mass of thick hair.

Death and its rituals and all the natural processes that went along with it amazed him. No matter how many dead bodies he saw, he continued to be fascinated. Less than twenty-four hours ago something warm and pulsating had been housed within this body. In New Caledonia the old men called this a word that meant *shadow soul.* The Esquimaux of Bering Strait referred to it as a person's shade. In Christian faith it was simply referred to as the soul. But now, whatever it was, it was gone. It had disappeared into thin air, leaving behind an empty, hollow carcass for insects to feed upon.

He remembered reading somewhere that in a week's time, a human cadaver could lose about ninety percent of its original weight when left exposed to insects during a hot summer. Insects were certainly efficient and predictable. Too bad human beings weren't. It would make his job so much easier.

"Hey, watch where you're stepping!" a uniformed cop yelled at him.

"Who the hell are you, buddy?" a guy in a navy windbreaker and baseball cap wanted to know. He looked more like a third baseman than a cop. When Ben didn't answer and continued to snap shots, the man grabbed him by the elbow. "Who let this guy back here?"

"Wait a fucking minute." Ben twisted free and was immediately accosted by two uniforms. Now he could see the white letters on the back of the guy's windbreaker. FBI. Shit, how was he supposed to know? The guy looked like a clean-cut, fucking Boy Scout.

"It's okay." Racine finally appeared to rescue him. The knees of her carefully pressed trousers had leaves sticking to them and her short blond hair had been tangled by the wind. "I know the guy. He used to shoot crime scenes for us before he became a big-shot freelancer. Steinberg isn't here yet. He's across town at another scene. We've gotta get some shots before the rain starts. Hell, we lucked out. Garrison just happened to be in the neighborhood."

The officers let go of Ben's arms, giving him a shove just as a reminder that they could. He checked his camera settings to make sure they didn't get all fucked up. Assholes. He was doing them a goddamn favor, and they still treated him like shit.

"Come on, boys. Show's over," Racine told the mobile-crime-lab guys who had stopped crawling around in the grass to watch the commotion. "We've got to hurry up before our evidence gets washed away. That goes for you, too, Garrison."

He nodded but wasn't paying much attention. He had only now noticed that no matter where he stood, the dead woman's eyes seemed to follow him. It had to be one of those strange illusion things, right? Or was he getting paranoid?

"Hey, camera guy," the FBI agent called to him. "Get a shot of this."

The guy stood behind Ben, pointing to a spot on the ground about five feet away from the body.

"The name's Garrison," Ben said, waiting for the guy to meet his eyes, and when he did, Ben made it clear that he wouldn't proceed until the guy acknowledged him with a little respect.

He tipped back his baseball cap and smiled. "And you just happened to be in the neighborhood, is that what Detective Racine said?"

"Yeah. What about it? I was getting some fucking stock shots of the monuments."

"On a Sunday morning?"

"Best time to do it. No oddballs monkeying around, thinking it's funny to screw up my shots. Hey, I'm helping you guys out here. Maybe you could quit busting my balls." Ben kept his tone calm, confining the anger, when he really wanted to tell this guy to go fuck himself.

"Okay, Mr. Garrison, could you please take a shot of these indentations in the dirt?" He pointed to the ground again. He was tall, over six feet, and lanky but athletic-looking. The sarcasm and his eyes told Ben he'd better not push it. Fucking feebie. Ben glanced at the guy's windbreaker and wondered where his gun was hidden. He bet the asshole wouldn't be such a macho prick without his government-issued Glock.

"No problem," Ben finally said. He checked out the area where the agent pointed. Immediately he saw two, maybe three small circular indentations in the ground. They were about five to six inches apart.

"What is it?" Racine joined them, looking over Ben's shoulder just as he felt the first raindrops on the back of his neck.

"Not sure," the agent told her. "Something was set down here. Or maybe it's some sort of signature."

"Jesus, Tully, you're always thinking serial killers, aren't you? Maybe the killer set down a suitcase or something."

"With little circular feet?" Ben laughed and snapped a couple of more shots.

"Everyone's a goddamn expert." Racine was getting pissed.

Ben smiled, his bent back to her and his face to the ground. He liked when Racine got pissed, and he imagined her mouth making that sexy little pout.

"That should be enough photos, Garrison. Now, play nice and hand over the film."

When he glanced up at her, she was holding out her hand.

"I didn't get very many angles of the body," he protested. "And I have a few more exposures left."

"I'm sure we have enough. Besides, the medical examiner's here." She waved to the small, pudgy man in the houndstooth jacket and wool cap making his way up the overgrown incline. The guy took small, careful steps, watching his feet the entire time. He reminded Ben of some cartoon character with a little black bag.

"Come on, Garrison." Her hands had moved to her hips while she waited. Maybe she thought it made her look authoritive. Racine had boyish, straight hips, probably even wore men's trousers with those long legs. What she lacked in hips, she made up for in tits. He stared at them now as she waited. Something about those soft tits next to that holstered metal gave him a hard-on every time. He wondered if she knew and liked it, because she didn't budge to close her jacket. Instead, she stood there, same stance, pretending to get impatient but not denying him access.

"Garrison, I don't have all fucking day."

Reluctantly, he tapped the release button and rewound the film, snapped the camera open and handed her the roll. "No problem. Not like I don't have better places to be."

She stuffed the film into her pocket, then buttoned the jacket as if to tell him the show was over now that she had what she wanted.

"So you owe me one, Racine. How about dinner?"

"In your dreams, Garrison. Just send me a bill." She turned to meet the medical examiner, dismissing Ben as though he were one of her lackeys.

Ben scratched his bristled jaw, feeling like he had been sucker punched. The ungrateful cunt. One of these days she wouldn't get away with jacking men around. Actually, Ben had heard rumors that she did the same thing to women. Yeah, he could see Racine doing both, maybe even at the same time. The thought threatened to give him another hard-on. He felt the feebie staring at him. It was time to get the hell out of here. After all, he had gotten what he wanted.

He started down the path, knowing without looking where to step so he wouldn't slip. Before he turned around the granite boulders, he glanced over his shoulder. Racine and the rest of them were already occupied with the medical examiner. Ben stuffed his hand deep into his pocket, found the smooth cylinder. Then he smiled as he squeezed the roll of film into the palm of his hand. Poor Racine. It had never occurred to her that he may have taken more than one roll.

CHAPTER 22

Maggie felt an immediate sense of relief. How awful was that? She preferred examining a dead body to having breakfast with her mother. Surely, that had to be a mortal sin for which she'd burn in hell. Or perhaps she'd be struck by lightning—maybe by one of the thickening gray thunderheads gathering now.

She flashed her badge to the first uniformed officer blocking the sidewalk next to the information center. He nodded, and she ducked under the crime scene tape. It was her first visit to the monument, though it had been finished and dedicated in 1997. She guessed she wasn't much different from other District suburbanites. Who had time to tour monuments except on vacation? And even if she took vacations, she certainly wouldn't choose to stay in the District.

Unlike the other presidential monuments, the FDR Memorial included trees, waterfalls, grassy berms, alcoves and gardens, all spread out over a long, expansive area rather than grouped in one imposing structure. As Maggie walked through the galleries or rooms, she paid little attention to the sculptures and bronzes. Instead her attention went to the granite walls, the ledges above and behind. She noticed plenty of trees and bushes. From down here, the area looked like a private haven for murder. Had the designers not given that a thought or had she simply become cynical after years of trying to think like a killer?

Maggie stopped at the bigger-than-life bronze of the seated Roosevelt with a little bronze dog next to him. She checked the position of the spotlights around it and wondered how far up they would shine. If the sky continued to darken, perhaps she'd soon get her answer. However, the granite walls had to be ten to fifteen feet tall. She doubted the lights illuminated any of the trees and bushes above and behind. From where she stood, craning her neck, she wondered if it was possible to even notice someone in those woods? She could faintly hear the commotion of detectives over the rushing sound of the waterfall. The voices came from above and farther in the bushes, but she couldn't see them. Not a single motion.

"The little dog's name is Fala."

She startled and turned to find a man with a camera hanging from his neck.

"Excuse me?"

"Most people don't know that. The dog. It was Roosevelt's favorite."

"The monument's closed this morning," she told him, and immediately saw his expression change to anger.

"I'm not some fucking tourist. I'm here taking crime scene shots. Just ask Racine.

"Okay, my mistake." But his quick temper drew her attention, and she found herself assessing his bristled jaw and tousled dark hair, the worn knees of his blue jeans and the toe tips of shiny, expensive cowboy boots. He could easily pass for a tourist or an aging college student.

"See, I could make a snap judgment, too, and wonder what a babe like you was doing here. I thought Racine liked being the only babe on the scene." He returned her assessment by letting his eyes slowly run the length of her.

"New police procedure. We like to have at least one backup."

"Excuse me?"

"I'm the backup babe."

He smiled, more of a smirk than a smile, and his eyes traveled the same path.

"Sorta like cameramen," she continued. "Every police station needs a backup. You know, a second stringer, some lackey they call when they're in a pinch and the real cameraman can't make it."

His eyes shot up to hers, and she could see the flash of anger return. This guy was as much a crime scene photographer as she was a police babe. What the hell was Racine thinking? Or perhaps that was the problem. Racine hadn't been thinking, as usual.

"I'm tired of this fucking treatment," he said, with his hands swiping the air as if to show her what he had endured. "I do you assholes a favor and what do I get? I don't fucking need this shit. I'm outta here."

He didn't wait for a response. Instead, he turned on the heels of his polished boots and left with enough of a strut that Maggie knew he had gotten something for his early morning trouble. Just what, she wasn't sure. Perhaps some promise from Racine, some token quid pro quo. The woman had it down to an art form. Maggie remembered the last time she and Racine had worked a case, not that long ago. It was still too fresh in her memory bank to shrug off the distasteful experience. She had almost found herself on the other end of one of Racine's quid pro quos.

"O'Dell." This time the voice came from above. Agent Tully leaned over the ledge. "I want you to take a look at this before they bag the body."

"What's the best route up?"

"Around the fourth gallery. There's a set of rest rooms. Come all the way around them and to the back." He pointed to a place she couldn't see—too many granite walls. She found her way past another waterfall and more granite, then climbed a path that looked freshly made.

They were waiting for her, keeping their distance from the body, though Stan Wenhoff looked anxious to get on with his job. The forensics team was packing up what they had gathered so far in larger plastic bags. Maggie understood their urgency even before a low rumble of thunder came from overhead.

The girl sat against a tree with her back to the ledge of the monument. Her head lolled on her neck, exposing one side of deep raw tracks. Her eyes stared out despite the mass of whitish yellow in the corner of one. Without closer examination, Maggie knew the mass to be maggots. Her legs were extended straight out in front of her and spread apart. Black, shiny-backed blowflies were already taking their posts in her pubic area and up her nostrils.

The girl wore only a black bra, still clasped but pushed up to expose her small white breasts. A piece of gray duct tape covered her mouth. Her short dark hair was tangled with bits and pieces of dried leaves and pine needles. Despite the horror of the scene, the girl's hands were folded together, lying neatly and calmly across her lap, resting just below the nest of blowflies. The hands reminded Maggie of someone praying. Was it supposed to mean something?

"We don't have much time, Agent O'Dell." Stan was the first to get impatient.

Poor Stan. Another early morning call-in for him in less than a week.

Tully was alongside her now, pointing to the ground in front of her.

"There's these weird marks, circular indentations."

At first she couldn't see them. It looked as if something may have been set down, though the object had not been very heavy. The marks Tully referred to were not deep, barely leaving impressions on the surface.

"Mean anything to you?" he asked.

"No. Should it?"

"I think so, but I can't figure out what."

"Tully's all gloom and doom today." Julia Racine approached on Maggie's other side. She smiled down at her, hands on her hips. "He's already looking for a serial killer."

Maggie took one last look at the indentations, stood up and glanced at the girl's body again, then she faced the detective. "I think Agent Tully's right. And judging by this scene, I'd say this guy's just getting started."

CHAPTER 23

"If you ask me, it looks like a rape that got carried away."

Tully winced at Detective Racine's assessment, but he didn't need to argue with her. All he had to do was wait for O'Dell to do it.

"If that's what you think, then why did Agent Tully and I get called in to check it out?"

"Beats me." Racine shrugged, lifting the collar of her jacket as another rumble of thunder echoed through the air. "It's federal property."

"Then someone at the field office would have been called. Still doesn't explain why BSU would be consulted."

Tully stared up at the rolling gray thunderheads. O'Dell was right. The two of them specialized in criminal analysis, coming up with profiles, especially of repeat offenders or serial killers. Someone other than Detective Racine must have thought it important to call Cunningham. Whoever it was hadn't bothered to let Racine in on it. Didn't make much sense.

"The scuffle happened over here." Racine, anxious to prove her theory, pointed to a spot where leaves were smashed and crumbled. The mobile crime lab people had spent a good deal of time sifting and collecting from that area.

"Doesn't look like much of a scuffle." O'Dell squatted at the edge of the perimeter and examined the area without touching anything. "Someone definitely lay down here. Maybe even rolled around. The leaves and grass are packed down. But I don't see any torn grass, any scuffs in the dirt or heel marks for the type of violent scuffle you're talking about."

Detective Racine snorted under her breath, and Tully couldn't help thinking how unladylike it sounded. These two were strutting around each other like a couple of cockfighters. Sort of the equivalent of two men having a pissing contest.

"Look, O'Dell, I know a thing or two about rape scenes." Racine sounded as though her patience was wearing thin. "Posing the body like that is just one more way for him to degrade his victim."

"Oh, really?"

Tully turned away. Oh, Jesus! Here it comes. He recognized that tone of sarcasm. Had even had it launched at him a time or two.

"Did you ever think the unsub may have posed the body to alter the crime scene?" O'Dell asked the detective.

"Alter? You mean like on purpose, to throw us off?"

With his back to the two women, Tully rolled his eyes and hoped that O'Dell didn't say "Oh, duh." Detective Racine was in charge. Just once, couldn't O'Dell remember that?

"Maybe he posed the body," O'Dell was saying slowly as

if speaking to a small child, "to redirect the investigation away from himself."

Another snort from Racine. "You know what your problem is, O'Dell? You give criminals too much credit. Most of them are stupid bastards. That's the premise I work from."

Tully walked away. He couldn't take any more. It had been entertaining at first. Now he no longer cared who won the pissing contest, although he'd place his money on O'Dell. He wandered over to Wenhoff, who was finishing his examination of the young woman's body.

"Any guess on time of death?"

"My best guesstimate right now judging from the stage of rigor, the rectal temp and the invasion of only the early feeders—" he batted away a few of the persistent blowflies "—is less than twenty-four hours. Maybe about twelve hours. I'll need to do some other tests. I also want to check with the weather service and see how cold it got last night."

"Twelve hours?" Tully knew enough about dead bodies to have estimated on his own that the murder had been recent; however, he hadn't expected it to have been that recent. Suddenly, he felt a knot twist in his stomach. "That would make it last night, maybe somewhere between what—eight and midnight?"

"That's a good guess." Wenhoff pushed himself up with great effort and waved over a couple of uniformed officers. "She's ready to bag, boys, but she's stiff as a board. Be careful you don't break something."

Tully moved out of the way, not wanting to watch how they'd get her from a sitting position into the black nylon bag. He looked out over a clearing in the woods. In the distance he could see tourists wandering along the Vietnam Wall. Buses were winding around the police blockade to bypass the FDR Memorial and snake around to the Lincoln Memorial. Last night Emma and her friends had been here, walking those same sidewalks. Had the killer watched them while choosing his target? Hell, this girl didn't look much older than Emma.

"Tully." O'Dell came up beside him, startling him. "I'm heading over to the morgue. Stan's going to do the autopsy today. You want to meet me there, or should I just fill you in tomorrow?"

He only heard about half of what she had said.

"Tully? Are you okay?"

"Sure. I'm fine." He rubbed his hand over his face to cover up the sense of panic he was feeling. "I'll meet you over there." When she didn't move and continued to stare at him, he decided he needed to convince her. No better way to do that than to change the subject. "What's with you and Racine? I get the feeling there's some history there?"

She looked away, and immediately Tully knew he was right. But instead she said, "I just don't like her."

"How come?"

"Do I need a reason?"

"I know I probably don't know you very well, but yeah, I'd say you're the type of person who needs a reason to not like someone."

"You're right," she said, then added, "You don't know me very well." She started to leave but said over her shoulder, "I'll see you at the morgue, okay?" She didn't look back, only waved a hand at him, a gesture that said it was a done deal and that any conversation about her and Racine was over. Yes, there was definitely something there.

Now, as he watched everyone pack up, including the officers with the body bag, he could allow the nausea to take over his stomach. He walked to the ledge and looked out over Potomac Park. This time a rumble of thunder cracked open the sky—as if it had been waiting out of respect—and the rain came pouring down.

Tully stood still, watching the tourists below, scattering for shelter or popping open umbrellas. The rain felt good, and he lifted his face to it, letting it cool the sweaty, clammy feeling that had taken over his body. Yet, all he could think about was—Jesus—how close had his daughter come to being this guy's victim?

CHAPTER 24

Maggie kicked off her leather pumps and put plastic shoe covers over her stockinged feet. She'd chosen the pumps for breakfast with her mother at the Crystal City Hyatt, not ones she would have picked had she known she would be working. Stan watched but said nothing. Perhaps he didn't want to push his luck. After all, she was wearing her goggles without being told. Usually they stayed on top of her head. But there was something different about Stan's behavior toward her; he seemed quieter. He hadn't yet muttered a single "humph" or heavy sigh. Not yet, anyway. Was he worried she'd freak out on him again?

She had to admit, she wasn't exactly comfortable being back here this soon. With little effort she could still conjure up the image of Delaney's gray death mask. But lately, she was able to do that anytime, anyplace—being back at the morgue probably wouldn't make it any worse. Or at least, that's what she told herself. She needed to stop thinking about Delaney. It wasn't just Delaney, though. It was all the memories his death had unleashed. Memories of her father that, after all these years, still left her feeling empty and hollow and, worst of all, alone.

It made her realize that with her impending divorce from Greg, she was on the verge of losing any sense of family that she had tried to construct. Or had she honestly ever tried? Gwen was constantly telling her that she kept too many people who cared about her at arm's length. Is that what happened with her and Greg? Had she kept her own husband at arm's length, not allowing him access to the vulnerable places inside her? Maybe her mother was right. Maybe the demise of her marriage *had* been all her fault. She felt a shiver. What a thought! That her mother could actually be right about something.

She joined Stan. He had already begun his external examination of the girl's body and was taking measurements. She helped him with the menial tasks of placing the body block and removing fluid samples. It felt good to concentrate on something concrete, something familiar and constructive. She had worked with Stan enough times to know which tasks he'd allowed her to do, and which she needed to stand back and simply watch.

Maggie carefully slipped the paper bags off each of the girl's hands and began scraping under the fingernails. There was plenty of material to scrape, which, ordinarily, would mean the girl might be able to tell them through DNA who her attacker had been. But from a preliminary look at the girl's neck, Maggie could see at least a dozen horizontal crescentic abrasions among the various raw and deep ligature tracks and massive bruising. Horizontal marks meant it was a safe guess that much of the skin behind the girl's fingernails was her own, caused by her clawing at the ligature.

Stan snapped enough Polaroids to fill the corkboard over the main sink. Then he removed his gloves, and for the third time since they had started, he scrubbed his hands, applying lotion and massaging it into his skin before putting on a fresh pair of gloves. Maggie was used to his strange ritual, but once in a while it made her acutely aware of the blood on her own gloves. Today would be one of those times.

"Sorry, I'm late," Agent Tully said from the doorway where he stood, hesitating. He was dripping wet—even the brim of his baseball cap was soaked. He took off the cap and raked the wetness from his close-cropped hair. At first, Maggie thought his hesitancy was because he didn't want to get the floor wet, which was crazy because it was cement with drains strategically positioned for nastier run-off than rainwater. But then, she saw he was waiting for someone. Detective Racine appeared behind Tully, looking too dry and refreshed to have come from the same place as him.

"Are we all here now?" Stan asked with the grumble he had suppressed until now.

"Yep. We're all here and ready," Racine sang out, rubbing her hands together as if they were gathering for a game of dodge ball.

Maggie had forgotten that Racine would be at the autopsy. It was her case—of course she'd want to be here. The last time Maggie worked with Racine the detective had been assigned to the sex crimes unit. Now she couldn't help wondering if Racine had ever watched an autopsy before. Suddenly, Maggie was anxious to get to work.

"Shoe covers, masks, everything's in the linen closet," Stan said, pointing. "No one watches without being properly gowned up. Got it?"

"No problem." Racine whipped off her leather bomber jacket and headed for the closet.

Tully lagged behind, taking more time than necessary to wring out his windbreaker and cap over one of the drains. He glanced several times at the girl's body, splayed out on the aluminum table. Maggie realized suddenly she may have been mistaken. Was it possible Tully was the one who had never witnessed an autopsy?

Before he transferred to Quantico, Tully had been doing criminal analysis at the Cleveland field office for five or six years. But she also knew much of that time was spent viewing crime scenes via photos, digital scans and video. He had admitted once that he hadn't physically attended many murder scenes until the Albert Stucky case. It was altogether possible he had never attended an autopsy until now. Damn it! And she had been so hoping it would be Racine who would upchuck her breakfast.

"Agent Tully." Maggie needed to get his mind off the dead body and onto the case. "Are we sure there was no ID found anywhere at the scene?"

She saw him glance at Racine, but the detective was busy, taking too much time finding a gown her size, like they came in anything other than large, too large and extra too large. At this rate, Maggie knew it would take the woman another ten minutes to accessorize. When Tully realized Racine wasn't paying enough attention to answer, he left his wet gear at the door and came over, grabbing a clean gown off a laundry rack and slipping it on.

"They found her handbag, but no ID. Her clothes were folded and stacked with the purse about ten yards away."

The absence of ID didn't surprise Maggie. Killers often disposed of any tangible identification in the hopes that if the victim couldn't be identified, perhaps neither could the killer. Then, there were always the freaks who took the IDs as trophies.

"Her clothes were folded? What a neat and tidy rapist," Maggie said for Racine's benefit. Now the woman glanced over and frowned at her. So she was listening, after all.

"The girl's underpants were ripped in the crotch area,"

Racine couldn't resist adding. She padded over to the table, tucking the goggles up onto her spiky blond hair.

Maggie waited for Stan to notice and reprimand Racine, but he was occupied with getting the nests of maggots out of the girl's pubic hair. Then she reminded herself that she needed to concentrate and not let Racine get under her skin. She continued scraping evidence from beneath each fingernail, bagging the findings and labeling each as to which finger it had been taken from.

Besides, why should she care if Racine insisted on sticking with her theory of this being a rape that got carried away? That the District PD hadn't noticed yet that their detective was incompetent shouldn't be Maggie's problem. Yet, it *did* matter if Maggie was going to be on this case, even as a consultant. The last case she'd worked with Racine had left Maggie with a bad taste in her mouth—Racine's mistakes had almost cost them an indictment.

Maggie swatted a strand of hair off her perspiring forehead with the back of her wrist, so as not to contaminate her latexed hands. She caught Racine watching her. Maggie looked away.

Quite honestly, other than the one botched case, Maggie knew little about Julia Racine except what she had heard through rumors. She probably had no right to judge the woman, but if there was any truth to the rumors, Detective Racine represented a breed of woman that Maggie despised, especially in law enforcement, where playing games could get someone hurt, or even killed.

Since day one of her forensics fellowship, Maggie had worked hard to be just one of the guys and to be treated as such. But women like Racine used their sex as some sort of entitlement or bribe, a means to an end. Now, as she felt Racine's eyes watching her, Maggie hated that Racine still thought she could use that tactic, especially with her. After the last time they had worked together, Maggie thought Racine would know better—pouring on the charm or flirting wouldn't get her any favors from her. But when Maggie glanced up and caught the woman watching her, Racine didn't look away. Instead, she met Maggie's eyes, held her glance and smiled.

CHAPTER 25

Ben Garrison strung the dripping prints on a short length of clothesline in his cramped darkroom. The first two rolls of film had been disappointing, but this roll...this one was incredible. He was back in the saddle again. Maybe he'd even be able to get a little bidding war started, though he wouldn't be able to waste any time. His fingertips tingled with excitement, but his lungs ached from the fumes. He needed to take a break despite his impatience.

He took one of the prints with him, closing the door on the fumes and heading for the refrigerator. Of course, it was empty except for the regular array of condiments, some kiwi fruit he couldn't remember putting in the back, a container of mystery goop and four long-neck bottles of Budweiser. He grabbed one of the bottles, twisted off the cap and returned to the kitchen counter to admire his masterpiece in the shitty fluorescent lighting.

A knock at the door startled him. Who the hell? He rarely got visitors, and he thought he had trained his meddling neighbors to fuck off. His artistic process was time sensitive. He couldn't be disturbed if he had prints in the fix bath or a roll of film in the developing canister. No respect. What was fucking wrong with people?

He flipped all three locks and yanked open the door.

"What is it?" he growled, causing the small gray-haired woman to step backward and grab the railing. "Mrs. Fowler?" He scratched at his jaw and leaned against the doorjamb, blocking his landlady's wandering eyes. Apparently he hadn't trained everyone in this dilapidated old building to leave him alone. "Why, Mrs. Fowler, what can I help you with today?" He could turn on the charm when necessary.

"Mr. Garrison, I was just wandering by. I've been checking on Mrs. Stanislov down the hall." Her beady eyes were darting around him, trying to get a glimpse into his apartment.

Several weeks ago, she'd insisted on accompanying the plumber to fix his leaky faucet. The old woman's birdlike head pivoted around, trying to take in the African masks on his wall, the bronze fertility goddesses that adorned his bookcase and the other exotic trinkets he had amassed during his travels. That was when the money was flowing in, and there wasn't a photo he could shoot that someone at *Newsweek* or *Time* or *National Geographic* wouldn't pay top dollar for. He was the hottest new commodity to hit the photojournalism world. Now he was barely thirty and everyone seemed to consider him a has-been. Well, he'd show them all.

"I'm actually pretty busy, Mrs. Fowler. I'm working." He kept his voice pleasant, crossed his arms to stifle his irritation and waited, hoping she could see his impatience through her trifocals.

"I was checking on Mrs. Stanislov," she repeated, waving

a skeletal arm toward the door at the end of the hall. "She's been under the weather all week. There's that flu bug going around, you know."

If she was expecting some show of sympathy, they'd be here all night. That was above and beyond his ass-kissing ability, cheap apartment or not. He shifted his weight and waited. His mind wandered back to the print he had left on the kitchen counter. Over thirty exposures to finally capture that one image, that one—

"Mr. Garrison?"

Her small pinched face reminded him of the wrinkled kiwi fruit in the back of his frig.

"Yes, Mrs. Fowler? I really must get back to my work."

She stared at him with eyes magnified three times their size. Her thin lips pursed, wrinkling her skin beyond what he thought possible. Spoiled kiwi. He reminded himself to throw them out.

"I wondered if it might be important. That you might want to know."

"What are you talking about?" His politeness had but one level, and she was pushing it past its limits.

This time she backed away, and he knew his tone must have frightened her. She simply pointed at the package he hadn't noticed sitting next to his door. Before he stooped to pick it up, Mrs. Fowler's tiny bird feet shuffled down the stairs.

"Thank you, Mrs. Fowler," he called after her, smiling when he realized he sounded like Jack Nicholson in *The Shining*. Not that she would notice. The old bat probably hadn't even heard him.

The package was lightweight and wrapped in ordinary brown paper. Ben flipped it around. Nothing rattled, and there were no labels, only his name scrawled in black marker. Sometimes the photo lab down the street delivered supplies for him, but he couldn't remember ordering any.

He set it on the kitchen counter, grabbed a paring knife and started cutting the wrap. When he opened the lid of the box, he noticed the packing material's strange texture—it looked like brown packing peanuts. He didn't give it a second thought and stuck his hand into the box, feeling for what was buried inside.

The packing material began to move.

Or was it the exhaustion and too many fumes playing tricks on him?

In seconds the brown peanuts came to life. Shit! The entire contents started crawling out over the sides of the box. Several scurried up his arm. Ben swatted and slapped at them, knocking the box off the counter and releasing hundreds of cockroaches, racing and skittering across his living room floor.

CHAPTER 26

"Anything found that could have been used as a ligature? And what about handcuffs?" Maggie showed Tully and Racine the girl's wrists, but looked to Tully for answers. The bruises and marks on the wrists were undeniably made by handcuffs. She watched Tully's face, pretending to wait for the answer but really trying to see if he was okay.

This time Tully didn't glance at Racine, but Maggie did, and she could tell the detective wanted to answer, but stopped herself. Tully started pulling out his eyeglasses and pieces of paper from somewhere beneath the gown, tangling his hands in the process. Typical Tully, Maggie noted. He put the glasses on and began sorting through his slips of paper, an odd assortment that included some sort of pamphlet, a folded envelope, the back of a store receipt and a cocktail napkin.

"No handcuffs," he finally answered, and continued to search his scraps of paper.

She wished he would relax. Tully was usually the laid-back one. She was the quick-tempered, hotheaded one, the loose cannon. He was the steady, let's-think-before-we-leap type. It unnerved her how uptight he seemed to be. Something was wrong. Something more than his discomfort with witnessing an autopsy.

"You know, Tully," she said, "they make these really cool contraptions with sheets of paper all tacked together. They're called notebooks, and you can even get them small enough to fit into your pocket."

Tully frowned at her over his glasses and went back to his notes.

"Very funny. My system works just fine."

"Of course, it does. As long as you don't blow your nose." Racine laughed.

"Humpf." Stan Wenhoff didn't have time for a sense of humor. He motioned to Maggie for help, wanting to hoist the body onto its side for a quick search of any other lacerations.

"Why is her bottom so red?" Racine asked. "The rest of her seems to have this bluish tint, but her ass is all red. Is that weird or what?" Racine attempted a nervous laugh.

Stan sighed, exhaling what sounded like a day's worth of sighs. He was not the most patient medical examiner when it came to explanations. Maggie got the impression he would post No Visitors signs if allowed. They eased the body back. And Stan turned around to peel off his gloves and begin his hand-washing ritual again.

"It's called livor mortis, or the bruising of death," Maggie said when it was obvious Stan wasn't going to answer.

She watched and waited for him to stop her. Instead, he nodded for her to continue. "When the heart stops pumping, the blood stops circulating. All the red cells are literally pulled by the force of gravity to the lowest area, usually the area of the body that's in contact with the ground. The blood cells start breaking down and separating into the muscle tissue. After about two hours, the entire area looks like this, sort of one big reddish bruise. That is, if the body hasn't been moved."

"Wow!" Maggie could feel Racine staring at her. "Does that mean she died sitting up?"

Maggie hadn't thought about it before, but Racine was probably right. Why would the killer have positioned the girl's body while she was still alive? Without asking, she looked to Stan for him to confirm or deny Racine's observation. As the silence stretched out, he finally realized they were waiting for him to respond. He turned around, tugging on a fresh pair of gloves.

"My early guesstimate would be, yes. I'm curious, though. She has almost a pinkish-red tint to her. I'll need to have toxicology check for any poisons."

"Poisons?" Racine attempted another of her nervous laughs. "Stan, this kid was obviously strangled."

"Really, Detective? You believe that to be obvious, do you?"

"Well, maybe not entirely obvious."

Stan took this opportunity to choose a scalpel from the tray of instruments, and Racine's eyes grew wide. Maggie knew they had reached that moment Racine had been dreading since she arrived. Stan started the Y incision.

"Wait." Maggie stopped him, but it wasn't to save Racine. There was something she wanted to check, now curious. If the girl had still been alive when sitting up, maybe strangulation wasn't the cause of death. "Do you mind if we take a look at the ligature marks on her neck first?"

"Fine. Let's take a look at the ligature marks on her neck first." Wenhoff sighed again and set the scalpel aside, purposely clanking it against the other metal instruments.

Maggie knew he was doing his best to restrain his impatience, though his pudgy face betrayed him with its unnatural shade of red. Sweat beads filled his receding hairline. He was used to doing things his own way and his audiences keeping their mouths shut. That he humored her at all, Maggie regarded as Stan's ultimate show of respect. Now he stepped aside, giving her permission to proceed.

"So there was nothing left at the scene that could have been used as a ligature?" Maggie asked Tully while she searched the countertops.

This time she saw him check with Racine, and she was the one to answer. "Nothing. The girl wasn't even wearing panty hose. The purse strap was found intact and clean. Whatever he used, he took with him."

Maggie found what she was looking for and grabbed the tape dispenser from a desk in the corner. She peeled off her gloves so she could handle the tape, then ripped off a piece, holding each end carefully.

"Stan, could you tilt her head, so I can get a better look at her neck?"

Stan handled the girl's head as if it belonged to a mannequin. Rigor mortis was fully established and had stiffened the muscles. After about twenty-four more hours, the muscles would become pliable again, but at the moment, Stan had to twist the head in what looked like an irreverent way, but was, in fact, a necessity.

There were several ligature marks, some overlapping, some deeper than the others. The girl's neck, which probably hadn't contained a single age line, now looked like a road map in 3-D. In addition to the tracks were massive bruises, where the killer must have decided to use his hands, as well.

"Why do you suppose he had such a tough time getting the job done?" Maggie said out loud, not really expecting an answer.

"Maybe she put up a hell of a fight," Racine suggested.

The girl was small, barely sixty-two inches, according to

Stan's measurements. Maggie doubted that she could have managed much of a fight.

"Maybe he didn't want to get the job done right away." Tully surprised her with his hushed remark. She could feel him close by, looking over her shoulder.

"You mean he just wanted her unconscious?" Racine asked.

Maggie tried not to get distracted and pressed the transparent tape against the girl's skin, pushing it into one of the ligature grooves.

"He might simply have gotten off on watching her pass out," Tully said, exactly what Maggie had been thinking. "It could have been part of some autoerotic asphyxiation."

"That could explain her dying while sitting up," Maggie said. "Maybe her position was simply a part of his sick game."

"What are you doing with the tape?" Racine asked her.

Ah, so the good detective would finally admit to not knowing something. Maggie lifted the tape while Stan held a slide up for her to attach it to. When it was safely secure, Maggie raised it up to the light.

"Depending on what the killer used, we can sometimes pick up fibers left in the tracks."

"That's if he used a rope or some kind of clothing," Tully added.

"Or any sort of fabric or nylon. Doesn't look like any fibers here. But there is something odd. Looks like glitter."

"Glitter?" Stan was suddenly interested. She handed him the slide and went back to the girl's throat.

"He must have used something strong and thin." Maggie pulled on a fresh pair of gloves. "Probably a cord. Maybe something like a clothesline." She examined the sides of the neck. "Doesn't appear to be a knot."

"Does that mean anything?" Tully asked.

"It could help us if he's done this before. We might be able to match up something already on VICAP. Sometimes killers use the same kind of knot each time. That was one of the identifying factors of the Boston Strangler. He used the same knot on all thirteen of his victims."

"O'Dell, you sure know your trivia about serial killers," Racine jabbed.

Maggie knew she meant it as an innocent joke, but snapped back, "It wouldn't hurt you to know some. You can bet the killers know." As soon as the words were out of her mouth, she regretted them.

"Maybe I need to come to Quantico and take a couple of your classes."

Oh, wonderful, Maggie thought. That was all she needed—to have Julia Racine as a student. Or was that what Racine was hoping for? Did the detective have aspirations of being an FBI agent? Maggie shoved the thought aside and concentrated on the girl's throat.

She ran an index finger over the deep, red scars. As she did this, she noticed a bump. Not just a bump, but a swollen area in the soft underside of the girl's throat. "Wait a minute. Stan, did you check her mouth yet?"

"Not yet. But we'll need to get dental prints if there was no ID."

"I think there's something in her throat."

She hesitated. Both men and Racine hovered over the body and over Maggie, waiting and watching. As soon as Maggie pried open the mouth, she could smell it, a sweet almond scent. Again, she hesitated and glanced up at Stan.

"Do you smell that?"

He sniffed the air. Maggie knew not everyone was capable of smelling the scent, actually about fifty percent of the population. It was Tully who finally answered, "Cyanide?"

Maggie used an index finger to scoop inside both cheeks and removed a partially dissolved capsule. Stan held up an open plastic bag.

"What's with cyanide these days?" Stan said, then noticed the warning look Maggie shot him.

"What kind of crazy son of a bitch gives his victim a cyanide pill after he's strangled her? Or is that the cause of death?" Racine sounded impatient. She didn't seem to notice the exchange between Stan and Maggie, who had both recognized the red-and-white capsule. Enough of it was intact to see that the capsule bore the same brand name they had extracted from the five boys in the cabin just last weekend.

"I haven't gotten that far yet," Stan finally answered.

He was growing impatient, too, but for the moment he was keeping what he knew quiet. Evidently he had read Maggie's urgent look accurately. If there was a connection between this girl and those boys, Racine would know soon enough. For the moment, it was one of the few things they had managed to keep from the media, and Maggie wanted it to remain that way.

"Her mouth was taped shut," Stan continued. "I bagged the duct tape."

"He probably stuck the pill into her mouth and taped it shut while she was unconscious," Tully said, trying to explain the partially dissolved capsule. The girl's saliva glands would have still needed to be working for the capsule to have started dissolving.

Maggie glanced at Tully and could see that he had recognized the capsule, too, and had guessed what was going on. So Racine was the only one in the dark. Not a bad game plan. Maggie refused to feel an ounce of guilt over keeping this from the detective, especially after their last case together.

"Seems like overkill," Racine said.

"Or insurance." Stan was playing along.

"I hate to interrupt your brainstorming, everyone," Maggie said. "But there's something else in here. Stan, could you hand me those forceps?"

She opened the woman's mouth as wide as the rigored jaws

allowed, then squinted as she pinched onto an object that was lodged halfway down the girl's throat. What she extracted was covered with blood, folded and crinkled, but still recognizable.

"I think I just found her ID," Maggie told them, holding up what looked like a mangled driver's license.

CHAPTER 27

Tully sipped his Coke, grateful for the break. Wenhoff had taken the seventeen-year-old's driver's license and finger-prints upstairs to the lab. But Tully knew they wouldn't find any priors or runaway reports on Virginia Brier. From the bikini wax and the girl's mid-November tan lines, Tully knew Virginia was not the typical high-risk victim. She wasn't a prostitute or some throwaway or a homeless street kid. He guessed she came from a good home, a middle- to upper-class family. Somewhere a father and mother were still waiting for her to come home from last night or going crazy because it was too early to file a missing person's report. It reminded him of waiting up for Emma last night. She had been only twenty minutes late, but what if...

"Hey, Tully?"

He realized O'Dell was staring at him again with a look of concern.

"Are you feeling okay?"

"Yeah, I'm fine. Just tired. Stayed up too late last night."

"Oh, really? Hot date?" Racine hoisted herself up onto an empty countertop, her long legs allowing her to do it in one smooth motion.

"My daughter and I stayed up watching *Rear Window.*"

"Jimmy Stewart and Grace Kelly? I love that movie. I guess I didn't realize you were married, Tully."

"Divorced."

"Oh, okay." The detective smiled at him as if she was glad. Most people automatically mumbled some sort of apology, which he didn't really understand, either.

He glanced over at O'Dell, who was pretending to be occupied with some evidence bags instead of paying attention to Racine's flirting. Or at least, he *thought* Racine was flirting with him. He'd never been good at it himself or even good at detecting it, for that matter. At least O'Dell was trying to behave herself with Racine, as if being nice to the detective would make up for them keeping her in the dark about the cyanide capsule. He wasn't sure he agreed that they should be withholding information. This was Racine's case, after all. Not theirs. They were here only to assist and offer consultation.

Tully still wondered why Cunningham and BSU had even been called in on this case. Who had made that call and what did they know? Had someone already suggested a connection between this girl and the five young men from the cabin raid? And if so, who was it and how did they know? Evidently, it wasn't anyone at the District PD, because Racine seemed clueless.

His stomach still felt queasy, though the Coke was helping. He was fine as long as he concentrated on the case and not the fact that the dead girl could just as easily have been

Emma. He found himself wondering what had made this girl different. Why had the killer chosen her?

"Okay, you two," Racine said. "Tell me what you know."

Tully shot a look at O'Dell. Had Racine finally figured out they hadn't told her something? Before either of them could answer, Racine continued, "Since we have some time, tell me about this guy from what we've learned so far. I have to get out there and start looking for this fucking psycho. You guys are the profilers. Tell me what I'm supposed to look for."

Tully relaxed, almost sighing. O'Dell hadn't flinched. She was good, impressive. They hadn't known each other for very long, but he did know that O'Dell was a better liar than he was. He'd let her have the first shot at Racine's question.

"Everything so far points to him as being organized."

Racine nodded. "Okay, I know about organized versus disorganized. You can save me the textbook stuff. I'm after specifics."

"It's awfully early for specifics," O'Dell told her.

This time Tully could tell O'Dell was not just being difficult with the detective; she was being careful. Maybe too careful. They owed Racine something.

"I'd say he's between twenty-five to thirty years old, Tully said. "Above-average intelligence. He probably holds a regular job and appears to be socially competent to those who know him. Not necessarily a loner. Maybe even a bit arrogant, a braggart."

Racine flipped open a small notebook and was jotting the information down, though what he was giving her could be considered classic textbook generalities, exactly what she had said she didn't want.

"He knows a thing or two about police procedure," O'Dell added, obviously deciding it safe to divulge some of what they knew. "Probably why he likes to use handcuffs. Also, he knew how to ID-proof a body and that delaying her identity might delay us in identifying him, too."

Racine looked up. "Wait a minute. What are you saying? That he could be an ex-cop or something?"

"Not necessarily, but he could be someone who knows a thing or two about crime scenes," O'Dell said. "With some of these guys, it's a fascination. It's part of the cat-and-mouse chase. What they know about police procedure could be from cop shows or even suspense novels."

Tully watched. Racine seemed satisfied and continued writing. At least the two women weren't trying to contradict or outdo each other. For the moment, anyway.

"His posing the body is significant, too. I think it's something more than just gaining control or some sense of empowerment." O'Dell looked at Tully to see if he wanted to venture a guess. He motioned for her to go ahead. "It's possible," she continued, "that he wanted only for us to admire his handiwork, but I think there's something more to it. It may be symbolic."

"You said at the crime scene that it may have been to alter the scene, to throw us off."

"Oh my God, Racine! You mean you were actually listening to me?" This time the women smiled at each other, much to Tully's relief.

"Those circular indentations in the ground mean something, too," Tully reminded them, "but I have no idea what. Not yet, anyway."

"Oh, and he's left-handed," O'Dell added as an afterthought.

Both Tully and Racine stared at her, waiting for an explanation.

O'Dell walked back to the body and pointed to the right side of the girl's face.

"There's a bruise here along her jawline. Her lip is split in this corner. Even bled for a short time. It's her right side, which means, if he was facing her, he hit her from left to right, probably with his left fist."

"Couldn't he have used the back of his right hand?" Tully asked, trying to play out the possible scenarios.

"Maybe, but that would be more of an upward motion." She demonstrated, swiping a backhanded motion toward him. He could see what she meant. A person's natural tendency would be to start with the hand down and to bring it up and across. "This injury," O'Dell continued, "looks like a direct hit. I'd say a fist." She balled up her left hand and swiped again, this time straight in front. "Definitely, a left fist to the right jaw."

Throughout this demonstration Tully noticed Racine watching quietly, almost with awe or perhaps admiration. Then she went back to her notes. Whatever it was Tully had noticed in Racine's expression, it had been lost on O'Dell. She hadn't been paying any attention. But then she was like that when anyone seemed to be amazed by her. Most of the time, she drove him a little nuts with her anal-retentive habits, her hotshot tactics or her tendency to overlook procedure whenever it was convenient to do so. However, this—her ability to be impressive and not take note or make a big deal of it—this was one of the things he really liked about her.

"One thing," O'Dell said, addressing Racine, "and I really am not just saying this to bug the hell out of you. This is not a one-time thing. This guy's going to do it again. And I wouldn't be surprised to find that he may have already killed before this. We really should check VICAP."

The morgue door swung open behind them. All three of them jumped, spinning around to find Stan Wenhoff, his ruddy complexion pale. He held up what looked like a computer printout.

"We're in for a hell of a mess, kids." Stan wiped at the sweat on his forehead. "She's the daughter of Henry Franklin Brier…a goddamn U.S. senator."

CHAPTER 28

Everett's Compound

Justin Pratt felt an elbow poke his side, and only then did he realize he had dozed off. He glanced at Alice, who was sitting beside him, cross-legged like the rest of the members, but her head and eyes were facing ahead, her back straight. Two of her fingers tapped his ankle, her polite way of telling him to stay awake and pay attention.

He wanted to tell her he didn't give a fuck what Father had to say tonight or any night, for that matter. And after last night he wished that Alice didn't give a fuck, either. Jesus! He was so tired. All he wanted to do was close his eyes, just for a few minutes. He could still listen even if his eyes were closed. His eyelids started to droop, and this time he felt a pinch. He sat up and scrubbed a hand over his face, digging a thumb and index finger into his eyes. Another elbow. Jesus!

He glared at her, but she didn't flinch from her appropriately adoring attention on Father. Maybe she liked what the guy did to her last night. Maybe she had really gotten off on it, and what Justin thought was a grimace had actually been her expression of orgasm. Shit! He was just tired. He needed to stop thinking about last night. He sat up straight and folded his hands into his lap.

Tonight Father was going off on the government again, a favorite topic of his. Justin had to admit that some of the stuff the man said did make sense. He remembered his grandfather telling Eric and him stories about government conspiracies. How the government had murdered JFK. How the United Nations was really a conspiracy to take over the world.

Justin's dad had said, "The old man had a couple of loose screws," but Justin loved and admired his grandfather. He had been a war hero, getting the Congressional Medal of Honor for saving his whole squad in Vietnam. Justin had seen the medal, as well as the photos and letters, one from President Lyndon Johnson. It was pretty cool. But it was all stuff Justin knew his dad despised. Probably another reason Justin loved the old man—they had something in common: neither of them had ever been able to please Justin's dad. Then his grandfather up and died last year. Justin still felt pissed at him for leaving him. He knew that was a fucked-up attitude. It wasn't his granddad's fault, but he missed the old man. He didn't have anyone to talk to, especially after Eric left.

He knew Eric missed Granddad, too, even if he was too much of a macho-shithead to admit it. Less than three weeks after the funeral, Eric dropped out of Brown University. That was when all hell broke loose at home.

"Excuse me, am I boring you?" Father's voice boomed across the room.

Justin sat up, but he was already sitting about as straight as he could. He felt Alice gripping his ankle, so tight her fingernails dug into his sock and skin.

Shit! He was in trouble now. Alice had warned him that

daydreaming during Father's talks could lead to punishment. Oh, what the hell. So what if he sent him out into the woods again. Maybe this time he'd just take off. He didn't need this shit. Maybe he could meet up with Eric somewhere else.

"Answer me," Father demanded as the room grew quiet. No one dared turn to look at the guilty one. "Do you find what I say so boring you'd rather sleep?"

Justin looked up, ready to take his punishment, but Father's eyes were staring off to Justin's left. And now the old man sitting next to Justin began to fidget restlessly. Justin could see the man's callused hands wringing the hem of his blue work shirt. He recognized him from the building crew. No wonder the poor guy was dozing. The building crew had been working around the clock to remodel Father's living quarters before winter, which was ridiculous if all of them were to be moving to some paradise soon. Surely others on the crew would speak up and remind Father of the long hours they'd been working. But instead, everyone remained silent, waiting.

"Martin, what do you have to say for yourself?"

"I guess I—"

"Stand up when you address me."

The members all sat on the floor during the meetings. Justin couldn't figure out why the hell Father was the only one who got a chair. Alice had tried to explain that no one's head should be higher than Father's when Father spoke. Justin would have laughed out loud at that had it not been for the somber, almost reverent look on her face.

"We have traitors in our midst," Father bellowed. "We have a reporter trying to destroy us with ugly lies. This is no time for any of us to be caught sleeping. I said stand!"

Justin watched the old man untangle his legs and crawl to his feet. He could sympathize with the guy. After three hours, he, too, had problems with muscle cramps. The old guy reminded Justin of his grandfather, thin and small, but wiry. He was probably stronger and younger than his weathered skin suggested. He shot a look at Justin, then looked away quickly, reminding Justin that he shouldn't be watching. Out of the corner of his eyes Justin could see the others with their heads obediently facing the front of the room and their eyes cast down.

"Martin, you're wasting everyone's time. Perhaps instead of offering an explanation, you need a reminder of what happens when you waste everyone's time." Father waved to the two bodyguards, and the men disappeared out the back door. "Come here, Martin, and bring along Aaron."

"No, wait…" Martin protested as he made his way to the front, stepping carefully around the members who sat in an unorganized fashion on the floor. "Punish me," Martin said, weaving his way, "but leave my son out of this."

However, the fair-skinned, blond Aaron was already making his way to Father's side. Justin figured him to be about his age, only small and wiry like his dad, and strangely eager to assist Father.

"Martin, you know there are no fathers and sons here. No mothers and daughters. No brothers and sisters." Father's voice was back to its calm, soothing tone. "We all belong to one unit, one family."

"Of course, I just meant—" Martin stopped when he saw the guards return, carrying what Justin thought was a huge, long hose.

Then the hose moved.

"Shit!" he said under his breath, then quickly glanced around, grateful no one had heard him over their own gasps. Because what the guards carried between them was the biggest fucking snake Justin had ever seen.

He stole a glimpse at Father's face while everyone else returned to silence. Father was smiling, watching the crowd's reaction and nodding as if in satisfaction. Suddenly, Father caught Justin's eyes and the smile turned to a scowl. Justin looked away, lowering his head as well as his eyes. Jesus! Was *he* in trouble now? He waited for his name to be called and realized his heart had begun slamming against his ribs. In this fucking silence would the sound betray him?

"Aaron," Father called instead, "I want you to take this snake and place it around Martin's neck."

There were no gasps, only more silence, as though the entire room of people was collectively holding its breath.

"But Father..." Aaron's voice sounded like a small boy's, and Justin cringed. Stupid kid. Don't show weakness. Don't show him you're scared.

"Aaron, I'm surprised." The reverend's voice was soft and sweet, and it made Justin cringe even more. "Didn't you come to me just last week and tell me you were ready to become one of my soldiers? One of our warriors for justice?"

"Yes, but—"

"Stop your sniveling, then, and do as I say," he yelled, causing everyone to jump at the change in his tone.

Aaron looked from Father to Martin and then at the snake. Justin couldn't believe the kid was considering it. But what choice did he have if he didn't want that fucking snake around his own neck? Surely, this was only a test. Yeah, that was it. Justin didn't know much about the Bible, but wasn't there some story about God telling a father to kill his own son? Then at the last minute God stopped the guy. That had to be what this was.

Justin took a deep breath, but no relief seemed to come with his sudden realization. Instead, all he felt was Alice's fingernails digging deeper into his ankle.

Aaron took hold of the snake. Martin, who had stood tall and firm all this time, began to sob, so violently he shook as Aaron and one of the guards wound the snake across the old man's shoulders and neck.

"We must not be caught sleeping," Father was saying, his voice calm again as though this was just another one of his instructive lectures. "Our enemies are closer than you think.

Only those of us who are strong and obey the strictness of our rules will survive."

Justin wondered if anyone was listening to Father's words. He had difficulty hearing them over the pounding of his own heart, while he watched the snake squeeze and Martin's face swell, turning crimson-red. The old man's fingers clawed at the snake as panic overrode fear.

"All it takes is one person," Father continued, "to betray us, to destroy us."

Justin couldn't believe it. Father wasn't even looking at Martin. Surely, he'd call it off any second now. Wasn't this enough of a test? The old man's eyes started to roll back in his head, his tongue hung from his mouth. His head would explode. It was going to fucking explode all over the place.

"We must remember…" Father stopped and looked down at the puddle forming around his shoes. Martin had peed his pants. Father lifted one foot, his face contorting with disgust. He waved to his guards. "Remove the snake," he said, as if only because he didn't want his shoes soiled any more than they already were.

It took both guards and Aaron to pull off and unwrap the snake. Martin collapsed where he stood. But Father continued as though this had only been a minor distraction, stepping over Martin's body and turning his back to him as the old man crawled away.

"We must remember there are no loyalties, no bonds except for the greater good of our mission. We must free ourselves from petty desires of the material world."

Father seemed to be addressing a specific group, especially one woman, who sat in front. Justin recognized her. She was one of the entourage that the reverend kept close at prayer rallies, one of the group of about a dozen members that was bused in for the meetings. They all still lived and worked on the outside and had not yet entirely joined the community. Alice had explained that these were people with important ties to the outside, or ones who had not yet fully proved themselves to Father.

As the meeting ended, Justin watched Father go to the woman, giving her both his hands to help her stand and hugging her. Probably feeling her up and getting in a few extra squeezes. Justin couldn't help thinking she looked like one of his mom's country club friends, wearing a navy dress and that bright red scarf.

CHAPTER 29

It was at this time every evening that Kathleen O'Dell still craved a tumbler of bourbon, a stirred—not shaken—martini or even a snifter of brandy. She stared at the tray with the porcelain gold-trimmed pot and watched as Reverend Everett poured a cup of hot tea for her, Emily, Stephen and himself. All the while, she couldn't help thinking how much she hated tea. It didn't matter if it was herbal, spice or served with lemon or honey or milk. Just the aroma made her want to gag.

The tea reminded her of those first weeks from hell when she quit drinking. Father had stopped by her apartment several times a week, generously giving of his precious time to brew for her a pot of his special tea made from leaves shipped from some exotic place in South America. He claimed it had magical powers. Kathleen swore it made her hallucinate, causing painful flashes of bright light behind her eyes. That was before it made her stomach rock violently. Each time, Father stood patiently over her, telling her how God had different plans for her, or more precisely, telling the back of her head while she vomited her guts into the toilet.

Now she smiled up at him as he handed her a cup, pretending this was exactly what she craved. She owed this man so much, and yet he seemed to ask for so little in return. Pretending to enjoy his tea seemed a small sacrifice.

They all sat in front of the roaring fireplace in the soft leather chairs Father had received from a wealthy donor. Everyone sipped the tea, and Kathleen put the cup to her lips, making herself do the same. There had been little conversation. They were still a bit stunned from Father's powerful performance. No one doubted the need for Martin to be taught a lesson. How dare he fall asleep.

She could feel Father watching the three of them, his diplomats to the outside world, as he called them. Each played an important role, assigned tasks that only he or she could deliver. In return, Father allowed them these private meetings, gracing them with his time and his confidences, both rare and special commodities. He had so many obligations. There were so many people who needed him to heal their wounds and save their souls. Between weekend rallies and daily lectures, the man had little time to himself. So many pressures, so much to expect from one person.

"All of you are very quiet tonight." He smiled at them, sitting down in the large recliner set closest to the fire. "Did tonight's lesson shock you?"

There were quick glances between them. Kathleen sipped her tea again, suddenly a preferable action to saying the wrong thing. She watched over the rim of her cup. Earlier, during the meeting, Emily had almost fainted. Kathleen had felt the woman leaning into her while the boa constrictor choked Martin, turning his face into a puffy crimson balloon. But she knew Emily would never admit to such a thing.

And Stephen, with his soft and... She stopped, trying to keep a promise to herself not to think of Stephen in that way. After all, the man was quite smart and certainly had other qualities that had nothing to do with his... Well, with his sexual preference. But she knew Stephen had probably been shocked and too much in awe to say anything. Perhaps that's why Father's eyes now met Kathleen's and stayed there, as if the question had been addressed to only her. But they were friendly eyes, coaxing her, making her feel, once again, as though she was the only one whose opinion he cared about.

"Yes, I was shocked," she said, and saw Emily's eyes grow wide as if she were going to faint again. "But I understood the importance of the lesson. You were very wise in choosing a snake," she added.

"And why do you say that, Kathleen?" Father leaned forward, encouraging her to continue, as if anxious to hear why he was so wise. As if he didn't already know.

"Well, it was a snake, after all, that contributed to Eve's betrayal and the destruction of paradise, just like Martin's falling asleep could betray all of us and destroy our hopes for building our paradise."

He nodded, pleased, and rewarded her with a pat on the knee. His hand lingered a bit longer than usual tonight, the fingers splaying onto her thigh, caressing her, making her feel warm—so warm she could feel his power radiating through her panty hose, through her skin, almost sending a shiver through her veins.

Finally he removed his hand and turned his attention to Stephen. "And speaking of our paradise, what have you learned about our possible transportation to South America?"

"Just as you thought, we'll need to do it in several waves. Trips, perhaps of two or three dozen at a time."

"South America?" Kathleen didn't understand. "I thought we were going to Colorado."

Stephen wouldn't meet her eyes. He looked away, embarrassed, as if he had gotten caught revealing a secret. She looked to Father for an answer.

"Of course we're going to Colorado, Kathleen. This is merely a backup plan. No one else knows, and it must not leave this room," he instructed. She studied his face to see if he was angry, but then he smiled and said, "You three are the only ones I can trust."

"So we are still going to Colorado?" Kathleen had fallen in love with the slides he had shown them of the hot springs, the beautiful aspen trees and wildflowers. What did she know about South America? It seemed so far away, so remote, so primitive.

"Yes, of course," he reassured her. "This is just in case we need to leave the country."

She must have not looked convinced, because he reached for her hands, taking them delicately in his as though they were fragile rose petals.

"You must trust me, my dear Kathleen. I would never let any harm come to any of you. But there are people, evil people, in the media and in the government who would be pleased to destroy us."

"People like Ben Garrison," Stephen said with an uncharacteristic snarl that surprised Kathleen and garnered a smile from Father.

"Yes, people like Mr. Garrison. He was only able to spend a couple of days inside the compound before we discovered his true mission, but we're still not certain what he saw or what he knows. What lies he might tell the rest of the world."

Absently, he still held Kathleen's hands in his and began caressing the palms while he continued to address Stephen. "What do we know about the cabin? How did the feds even find out about it?"

"I'm still not sure. Perhaps a disgruntled ex-member?"

"Perhaps."

"Everything is lost," Stephen answered, looking at his hands, not able to meet Father's eyes.

"Everything?"

Stephen only nodded.

Kathleen had no idea what they were referring to, but Father and Stephen often talked of secret missions that didn't concern her. Right now all she could focus on was how Father's large hands seemed to be massaging her small ones, making her feel special but at the same time, much too warm and suddenly much too uncomfortable. She wanted to pull her hands away but knew that would be wrong. Father only meant it as a gesture of compassion. How dare she think otherwise. She felt her cheeks flush at the mere thought.

"We have one loose end," Stephen said.

"Yes, I know. I'll take care of that. Will we need to…" Father hesitated as if looking for the correct word. "Will we need to accelerate our departure?"

Stephen pulled out some papers, along with a map, went to Father's side and got down on one knee, showing him the items. Kathleen watched Stephen, concentrating on his gestures. He constantly amazed her. Though tall and lean with flawless brown skin, boyish features and a sharp mind, he appeared timid and quiet, as if always waiting for permission to speak. Father said Stephen was brilliant, but at the same time, he was too humble for his own good, slow to take credit and a little too ordinary in his mannerisms to stand out. He was the type of man who would not easily be noticed. And Kathleen wondered if that made his everyday job more or less difficult.

She tried to remember what it was that he did at the Capitol. Though she spent hours with Stephen and Emily in conversations like this, she knew little about either of them. Stephen's position sounded like an important one. She had heard him mention something about his level of security clearance, and he was always dropping the names of senators and their aides whom he had talked to or whom he would get in touch with. Whatever his position was, it obviously helped Father and the church.

Stephen finished with the papers, stood and retreated. Kathleen realized she hadn't paid attention to a word of the conversation. She looked to Father's face, checking to see if he had noticed. His olive skin and bristled jaw made him look older than his forty-six years. There were new lines at his eyes and at the corners of his mouth. So much pressure he was under, too much for one man. That was what he often told them, but then said he had no choice, really, that God had chosen him to lead his followers to a better life. He finally pulled his hands back, away from Kathleen's, and folded them together in his lap. At first, Kathleen thought it was in prayer until she noticed him kneading the hem of his jacket, a subtle but disturbing gesture.

"Those who want to destroy us draw closer each day," he said in a hushed tone, confiding in the three of them. "There are ways I can destroy some of our enemies, but others can simply be stifled for the time being. Everything stored at the cabin was for our protection, our security. If all is lost, we will need to find some other way to obtain protection. We must protect ourselves from those who wish to destroy us. Those who are jealous of my power. What concerns me most is that I sense betrayal within our own ranks."

Emily gasped, and Kathleen wanted to slap her. Couldn't she see this was hard enough for Father? He needed their strength and support, not their panic. Although she wasn't sure what Father meant by betrayal. She knew there had been members who had left, several recently. And then, of course, the reporter—that photographer who had pretended to be a lost soul to gain access to their compound.

"No one shall cross me and go unpunished." Instead of angry, Father looked sad when he said this, glancing at each of them as if appealing to them for help, though this strong, miraculous man would never ask for such a thing, at least not for himself. It made Kathleen want to say or do something to comfort him.

"I'm counting on the three of you," he continued. "Only you can help. We must not let lies destroy us. We cannot trust anyone. We mustn't let them break up our church." The calm slowly transformed to anger, his hands turning to fists and his face changing from olive to crimson. Still his voice remained steady. "Anyone who is not with us is against us. Those against us are jealous of our faith, jealous of our knowledge and of our special graces with God."

He pounded a fist on the chair arm, making Kathleen jump. He didn't seem to notice and continued as if the rage had taken control. She had never seen him like this before. Spittle drooled from the corner of his mouth as he said, "They're jealous of my power. They want to destroy me, because I know too many of their secrets. They will not destroy everything I worked so hard to build. How dare they even think they can outwit me. That they can destroy me. I see the end and it will come in a ball of fire if they choose to destroy me."

Kathleen watched, uncomfortable yet unflinching. Perhaps this was one of Father's prophetic fits. He had told them about his visions, his tremors, his talks with God, but no one had witnessed one. Is that what was happening now? Is that what caused the veins at his temples to bulge and his teeth to clench? Is this what it looked like to talk to God? How would she know? She had stopped talking to God ages ago. Right about the time she started believing in the power of Jack Daniel's and Jim Beam.

However, Father did seem to have special powers, certain knowledge, almost psychic abilities. How else was he able to so keenly zero in on people's fears? How else was he able to know so much about things the media and the government kept from everyone?

She had been shocked at first when he told them about the

government putting chemicals like fluoride in the water to cause cancer or about the government injecting healthy cows with E. coli to cause a national panic. About the government putting listening devices in cellular phones and cameras in ATM machines, all to record their every move. Even the magnetic strips on the back of credit cards contained personal tracking devices. And now with the Internet, the government could see inside people's homes anytime they went online.

At first she had found it all hard to believe, but each time, Father read to them articles from sources he said were unbiased, some in prestigious medical journals, and all backing up his knowledge.

He was one of the wisest men Kathleen had ever known. She still wasn't sure she cared whether or not her soul had been saved. What Kathleen O'Dell did care about was that, for the first time in more than two decades, she believed in someone again and that she was surrounded by people who cared about her. She was an integral part of a community, an integral part of something larger and more important than herself. That was something she had never experienced.

"Kathleen?"

"Yes, Father?"

He was pouring more tea for them and frowned when he noticed she had hardly touched hers. But instead of lecturing her on the healing qualities of his special tea, he said, "What can you tell me about breakfast with your daughter?"

"Oh, that. It was nice," she lied, not wanting to confess that they hadn't even ordered breakfast before Maggie bailed out on her. "I told Maggie that perhaps we could do Thanksgiving."

"And? I hope she won't make an excuse that she has to be off profiling some important case, will she?" He seemed so concerned that her relationship with her daughter work out. With all these other problems to deal with, Kathleen felt guilty that she had given him one more concern.

"Oh, no, I don't think so. She seemed very excited about it," she lied again, wanting to please him. After all, he often said the end justified the means. He had so many pressures of his own. She couldn't add to that. Besides, it would all work out just fine with her and Maggie. It always did.

"I'm excited about cooking a real holiday meal. Thanks so much for suggesting it."

"It's important for the two of you to repair your relationship," he told her.

He had been encouraging her to do so for months now. She was a bit confused by it. Usually, Father emphasized that members needed to let go of family. Even tonight with Martin and Aaron, he had lectured that there were no fathers and sons, no mothers and daughters. But she was sure Father had a good reason—if he was insisting it must be for her own good. He probably knew that she needed to repair the relationship before they left for Colorado. Yes, that was it. So that she could truly feel free.

Just then, she wondered how Father knew that Maggie was a profiler for the FBI. She was quite certain she hadn't told him. Half the time, she couldn't even remember what it was called. But, of course, Father would have taken it upon himself to know. She smiled to herself, pleased that he obviously cared a great deal about her to bother with such a small detail. Now she really would need to make an effort to have Thanksgiving with Maggie. It was the least she could do if it meant that much to Reverend Everett.

CHAPTER 30

Newburgh Heights, Virginia

Maggie leaned her forehead against the cool glass and watched the raindrops slide down her kitchen window. Wisps of fog descended upon her large, secluded backyard, reminding her for a second time in two days of swirling ghosts. It was ridiculous. She didn't believe in ghosts. She believed in things she knew, black-and-white things she could see and feel. Gray was much too complicated.

Yet each time she viewed a dead body, each time she helped slice into its flesh and remove what were once pulsating organs, she found herself reaffirming—or perhaps it was hoping—that there had been something eternal, something no one could see or even begin to understand, something that had escaped from the decaying shell left behind. If that's the way it worked, then Ginny Brier's spirit, her soul, was in another place, perhaps with Delaney and Maggie's father, all of them sharing the horrific last moments as they swirled in wisps of gray fog around the dogwoods in her backyard.

Jesus! She grabbed the tumbler of Scotch off the kitchen counter and drained what was left, trying to remember how many she had drunk since getting home from the morgue. Then she decided if she couldn't remember, it didn't matter. Besides, the familiar buzz was preferable to that annoying hollow feeling she couldn't shake off.

She poured another Scotch, this time noticing the wall calendar that hung alongside the small corkboard above the counter. The board was empty except for a few pushpins with nothing to hold up. Was there not one goddamn thing she needed to remind herself about? The wall calendar was still turned to September. She flipped the pages, bringing it to November. Thanksgiving was only days away. Had her mother been serious about cooking a dinner? Maggie couldn't remember the last time they had attempted a holiday together, though whenever it was, she was sure it had been disastrous. There were plenty of holidays in her memory bank she would just as soon forget. Like four years ago when she spent Christmas Eve on a hard, lumpy sofa outside the critical care unit of St. Anne's Hospital. While others had been buying last-minute gifts or stopping at parties for sugar cookies and eggnog, her mother had spent the day mixing red and green pills with her old friend, Jim Beam.

She stood at the window again, watching the fog swallow entire corners of her landscape. She could barely see the outline of the pine trees that lined her property. They reminded her of towering sentries, standing shoulder to shoulder, shielding her, protecting her. After a childhood of feeling lost and vulnerable, why wouldn't she spend her adulthood looking for ways to be in control, to protect herself? Sure, in some ways, it had also made her cautious, a bit skeptical and untrusting. Or as Gwen would put it, it made her inaccessible to anyone including those who cared about her. Which made her think of Nick Morrelli.

She leaned her forehead against the glass again. She didn't want to think of Nick. Her mother's accusation that morning still stung, probably because there was more truth in it than she wanted to admit. She hadn't talked to Nick in weeks, and it had been months since they had seen each other. Months since she had told him she didn't want to see him until after her divorce was final.

She checked her watch, took another sip of Scotch and found herself reaching for the phone. She could stop at any second, she could hang up before he answered. Or maybe just say hi. What harm was there in hearing his voice?

One ring, two, three... She would leave a brief and friendly message on his answering machine. Four rings...five—

"Hello?" It was a woman's voice.

"Yes," Maggie said, not recognizing the voice. Maybe she had the wrong number. It had been months, after all, since she had dialed it. "Is Nick Morrelli there?"

"Oh," the woman said, "is this the office? Can't it wait?"

"No, this is a friend. Is Nick there?"

The woman paused as if she needed to decide what information a friend was entitled to. Then finally she said, "Umm...he's in the shower. Can I take a message and have him call you back?"

"No, that's okay. I'll try back another time."

But when Maggie hung up the phone, she knew she would not try back anytime soon.

CHAPTER 31

Reston, Virginia

Tully hoped his gut instinct was wrong. He hoped he was being an overprotective father who was simply overreacting. That's what he kept telling himself, yet before he left the morgue he made a copy of Virginia Brier's driver's license photo and stuck it in his back pocket.

He had called Emma earlier to let her know he wouldn't be home until later, but if she wanted to wait for dinner, he'd pick up a pizza. He was pleased when she asked for lots of pepperoni on her side. At least they would be sharing a meal together, perhaps one they could both enjoy. Between the two of them, their culinary skills didn't extend much beyond grilled cheese sandwiches with soup. Sometimes when Tully was feeling a bit adventurous he'd throw a couple of chunks of meat on the grill. Unfortunately, he had never been able to figure out how to keep it from becoming a shrunken, charred hockey puck, and there wasn't much treat in that.

Their small two-bedroom bungalow in Reston, Virginia, was a far cry from the two-story colonial they'd lived in in Cleveland. Caroline had insisted on keeping the house, and now Tully wondered if Emma would ever want to come back here after spending Thanksgiving vacation in her old room. Only recently had this house begun to feel like home, though it had been almost a year since they'd made the move. No matter how much he complained about this parenting stuff, he couldn't imagine what this house, the move, the new town and new job—what any of it would have been like without Emma.

Thanks to his daughter, the house didn't have that bachelor look or smell to it, though, as Tully weaved his way through the living room clutter to the kitchen clutter, he wondered if there was a difference between bachelor clutter and teenager clutter. Maybe what he liked was having some feminine things around, even if the pink lava lamp on the bookcase, the purple Rollerblades sticking out from under the sofa or the smiley-face magnets on the refrigerator were not his style.

"Hey, Dad." As he stepped through the front door Emma appeared. He didn't kid himself. It was the power of pizza that drew her, not his lovable presence.

"Hi, sweat pea." He kissed her cheek, a gesture she tolerated only when they were alone.

She wore her headphones wrapped around her neck, a compromise that had taken much drilling and constant reminders, but was well worth it, although he could still hear the music blaring. The music, however, he couldn't complain about, since he still enjoyed some head-banging rock 'n' roll once in a while, only in the form of the Rolling Stones or the Doors.

Emma got out the paper plates and plastic cups that they had agreed long ago would be part of any take-out treat. What was the use of having someone else prepare the meal if you still had to wash dishes? As he scooped up pieces of pizza and watched her pour their Pepsis, he wondered when would be a good time to broach the subject about the dead girl.

"Kitchen or living room?" she asked, picking up her plate and cup.

"Living room, but no TV."

"Okay."

He followed her into the living room, and when she decided to sit on the floor, he joined her despite his thigh still being a bit tender. It reminded him that Agent O'Dell never once mentioned or complained about *her* scar, a memento from the legendary serial killer Albert Stucky. Although he had never seen it, Tully knew from rumors that the scar crossed the length of her abdomen, as if the man had tried to gut her. Now he and O'Dell had something in common. Tully had a scar of his own, a constant reminder of the bullet Albert Stucky had put into him last spring as he and O'Dell tried to recapture him.

The bullet had caused some damage, but he refused to let it stop him from his daily ritual run. Lately he hated to admit that it qualified more as jogging than running. That one bullet had messed up a lot of things, including his ability to sit cross-legged on the floor without feeling the muscles sting and pinch. There were some things worth a little pain, and having pizza on the floor with his daughter was one of them.

"Mom called," Emma said as if it were an everyday occurrence. "She said she talked to you about Thanksgiving and that you were cool with everything."

He clenched his jaw. He wasn't cool with everything, but then Emma didn't need to know that. He watched her swipe a strand of long blond hair from her face to keep it away from the strings of cheese that hung from the pizza slice.

"Are you cool about spending Thanksgiving in Cleveland?" he asked.

"I guess."

It seemed like a typical Emma response, a hint of indifference mixed with that you'd-never-understand-anyway shrug of the shoulders. He wished someone had told him long ago that he'd need a degree in psychology to be a parent of a teenager. Maybe that's why he enjoyed his job. Figuring out serial killers seemed like a piece of cake compared to figuring out teenage girls.

"If you don't want to go, you don't have to." He gulped his Pepsi, trying to replicate the art of indifference that his daughter seemed to have perfected.

"She's got it all planned and stuff."

"Doesn't matter."

"I just hope she didn't invite him over."

Tully wasn't sure who the new "him" was in his ex-wife's life. Maybe he didn't want to know. There had been several since their divorce.

"You have to understand, Emma, if your mom has someone new in her life, she's probably gonna want to include him for Thanksgiving."

Jeez! He couldn't believe he was defending Caroline's right to screw yet another guy. Just the thought made him angry, or worse, lose his appetite. Two years ago his wife decided one day that she was no longer in love with him, that the passion in their marriage was gone and that she needed to move on. Nothing better to destroy a guy's ego than to have his wife tell him she needed to move on and away from his passionless, unlovable self.

"What about you?"

For a minute Tully had forgotten what exactly they had been talking about.

"What do you mean?"

"What will you do for Thanksgiving?"

He caught himself staring at her, then grabbed for another piece of pizza, feeling his indifference slipping. Yet he couldn't help but smile. His daughter was worried about him spending Thanksgiving alone. Could there be anything more cool?

"Hey, I'm planning on a full day of fun, sitting in my underwear watching football all afternoon."

She frowned at him. "You hate college football."

"Well, then maybe I'll go to the movies."

This made her giggle, and she had to set her Pepsi aside so as not to spill it.

"What's so funny about that?"

"You, go to the movies by yourself? Come on, Dad. Get real."

"Actually, I'll probably need to work. There's a pretty important case we're working on. In fact, I wanted to talk to you about it."

He pulled the photocopy from his back pocket, unfolded it and handed it to Emma.

"Do you know this girl? Her name's Virginia Brier."

Emma took a careful look, then set the copy aside and began on another piece of pizza.

"Is she in some kind of trouble?"

"No, she's not in trouble." Tully felt a wave of relief. It looked like Emma didn't recognize the girl. Of course he had been crazy. There had been hundreds of people at the monuments Saturday night.

But before he could relax, Emma said, "She doesn't like to be called Virginia."

"What?"

"She uses Ginny."

Jesus! The nausea grabbed hold again.

"So you do know her?"

"Actually, Alesha and I just met her Saturday when we were on the field trip, but yeah, she was there Saturday night, too. She sorta made us mad, because she was flirting with this boy Alesha really liked. He was really cool and he seemed to be having a good time with us until that reverend guy fawned all over Ginny."

"Hold on a minute. Who was this boy?"

"His name's Brandon. He was with Alice and Justin and the reverend guy."

Tully got up and went to where he'd left his windbreaker. He started pulling everything out of his pockets and finally found the pamphlet he had picked up blowing around the FDR Memorial. He handed it to Emma.

"Is this the reverend guy?" He pointed to the color photograph on the back.

"Yeah, that's him. Reverend Everett," she read off the pamphlet. "Except they were all calling him Father. Seemed kinda creepy. I mean it's not like he's their dad or anything."

"It's not that weird, Emma. Catholics call priests Father. It's sort of a title, like pastor or reverend or Mr."

"Yeah, but it wasn't like they were using it as a title. They really were all talking about him as if he were their father, 'cause he's their leader and like he knows what's best for them and stuff."

"This Brandon guy, did you see him go off with Ginny?"

"You mean like to be alone?"

"Yes."

"Dad, there were like tons of people. Besides, Alesha and I left before the rally thing was over. It was so lame, all that singing and clapping."

"You think you might be able to give a detailed description of Brandon?"

She looked at him as if realizing for the first time there might be some connection to the questions about Ginny and his job as an FBI agent.

"Yeah, I guess I could," she said, her indifference changing to concern. "I thought you said Ginny wasn't in trouble."

He hesitated, wondering what to tell her. She wasn't a little girl anymore, and chances were she'd hear about it soon on TV. No matter how much of a protective father he wanted to be, he couldn't protect her from the truth. And she'd be upset with him if he lied.

He reached across the floor and took her hand, then said, "Ginny's dead. Someone murdered her Saturday night."

CHAPTER 32

MONDAY
November 25
FBI Academy
Quantico, Virginia

Maggie stole a glance at Agent Tully as they watched Agent Bobbi LaPlatz scratch several pencil lines. Magically the face on her sketch pad developed a thin, narrow nose.

"Does that look close?" she asked Emma Tully, who sat beside her, hands in her lap, her eyes examining the line drawing.

"I think so, but the lips aren't quite right." Emma glanced at her dad, as if waiting for him to comment. He only nodded at her.

"Too thin?" LaPlatz asked.

"Maybe it's the mouth, not the lips. You know, like he never smiled. He sorta had this…um…frown, but not like he was mad. Just maybe like he was too tough to smile." She flipped her hair back and gave her dad another glance. "Does that make sense?" she asked, turning back to Agent LaPlatz, her eyes darting back to check Tully's face before returning to the paper.

"I think so. Let me give it a try." And LaPlatz's hand went to work, making quick, short movements. A line here, one there, transforming the entire face again with her simple number two pencil, a magic wand with teeth marks embedded in its sides.

Maggie could see Tully had that worried indent in his forehead. She had noticed it earlier, even before he now started rubbing at it as if he could make it disappear. Earlier when he stopped by her office he seemed more than just worried. *Disoriented* was the best word Maggie could come up with.

His daughter, Emma, had never been to Quantico before, and this morning, unfortunately, was not going to be one of those fun tours to see where Daddy worked. Emma seemed to be handling the situation just fine, but Tully was still fidgeting. His toe kept tapping. When he wasn't rubbing the indent off his forehead, he was pushing up the bridge of his glasses. He remained silent, saying not a word since Agent LaPlatz had sat down. Once in a while his eyes strayed from the face materializing on the paper to Emma's. Maggie watched as his fingers found a paper in his breast pocket and he began an accordion fold. His fingers worked without the aid of his eyes, as if on a mission of their own.

Maggie had a good idea why her normally laid-back partner looked like he had been injected with caffeine. It wasn't just that Emma had known the dead girl, but that she had also been at the rally Ginny had supposedly attended. Some rally held at the monument Saturday evening. This was probably why he had been on edge at the crime scene and at the autopsy. Was Tully wondering how close Emma had come to being the killer's target?

"How's that?" LaPlatz asked.

"Close. Is there any way I can see it in color?" Emma

looked back at Tully again, as if waiting for an answer from him.

"Sure." LaPlatz stood. "Let me scan it into the computer. I like to use the old-fashioned method first, but if you think we're close, we can let the computer mess around with what we have." She started for the door with Emma alongside of her, but turned just as Tully was getting to his feet to follow. "Why don't you two wait here," LaPlatz said casually, but her eyes looked from Tully to Maggie.

When Tully looked like he might still follow, Maggie put a gentle hand on his arm. He looked down at it, a sleepwalker suddenly waking.

"We'll wait here," he said, and watched the door close before sitting down again. Maggie stood in front of him, leaning against the table, studying him. He didn't seem to mind. If he even noticed. He was off somewhere else, if not in the other room with Emma, then back conjuring up that horrible murder scene.

"She's doing an excellent job."

"What?" He looked up at her as if only now realizing she was still there.

"Emma might be providing the only clue we have as to who this killer is."

"Yeah. I know." He rubbed his jaw, pushed up his glasses for the tenth time.

"Are you okay?"

"Me?" This time there was surprise in his tone.

"I know you're worried about her, Tully, but she seems to be okay."

He hesitated and took off his glasses, rubbed his eyes. "I just worry about her." Back went the glasses. The hands found the pamphlet again and the folds began in the other direction, putting new creases in a picture of a man's face. "Sometimes I feel like I don't have a clue how to do this parenting thing."

"Emma's a brave, smart girl, who came here today to help

in a murder investigation. And she's doing a great job while remaining calm and diligent. Judging from that alone, I'd say you've done a damn good job with her."

He looked up at her, met her eyes and managed a weak smile. "Yeah? So you don't think it's totally obvious that I'm winging it?"

"If you are, it'll be our secret. Okay? Hey, didn't you tell me once that there are some things, some secrets, that only partners should share?"

Finally a real smile appeared. "I said that? I can't believe I would ever encourage secrets or withholding information."

"Maybe I'm becoming a bad influence on you." She checked her watch and started to leave. "I need to go rescue Gwen from Security. I'll see you in the conference room."

"Hey, Maggie?"

"Yep?"

"Thanks."

She stopped at the door and gave him a quick glance over her shoulder, just enough to check his eyes, and was immediately relieved to see that deer-in-the-headlights daze gone. "Any time, partner."

CHAPTER 33

Gwen Patterson hurried up the steps of the Jefferson Building. As usual, she was late. Kyle Cunningham and BSU hadn't called her in as a consultant on a case for more than a year. She knew this time it was probably only at Maggie's request. In fact, it had been such a long time since her last visit to Quantico that she almost expected to be strip-searched at the guard hut. But apparently Maggie had seen to it that her credentials had been updated and kept on file. She stopped at the counter to sign in, but before she picked up the pen the young woman sitting at the computer stopped her.

"Dr. Patterson?"

"Yes."

"Here you are." The woman handed her a visitor's badge. "I do still need for you to sign in with your check-in time."

"Yes, of course." Gwen signed the sheet as she noticed the

badge. It had her name printed on it—Dr. and even Ph.D. at the end—instead of the standard Visitor. Okay, so Maggie was trying hard to make her feel at home. Gwen still wasn't convinced, though, she'd be much help with the investigation.

That Cunningham had even agreed to Maggie's request for Gwen to be a part of the case meant he was feeling desperate. He usually didn't call in outsiders. In the early days, yes, but not now, not since the FBI had come under considerable scrutiny. Gwen knew Cunningham well enough to detect a hint of desperation in his voice yesterday when he called. He had asked if she would share her new research and expertise. Her response was that he had some amazing agents in his Behavioral Science Unit, including Maggie, who could tell him just as much, if not more, about the criminal workings of the adolescent male's mind. She told him she wasn't sure she could add much to the investigation.

"As an outsider, you might be able to point out things we're missing," he countered. "You've done that with some of our cases in the past. I'm hoping you'll be able to work your magic on this one."

Flattery. Gwen smiled as she clipped on her badge. The man could be charming as hell when he wanted to be. Then she read the words on the badge under her name and immediately frowned: Member, Special Task Force.

Task force. Gwen hated the term. It reeked with bureaucracy and brought to mind visions of red tape. Already the media had trounced every tidbit of information that had been released on this case, hounding poor Senator Brier from outside his apartment to the Capitol. When Gwen checked her office this morning for messages, her assistant, Amelia, had already received calls from the *Washington Times* and the *Post* wanting to know about Gwen's involvement. How the hell did they find out these things so quickly? It had been less than twelve hours since Cunningham had even called her.

Supposedly, it was one of the reasons they were meeting

at Quantico instead of in the District. The murder of a senator's daughter—let alone having it occur on federal property—warranted a federal investigation. Yet, it surprised Gwen that Cunningham had been asked to head the task force. Now she wished she had been able to get ahold of Maggie last night. Her friend may have answered some of the questions Cunningham wouldn't.

"Gwen, you're here."

She leaned around the counter to find Maggie coming down the hall. She looked good, dressed in burgundy trousers, matching jacket and a white turtleneck sweater. Only now did Gwen notice that her friend had finally put back on some of the weight she had lost last winter. She looked more her athletically trim but strong self rather than the emaciated waif Albert Stucky had driven her to become.

"Hi, kiddo," Gwen said while she managed a one-armed hug, her briefcase and umbrella occupying her other arm.

She knew Maggie only tolerated the gesture, but this morning she felt the younger woman hugging her back. As Maggie pulled away, Gwen kept a hand on her shoulder, keeping Maggie from escaping too quickly. The hand moved to Maggie's face, gently lifting her chin for a closer inspection. Maggie put up with this, too, even managing a smile while Gwen examined the red lines in Maggie's eyes and the puffiness underneath that was concealed with makeup to fool those who were less adept at reading this intensely personal and private woman.

"Are you okay? You look like you didn't get much sleep."

This time she casually shifted away from Gwen's touch. "I'm fine." There went the eyes—someplace, anyplace, as long as they could no longer be scrutinized.

"You didn't return my call last night," Gwen said, treating it like no big deal and trying to keep the concern from her voice.

"Harvey and I didn't get back from our run until late."

"Jesus! Maggie, I wish you wouldn't go out running that late at night."

"It's not like I was alone." She started back down the hall. "Come on, Cunningham's waiting.

"I figured as much. I can feel him frowning at me through the walls."

As they walked, Gwen found herself absently patting at her hair, which felt in place, and smoothing her skirt, which began the day without a single wrinkle, but after an hour-long drive... She caught Maggie watching her.

"You look sensational as always," Maggie told her.

"Hey, it's not every day I meet a United States senator."

"Oh, right," Maggie said with just enough sarcasm for Gwen to smile.

Of course, Maggie wouldn't let her get away with a comment like that. Gwen's past and present clients included enough embassy, White House and congressional members to start her own political caucus. Okay, so her friend was not getting enough sleep. Probably still upset about her fallen colleague—a certain amount of depression could develop from such a circumstance. But that Maggie was feeling up to some repartee was a good sign. Maybe Gwen had been worried for no reason.

Two blue-polo-shirt academy recruits held a set of doors open for them. Gwen smiled and thanked them. Maggie only nodded. They started down one of the walkways. Gwen knew they had a long way to go. What would it hurt to make another attempt at finding out if Maggie was, indeed, okay?

"How did breakfast go with your mom yesterday?"

"Fine."

Too short, too easy. This was it. She knew it.

"It was fine? Really?"

"We didn't actually have breakfast."

A group of law enforcement officers in green polo shirts and khakis moved to the side of the walkway and let the two women pass. Used to living in the hustle and bustle of the District, Gwen always felt the treatment she received at Quantico was over the top on the polite-and-courteous Richter scale. Maggie waited for her at the next door before they started down another hallway.

"Let me guess," Gwen continued as though there had been no interruption, "she didn't show up."

"No, she showed up. Boy, did she show up. But I had to leave early. For this case, as a matter of fact."

Gwen felt that annoying maternal instinct begin to stir— the one that only reared its ugly head when she was feeling protective of her friend. She didn't dare ask the question for fear she'd get the answer she expected. She asked, anyway. "What do you mean, boy, did she show up? She wasn't drunk, was she?"

"Can we talk about this later?" Maggie said, then greeted a couple of official-looking men in suits.

Gwen recognized them as other agents. Yes, this probably wasn't the best place to air the family laundry. They turned a corner and approached another walkway, this one empty. Gwen took advantage of it.

"Yes, we can talk later. But just tell me now what you meant, okay?"

"Jesus! Did anyone ever tell you you're a pain in the ass?"

"Of course, but you must admit, it's one of my more endearing qualities."

She could see Maggie smile, though she kept her attention and her eyes ahead and safely away from Gwen's.

"She wants us to have Thanksgiving together."

It was the last thing Gwen expected. When the silence lasted too long, she felt Maggie glance over at her.

"That was sort of my response, too," Maggie said with another smile.

"Well, you've been saying for some time now that she's trying to change."

"Yes, her friends and her clothes and her hair. Reverend Everett seems to have helped her change quite a few things in her life, many of them for the better. But no matter what she does, she can't change history."

They got to the end of the walkway, and Maggie pointed to the last door on their right. "We're here."

Gwen wished they had more time. If she wasn't eternally late, maybe they would have. As they entered the conference room, the man at the end of the table stood, though it took effort and he leaned on a walking cane. His gesture prompted the other men around the table to stand, as well; Agent Tully, Keith Ganza, whom Gwen recognized as the head of the FBI crime lab, and Assistant Director Cunningham. Detective Julia Racine shifted impatiently in her chair. Maggie ignored her colleagues' clumsy attempt at courtesy and walked ahead, directly to the senator, her hand outstretched to him.

"Senator Brier, I'm Special Agent Maggie O'Dell and this is Dr. Gwen Patterson. Please excuse us for being late."

"That's quite all right"

He shook both their hands with a brisk but bone-crushing strength, as if making up for his disabled left leg. It had been the result of a car accident, Gwen remembered, not a war injury as the media seemed quick to point out during the last election.

"I'm so sorry for your loss, Senator," Gwen said and immediately saw him flinch, uncomfortable with the rise of emotion her simple condolence seemed to spark.

"Thank you," he said quietly in a tone that suddenly lacked the control and strength that his greeting had projected.

Other than the dark circles under his eyes, Senator Brier looked impeccable, dressed in an expensive navy suit, crisp white shirt and purple silk tie with an initialed gold tie bar. Hoping to put him back at ease, Gwen noticed four initials—WWJD—instead of the traditional three engraved there.

"That's a lovely tie bar," she said. "If you don't mind me asking, what are the initials?"

He looked down as if needing a reminder. "Oh, no, I don't mind at all. It was a gift from my assistant. He said it's supposed to help me make important decisions. I'm not much of a spiritual man, but he is, and well, it was a gift."

"And the initials?" Gwen insisted, despite Cunningham's frown of impatience.

"I believe it's the acronym for What Would Jesus Do."

"Let's get started," Cunningham announced, waving them to their places before there could be any more wasted chitchat.

Gwen took a seat close to the senator and noticed that Maggie walked clear around the table, taking a seat next to Keith Ganza and avoiding the empty one next to Racine. However, in doing so, she now sat directly across from the detective. Racine smiled at her and nodded. Maggie looked away. Gwen had forgotten why Maggie disliked the woman so much. She was certain it had something to do with a previous case they had worked together, but there was something else. Something more. What was it? She studied Racine, trying to remember. The detective was a little younger than Maggie. Maybe in her middle or late twenties, fairly young for a detective.

"Senator, I know I speak for all of us when I say I'm sorry for your loss," Cunningham said, interrupting Gwen's thoughts and bringing her back to the group in front of her.

"I appreciate that, Kyle. I know having me here is out of the ordinary. I don't want to get in the way, but I want to be involved." He pulled at the cuffs of his shirt and leaned his arms on the table. A nervous gesture of a man trying to keep himself together. "I need to be involved."

Cunningham nodded, began opening file folders and distributing handouts across the table to each of them. "This is what we know so far."

Before looking at the papers, Gwen knew this would be a

watered-down version of the real story. She would need to wait until later to be filled in on the details, which only made her fidget in her chair. She hated not being prepared and wondered why Cunningham hadn't scheduled a later meeting with the senator, after the task force had had time to discuss the case. Or didn't he have a choice? Already Gwen could feel there was something about this case that didn't fit neatly into any of the regular rules and procedures. She glanced at Cunningham and found herself wondering if he really was in charge of this case.

Gwen flipped through the pages and with only a glance began picking out the ambiguous terms, the safe posts that specified approximate time and cause of death, giving information without giving details. Whatever clearance or special permission Senator Brier may have gotten from Director Mueller himself, Gwen knew he would be spared the real facts. Yes, Cunningham would do his best to dilute the gruesome details, no matter who might be calling the shots. And Gwen didn't blame him. Senator or not, no father should hear about the frightening and brutal last minutes of his daughter's life.

"There is one thing I need to ask up front." The senator stopped riffling through the papers, but did not look up. "Was she…was she raped?"

Gwen watched all the men's faces, their eyes avoiding the senator's. This was something that fascinated her about men who were close to a victim, whether it be husband, father or son. Their loved one could have been beaten and stabbed beyond recognition, tortured, mutilated and brutally murdered, but somehow none of that was as awful to them as the mere thought that she may have been raped, that she may have been violated in a way incomprehensible to them.

When nobody spoke, Maggie said, "The evidence is inconclusive."

Senator Brier stared at her, then shook his head. "You need not spare me. I need to know."

Like hell he needed to know. Gwen stopped herself as Maggie caught her eyes. Maggie looked to Cunningham as if for permission to proceed. He sat, eyes straight ahead, his hands folded over each other on the table, no indication that he wanted her to stop.

Maggie continued, "We did find some vaginal semen, but there was no bruising, no tearing. Is it possible Ginny may have been with someone earlier in the evening?"

Gwen saw Cunningham shoot Maggie a look of warning. He obviously hadn't expected her to ask the question. But now Maggie was no longer paying attention. Instead, she focused on the senator, waiting for his answer. Gwen wanted to smile. Good for you, Maggie. The senator looked flustered. He seemed more willing and comfortable talking about his daughter's possible rape than he did about her normal sex life.

"I don't know for sure. Some of her friends might know."

"It would be helpful for us to find out," Maggie continued, despite Cunningham fidgeting at the end of the table.

"You can't possibly believe some boyfriend of hers did this to her, can you?" Senator Brier leaned forward, a hand twisting into a fist, crumpling a piece of paper. "That's absolutely absurd."

"No, we don't believe that. Not at all, sir," Cunningham said, jumping in. "That's not what Agent O'Dell meant." He looked at Maggie, and Gwen recognized the scowl that barely transformed his always stoic face. "Is it, Agent O'Dell?"

"No, of course not." Maggie appeared calm and unflustered, and Gwen was relieved. "What I meant was that we will need to determine whether or not Virginia did, in fact, have consensual sex that evening. Otherwise the semen could be important evidence in finding her murderer."

The senator finally nodded, then he sat back an inch,

maybe two. Gwen imagined this was his style on the Senate floor, too, always ready, never relaxed.

"On that same note, Senator Brier," Cunningham said, pushing up his glasses and planting his elbows on the table, "I have to ask you, is there anyone you know of who would want to hurt you or your daughter?"

The senator flinched, stunned by the question. He rubbed at his temple as if warding off a headache. When he finally spoke there was an unmistakable quiver. "So you *are* saying this wasn't random? That it may have been someone Ginny knew?"

Chairs creaked with the shifting of uncomfortable bodies. Nervous fingers rustled papers. Without knowing much about the case, even Gwen realized that, whether it was a crazed boyfriend or not, no one around the table believed Virginia Brier had simply been in the wrong place at the wrong time. No one, that is, except for Senator Brier, who either believed it had been random, or wanted badly to convince himself that it had been. Gwen watched the man wring his hands as he waited for Cunningham to tell him the obvious.

"We don't know anything for certain, Senator. We need to eliminate all possibilities. And, yes, we'll need a list of all your daughter's friends, anyone who may have seen or talked to her Saturday or even Friday."

There was a muffled knock at the door and a tall, handsome black man came in, apologizing as he went to the senator's side without waiting for an invitation. He leaned down and whispered something in his boss's ear, a gesture that appeared familiar and comfortable for both men, despite the audience that waited quietly around the table.

The senator nodded and without looking up at his assistant said, "Thank you, Stephen." Then he looked across the table to Cunningham while he stood, leaning on the young man's outstretched arm. "I apologize, Kyle. I must get back to the Capitol. I expect you'll keep me informed."

"Of course, Senator. I'll give you all the details you need to know, as soon as we know them."

Senator Brier seemed satisfied. Gwen smiled at Cunningham's choice of words—"all the details you *need* to know." Cunningham should have been a politician. He was good at this, telling people what they wanted to hear while telling them absolutely nothing at all.

CHAPTER 34

Richmond, Virginia

Kathleen O'Dell shoved the papers aside and grabbed for her mug of coffee. She took a sip, closed her eyes and took another. This was much better than that god-awful tea, although Reverend Everett would be scolding her if he knew how much caffeine she had poured into her system, and it wasn't even noon. How could she be expected to give up alcohol *and* caffeine?

She shuffled through the pages again. Stephen had been very considerate in getting all the government forms she needed. If only it didn't take so long to fill them out. Who would ever guess that it took so much work to transfer what little assets she had: a meager money market and savings account along with Thomas's pension. She had even forgotten about Thomas's pension, a small monthly amount, but enough that Reverend Everett seemed quite pleased when she had remembered it. That was when he'd told her once again she played an integral part in his mission. That God had sent her to him as a special favor. She'd never before been an integral anything to anyone, let alone to such an important man as Reverend Everett.

After spending the morning sorting through her assets, she realized that she also had never had much of anything. But then, she had never really expected much, either. Just what was necessary to get by—that was enough.

After Thomas's death, Kathleen had sold their house and all their belongings so that she could move Maggie as far away as possible and as soon as possible. With Thomas's life insurance, she thought they would be okay, and they had been comfortable in the small Richmond apartment. They never had much, but it wasn't like Maggie went hungry or wore rags.

Kathleen looked around her current apartment, a sunny one-bedroom she had recently decorated herself with bright and cheerful colors that she no longer saw through blurry, hungover eyes. She hadn't had a drink in ten months, two weeks and… She checked the desk calendar—four days. Though it still wasn't easy. She reached for the coffee mug again and took a swallow.

Looking at the calendar reminded her how close Thanksgiving was. She checked her watch. She would need to call Maggie. It was important to Reverend Everett that she and Maggie have a family Thanksgiving together. Surely they could do it, just this once. How difficult could it be to get through one day together? It's not like they hadn't done it before. They had spent plenty of holidays together, though at the moment, Kathleen couldn't remember any vividly enough to feel reassured. Holidays had usually been sort of a blur to her.

She checked the time again. If she called during the day, she'd get Maggie's voice messaging service, and she wouldn't get to talk to Maggie.

Kathleen thought about their breakfast yesterday. The girl

had fidgeted as if she couldn't wait to leave, and now Kathleen wondered if Maggie really had been called away. Or had she simply not wanted to spend another minute with her own mother? How did they ever get to this place? How did they ever get to be enemies? No, not enemies. But not friends, either. And why could they not even talk to each other?

She checked her watch again. Sat quietly. Tapped her fingers on the papers, then glanced at the phone on the counter. If she called while Maggie was at work, she'd only be able to leave a message. She sat for a while longer, staring at the phone. Okay, so this wasn't going to be easy—she was still a coward. She got up and went to the counter. She'd leave a message, and she picked up the phone.

CHAPTER 35

Maggie stood up to stretch her legs and automatically began her ritual pacing. The real meeting hadn't begun until the senator was safely in his limousine and on his way back to the District. Now the uncensored reports and photos were strewn across the conference room's table alongside coffee mugs, cans of Pepsi, bottles of water and sandwiches Cunningham had ordered up from the cafeteria.

The old easel-backed chalkboard Cunningham liked to use was almost filled. On one side were the words:

duct tape
cyanide capsule
semen residue
handcuff marks: none found on the victim
ligature tracks: possible cord with glittery residue

    possible DNA under nails
    scene posed/staged
    unidentified circular marks in dirt

On the other side under the heading Unsub was a shorter list, the beginning of a profile:

    left-handed
    organized, although a risk-taker
    knows police procedure
    prepared: brought weapon to scene
    may interact well with society, but no regard
    for others
    draws satisfaction from seeing his victim suffer
    strong sense of grandiosity and entitlement

Cunningham had peeled off his jacket and gotten down to work as soon as Senator Brier had left the conference room, yet he still hadn't explained why they had gathered out here at Quantico instead of at FBI headquarters. Nor had he bothered to explain why he had been chosen to head the task force rather than the Special Agent in Charge (SAC) of the District's field office or why BSU had even been called in to take a look at the scene before they knew the victim was a daughter of a United States senator. He hadn't bothered to explain any of it, and neither Maggie, nor the rest of them, seemed willing to call him on it.

    There was plenty he wasn't telling them. Yet, what he had told them, at least three times, was that all information was to remain shared with only the six members of the task force and with absolutely no exceptions. Redundant, really. They were all professionals. They knew the rules. Well, maybe all of them except Racine. Maggie wondered if perhaps Cunningham didn't trust Racine, either. Could that be why he was holding back on an explanation? Of course, he had no choice about including Racine. The task force had to have someone from the District PD, and since Racine had already been assigned to the case, it made sense she would continue as liaison.

"According to Wenhoff, cause of death was asphyxiation due to manual strangulation," Keith Ganza said with his usual monotone, continuing their list.

Cunningham found the word *ligature* on the chalkboard and scrawled underneath *manual strangulation—COD*.

"Manual strangulation? What about all the ligature marks?" Tully pointed them out in the autopsy photos of the young woman's neck.

Keith reached for several of the photos, pulled one out and slid it back to Tully. "See that bruising and the vertical crescent marks? The bruising was made by the pressure of his thumbs. The vertical crescentic abrasions were made by his fingernails. The horizontal ones are all hers. The bruising and the abrasions are in the perfect position to break the hyoid bone. That's the curved bone at the base of the tongue." He indicated the area in one of the photos. "There were also fractures to the cartilage of the windpipe and the larynx. All are signs of excessive force and signs of manual strangulation."

"The guy obviously had been using some kind of cord, over and over again." Racine stood now to look over Tully's shoulder at the photos. "Why the hell would he suddenly decide to use his hands?"

Maggie noticed that Racine was leaning close enough into Tully to brush her breasts against his back. She looked away and caught Gwen watching. Gwen's eyes told her she knew exactly what she was thinking, and Gwen's sudden frown warned Maggie to be careful and keep any sarcasm to herself.

"Maybe he used his hands when he was finished with whatever little game of pass out and wake up he was playing with her. He may have felt like he had more control with his hands to complete the job," Maggie said, then turned away from them and stared out the window. She remembered the girl's neck without looking at any photos, and she could easily conjure up an image of how it came to its mangled black-and-blue state. Black and blue, almost the color the sky had now turned, swollen with dark clouds. A light rain began tapping against the glass. "Maybe the cord simply wasn't personal enough," she added without looking back at any of them.

"She may have gotten personal enough to get a piece of him under her fingernails," Ganza said, and immediately had Maggie's attention. "Most of the skin was her own, but she managed to get in a scratch or two. Enough for DNA. We're checking to see if it matches the semen."

"Also, what about the cyanide capsule?" Racine asked. "And that pinkish tint. Stan made it sound like it could have been the poison."

Now Maggie turned and glanced at Tully. The two of them looked to Cunningham. Yes, what about the cyanide capsule? They had avoided discussing the possible connection between the senator's daughter and those five suicidal boys from the cabin in the Massachusetts woods. No way was it a coincidence—not that Maggie even believed in coincidences. Someone had gone to an awful lot of trouble to make sure they made a connection. Someone, perhaps, wanting to point out his deed, or rather, his revenge.

"Poison does leave a pinkish tint. Some of the cyanide had been absorbed into her system, but very little," Keith answered, though no one except Racine seemed interested.

"So," Racine said, rubbing her temple as if genuinely trying to figure it out. "Why strangle her if you've put cyanide in her mouth and taped it shut? Am I the only who thinks that doesn't make sense?"

"The capsule was strictly for show," Cunningham finally offered without looking at the detective, making the explanation sound commonplace. He wiped the chalk from his hands, taking a break and picking up his ham on rye. He took a bite without looking at the sandwich, concentrating instead on the diagrams and police reports spread out on the table.

Racine, now back in her chair, shifted impatiently, waiting.

"You must have heard about the standoff last week in Massachusetts." Cunningham, still wouldn't meet her gaze and flipped through the reports. "Five young men used the same kind of capsule filled with cyanide to commit suicide before they opened fire on ATF and FBI agents. For some reason, someone wants us to know there's a connection with Senator Brier's daughter."

Racine looked around the table, only now realizing this was news only to her. "You all fucking knew about this?"

"The information about the cyanide is classified and so far has been successfully held back from the media." Cunningham's tone made Racine sit back. "We need to keep it that way, Detective Racine. Is that understood?"

"Of course. But if I'm to be a part of this task force, I don't expect information to be held back from me."

"Fair enough."

"So was this some sort of revenge killing?" Racine caught on quickly. Maggie couldn't help but be impressed, and she turned back to the window when Racine looked her way.

"Or is that too obvious?" Racine asked. "The life of a senator's daughter in exchange for five?"

"Revenge certainly can't be discounted," Cunningham answered between bites of his sandwich.

"Maybe now you can also tell me how you knew about it before we discovered it was the senator's daughter?"

"Excuse me?"

Maggie looked back at Cunningham. Racine dared to ask the question all of them had been thinking. The woman certainly had more guts than brains.

"Why was BSU called in on this?" Racine asked, apparently unaffected by Cunningham's position of power or his scowl. Maggie couldn't help thinking that if Racine did have aspirations of getting into the FBI, she may be squashing an important reference.

"A homicide on federal property is a federal matter," he told Racine in his best cool, authoritarian tone, "and therefore, the FBI is in charge of the investigation."

"Yeah, I know that. But why BSU?" Racine didn't flinch. Maggie watched to see if Cunningham would. By now, everyone was watching to see if Cunningham would.

He pushed up the bridge of his glasses and looked around at each of them. "There was an anonymous phone call early yesterday morning," he finally confessed, digging his hands into his pockets and leaning against a seldom-used podium next to the chalkboard. "It was traced to a pay phone at the monument. The caller simply said we'd find something interesting at the FDR Memorial. The call came in on my direct line."

No one said anything.

"I'm not certain why the caller chose to tell me," Cunningham added when no one, not even Racine, dared to ask. "Perhaps they knew I was at the crime scene at the cabin. Perhaps they knew we had been asked to profile that case." He looked over at Maggie. "You were quoted in the *Times*. Anyone could have made the assumption we were on the case."

Maggie felt a sudden flush, regretting that she had said anything. That morning a reporter had caught her off guard, coming down the steps of the J. Edgar Hoover Building. He had asked about Agent Delaney. She hadn't been able to mask her anger and simply told him that they would catch the responsible party. That was all she had said, but in that evening's edition of the *Washington Times,* the reporter had identified her as a criminal profiler, insinuating that BSU was somehow involved.

"It doesn't matter." Cunningham tried to relieve her discomfort with a wave of his hand. "The important thing is for us to find this bastard. Agent Tully, how did it go with Emma and Agent LaPlatz?"

"I think it went well." Maggie noticed Tully seemed back to his normal self. He pulled out a copy of the line drawing from a folder and added it to the mess in the middle of the table. "Whether this Brandon is involved or not, Emma knows she saw him with Ginny Brier that evening. Agent LaPlatz is in the process of faxing the sketch to all law enforcement within a hundred-mile radius with a note that he's wanted for questioning."

"Questioning and perhaps a voluntary DNA sample. We need to find him. Detective Racine," Cunningham said, picking up the sketch, "perhaps you could have some officers take a copy of this and check if anyone saw this Brandon around the monuments Sunday morning. Maybe he's also our mystery caller."

Racine nodded.

"And we need to know what group those boys in that cabin belonged to. We keep coming up empty-handed." He looked to Gwen. "There's one survivor. He's refused to talk to anyone. He may have important information. Would you give it a shot?"

"Of course," Gwen said without hesitation.

Just then, Tully pulled out the pamphlet Maggie had seen him folding earlier. It still had the accordion folds, and he tried smoothing out the creases on the side with the man's picture. "I forgot about this. I found it at the monument Sunday morning. It's from the group that held the prayer rally Saturday night. Emma thinks Brandon might be a member. And in fact, if Wenhoff's time of death is accurate, the murderer was killing the Brier girl while the rally was still taking place down below."

Cunningham leaned over the table to take a look. Maggie left her perch at the window.

"That's it," Maggie said as she read the block type: Church of Spiritual Freedom. "That's the nonprofit organization that owns the cabin."

"Are you sure?"

She nodded, looking to Ganza for confirmation as they all stood, leaning over Tully for a closer look. Now Maggie glanced at the man's photo, a handsome, dark-haired man in his forties with a movie star's slick looks. Then she read the caption, and she felt her stomach flip. Reverend Joseph Everett. Jesus! The man who might be at the center of these murders was her mother's savior.

CHAPTER 36

Justin couldn't believe his eyes. Compared to the rest of the compound, Father's small cottage looked like a fucking palace. There was a fireplace and expensive leather chairs. Bookcases were filled with books, something members were not allowed to own or keep, except for a personal copy of the Bible. The walls were covered with framed artwork and the windows with flowing drapes. A bowl with fresh fruit, another rare commodity, sat on a hand-carved sofa table. Next to the bowl was a can of Pepsi. Shit! Alice had led him to believe that junk food was like the Antichrist or some fucking thing.

He sat in one of the leather chairs, waiting as he had been instructed to do by Cassie, Father's personal assistant. He should have been nervous about being asked here—no, summoned. That was the word Darren had used when he came to get him. Had to be Father's word. Not likely an idiot like Darren would come up with a word like that all on his own.

He could hear Father's voice in the room next door, Father's office. He couldn't hear another voice, though it was obvious Father was having a conversation with someone. He had to be on the phone. Another surprise. Had to be a cellular phone, since there weren't any fucking phone lines running into the compound.

"I don't like the sounds of this, Stephen," Father was saying.

Yeah, he had to be on the phone, 'cause Justin wasn't hearing Stephen answer.

"How could this have happened?" Father asked, sounding impatient. He didn't wait for an answer. "He made a big mistake this time."

Justin wondered who'd fucked up. Then he heard Father say, "No, no. Brandon's being taken care of. Don't worry about him. He won't make the same mistake twice."

Brandon? So it was the golden boy who fucked up? Justin smiled, then caught himself. There could be cameras.

He tried to sit still, but his eyes kept pivoting around at the amazing surroundings. Office, bedroom, huge fucking living room. He knew Father even had his own bathroom. Now he wondered if the man had a fucking whirlpool bath and... Oh, shit. He hadn't even thought about it before—the man probably had toilet paper. Not just toilet paper but that white, soft, cushiony stuff. And no way was he restricted to two-minute showers. The thought had Justin raking his fingers through his hair. At least this morning he had gotten all the shampoo out before the water shut off. Maybe he was finally getting the hang of it. But he would never get used to brushing his teeth without water. The antiseptic taste of that generic paste stayed with him throughout the day.

"Justin." Father entered the room without a sound, no footstep, no warning. He wore a black turtleneck sweater and dark trousers that looked freshly pressed.

Justin jumped at the sound of his voice, then automatically stood, wondering if he would need to sit on the floor now. Hadn't Alice told him that Father's head had to be above everyone else's? Or did it not count when no one else was around to see? Shit! He wished he had talked to Alice before coming.

"Sit down," Father said, pointing to Justin's chair. "I've been meaning to talk to you since Saturday night." He sat in the leather chair facing Justin's.

He watched the reverend's face, looking for signs of anger or that scowl he had perfected, the one that could turn men to stone and probably make women sterile. Who knew what powers this guy possessed. But, instead, Father's face was calm and serious but friendly.

"I know you must be confused by what you think you saw on the bus coming back Saturday evening."

Oh, shit! He was actually going to make them discuss this. Justin shifted, making the leather of his chair crackle. "I was sorta half-asleep," he attempted.

"Yes, I thought perhaps you had been. That's why I think you may have misunderstood what you saw." Father sat back and crossed his leg with his right ankle resting on the knee of his left leg, making himself comfortable yet looking in complete control. "You know, Justin, I must constantly test all my followers. Just one among us who shows weakness could destroy us all."

Justin nodded, pretending to understand this bullshit.

"It's not something I enjoy, and sometimes my tests probably look odd to those who don't fully understand. But no one can be exempt. No one, not even sweet, dear Alice." He folded his hands together as if trying to decide whether or not to proceed. "There are things you don't know about Alice. Things no one else knows."

Justin had to admit he didn't know much about Alice's past. She never talked about it or mentioned her family, even though she was always trying to get him to talk about his. It had taken days of probing to finally get her to tell him she was twenty years old, three years older than he was. Now that he thought about it, he didn't even know where she had grown up.

"Alice was a very troubled girl when she came here. Her parents had thrown her out of the house. She had nowhere else to go. I took a special interest in her, because I knew there was such good inside her, wanting to come out. But there were things she has done in her past, things that...well, all I will tell you, Justin, is that she has been used to receiving anything she wanted in exchange for sexual favors."

Justin felt a knot twisting in his stomach. Father's eyes were searching his, making sure Justin understood what he was saying.

"I know it's hard to believe." Father seemed satisfied with what he saw and sat back, shaking his head as if he, too, still couldn't believe it. "Looking at her now and seeing what progress she's made, yes, it is so hard to believe what a slut she was."

Justin caught himself from grimacing at the word. He blinked and swallowed hard. His mouth had gone dry and suddenly the room had grown much too hot. He remembered that tight pink sweater Alice had worn Saturday and how inappropriate he thought it was. Then he remembered her shaking her head no the entire time Father had his hand in her crotch. But there had also been such a pained look on her face, almost a sort of fear in her eyes. Had he imagined all that? Or had she simply been afraid of failing Father's test? Jesus!

"So now you understand the manner of testing I must use with Alice. It's so important to make certain that she has grown beyond that lifestyle, that she isn't continuing to lead other members into temptation. That she recognizes she has so much more to offer. That's also why I put her in charge of recruiting, so that she can experience successes from using her other talents and not just her body."

Justin didn't know what to say. Father was watching him, waiting, but what the hell kind of response did he expect?

"You must never speak of this, Justin. It must never leave this room. Do you understand?"

"Sure. No, I won't tell anyone."

"Not even Alice. It would devastate her to realize that anyone knows. Can I trust you, Justin?"

"Yeah, sure. I mean…yes, you can trust me."

"Good." He smiled, and Justin couldn't remember Father ever smiling at him. It actually felt pretty good. "I knew you could be trusted. You're a good man, just like your brother, Eric." He sat forward, suddenly serious. "I knew you were special, Justin, when you survived my test."

Justin stared at him, looking for signs that the man knew he hadn't really survived but had spent the time with some campers. But Father was serious, his eyes warm and friendly.

"You must never repeat this, Justin, not even to your brother, but I knew from the day you stepped onto the compound that God had sent you."

"Sent me?"

"Yes. You're not like the rest. You see things, know things. You're not easily fooled."

Maybe the man honestly could read minds. Justin swallowed and nodded.

"You were sent by God to play an integral part in this mission, Justin. God sent you to me as a favor. You are a blessing."

Justin wasn't sure what to say. He couldn't help feeling… Hell, he couldn't help feeling special. He had never heard Father say such things to anyone else.

"That's why I want you to join the ranks of my warriors. I have the feeling you will be a very special warrior." He leaned even closer and lowered his voice. "I need your help,

Justin. There are those who would like to destroy me, even here within our ranks. Are you willing to help me?"

Justin didn't know much about Father's warriors, except that they did get special treatment, rewards. Eric was a warrior and took great pride in the title. Justin tried to remember if anyone had ever told him they needed him before. It felt good. It felt damn good.

Father was waiting for an answer.

"Yeah," Justin said, and found the answer came quite easily. "Yeah, I guess I could help."

"Good. Excellent." He smiled and slapped Justin on the knee, then sat back in the recliner. "Brandon and I are taking a group to Boston for initiation. I'd like you to go, too.

"Sure, okay." He had no idea what he was getting himself into, but maybe it was a good idea to be away from Alice for a while. Just to think and sort through everything Father had told him. Besides, he really was kind of excited about this. Eric would be so proud when he heard the news. "About Eric," he said, "any idea when he'll be back?"

"Could be any day now," Father said. But his eyes suddenly drifted off to look out the window, as if his mind had wandered somewhere else.

CHAPTER 37

John F. Kennedy Federal Building
Boston, Massachusetts

When the guard told Eric Pratt he had a visitor, Eric knew Father had sent someone to kill him. He sat down next to the thick glass partition and stared at the door on the other side, waiting to see who his executioner would be. His best friend, Brandon, walked through the door, stopped to be patted down by a guard then waved a hello. He sat in the yellow plastic chair and scooted as close as allowed to the barrier. Brandon was clean shaven, his wild, red hair wet with some sort of gel, combed and plastered to his head. He smiled at Eric as he picked up the telephone receiver.

"Hi, buddy," Brandon said, his voice muffled, though he sat right across from him. "They treatin' you okay in here?" His eyes flicked everywhere except to meet Eric's, and right then, Eric knew. It was Brandon. Brandon had come to deliver his death warrant.

After those first days of questioning when Eric refused to answer any questions, they had thrown him into solitary confinement. What they hadn't realized was that they were giving him exactly what he wanted—to be left alone. After months of being surrounded by people, of not being able to go anywhere without a tagalong, the solitary confinement was a reward, not a punishment. But he wouldn't dare tell Brandon. That would only give his friend more reason to want him dead.

"I'm fine," Eric said, not caring that his tone probably didn't back up his words.

"Heard the food in here is worse than the crap we eat every day." Brandon laughed, but it was a manufactured one.

Had he forgotten that Eric would be able to recognize it as such? Did he really believe he could dupe him into exchanging confidences? Oh, Father was good. Of course, he would send Eric's best friend to do the job. What sweet poetic justice, like sending Judas to betray Jesus, or rather, Cain to slaughter Abel.

"The food's okay."

Brandon glanced around, then leaned close to the glass. Eric stayed put, sitting straight-backed in the hard plastic chair. This was it. But how…how would he choose to destroy him?

"What the hell happened out there, Eric? Why didn't you take the pill?" He kept his voice hushed, but there was no mistaking the anger. Eric had expected nothing less than anger. And no matter how honest he tried to be with him, Brandon would never understand, because *he* would not have hesitated. Brandon would have swallowed ten cyanide capsules for Father. And now he wouldn't hesitate for a second to kill his best friend, whose only sin had been that he wanted to live.

"I did take it," Eric offered as a weak defense.

It was the truth, or at least part of the truth. Besides, hadn't Father taught them that it was okay to lie, cheat and steal as long as the end justified the means? Well, the end was now Eric's own survival. Then he realized something for the first time. How stupid of him to not realize it sooner. Neither Brandon nor Father had any idea what had happened after the shoot-out. They had no idea what the agents had asked him or what he had told them. How could they? All they knew was that he was still alive and in the midst of the enemy.

But maybe they didn't care about what had happened. They certainly didn't care about him or it wouldn't have taken this long for Father to send someone. No, the only thing they cared about was what he might confess, though there was nothing he could say. What could he tell them? That Father had tricked them? That he cared more about guns and his own protection than he did about his own followers? And why would the FBI care to hear about that?

"I don't get it," Brandon whispered. "Those capsules are supposed to be enough to drop a horse."

Eric looked into his friend's eyes. He could see Brandon didn't believe him. His friend's jaw was taut. One hand clenched the phone, the other was a fist on the small ledge.

"Maybe mine didn't have as much," Eric said, continuing the lie. "Lowell packs dozens of those. Maybe he didn't pack enough into the one I got." But even Eric wasn't convinced by his own emotionless voice.

Brandon looked around again. Two seats down a large, greasy-haired woman began to sob in loud, sloppy gulps. He leaned even closer to the glass, and this time he didn't bother to hide the anger. "That's bullshit!" he spat in a low, careful voice.

Eric didn't blink. He didn't answer. He could be silent. He had done it for two whole days while prosecutors and FBI agents screamed into his face. He continued to sit quiet and straight, telling himself, commanding himself not to flinch, while his heart pounded against his rib cage.

"You know what happens to traitors," Brandon whispered

into the phone. Those same eyes that only moments ago couldn't meet Eric's were now holding him, pinning him to his chair with their hate. When had Brandon's eyes become so black, so hollow, so evil? "Look for the signs of the end," Brandon said, "and just remember, this could be the day."

Then Father's messenger slapped the phone's receiver into its cradle. He shoved back the chair, its metal legs screeching against the floor. But he walked out with his usual calm, cocky strut, so that no one else would notice that he had just personally delivered Father's curse of death.

Eric should have felt relief that he had survived Brandon's visit. Instead he felt sick to his stomach. He knew what Father was capable of doing. The man seemed to have special powers. In the past, there had been members who had left, all of them traitors. No one left without being a traitor. Eric had heard plenty of stories, and then there were the ones he knew firsthand.

The most recent one to leave was Dara Hardy. She had given the excuse that her mother had cancer and Dara wanted to spend her last days with her. But Father insisted that if her story had been true, Dara certainly would have taken him up on his generous offer to bring the ill woman to the compound. Never mind that Father didn't allow any medications and preached that doctors were a selfish indulgence. After all, he alone could heal and would take care of his members. Dara Hardy left. Exactly one week later, she was killed in a car accident. Her mother died without Dara at her bedside.

Eric wondered what freak accident they would use with him. Would another prisoner accidently scald him in the shower? Would more cyanide find its way into his food? Or would a guard come into his cell late at night and make it look like he had hanged himself? One thing he knew for certain; his killer would be someone he least expected. Just as his messenger of death had been his best friend. How could he survive in this snake pit of the enemy and constantly be looking over his shoulder?

But it wasn't his enemy who wanted him dead. It was the man who, even as he killed Eric, would still claim to be his savior, the redeemer of his soul. No, he had that wrong—the owner of his soul, not the redeemer. Because that was the price Father charged all his followers in order for them to come into his fold. Their soul.

For the first time, Eric felt grateful that Justin was dead, reduced to a cardboard box full of unidentifiable bones. At least Father could no longer pull the two brothers apart, make them wage war against each other like he had with so many other family members. And, perhaps, just maybe, he had not had time to steal Justin's soul. If that was true then Justin was, indeed, the lucky one.

CHAPTER 38

"**Y**ou don't know it's the same Joseph Everett," Tully said from the doorway, watching O'Dell's fingers fly over her computer keyboard.

"Unlikely that there are two Reverend Joseph Everetts in the Virginia area," she said without a glance, but he recognized that anxious tone in her voice, and he couldn't help thinking, "Here we go again."

He became a little nervous whenever O'Dell got that tone in her voice and a certain look in her eyes, like she was on a personal mission. The last time it happened, the two of them ended up in a burning house with O'Dell saving his life—*after* he took a bullet to his thigh.

He was relieved however, that they might actually have some answers. And also relieved that Emma had gotten through the morning. O'Dell was right. Emma was an incredibly brave and smart girl. And before Agent LaPlatz volunteered to drive her back to Reston High, he embarrassed his brave, smart daughter with a hug and told her how proud he was of her.

Tully watched as O'Dell brought up some sort of document and began scrolling through it. He looked over at Dr. Patterson, who sat in the overstuffed lounge chair O'Dell had managed to squeeze into her small office. There had been several late nights when he had found his partner curled up and asleep in it. All of their offices in BSU were small, but O'Dell had a knack for organizing, using every inch of the floor-to-ceiling bookshelves and little cubbyholes to keep piles off chairs and off the floor, so that even with the lounge chair, her office looked cozy but not overcrowded. Not like his own, which reminded him some days of a storage closet with walking paths to his desk.

Dr. Patterson had removed her heels, and Tully watched absently as she made herself comfortable, tucking her legs underneath her. In doing so, she hiked up her skirt. She had great legs. Trim ankles. Firm, smooth thighs. Jeez! What the hell was wrong with him? He looked away as if caught doing something he shouldn't.

Usually Gwen Patterson bugged the hell out of him. There seemed to be nothing they agreed on. The last time he and O'Dell were working late, they stopped at her huge Tudor in Newburgh Heights, where Dr. Patterson had been dog-sitting. The three of them decided to order takeout. If he remembered correctly, he and Patterson had gotten into an argument over Chinese or pizza, debating each food's nonnutritional value. Of course, she was supposed to be the expert, being a so-called gourmet cook. Yeah, she irritated the hell out of him. Didn't mean she couldn't have great legs, though. Maybe thinking about Caroline over the weekend had simply reminded him—

"Here's something." O'Dell interrupted his rambling

thoughts. "It's a court document. It's old—1975. That's over twenty-five years ago. Everett would have been…what do you think…in his twenties?"

"We don't even know yet if Everett is involved."

"Cunningham must think so or he wouldn't be sending you and Gwen to Boston to interview the lone survivor. And he didn't hesitate when I asked to arrange a meeting with someone from Everett's organization. Maybe even an ex-member. In fact, he told me he'd call Senator Brier and see if he had any connections."

O'Dell kept her back to them while she read. Dr. Patterson was ignoring the two of them, rolling her shoulders and slowly massaging her temples—perhaps some relaxation routine she was used to doing to unwind. Tully found it distracting as hell. He finally gave in and came to O'Dell's side to look at what she had found.

"Not like a trip to Boston will do much good," Tully said. "The kid wasn't willing to talk at the cabin when we had him scared out of his wits. I can't imagine he'll spill anything now after he's had a nice warm place to sleep and three square meals."

"What makes you think that fear can be the only motivating force to get a suspect to talk?" Dr. Patterson asked without disturbing her temple rubbing.

Now that Tully was out of her line of vision he could safely steal a glance at her shiny, strawberry-blond hair. The woman was definitely attractive. Suddenly, she turned to look up at him.

"No really, what makes you think fear is the only way to go?"

"Fear's usually what works best on that age group," he told her.

This time O'Dell looked over her shoulder. "Isn't that exactly what you told me the other day, Gwen?"

"Not exactly. I said fear most likely made them think they

didn't have an alternative when their natural instinct should have been to fight. But from what I understand, this boy spit his cyanide capsule out. Which would tell me that fear might not be a motivating factor for him."

"That's not necessarily true," Tully said, and realized he was already feeling defensive. Why did she do that to him? He wasn't a defensive kind of guy. But now both Patterson and O'Dell were waiting for an explanation. "I know you think spitting the cyanide out could be a sign of him wanting to stick around to fight. But maybe he was simply scared to die. Isn't that possible?"

"Whoever convinced these boys to take cyanide certainly would have convinced them that they would be tortured and killed if taken alive." Dr. Patterson was no longer relaxing. Even her legs had come out from under her. "That this boy was willing to take that chance tells me that he's looking for and hoping for a safe haven."

"Really? You can tell all that even before you've met the kid."

"Okay, you two." O'Dell put up her hands in mock surrender. "Maybe I should be going to Boston with you, Gwen."

"You need to talk to your mother," Gwen answered, keeping her eyes on Tully as if planning her next offensive.

"You promise you two won't kill each other?" O'Dell smiled.

"I'm sure we'll be fine," Gwen said, smiling at O'Dell. However, O'Dell seemed to be waiting for confirmation from Tully.

"We'll be fine," he said, now anxious to change the subject, because even though Patterson made him defensive, she hadn't realized her skirt was still hiked up to her thighs. He turned back to the computer screen. "What did you find?"

"I have no idea if it's the same Joseph Everett, but at twenty-two years of age and from Arlington, Virginia, it could very well be. He was charged with rape. The nineteen-year-old girl was a second-year journalism student at the University of Virginia."

The phone suddenly rang, and O'Dell grabbed it. "O'Dell."

Tully pretended to read the computer screen, trying to keep his attention away from Patterson.

"What makes you think that?" O'Dell asked, then waited. Whoever it was hadn't given much of an explanation. O'Dell frowned as she said, "Okay, I'll be there."

She hung up the phone. "That was Racine," she said, swiveling her chair back to the computer. "I'll print out copies," she told Tully as she hit the print icon, listened for the printer to groan into action, then started closing down the Internet site. "She thinks she has something I need to take a look at."

There was an emphasis on "she thinks" and enough sarcasm to prompt Tully to try again. "What is it with you and Racine?"

"I told you. I don't trust her."

"No. You told me you didn't like her."

"Same thing," she said as she whipped two copies from the printer tray, handing one to Tully and folding the other for herself. "Any chance you could check if this is our Joseph Everett before you leave?"

"Sure. If he has a criminal conviction for rape, it'll be easy to track."

"Unfortunately, this is all we've got." She held up her copy. "There won't be any other documents. The girl dropped the charges." She put on her jacket, then stopped and looked from Tully to Gwen. "Everett must have been good at instilling fear, even back then."

CHAPTER 39

He knew he shouldn't be taking the concoction in between kills. Too much recreational usage would water down the effects, but he needed something to calm him. He needed something to battle the anger and fear…no, not fear. They couldn't scare him. He simply wouldn't allow it. They were out to stop him, to keep him from his mission, but he couldn't let them get to him. He was stronger than that. He simply needed a reminder that he was stronger. That was all this was. A simple reminder.

He sat back and waited. He knew he could count on the exotic concoction's special effects, its healing magic, its hidden strength. Already he was using almost twice the original dosage. But right now, none of that mattered. Right now, all he wanted to do was sit quietly and enjoy the psychedelic light show that always occurred afterward. Yes. After he accessed the strength and the rush of adrenaline, then came the light show. It flashed behind his eyes and caused the zinging inside his head. The flashes looked like tiny little angels shaped like stars, flitting from one side of the room to the other. It was absolutely beautiful.

He grasped the book and caressed the smooth leather. The book. How could he have done any of this without it? It had inspired the heat, the passion, the anger, the need, the justification. And it would provide the validation, as well.

He took deep breaths and closed his eyes, enjoying the warm, calm sweep through him. Yes, now he was prepared for the next step.

CHAPTER 40

The moon peeked over the District skyline just as Maggie pulled her Toyota into the empty parking lot. She could see the yellow crime scene tape, flapping in the wind, blocking off the entrance to the viaduct. Several officers paced and waited, but she couldn't see Racine. A mobile crime scene lab passed by as Maggie finished the last bite of her drive-thru dinner, a McDonald's Quarter Pounder and fries. She got out of the car and brushed the excess salt from her knit shirt, then exchanged her suit jacket for her navy FBI windbreaker.

She dug under the front seat and pulled out a pair of rubber boots, low-tops that she slipped over her leather shoes. Out of habit, she started to reach for her forensic kit, too, then stopped. The medical examiner's station wagon was already parked alongside the concrete wall, next to the opening of the viaduct. No sense in ticking off Stan any more than she already had.

However, as Maggie walked toward the scene, she wasn't surprised to see Wayne Prashard emerging from the viaduct entrance instead of Stan. Not only had Stan probably had his share of after-hours call-ins for one week, but he certainly wouldn't make the trip himself for some homeless woman. Maggie wasn't quite sure why Racine was so certain she should be here, either. She hoped it wasn't some ploy. Who knew what Racine could be up to.

Prashard nodded at Maggie as he opened the back of the wagon. "She won't let me touch a goddamn thing until you take a look."

"Good to see you, too, Wayne."

"Sorry." He surrendered a smile and his normal bulldog face creased into friendly lines. "It's just that sometimes she can be such a pain in the ass, you know what I mean?"

Yes, she knew exactly what he meant, but she only smiled. Prashard wasn't finished, though. "She never used to be that way."

"Really?" Maggie couldn't imagine Racine any other way.

"All she cares about now is making sure everyone knows she's in charge. But before she made detective she was actually nice," he said while he brought out a body bag from the back of the wagon. "Maybe a little too nice, if you know what I mean." He glanced at Maggie and winked.

She ignored his invitation to join in trashing the detective. She might not like Racine, but she had never resorted to idle gossip about other law enforcement officers. She wasn't about to start now. And it did look as if Prashard had a story or two he wanted to share. Instead, she turned to leave. "I wouldn't know," she said. "I didn't know Racine before she made detective." And she left it at that.

As she continued toward the entrance, she checked the area, aware of the noisy traffic overhead, flashes of headlights between six-foot guardrails. The smell of diesel emanated from the bus terminal on the other side of the small empty parking lot where engines were left running and several mechanics climbed in and around the Greyhound buses. About a half-dozen broken-down buses lined the chain-link fence, blocking a direct view of the viaduct's entrance.

Except for where the mechanics worked, the place was badly lit. It was dark and noisy, but deserted, and Maggie wondered why anyone would come here voluntarily. Except that the arch of concrete—more a tunnel than an arch—would provide shelter from the wind, if not some warmth. She could understand why it might be an enticing spot for someone looking to set up her cardboard home. Also an enticing spot for someone looking for a victim.

"Oh, good! You're here." Racine appeared and held up a section of crime scene tape for Maggie to crawl under.

Maggie could smell the body as soon as she walked into the tunnel. Racine led the way, carefully stepping around two crime lab technicians, one crawling the grid pattern with a flashlight, brush and plastic bags while the other set up several spotlights.

At the other opening, leaning against the cold concrete wall, sat a naked woman, stark and gray in the sharp glare of a spotlight. Her eyes were wide open, the corners already filled with white clusters of maggot larvae. Her head lolled to one side, revealing several ligature marks across her neck. Her dirty-and-smudged face was bloated, her mouth duct-taped shut. Her hands were folded into her lap, the wrists facing forward as if to show off the welts from where handcuffs had restrained her. Maggie noticed the insides of her elbows were clean, no track marks from needles. She hadn't been lured here by the promise of drugs. There was no cardboard box, no shopping cart, no other personal belongings, other than the carefully folded rags stacked about a yard away.

"What do you think?"

She realized Racine was watching her and waiting while Maggie examined the scene, careful where she stepped and letting her eyes collect the evidence.

"The posing of the body looks very similar."

"Looks fucking identical," Racine said. "Although I get the idea we won't find any ID stuffed down her throat."

"She certainly doesn't fit the victimology of our guy," Maggie said, squatting in front of the body to get a better look. She was staring directly into the corpse's empty eyes. The woman had been dead for more than thirty-six hours, the rigor mortis already leaving the body pliable again. Maggie could tell this by gently lifting one hand and carefully letting it fall back into place.

"I wish the hell you wouldn't touch the stiff," Prashard said from the entrance, making his way inside, staying close to the concrete wall.

"But she's not stiff anymore. She's been dead for a while. You have any estimates?" Maggie asked without getting up.

"I'm guessing forty-eight hours, but it's a major guess since I haven't been able to touch a fucking thing yet." He shot a look at Racine, but she wasn't paying attention. Instead, she was still watching Maggie.

"Check this out," Racine said, bringing out a penlight and shining it at the dirt floor of the tunnel.

Maggie got up and went to Racine's side. About five feet in front of the body was what looked like a circular indent in the dirt, although it and the area around it looked scuffed on purpose as if in an attempt to erase it and possibly other marks like it.

"Tully's signature," Racine said. "I don't know what the hell it is, but tell me that's not the exact weird imprint we found at the monument yesterday morning."

Maggie looked around the tunnel again. The scene looked too similar to be a coincidence. "Forty-eight hours ago would put time of death at Saturday night. Why in the world would he target and kill a senator's daughter and then some random homeless woman?"

"Maybe the guy's just really fucked up?" Racine suggested.

"No. Both scenes are much too organized." Maggie looked to Prashard. "Wayne, would you mind checking the victim's mouth?"

"Out here?"

"Yes. It would be helpful and speed things up if we can check to see if anything is left inside her mouth."

"I don't know." Prashard shrugged and scratched his head as though Maggie was asking him to do the autopsy out in the field. "It's highly unusual."

"Oh, for fuck's sake, Prashard," Racine yelled at him. "Just do it."

To Maggie's stunned surprise, Prashard started getting out latex gloves and a pair of forceps from his bag. Then he took position over the body, bending stiffly at the waist instead of getting down on his knees.

Maggie glanced at Racine, who seemed neither pleased nor angry with the assistant medical examiner. Instead, the detective came in closer, crossed her arms over her chest and waited, pointing the penlight, ready to peek inside. Suddenly moonlight streamed into the exit, just above the arch, and illuminating the woman's whole face, making her eyes glitter.

"Jesus!" Racine said. "That's pretty freaky." She glanced back at Maggie, and Maggie tried to remember when there had been a full moon, or if it was still to come. And did it mean anything?

"What exactly are we looking for?" Prashard asked, ignoring Racine and the sudden moonlight as he continued to peel back the gray duct tape, inch by inch, taking care to not lift away any skin. Maggie grabbed a plastic evidence bag from Prashard's case and held it open for him to put the tape in.

"Should be a capsule," Racine answered. "Check the inside of her cheeks."

"You mean like poison?"

"Just check, Prashard. Jesus!" The detective seemed a bit unnerved and impatient.

Prashard finally opened the woman's mouth, but before he could insert a gloved finger, quarters came spilling out.

"What the hell?" Racine shined the penlight, so that even standing over Racine's shoulder, Maggie could see quite clearly. The woman's mouth looked like a black, decaying slot machine filled with shiny coins, spilling out like she'd just hit the jackpot.

CHAPTER 41

TUESDAY
November 26
Boston, Massachusetts

From his corner suite at the Ritz-Carlton, Ben Garrison could see the Boston Common in one direction and the Charles River in the other. The lush suite was a long-overdue reward to himself and hopefully a good-luck charm for more good things to come. Not that he was superstitious, but he did believe that attitude could be a powerful tool. There was no harm in a few rewards and props now and then to boost that attitude. It made all the crap he had to deal with worthwhile; crap like crank phone calls and cockroaches. Small stuff compared to what he had dealt with in the past.

He remembered several years ago living out of a leaky one-man tent in a smelly, rat-infested warehouse in Kampala, Uganda. It had taken him months to learn Swahili and gain the locals' trust. But it paid off. In no time, he had enough explicit photographs to break the story about a mad scientist luring homeless people from the streets of Kampala for his radical experiments.

Ben still had several of those photos tacked up on the walls of his darkroom. In order to feed her family of five kids, one woman had allowed the so-called scientist to remove her perfectly healthy breast, leaving a scar that looked like the asshole had chopped it off with a machete. An old man had sold the use of his right ear, now mutilated beyond repair, for a carton of cigarettes.

Ben had chosen a slow-speed black-and-white film to bring out the textures and details with natural side lighting. When he developed the prints, he had used high-contrast-grade paper to accentuate the dramatic effect, making the blacks dense and silky and the whites blindingly bright. Through his magic, he had managed to transform those hideous scars into art.

He was a genius when it came to catching hopelessness, that flicker of despair that, if he waited long enough, would always reveal itself in his subjects' eyes. All it took was patience. Yes, he was truly a master at capturing on film the whole spectrum of emotions, from terror to jealousy to fear and evil. After all, the eyes were the window to the soul, and Ben knew he could one day capture the image of the soul on film. Patience.

At the time, both *Newsweek* and *Time* had been working on the mad scientist story, but neither of them had photos, not ones like Ben's. His reward to himself after selling those photos for a nice chunk of change had been a week on a yacht with some waitress whose name he couldn't remember. He did, however, still remember the cute rose tattoo on her tight little ass. Even had a photo of her on his darkroom wall, or rather a photo of her tattoo.

That was back in the days when kinky sex gave him a rush and kept him satisfied for a while. But there wasn't anything that could equal the rush of these past several weeks.

Of course, the best rush of all would be to see the Reverend fucking Everett's smug face when he finally got a visit from the FBI. Surely, even Racine and her bunch of Keystone Kops would make the connection and soon. Although if and when the feebies attempted to raid Everett's precious compound, there probably wouldn't be much left to investigate. If Everett truly believed he was in danger of being arrested, Ben knew the good reverend's blind little sheep would be prepared for a suicide drill, like during the raid on that shitty little cabin on the Neponset River.

He had heard about the cyanide capsules from an ATF agent who had been on the scene. Couple more drinks and the guy probably would have given Ben more details. But mentioning the capsules had been enough. Besides, he had seen them firsthand when he spent two days inside Everett's little compound, that concrete barricade that looked more like a prison than the utopia Everett professed it to be.

He'd also discovered that Everett had enough explosives to blow a nice-size hole in the Appalachian Mountains. The crazy thing was, Everett didn't have the explosives for some terrorist attack. Just like the stockpile at that cabin in the woods—no complex, intricate conspiracy takeover. No, not at all. Instead, it was all for protection, all to protect his fucking fortress if anyone dared try to come in and take away his flock. It would be sort of a cross between Jim Jones's purple Kool-Aid and Timothy McVeigh's fertilizer bomb. What a mess the feebies would have to clean up. And boy, would they have some explaining to do. Probably make Waco look like a cakewalk.

That's if the FBI even made it past all of Everett's booby traps. The asshole had the entire woods filled with Viet Cong-like surprises. Ben couldn't help wondering if his making shingle-nail pipe bombs and chemical-burn grass rags were a few of the reasons the guy had gotten kicked out of the military. Oh, but for good measure, the thoughtful reverend had posted what he probably believed to be disclaimer signs outside the area. Signs that said stuff like Survivors Will Be Prosecuted and Step Beyond This Point Only at Your Own Risk.

It was when Ben had seen the signs that he'd made the decision to gain entrance as a pathetic lost soul rather than as a renegade journalist sneaking through the woods. Weeks before he began his pathetic lost soul's charade, he had muddied himself up like the Three Hills tribe of Mozambique had shown him, covering every inch of his body with a paste mixture, surprised that he could still remember its basic recipe. Even Everett's ex-World Wrestling Federation bodyguards hadn't seen him sliding through the tall grass and blending in with the tree bark. He had learned a lot that visit. The main thing had been that no one could sneak in—or out, for that matter—without getting his fucking head or leg blown off.

Ben checked his wristwatch. He had plenty of time. From what he had overheard at the District rally Saturday night, Everett's boys wouldn't be ready yet for a few hours. He decided to call down to room service. Maybe even check out the whirlpool bath. He'd enjoy himself, reward himself for a short time, then get back to work.

CHAPTER 42

John F. Kennedy Federal Building
Boston, Massachusetts

Gwen Patterson watched Agent Tully wrestle their suitcases out of the taxi cab's trunk while the driver stood beside him. He was directing Tully, just as he had when he picked them up at the airport in Boston, pointing with a gnarled right hand, his excuse for not lifting the cases himself. Tully didn't seem to mind. Instead, he simply asked for a receipt while he dug in his trench coat's pockets, pulling out a wad and separating dollar bills from other crumpled receipts and a couple of Mc-Donald's napkins.

Gwen waited, her patience wearing thin. She wanted to snap open her handbag and pay the fare herself. It would be quicker. It was bad enough she was wasting two days, volunteering her services to the bureau and to Kyle Cunningham. Why was it that her colleagues wrote books and garnered interviews with Matt Laurer and Katie Couric? She wrote a book and what did she get? An interview with an adolescent killer.

She reached for her overnight case, but Tully snatched it away.

"No, I've got it," he insisted, tucking it under his arm while he wrapped the strap of her laptop computer's case around his other shoulder and grabbed his duffel bag.

Rather than argue with him, she led the way up the steps, letting him pass her at the last stretch so he could shuffle the bags and still open the heavy door. She wondered if he was overcompensating after Maggie had pointed out that perhaps the two of them couldn't do this trip without being at each other's throats the entire time. Whatever his reason for all the chivalry, Tully had been nothing but polite since they boarded their flight for Boston.

Maggie had assured Gwen time and again that Tully was one of the good guys, a smart, decent agent who wanted to do the right thing. Maggie always added that he was simply a little green, having spent much of his short time with the bureau behind a desk in Cleveland. But that his instincts and his motives were genuine. Yet, there was still something about the tall, lanky agent that rubbed Gwen the wrong way.

What she did know was that his polite, Midwestern manner grated on her. Perhaps he seemed too good to be real. Too honest. Too much of a Boy Scout. The kind of guy who would never drive over the speed limit or have one too many drinks. The kind of guy who went out of his way to open doors for women, but couldn't remember to keep his dollar bills in a money clip or take time to shine his shoes. Maybe that was why she insisted on ruffling his feathers, pushing his buttons. Maybe she wanted to expose that calm, polite, naive Boy Scout's facade, rip it just a bit and see what was underneath, discover what he was really made of. Had too many years as a psychologist made her cynical?

"Dr. Patterson?"

Gwen and Tully stopped and looked up at the man leaning over the second-floor railing. When he realized he was right, he bounded down the stairs with an athletic gait. Gwen knew immediately, before any introductions, that this had to be Nick Morrelli, the man who managed to make Maggie O'Dell blush at just a mention of his name. And now Gwen could understand why. He was more handsome than Maggie's description, the epitome of the cliché tall, dark and handsome, with a strong square jaw, warm blue eyes and dimples when he smiled.

"You must be Nick Morrelli," she said, offering her hand as he got to the bottom of the steps. "I'm Gwen Patterson."

"And I'm Agent R.J. Tully." Tully had to reshuffle the bags to free a hand, nearly dropping her overnight case in the process.

"Here, let me take one of those," Nick said, helping Tully peel the laptop case's strap from his shoulder. "District Attorney Richardson is still in court, so you're stuck with me. I'll take you upstairs. We can put your bags in a safe place. Why don't we take the elevator." He led them farther into the lobby to a bank of elevators and pushed the up button. "How was your flight?"

"It was fine," Gwen said. She hated small talk, but Nick made it seem as if he was genuinely interested, so she humored him. "Not much of a lunch, so I hope you have some good coffee waiting for us."

"There's a Starbucks across the street. I'll send someone out. What would you like?"

"A café mocha would be lovely." She smiled at Nick as he held the elevator door open and let her squeeze past him. As she did so, she noticed Tully watching her, and from his frown, she knew exactly what he was thinking. But she didn't care if he was disgusted by her shameless flirting. The least she could get out of this trip was a good cup of coffee.

"How about you, Agent Tully?"

"Just regular coffee is fine," he said, in what almost sounded like a grumble. Gwen watched him lean against the far corner of the elevator car with his eyes glued to the numbers above the door. What happened to the polite Boy Scout?

Now Gwen did the same—watched the numbers light up, one floor at a time—suddenly uncomfortable with the tension between the two men and feeling somewhat responsible.

"How's Maggie?" Morrelli asked without taking his eyes from the numbers above the door.

"She's good." She waited for him to ask more, but he didn't. Maybe he wasn't comfortable asking for more information with Agent Tully sulking nearby. She glanced at Tully and wondered if he knew about Nick and Maggie. Although, what was there really to know, since Maggie herself didn't seem to know what to do with the handsome assistant district attorney?

With Nick being in Boston and Maggie living in Newburgh Heights, Virginia, the two of them had little opportunity to spend any time together. It had been months since they had seen each other. Months since Maggie had even mentioned him. Even knowing that he'd been assigned this case and that Gwen would be seeing him today, Maggie had barely acknowledged the fact. Hadn't even given Gwen any messages to relay.

Gwen knew Maggie's divorce from Greg was dragging on, and that Maggie had purposely kept things from progressing with Nick, or as she would say, "getting messy." But there was something more, something her friend was keeping to herself. Why did Maggie insist on doing that? She had real problems with intimacy but refused to see it. Instead, she called it professional distancing and used her career as an excuse to keep everyone in her life at a safe distance.

"He's had only one visitor since he's been here," Nick was telling them, and Gwen forced herself to refocus on the reason for their trip. "He's refused to talk to a public defender and hasn't even made his one phone call."

"Who was the visitor?" Tully asked.

"I'm not sure. D.A. Richardson is personally handling this case. I haven't been involved until now, so I don't know all the details. I think the kid—the visitor—checked out as a college friend of Pratt's."

The elevator's doors opened and Nick held them again for Gwen to pass. Tully stayed for a moment, leaning in the corner of the elevator car, then trailed behind them as though he didn't need anyone's help, keeping his distance while Nick led them down a busy corridor. She hated how men played their territorial games, especially in the presence of a woman. If she hadn't been here, they'd be exchanging football scores and pretending to be old buddies.

"How did he know he was here?" Tully asked, now catching up with them.

"Excuse me?"

"How did the college friend know Pratt was here if Pratt hadn't made any phone calls?"

Nick slowed and glanced at Tully over his shoulder. The look on his face told Gwen Nick wished he had had more time to equip himself with the details of the case. She found herself wanting to defend him and at the same time wondered if Tully ever tried to make a good first impression.

"Good question. I can find that out for you." Nick finally said. "Here we are." He pointed to the door at the end of the hall.

This time Tully was on the right side, grabbing the handle before Nick had a chance and opening it wide for both Gwen and Nick. She stopped herself from rolling her eyes at him. It would probably only encourage him.

"We've got him ready to see you," Nick explained, "but if you'd like to take some time to unwind—"

"No," Gwen stopped him. "Let's go ahead."

He led her down another hallway to a door where a uniformed guard stood.

"Agent Tully and I will be watching from next door," Nick said, pointing to another door. "Burt, here, will be right outside, so you start feeling uncomfortable or want to stop and get the hell out, just say the word, okay?"

"Thanks, Nick." She smiled at him, hoping to relieve his concern. "I know the drill, so don't worry. I'll be fine."

She did know the drill. She had interviewed numerous criminals, tougher, cruder men than this boy. She slipped out of her London Fog trench coat, unsnapped her watch, plucked off her earrings and pearls, placing the items in her handbag, then surrendered the coat and handbag to Nick. She checked her suit jacket and unlatched a gold pin of a dove from her lapel. Nick opened the handbag for her, and she carefully placed it inside.

After inspecting her skirt and shoes and buttons, making certain there were no sharp edges, she bent down to her overnight case and pulled out a plain yellow legal pad—no wire spiral notebooks—and a simple number two lead pencil. She had learned the hard way that the simplest pen could be dismantled in seconds, its insides used to pick the lock of even the best set of handcuffs.

Finally prepared, she took a deep breath and nodded to Burt to open the door. Yes, she knew the drill. Don't show any signs of vulnerability. Let him know immediately that she wouldn't be intimidated by any of his bullshit, crude comments or lewd glares. However, when the young man sitting across the wooden table looked up at her, Gwen saw something that threatened to unravel her calm more than any obscene gesture or wolf-call whistle. What she saw in Eric Pratt's eyes was pure, undeniable fear. And that fear seemed to be directed at her.

CHAPTER 43

FBI Headquarters
Washington, D.C.

Maggie spread out the files on the counter Keith Ganza had cleared for her, shoving high-tech microscopes out of the way and setting empty racks of vials clinking.

"Should we wait for Detective Racine?" Ganza asked, glancing at his watch.

"She knew what time we were going to get started." Maggie tried to keep the impatience out of her voice. Just when she was starting to be impressed with Racine, the detective did something to annoy her all over again. "The only case I could find on VICAP," Maggie began, "is a floater fished out of Falls Lake just north of Raleigh. They found her about ten days ago." She pulled out the scanned photos she had downloaded. "She was a twenty-two-year-old college student at Wake Forest."

"A floater?" Ganza hovered over her shoulder. "How long had she been in the water?"

"Coroner's report says several days." She showed him a faxed copy. "But you know as well as I do that it's pretty tough to figure time of death with a floater."

"This doesn't sound like our guy. What was VICAP's match?"

"Actually there're quite a few things. Her mouth was taped shut with duct tape and a piece of paper was found shoved down her throat. There're handcuff marks on the wrist and several ligature tracks on her throat." Again, she pulled out more scanned photos, close-ups of a mutilated neck and welted wrists.

"Was the hyoid crushed?"

Maggie ran her index finger down the coroner's report until she came to the notation. "Yes. And check the photo. There's a lot more bruising than from a cord. This guy likes to use his hands when he's ready for the kill."

Ganza held up a full-length scan. "Looks like livor mortis on her backside. She may have been sitting when she died. Would have had to be sitting for hours before he came back and tossed her in the water. But why toss her? Our guy likes to pose his victims."

"He may not have tossed her," Maggie said. "The Wake County sheriff told me they had some flooding in that area about two weeks ago. The lake came up over its banks."

"Well, she's washed pretty clean. Any DNA samples found at all? How 'bout under her nails?"

"Nope. All washed away."

"I have the preliminary DNA results from the Brier girl," Ganza said while he shifted through the documents Maggie had laid out.

"And?"

"There was some foreign DNA under her fingernails, but it doesn't match the semen." Ganza didn't sound surprised.

Maggie wasn't, either. Whether Senator Brier wanted to believe it or not, the evidence seemed to point to consensual sex, probably earlier in the evening.

"Also found some foreign fingerprints on the Brier girl's purse. We'll check them against what we have in AFIS," Ganza continued. "'Course, the way you girls share your belongings with one another, it might not lead us anywhere."

"Goes to show you what you know about girls, Ganza. I don't share my things with anyone, let alone something as personal as a purse."

"Goes to show what you know about girls, O'Dell. When was the last time you carried a purse?"

"Okay, good point." She felt her cheeks flush, surprised that he had noticed such a detail about her. Yes, she hated to admit it, but it was true that she had been anything but the typical teenage girl, and it looked like she was far from the typical woman. Still, it was embarrassing that this scruffy, weathered, forensics relic knew more about women and their accessories than she did.

"One other thing." This time he went to the metal cabinet in the corner and brought back a plastic evidence bag. Inside, Maggie recognized the slide with a piece of transparent tape attached. It was the slide she and Stan had made from the residue found on Ginny Brier's neck. "Hang on to that for a minute," he told her as he walked to the door and reached for the light switch. "Now, keep in mind that whatever cord or wire or rope this guy is using has to be covered with this crap, okay?"

He shut off the light and the glittery substance on the slide began to glow in the dark.

"What in the world?"

"If we can figure out what it came off of, it might be able to tell us something about our guy."

He snapped the lights back on.

"What about something used in a magic act or for a theater production?" Maggie asked. "Maybe some novelty store or costume shop might be able to tell us."

"Could be. But I'm wondering, does he use it because it's a nifty prop or because it's something he has handy all the time?"

"My guess is it's a nifty prop." Maggie held up the slide again. "This guy likes attention. He likes putting on a performance."

When she looked back at Ganza, he was picking through the assortment of documents again. He pointed to the fax copy of the crumpled piece of paper found in the floater's throat. "No ID, no cyanide capsule, no quarters. What was this?"

Despite the wrinkles and creases, it looked like some kind of schedule with a list of dates and cities. Maggie pulled out another piece of paper from her jacket pocket.

"Recognize this?" she asked as she unfolded a copy of the Church of Spiritual Freedom's pamphlet. The one Tully had found after Reverend Everett's Saturday night rally. On the inside was listed the dates and cities for the organization's fall schedule of rallies. "Take a look at the first of November. That week's designated rally was at Falls Lake State Recreation Area in Raleigh, North Carolina. Don't tell me it's a coincidence, because you know—"

"Yeah, yeah, I know. You don't believe in coincidences. So how does the homeless woman fit into all this? There was no rally close by. And if Prashard's early assessment is correct, she was also killed Saturday night."

"I haven't figured that out yet."

"Maggie, you know all this means is that someone wants us to make a connection to Everett. The murder of Senator Brier's daughter looked like it could be revenge for the deaths of those boys in the cabin. But the rest—the floater, the homeless woman…" Ganza waved his hand over the spread of photos and reports and faxes. "All it means is that someone wants us to make a connection to Everett. Doesn't mean he's involved."

"Oh, he's involved," Maggie said, surprised by the hint of anger in her voice. "I don't know how or why, but my gut tells me the good Reverend Joseph Everett is somehow responsible. Maybe not directly."

"Or maybe even directly," Racine said, appearing at the doorway. Her spiky blond hair looked windblown, her face flushed, and she seemed a bit out of breath. She came in and held up a copy of the *National Enquirer.* The front-page photo showed Ginny Brier holding hands with Reverend Everett. Without looking at the newspaper, Racine read the headline aloud. "Moments Before Her Death, Senator's Daughter Attends Prayer Rally. Photo credit by our good pal Benjamin fucking Garrison."

"Garrison?" Maggie wasn't surprised. Though she had met him only briefly at the monument Sunday morning, she hadn't trusted him or his reasons for being there. "Okay, so Everett met Ginny Brier. No incriminating evidence there. And no harm done. We already knew she was at the rally. Why so steamed, Detective Racine?"

"Oh, it gets much better." Racine practically ripped the pages, flipping to the inside, creasing the fold before turning it back around. This time both Maggie and Ganza came in for a closer look.

"Son of a bitch," Ganza muttered.

"I should have known I couldn't trust that bastard," Racine said through gritted teeth.

Maggie couldn't believe it. The page was filled with crime scene photos, photos of Ginny Brier's dead body, black boxes strategically placed over her private parts, but nothing to hide the horrible, brutal rest. Nothing to cover those terrified eyes—frozen in time, eyes wide open.

CHAPTER 44

Eric Pratt could hear and feel the chipping and splintering of his fingernails as he dug them into the grooves of his handcuffs. It had become a new habit, useful only in that it prevented him from digging the jagged nails into his own flesh.

He should have been grateful that the guard had let him keep his hands together instead of locking them at his waist to each side. He knew his captors had misread his polite behavior, perhaps even thought he was harmless. Though not entirely harmless—he rattled the shackles on his ankles, reminding himself they were there, readjusted himself in the chair. He needed to stop squirming. Why couldn't he sit still?

As soon as the woman entered the room, Eric had felt a wet chill sweep over his body. She had introduced herself as a doctor, but Eric knew better. The woman was small, well dressed, about his mother's age, but very attractive. She carried herself with confidence and ease despite the high-heeled shoes she wore. He found himself watching her legs as she crossed them, making herself comfortable in the steel folding chair. She had smooth, firm calves, and from what he could see of her thighs, she was really nothing like his mother.

She was explaining why she was here. He glanced at her mouth, but he didn't need to listen. He knew exactly why she was here. He had known the second she walked in the door.

She was the woman clothed with the sun. Her reddish-blond hair had been a dead giveaway. It circled her face like the rays of the sun. Of course, she would possess warm green eyes and a quiet, captivating manner, a polite and hypnotic voice and a body that could distract and tempt. Father Joseph had outdone himself this time. He had sent a vision straight out of John's description of the Apocalypse. Had he honestly believed Eric wouldn't recognize her?

Sweat trickled down his back. Her voice hummed in his ears, the words no longer separate but strung together as melody—Satan's death song, lovely and mesmerizing. He wouldn't let it hypnotize him. He wouldn't let her draw him in and incapacitate him. But she was good. Oh, she was clever with that kind smile and those sexy legs. If Brandon's visit hadn't prepared him, he may very well have been taken into her web, ensnared before he realized what the true purpose of this visit really was.

Click, click—his fingernails picked at the metal. One of them was bleeding. He could feel it, but he kept his hands in his lap, pretending to be calm, pretending the fear wasn't clawing inside him, ripping at the walls of his stomach and trying to race up his throat to strangle him.

He looked into her eyes, saw her smile and quickly looked away. Was that her secret weapon? If she couldn't hypnotize him with her voice, would she use her eyes? He wondered how she might kill him, and his eyes scanned the length of her, looking for bulges in her clothing.

The guards would have allowed her in with anything she

cared to conceal. They would want no part of the mess, even if they were able to stop her. After all, Father had told them the woman clothed with the sun had special powers, according to the gospel of John, St. John the Divine, Revelation 12:1–6. She was light. She was dark. She was good and evil. She was a messenger of Satan and could disguise herself easily.

Suddenly, Eric remembered a newspaper article Father had read them just months ago. No member was allowed newspapers or magazines. There was no need when Father took the burden upon himself to relay those news items that were relevant and from sources that could be trusted.

But now Eric remembered the story of a foreign diplomat who had been visiting the States from some evil empire. Eric couldn't recall the country. The diplomat had been slain in his hotel bed and reports were that the woman who killed him did it while straddling him, waiting for him to come and then slitting his neck. Father Joseph had used it as an example of justice being done. Was that where he had gotten the idea of sending this woman?

Eric noticed her tapping the pencil, the eraser smacking the notepad—the notepad, a decoy left on the table, not a single note scrawled on it. The pencil had been freshly sharpened, its lead a dagger's point. He could distinguish some of the words that came out of her mouth, words like *help* and *cooperate*. He knew better. He refused to be sucked in by her code words. They could just as well have been words like *kill* and *mutilate*. He knew their true meaning.

Tap-tap, tap-tap—he watched the pencil and tried to ignore the panic squeezing the air out of his lungs. The room felt smaller. Her voice droned on. *Tap-tap, tap-tap*. His heart pounded in his ears. Or was that the pencil?

He made himself look into her eyes. He had cheated Satan once before. Could he do it again?

CHAPTER 45

Gwen shifted in her chair and recrossed her legs. Pratt was watching her again, staring at her legs. The horny bastard wasn't listening to a word she was saying. Had she misread his initial reaction, that look of absolute fear in his eyes when she entered the room? If it hadn't been fear, what the hell had it been? Had she been wrong about him wanting to survive, wanting to find a safe haven?

He hadn't answered a single one of her questions. Instead, he looked everywhere except into her eyes, as if she were Medusa and doing so would turn him to stone. Or did he simply hate psychologists? Maybe the kid was sick of shrinks or didn't trust any authority figures. Yet deep down she wondered if the real reason for his distraction, for his avoidance, was because he was worried she wielded some sort of power he couldn't stand up to.

If their theory was correct, Eric Pratt had been manipulated and controlled by someone other than himself for some time now. He had been a puppet willing to kill and be killed. Perhaps that someone—the Reverend Joseph Everett, most likely—still had a strong hold on him, despite Eric being locked away. But something had made the boy spit out that cyanide capsule. Self-preservation had won. She needed to follow her instinct. And she needed to believe his instinct to live was stronger than his fear of Everett.

"You are a survivor, Eric. That's why you're still here. I want to help you. Do you believe I can help you?"

She waited, tapping out her impatience with the pencil against her notepad. The kid seemed mesmerized by the motion. She tried to remember the reports she had glanced at, whether or not toxicology had shown any drug use. Yet that was what he reminded her of; some spaced-out coke-head. If he'd look at her, she might be able to tell from the dilation of his pupils. Was that why he kept his eyes away from hers?

"You don't need to be in this all alone, Eric. You can talk to me." She kept her voice low and soft, careful not to sound like she was addressing a small child. She didn't want to insult him. And if he was afraid, she needed to convince him he could trust her. Right now that looked like a dim prospect.

She noticed drops of sweat on his forehead and his upper lip. A glimpse into his eyes made her wonder if he was even here in the room with her. An annoying clicking came from under the table. This would be a wasted trip, she realized, and she thought of all the billable hours she had rescheduled back at her office.

Then she accidentally dropped the pencil.

His chair screeched as he lunged for the floor. The leg shackles clattered and his body flew so quickly, all Gwen saw was the streak of his orange jumpsuit. Her own impulse was to dive for the pencil, as well, sending her chair tumbling behind her. But she was too late. He had beaten her to it. She scrambled on hands and knees, trying to get to her feet. But just as she heard running footsteps and locks sliding open, she felt her head jerked backward.

He was sprawled on the floor but had managed to grab a handful of her hair before she could pull away. He yanked her hard, throwing her off balance. He yanked her again, and she slammed against his chest. All she could see were three sets of shoes come sliding to a halt. That's when she felt the pencil at her throat, the sharp point pressed against her carotid artery, threatening to penetrate through flesh and veins. And, despite the fear that shot through her, the first thing that came to mind was how stupid she had been to have sharpened the pencil just that morning.

CHAPTER 46

Tully kept his Glock aimed at the kid's head. At this angle, it would be a clean shot. He could do it, but would the bastard's jerking muscles still plunge the pencil into Dr. Patterson's neck. Shit! Why hadn't he thought of that damn pencil?

"Eric, come on now." Morrelli was trying to talk sense to the kid. From the crazed look in Pratt's eyes, Tully knew there would be no talking him out of anything. But Morrelli continued. "You don't want to do this, Eric. You're in enough trouble. We can help you, but not—"

"Stop it! Shut the fuck up!" the boy yelled, and yanked Dr. Patterson's head back, exposing her neck even more.

His cuffed hands only allowed him to hang on to a clump of her hair with one hand, keeping her close to him while his other hand held the pencil, its razor point pressing into her skin. So far Tully could see no blood. But one good shove, and he knew it would be a major gusher. Jesus!

Tully tried to figure out the doctor's position without taking his sight off Pratt. One of her legs was twisted under her body. One hand had instinctively shot up to grab at her assailant's arm, and she kept her fingers tightly grasping the sleeve of the orange jumpsuit. Pratt either didn't notice or didn't care. That was good. She had some sense of control, though she was holding on to the arm that held her hair and not the pencil. He glanced at her face. She seemed calm and steady. But then her eyes caught his, and he could see the fear. Fear was good. Panic was not.

"What do you want us to do, Eric?" Morrelli tried again.

It was obvious he was bugging the hell out of the kid, but at least he was keeping him distracted. Tully was impressed with Morrelli's demeanor, hands quietly at his side, despite two men with guns drawn on either side of him. He talked to the kid as if he had a jumper on a ledge.

"Just talk to us, Eric. Tell us what you need."

"Eric," Dr. Patterson said quietly, "you know you don't want to hurt me." She said it slowly—making a noticeable effort to say the words without moving or swallowing—but she managed it without a trace of fear.

Tully couldn't help wondering if she had been through this before.

"No, I don't want to hurt you," Pratt answered. But before any of them could relax, he added, "I need to kill you."

Out of the corner of his eye, Tully saw Morrelli shift just slightly, and he hoped to God the prosecutor wasn't thinking of doing something stupid. He glanced at Dr. Patterson again, this time trying to draw her eyes to his. When she did, he gave her a slight nod, hoping she would understand. She watched him, keeping her eyes on his face, then finally moving her gaze down the length of his arm and to his trigger finger.

"Eric." Morrelli had decided to try one more time. "So far

there's no murder charge against you. Only weapons charges. You don't want to do this. Dr. Patterson only wants to help you. She isn't here to hurt you."

Tully focused his aim and kept it steady. His finger wanted to squeeze now. He waited, checked Dr. Patterson's grip on the orange sleeve.

"She's Satan," Eric whispered this time. "Can't any of you see that? Father Joseph sent her." He adjusted his grip on the pencil, puncturing the skin and drawing blood. "She's come to kill me. I need to kill her first."

Tully heard Burt's safety click off. Shit! He couldn't signal the guard with Morrelli standing between them. Instead, he found Dr. Patterson's eyes again. She was ready despite the fear. He gave her another slight nod.

"I have to kill her," Eric said, and something in his voice told Tully he meant it. "I have to kill her before she kills me. I have to. I don't have a choice. It's kill or be killed."

Tully saw her fingers tighten on the orange sleeve. Good. She was getting a better grip. He watched her fingers while still looking down the sight of his Glock. Then suddenly she yanked downward and hard. Pratt didn't let go of her hair, and the motion caused her head to twist down and away from the pencil. Tully wasted no time. He squeezed the trigger, shattering Pratt's left shoulder. The boy's fingers opened. The pencil dropped. Dr. Patterson slammed an elbow into his chest, causing him to release his grip on her hair. She scrambled away on hands and knees. In seconds, Burt was on Pratt, smashing his face against the floor. The angry guard had a huge black boot pressed on top of Pratt's bleeding shoulder and a gun to the kid's temple.

"Easy, Burt." Morrelli was at the guard's side, keeping him in line.

Tully hesitated before going to Dr. Patterson. She remained hunched on her knees, sitting back on her feet as if waiting for the strength to stand. He knelt down in front of her, but she avoided his eyes. He touched her cheek, cupped her jaw and lifted it gently, to get a good look at her neck. She allowed him the examination, now watching his eyes and gripping his arm as though she didn't want to let go.

He wiped the drops of blood away. The puncture had only broken the skin.

"You're gonna have a hell of a bruise, Doc." He met her eyes and looked for the fear he could see her already stowing away. Or trying to, anyway.

"We should get you to an emergency room," Morrelli said from behind them.

"I'll be fine," she reassured Morrelli while giving Tully a quick and restrained smile before she pulled away from him, removing her hand from his arm. She didn't, however, resist his help as she climbed to her bare feet. Sometime during the scuffle she had lost both shoes.

"She's Satan, she's the Antichrist. Father Joseph sent her to kill me," Pratt was still yelling. "Why can't any of you see that?"

"Get him the hell out of here," Morrelli told Burt, who swung the kid up to his feet and shoved him along, pushing harder when Pratt began to mutter again.

Tully picked up the folding chair and brought it over for Dr. Patterson. She waved him off, looking around the room in search of her shoes. Tully saw one and crawled under the table for it. When he stood up again, Morrelli was on one knee placing the other shoe on the good doctor's foot, holding her ankle and looking like Prince Charming. It only reminded Tully how much he didn't like this guy or guys like him. Morrelli turned to him, staying on his goddamn knee and gesturing for the other shoe. Tully surrendered it.

However, when he glanced at Dr. Patterson's face, she was watching him and not Morrelli.

CHAPTER 47

West Potomac Park
Washington D.C.

Maggie stopped at the drinking fountain and took long, slow gulps. The afternoon had turned unseasonably warm for November. She hadn't been far into her run when she peeled off her sweatshirt and knotted it around her waist.

Now she pulled the sweatshirt loose and wiped the dripping sweat from her forehead and the water from her chin as she scanned the surroundings. She looked up and down the Mall, watching for the woman she had talked to earlier, who had given her a long list of instructions but failed to include a single description of what she looked like.

Maggie found the wooden bench on the grassy knoll overlooking the Vietnam Wall, exactly where the woman told her it would be. Then she put a foot up on the bench's back rail and began her leg stretches, something she seldom did after running, always feeling like she didn't have time. But this, too, had been requested, as well as the strict instructions to wear nothing that would give her away as a law enforcement officer: no FBI T-shirts, no bulging holsters, guns or badges, no navy-blue. Not even a baseball cap or sunglasses.

Maggie wondered—and not for the first time—what good it would do to talk to someone so paranoid. Chances were, she'd get some delusional perspective, some skewed vision of reality. Yet she felt fortunate that Cunningham and Senator Brier had found someone willing to talk. An aid in Senator Brier's office had tracked the woman down, and although she had agreed to meet Maggie, she had insisted on remaining anonymous. The cloak-and-dagger game didn't bother Maggie. As long as this woman, an ex-member of Everett's church, could provide a view of Everett that Maggie knew she'd never find in any FBI file. And certainly a view she'd never get from her mother.

High school kids outnumbered tourists, scattered all along the sidewalks, hiking up the Lincoln Memorial steps and winding around the bronze sculptures of the Korean Veterans and Vietnam Women's Memorials. More field trips. Wasn't that why Emma Tully had been at the monuments the other day? November must be prime time for school field trips, though the educational significance seemed to be lost on most of them. Yes, other than the students there were very few tourists.

Then Maggie saw her. The woman wore faded blue jeans, too loose for her tall, thin frame, a long-sleeved chambray shirt and dark aviator sunglasses. Her long brown hair was pulled back into a ponytail, and Maggie could see that she wore little, if any, makeup. A camera hung from her neck and a backpack from her shoulder while she stopped and reached with paper and pencil to do a rubbing against the Wall.

She looked like any other tourist, a family member completing her journey and paying homage to a loved one, a fallen soldier. The woman took three rubbings before she came over and sat on the bench next to Maggie. She started pulling out of her backpack a sandwich wrapped in wax paper, a bag of Doritos and a bottled water. Without a word, she began eating, looking out over the park and watching. For a minute, Maggie wondered if she had been wrong about this being her mysterious contact. She took another look at the tourists at the Wall. Was it possible the woman had changed her mind and not come?

"Do you know anyone on the wall?" the woman asked without looking at Maggie while she sipped her water.

"Yes," Maggie answered, expecting the question. "My uncle, my father's brother."

"What was his name?"

The exchange was casual, an everyday occurrence between two complete strangers sitting on a park bench in front of the one monument that seemed to touch every American's life somehow. An everyday exchange and yet so very clever. No way to mistake the details of this question.

"His name was Patrick O'Dell."

The woman seemed neither pleased nor especially interested and picked up her sandwich again. "And so you are Maggie," she said with a slight nod, taking a bite and keeping her eyes on a game of tag that had broken out between several of the teenagers up on the hill.

"What should I call you?" Maggie asked, since she'd been given only the woman's initials.

"You can call me…" She hesitated, took another sip of water and glanced at the bottle. "Call me Eve," she said.

Maggie caught a glimpse of the bottle's label: Evian. This was ridiculous. But names didn't matter as long as she answered her questions.

"Okay, Eve." She waited. No one was within earshot, and the game of tag was drawing everyone's attention. "What can you tell me about Everett and his so-called church?"

"Well." She crunched several chips, offering the bag to

Maggie. Maggie accepted. "The church is a ruse to get donations and stockpile money and arms. But he's not interested in taking over the world or the government. He preaches the word of the Lord only to get what he wants."

"So if it's not to overtake the government or even terrorize the government, what is it he wants?"

"Power, of course. Power over his own little world."

"So he doesn't even believe?"

"Oh, he believes." Eve set aside her sandwich and dug in her backpack until she found another bottle of Evian water and handed it to Maggie. "He believes he is God." She hesitated, picking up her own bottle, wrapping both hands around it, cradling it as if looking for something to hang on to. "He preys on those of us who have no clue who we are, those who are weak and searching and have nowhere else to go. He tells us what to eat, what to wear, who we can and can't talk to, what we should believe.

"He convinces us that no one outside the church understands or loves us and that those who are not with us are against us and only want to hurt us. We're told we must forsake family and friends and all worldly materialistic things in order to find true peace and be worthy of his love. And by this time, he's stripped us of every single individual thing that defined us, until we are absolutely nothing without him and without his church."

Maggie listened quietly. None of this was news. It only followed the same profile of every other cult she had read about. It simply confirmed their beliefs that Everett's church was a bogus organization, a smoke screen for his own power-hungry maneuvers. But there was something she didn't understand. Something she needed to ask. A hint of impatience seeped out in her question. "Why in the world does anyone join?"

"In the beginning," Eve said in a calm voice, taking her time, appearing to be neither insulted nor intimidated by the question, "you want to believe that you've found a place where you finally belong. Where you're a part of something bigger than you. In not so different ways, we're all lost souls, looking and searching for something that's missing in our lives. Self-identity or self-esteem—whatever you want to call it—it's such a fragile commodity. When you have no idea who you are to begin with, it's so easy and tempting to become your surroundings. When you feel lost and alone, sometimes you're willing to give anything to belong. Sometimes you're even willing to give your soul."

Maggie fidgeted, growing weary and suspicious of the woman's overly calm manner. It seemed too well rehearsed. Was this meeting a ploy, maybe even orchestrated by Everett to convince her the organization, though definitely screwed up, was not dangerous? Maggie was looking for a murderer, and this woman was talking like Everett's only crime was snatching souls.

"It doesn't sound so bad," she told Eve, and took a sip of her water, watching the woman from the corner of her eye. "Everett takes good care of you, feeds and clothes you, makes all your decisions and gives you a place to stay free of charge. All he asks for in return is for you to indulge in his delusions of grandeur. Nope. Doesn't sound bad to me. And quite honestly, no one can really take away your soul without your permission, can they?"

She waited out the silence, helping herself to the bag of chips left on the bench between them. Finally, the woman looked over at her, pushed her sunglasses on top of her head and examined Maggie, holding her gaze as if searching for something hidden within her. She looked older than Maggie had guessed. Now without the dark glasses, Maggie could see the wrinkles at Eve's eyes and lines around her mouth. There was another smile, again just a twist at the corner of her mouth. It occurred to Maggie that this woman was used to keeping her expressions and emotions in check. Even her eyes refused to show any hint of feeling, though they were not cold, just empty.

Eve looked away suddenly, as if she had exposed too much, and flipped the dark glasses back down into place.

"You look a lot like her," she said in that same even tone.

"Excuse me?"

"Kathleen. She's your mother, isn't she?"

"You know my mother?"

"She joined just before I escaped."

Maggie felt herself wince at Eve's use of the word *escape,* though she had said it as casually as if they were talking about going home after a day at work.

"Don't think for a minute—" Eve began unbuttoning and rolling up the sleeves of her shirt as if suddenly too warm "—that there is anything harmless about Everett. He saves you, builds you up, tells you he loves you, trusts you, that you are special, a favor to him from God. Then he turns on you and rips you to shreds. He discovers your weaknesses and your fears, then uses them to humiliate you and to destroy any last piece of self-respect you think you deserve."

With her shirtsleeves now rolled up, she held out her wrists in front of her for Maggie to see.

"He calls it being sent to the Well," she said, her voice still annoyingly calm and level. Red welts circled both her wrists where the skin had flayed and bled from rope or handcuffs cutting into the flesh. The wounds looked recent. Eve's head pivoted around, and she pulled the sleeves back in place, picking up her sandwich and unwrapping it to continue her lunch as though there had been no interruptions.

Again Maggie waited, this time out of respect and not impatience. She followed Eve's lead and sipped at her own water and managed a few more chips.

"It's an actual well," Eve said. "Though I doubt he ever intended to use it for anything more than a punishment chamber. He knew I was terrified of the dark, closed places, so it was a perfect punishment."

She stared out at the teenagers up on the hill, though Maggie wondered what the woman really saw. Her voice remained calm but now almost disconnected. "He had them tie me by the wrists and lower me into the well. When I kicked and clawed and tried to climb out, he had them spill buckets of spiders down on top of me. At least that's what I think they were. It was too dark to see them. But I could feel them. I could feel them all over me. Every inch of my hair and face and skin seemed to be crawling. I couldn't even scream anymore because I was afraid they'd crawl inside my mouth. I closed my eyes and tried to stay still, so they wouldn't bite me as much. And for hours I tried to retreat to somewhere else inside my mind. I remember reciting an old Emily Dickinson poem over and over again in my head. It was probably the one thing that saved me from losing my mind. 'I'm nobody. Who are you?' Do you know it?"

"'Are you nobody, too?'" Maggie answered with the next line of the poem.

"'Then there's a pair of us,'" Eve continued. "'Don't tell. They'd banish us.'"

"The mind's a powerful tool," Maggie said, thinking of her own childhood and how many times she had resorted to going away—far, far away inside her own mind.

"Everett took everything away from me but still wasn't able to take away my mind." Eve looked over at her and this time when she spoke there was a spark of anger. "Don't let anyone tell you Everett is harmless. He makes them believe he only wants to take care of them while he has them sign over their homes and property, their social security and pension and child support checks. He rewards them with fear. Fear of the real world. Fear of being hunted down if they betray him. Fear of the FBI. So much fear that they're more willing to go through his suicide drills than be captured alive."

"Suicide drills?" Despite Eve's story, Maggie couldn't help thinking this didn't sound like the man who had gotten her mother to stop drinking. All the changes she'd seen in her mother seemed so positive. "My mother doesn't seem frightened," she told Eve.

"He may still be looking for ways to use her. Is she living at the compound yet?"

"No. She has an apartment in Richmond and has made no mention of leaving it." Only now did that realization bring relief to Maggie. Perhaps her mother wasn't in too deep. She couldn't possibly be in as much danger as this woman had been. "She loves her apartment. I doubt very much she'll be willing to move to the compound."

The woman shook her head and there was that smile again. "She's more valuable to him on the outside," she said, without looking at Maggie. "He's hoping to find a way to use you."

"Me?"

"Believe me, he knows Kathleen has a daughter who is an FBI agent. He knows all about you. He knows everything. It could be why he's been so good to her. But if he finds out you're of no use to him, or if he finds out you're trying to hurt him... Well, just be careful. For your mother's sake."

"I just need to convince my mother to stay the hell away from him."

"And, of course, she'll listen to you because the two of you are so close."

Maggie felt the sting of Eve's sarcasm, despite Eve's calm, friendly tone.

"I need to go," the woman said, suddenly packing up her things and getting to her feet.

"But wait. There's got to be something you can tell me that could help me bring down Everett."

"Bring him down?"

"Yes. Exactly."

"You'll never get him. Most of what he does is legit, and

what he does that isn't.... Well, you don't see any of us lining up to press charges, do you?"

"Only because you're still afraid of him. Why let him control your life? We can protect you."

"We? You mean the government?" She laughed, a true, genuine laugh. Then she slung her backpack over her shoulder. "You can't protect me until you get Everett. And you'll never get him. Even if you try, he'll know. He'll have them all lined up for their cyanide capsules and dead before you step foot inside the compound." She hesitated, glancing around the park as if making certain it was safe. As if she expected Everett to appear from behind a monument or a tree.

"What did you do?" Maggie asked.

"Excuse me?"

"What was it that you did to deserve the Well?"

"I wouldn't stop trying to take care of my mom. She was the only reason I was there. And she was sick. I kept sneaking her my food. The breaking point was when I stole some of her heart medicine to give to her. It was her own medicine that had been confiscated from her, because, of course, Father's love is the only medicine anyone needs."

"Where is your mom now?"

Maggie watched Eve disconnect as she stared out over her head. It was like turning an on-off switch.

"She died the day after he put me in the Well. I think she felt so guilty, she had a heart attack. I'll never know for sure." She looked at Maggie through her dark glasses, reflecting back the Wall. "In the end, he always wins. Just be careful for yourself and especially for your mom."

Then she turned and left.

CHAPTER 48

Boston, Massachusetts

Maria Leonetti took a shortcut through Boston Common, wishing she had brought a pair of running shoes. But she hated wearing them with her expensive suits and thought the other women at the brokerage firm gave up a piece of their credibility as soon as they put on their Nikes and Reeboks at the end of the day. After all, none of the male brokers changed their shoes just to walk home. Why couldn't women simply buy comfortable shoes? And why the hell couldn't shoe designers create something both stylish and comfortable?

She noticed a crowd at the fountain and wondered what kind of celebration could be taking place on a Tuesday afternoon. The day had been unseasonably warm, bringing out in-line skaters, joggers and all sorts of riffraff, too. This group of rowdy young guys looked like a fraternity party. Maybe college kids were out already for the Thanksgiving holiday.

She probably should have taken another trail, but she was exhausted. Her feet hurt. All she wanted to do was get home, snuggle with Izzy, her calico cat, and veg out. Maybe put on an old Cary Grant movie and make popcorn. That was as much of a party as she wanted.

Suddenly, she felt someone grab her elbow.

"Hey," she yelled, and jerked away. Before she could turn around, two men were on either side of her, each grabbing an arm. One of them pulled at her purse, ripping the strap and tossing it to the ground. Jesus! They weren't interested in robbing her. A fresh panic took hold.

"Hey! Look what we found," one of them shouted to the others.

"Get your fucking hands off me," Maria screamed, pulling and tugging as they dragged her into the crowd.

Arms and hands and faces came at her from all directions. They were laughing and egging one another on, chanting, "Bitch, bitch."

She screamed and kicked, losing a shoe but connecting with one groin. It only infuriated them into holding her feet as well as her arms. Someone sprayed her with beer, dousing her face and blouse. Then she heard the rips of her clothing, and she screamed louder. No one seemed to care—or could they just not hear over the laughter and yelling? Hands squeezed her breasts and ran up her thighs. Fingers poked and prodded into her underpants, and soon they were being ripped off her, too. She could see a glint of a camera lens and then saw its owner, pushing between shoulders to get a better view.

Oh, dear God. They were going to kill her. They were going to rape her and then they were going to kill her. And it would all be on film for someone's entertainment.

She clawed at their faces and got slapped so hard, blood trickled down her mouth. She managed to pull one hand free, and clung to her bra as the rest of her blouse was ripped away. Her shoes were gone. She could feel her panty hose shredded around her ankles, where they were using them to hold her down. They gripped her so tight she could already feel the bruises and her skin rubbed raw.

"Hey, here comes another bitch."

One by one, they let go. They left her as suddenly as they had attacked, rising up and moving like a swarm. She lay heaped on the grass in only her bra and her skirt, which was slit up the side seam, hanging together only by the waistband. Her underpants were gone. She hurt everywhere and couldn't see through the tears. She wanted to curl up and die. Then she heard the woman's scream and realized they had found another victim. Her stomach knotted up and she felt dizzy, but she knew she needed to leave before they decided to come back to her.

She tried to stand, but her knees collapsed as her head began to spin. Another hand grabbed her arm, and she jerked away, falling back on the grass.

"No, wait. I just want to help."

She stared up at the young man, but the spinning in her head wouldn't let her eyes focus. All she could see was that he wore a blue baseball cap, jeans and a T-shirt that smelled of beer. Oh, God! He was one of them. She tried to crawl away, but he took her by the arm and lifted her to her feet.

"We need to get you away from here." He was holding her up and wrapping her in a scratchy jacket.

She had no energy left to fight him. She walked as best she could as he led her up the trail and away from the crowd, away from the laughter and that continuous scream for help that made her sick to her stomach. They barely got to the edge of the park before she pulled away from him, retching and vomiting behind a nearby bush. When she turned around, he was gone.

Maria sat down, safely hidden behind the trees, trying to calm her stomach and catch her breath. The rumble of nearby traffic seemed to soothe her, as if reminding her that civilization was, indeed, close by. That she hadn't fallen off the edge of the world. A breeze chilled her wet body, and she could smell the stale beer that had doused her skin. It made her gag again, but she was able to contain the urge to vomit. She hugged herself, listening to the sound of car horns and the hydraulic screech of brakes, listening for anything that would help shut out the sounds of laughter, the chants of "bitch, bitch" and the poor woman's stifled cries. Why couldn't anyone else hear that? Why wasn't anyone stopping them? Had the whole world suddenly gone mad?

She pushed her arms into the jacket sleeves and discovered most of the buttons were missing. Still it was better than nothing. It smelled of peppermint. She dug into the pockets and found two quarters, a McDonald's napkin and half a roll of peppermint Life Savers. God, her fingers were still shaking so bad, it took a concentrated effort to unwrap one of the mints and pop it into her mouth. Hopefully it would settle her stomach. As soon as her knees were strong enough, she'd get out of the park, onto the street, and find a cop. Where the hell were the cops, anyway? It was getting dark. There was usually at least one hanging around in the evenings.

Then from behind her, something came over her head and around her neck. Maria clawed at it. It dug into the skin of her throat. She gasped for air, kicking and twisting her body. Her fingers tried to get hold of the cord. God! It was so tight. It was already embedded into her neck, so deep that her fingernails were ripping at her own skin as she tried to dig it out.

She couldn't breathe. Couldn't pull away. My God, he was strong. And now he was pulling her back farther into the trees, dragging her, because her feet wouldn't work. She had no energy left.

Air. She needed air. She couldn't breathe. Couldn't focus. Couldn't even see straight. Her head was spinning again, a blur of trees and grass and sky. She felt herself slipping away. She could no longer hear the chants or the laughter or even the woman's screams. Where were the sounds of traffic? Why did everything sound so muffled? So far away? The cord drew tighter, and soon she couldn't hear anything at all.

CHAPTER 49

Justin's hands were still shaking when he got back to the bus. He hadn't bothered to wait for the rest of them. He still couldn't believe this was what Father had meant by an initiation trip. He imagined it to be some test of survival like his so-called week alone in the woods. Or some marathon lecture series like their weekend revival meetings. But, Jesus! He had never imagined something like this.

He felt sick to his stomach, remembering that poor woman vomiting and all those screams. He yanked off his cap and wiped the sweat from his forehead with the back of his arm. The bus was empty. Thank God! Though he could see Dave, their driver, inside the McDonald's, keeping an eye on things as he probably wolfed down an illicit Big Mac.

Justin slumped into one of the seats, crossing his arms over his chest and trying to stop shaking. He was sweating up a storm, so why was he shivering like he was cold? Fuck! He couldn't get those screams out of his head. Those poor women. That wasn't the way his grandfather had taught him to treat women. Even his dad could be an asshole sometimes, but he was good to Justin's mom. No woman deserved to be treated that way. He didn't care what the hell Father's instructions were.

While he handed out Quarter Pounders and beer, Brandon had told them that they were about to learn an important lesson. All Justin had cared about was that finally he had some decent food and that being a warrior wasn't such a bad thing. He'd hardly paid attention to what Brandon was saying. He must have eaten three Quarter Pounders and drunk four or five beers.

He had been feeling a pleasant buzz by the time Brandon led them to the park, where he continued his lecture about how they needed to put all bitches in their place, make them understand that men were still in power. He said women were the reason everything was going so haywire in the world. Women thought they didn't need men, were off being lesbos, having babies on their own, taking good jobs away from family men and then crying to the government to protect them. The sluts and whores were responsible for spreading AIDS. They needed to be punished. They needed to be taught a lesson.

They sprayed the first woman who came by with beer, and Justin remembered laughing at her. By the third woman, they were grabbing and fondling and ripping. Her screams shook Justin as if waking him from a nightmare. He couldn't believe what he was doing. That was when he started to think about Alice. What if Alice had been one of the women walking through that park? What if the others knew about her past? Jesus! Would they swarm her like a pack of wolves?

No one had seen him slip behind the trees to vomit up all those precious hamburgers. He stayed there, and when they were finished with the third woman and heading for a fourth, Justin helped her away, trying to make up for his part in the nightmare. When he knew she was safe, he left, sneaking back to the bus, still hearing the laughter and the screams ringing in his ears.

He didn't want to think about it. He brought his knees up and hugged them to his chest. He needed to think about something, anything else.

He had only been to Boston once before when Eric was still at Brown. It had been one of their last family trips together. They had stayed at the Radisson. He and Eric had even gotten a room to themselves. Their dad let them order room service, which blew them away because he'd always been so tight with money.

They spent one day at a Red Sox game, then the Metropolitan Museum to satisfy his mom. But even that didn't suck. It had actually been a good time, one of the few that hadn't ended in a huge argument of some kind. It had left Justin with good feelings about Boston; feelings that now were replaced with sounds of women's screams for help and the smell of warm beer.

He jumped off the seat and into the aisle, pulling off his T-shirt, wadding it up and kicking it under seat. Then he peeled off the rest of his clothes until he was standing in the bus aisle, wearing only his jockey shorts. That was when he saw Brandon standing in the bus's door, staring at him. But instead of getting angry, Brandon started laughing.

"I knew it," he finally said as Justin wrestled back into his blue jeans. "I knew you didn't have the stomach for this. You're a coward, just like your fucking brother, Eric. I need to get back and finish things like a real man."

Then he turned and left, heading toward the park.

CHAPTER 50

Calm. He needed to stay calm and let the liquid coarse through his veins. Let it do its magic. Already he could feel its strength, its power.

Not that he needed much physical strength. The woman was small, easy to drag. And with the noise and excitement still going on close by, no one would notice the rustling of leaves and snapping of twigs.

But he needed to hurry. He needed to find a more isolated area. The sun was sinking behind the buildings. He didn't have much time to set up, to get ready. Tonight would be different. He could feel it. Tonight would be the night. Somehow he just knew it.

He stopped, turned and waited while he stared at the woman's half-naked body, leaves and brush dragging along between her legs. He smiled when he finally saw her exposed chest move just slightly, shallow breaths, barely noticeable. Oh, good. She was still alive. Then he continued dragging her. Yes, tonight he felt quite certain it would happen. He would finally see it tonight.

CHAPTER 51

Maggie drove with the windows rolled down, hoping it would squelch the churning in the pit of her stomach. As she drove, she tried to make sense of all that she had learned from the woman called Eve about the Reverend Joseph Everett. She needed to prepare herself before she confronted her mother. She'd need to arm herself with information for when her mother started to defend the man, because Maggie knew her mother would defend him.

She tried to put aside the horrible images Eve had conjured up. Instead, she should concentrate on the facts. Most of her arsenal of facts was general biographical stuff. As a young man, Everett had been kicked out of the army, an honorable discharge with no further explanation. There was no police record, despite the rape charge that was later dropped by the journalism student herself. At thirty-five he ran for the Virginia state senate and lost. Then three years later he started the Church of Spiritual Freedom, a nonprofit organization that allowed him to amass stockpiles of tax-free donations. Everett finally found his calling, but there seemed to be no information on where or if he had actually been ordained as a minister.

In less than ten short years, the Church of Spiritual Freedom claimed more than five hundred members with almost two hundred of them living on a compound he had built in Virginia's Shenandoah Valley. Ironically, the area was only a few miles from where the journalism student had been raped twenty-seven years earlier. Everett had either been innocent and had nothing to hide, or perhaps, Maggie couldn't help thinking, he was superstitious and didn't think lightning could strike in the same place twice.

If it was the latter, he had good reason to believe it. In the past ten years, he and his church had not been in any kind of trouble with the law—no IRS audits, no weapons violations, no building permit or zoning violations. The illegal-weapons summon at the Massachusetts cabin was the first violation, and even that could only loosely be connected to Everett's church. In fact, everything seemed to be going quite nicely for the good reverend. He had even made some close and powerful friends in Congress, permitting him to buy a parcel of government land in Colorado for a sinfully low price. If things were going so well, why did he want to uproot and move to Colorado?

Maggie wasn't certain what her mother's involvement was with Everett and his so-called church. One thing Maggie did feel certain about, however, was that the man could be a time bomb waiting to explode. And despite only circumstantial evidence, she knew he was somehow involved in, at least, Ginny Brier's death and possibly the floater in North Carolina. It was too much of a coincidence that these women died while

Everett's rallies were taking place just footsteps away. As for the nameless transient, well, she was still a mystery.

The crisp autumn air chilled her, but she kept the windows down. She took deep breaths, filling her lungs with the scent of pine and the exhaust fumes of the traffic on I-95. She'd need to have all her senses on alert and in overdrive for this mission. Even without a confrontation, being in the same room with her mother was difficult enough. There were too many memories. Too much past left behind, and that's just the way Maggie preferred it.

It had been more than a year since she had visited her mother's apartment, although she doubted her mother would remember that visit. How could she remember? She had been passed out for most of it. Now Maggie wondered how she would begin to explain this visit. What did she think she could do, just drop by and say, "Gee, Mom, I was passing through and thought I'd stop and see how you were? Oh, and by the way, did you realize your precious Reverend Everett may be a dangerous maniac?" No, somehow she didn't think that would get her anywhere.

Maggie tried to put aside what she had learned in the FBI file and what she had just learned from Eve. Instead, she tried to remember everything in the past year that her mother may have told her about Reverend Joseph Everett. She was embarrassed to admit that she hadn't paid much attention. In the beginning she had simply been relieved that there was someone else to watch over her mother. Months went by without a suicide attempt, and Maggie hoped that the woman had finally found a less destructive addiction. Perhaps she had finally found a way to get the attention she so craved, and it didn't include a trip to the ER.

Later, when she discovered that her mother had stopped drinking, Maggie was skeptical. It seemed too good to be true. There had to be a catch. And, of course, there was one. The sudden sobriety had changed the habits but hadn't changed

Kathleen O'Dell's personality. She was still as selfish, needy and narrow-minded as she had always been, only now Maggie couldn't explain it away as drunken drivel.

It didn't make sense that her mother had suddenly found God. Maggie could count on one hand the times her mother had insisted they attend mass. Her entire childhood, she couldn't remember her mother doing or saying anything that could remotely be misconstrued as religious.

The only time Maggie remembered her mother mentioning religion was when she was drunk, often times joking that she was a recovering Catholic from which there was no cure. Then she would snort and laugh, telling anyone who would listen that being a little bit Catholic was like being a little bit pregnant.

For Kathleen O'Dell, being a Catholic was something she had held on to simply as a party favor. Which led Maggie to believe that Everett's Bible-thumping would probably be lost on the woman. In the last several months, she had not heard her mother suddenly start spouting off psalms or scripture. There certainly hadn't been a miraculous religious conversion. At least not one Maggie could see.

What she did see was the same compulsive, judgmental, addictive woman finally finding someone or something to blame for all her hardships and bad luck. And Reverend Everett provided for her the sinister, evil culprit in the form of the United States government, a faceless entity, an easy target as long as Kathleen O'Dell could reason that her daughter was not a part of that entity.

Now that Maggie thought about it, why would she find it odd that her mother be attracted to Everett's brand of religion, to Everett's version of reality? After all, hadn't Kathleen O'Dell spent years worshipping at the altar of BCD: Beam, Ceurvo and Daniel's? There had been times in the past when the woman would have sold her soul for a bottle of Jack Daniel's. Just because she was no longer drinking didn't necessarily mean her soul was no longer for sale. She had handed in one skewed sense of reality for a different one, one addiction for another.

Maggie could understand the seductive lure for her mother, whose version of current events came from the *National Enquirer* or watching *Hard Copy.* What a rush it must now be for her to believe that she had the inside scoop on national issues; that she was respected and trusted by someone with the charisma and charm of the good reverend; and that she could have the easy answers to questions so many people spent a lifetime in search of.

She had heard some of those answers, the paranoid delusions that men like Reverend Everett spread. There was power in hate, and control by fear was one of the most successful manipulations. Why had Maggie shrugged off her mother's comments about chemicals in her drinking water, hidden government cameras in ATM machines and oh, yes, several weeks ago a hysteria about not wanting to talk to Maggie if she was calling on her cellular phone because "they had ways of listening in to those conversations?"

Why hadn't she seen the danger signs long ago? Or had she seen them but been so relieved to no longer be picking up the shattered pieces her mother left behind that she didn't care, or that she simply didn't want to know?

Somewhere Maggie had read that alcohol only emphasized an alcoholic's personality, bringing out and highlighting characteristics that already existed. It made sense with her mother. The alcohol only seemed to make her more needy, more hungry for attention. Yet, if that was indeed true, Maggie realized the irony in her own drinking habits. She usually drank to forget the empty feeling inside her, and to not feel so alone. If the alcohol only emphasized those very same things, then no wonder she was so fucked up.

Like mother, like daughter.

Maggie shook her head, trying to prevent the memory.

You two could be sisters. I never fucked a mother and daughter before.

Those goddamn crumbling walls. She grabbed the Pepsi can in her cup holder and gulped the warm, flat remainder. Why was it that she could not remember the sound of her father's voice, but she could still feel this stranger's breath on her face? With little effort, she could smell the sour odor of whiskey and feel the scrape of his beard as he pinned her small body to the wall and tried to kiss her. She remembered his hands fondling her preadolescent breasts, laughing and telling her he bet she was "gonna have some big tits just like her mama."

And all the while her mother stood back with her glass of Jack Daniel's, watching and telling him to cut it out but not making him stop. She didn't make him stop. Why didn't she make him stop?

Somehow Maggie had escaped on her own. She couldn't even remember how. That was when her mother started insisting her men friends take her to a hotel. She stayed out all night, sometimes was gone for days at a time, leaving Maggie home alone. Alone. It was good to be alone, a little scary but less painful. She had learned early on how to be a survivor. Being alone was simply the price of survival.

As she approached Richmond, she started paying attention and watching for her exit. She tried to ignore the growing nausea in the pit of her stomach and was annoyed that it was there at all. What the hell was wrong with her? She chased killers for a living, examined their gruesome handiwork and traveled into their worlds of evil. What could be so difficult about one goddamn visit to her mother's?

CHAPTER 52

Richmond, Virginia

Kathleen O'Dell finished packing the last of her grandmother's porcelain figurines. The man from Al and Frank's Antiques and Secondhand Treasures would be picking them up in the morning with the other items. Now she couldn't remember if the man's name was even Al or Frank, although he had told her, while he appraised her things, that he was one of the co-owners.

It bothered her that she felt sad about giving up the items. She still remembered her grandmother letting her handle the figurines when she was just a child, allowing her to gently turn them around in her small hands in order to admire and touch them.

Several of the figurines had come over with her grandmother from Ireland, stuffed in an old suitcase with few other belongings. They were a part of her family's heritage, and it seemed wrong to sell them for something as meaningless as money. But then, Reverend Everett constantly reminded them that they needed to divorce themselves from the materialism of the world in order to be truly free. That it was sinful to admire and covet material items even if they held some sentimental value.

More important, Kathleen knew she couldn't very well cart all these things with her when they left for their new paradise in Colorado. Besides, she wouldn't need them. Reverend Everett had promised that everything would be provided for them, their every need and desire would be attended to. She hoped that meant it would be much cleaner and luxurious than the compound. Most of the time the place smelled bad. And on her last trip there, she could swear she had seen a rat scurrying along the side of the conference hall. She hated rats.

She left the boxes and walked through the rooms, looking to see if she had forgotten any of the items she had agreed to sell to the man from Al and Frank's. The man whose name she couldn't remember. She decided she would miss this apartment, though she hadn't lived here very long. It was one of the few places she had bothered to decorate and make into a home. And it was one of the few places that didn't remind her how trapped and alone she could feel. Although some evenings nothing could prevent her from feeling the walls closing in on her.

She told herself that it would be nice to live in a community where her new friends lived just across the hall. But hopefully not Emily. Dear God, Emily's constant complaining would drive her nuts if she had to live across the hall from the woman. It would also be nice to have people she could talk to, rather than spending her evenings answering Regis Philbin's million-dollar questions. Yes, she was tired of being alone, and she certainly didn't want to grow old alone. So if the price was a few rare figurines her grandmother had willed to her, then so be it. It wasn't like those silly things had done anything for her lately.

There was a knock at the door, and for a moment she wondered if perhaps she had gotten the days mixed up. Was it possible the man from Al and Frank's meant to come today and not tomorrow? She'd just have to tell him that she'd changed her mind. That's what she would do. She couldn't possibly sell them to him today. She needed time, after all, to get used to the idea.

She opened the door, ready to say just that, and found herself staring at her daughter, instead.

"Maggie? What on earth are you doing here?"

"Sorry I didn't call."

"What's wrong? Did something happen? Is Greg okay?"

She saw Maggie flinch. It was the wrong thing to say. Why did her daughter always have to make her feel like she was saying the wrong thing?

"Nothing's wrong, but I do need to talk to you. Is it okay if I come in?"

"Oh, sure." She opened the door and waved her in. "The place is a mess."

"Are you moving?" Maggie walked over to the stacked boxes.

Thank God the boxes weren't labeled. Her daughter would never understand about the materialism and divorcing it to feel free or not coveting, or whatever it was… Oh, it didn't matter. Maggie would never understand, and no one outside the church was supposed to know about Colorado.

"I'm just cleaning out some old stuff."

"Oh, okay."

Maggie gave up her questioning and stood at the window, looking out over the parking lot. Kathleen couldn't help wondering if the girl already wanted to escape. Well, it wasn't like it was a day at the circus for her, either. At least, she didn't expect anything from Maggie. Not anymore, that is.

"Would you like some iced tea?"

"Only if it's no trouble."

"I just brewed some. It's raspberry. Is that okay?" But she didn't wait for an answer. She retreated to her small kitchen, hoping its cozy warmth would soothe her nerves.

When she reached for the tall iced tea glasses, she noticed a bottle in the far corner of the cupboard. She had forgotten she even had it. It was for emergencies. She hesitated, then stretched to grab it. This was feeling like an emergency day. First her grandmother's figurines and now an unexpected visit from her daughter.

She poured a quarter of a glass for herself, closed her eyes and gulped it, savoring the burning sensation sliding down her throat and all the way to her stomach. What a wonderful, warm feeling. She had another, then filled her glass one last time about halfway, tucked the bottle back into its hiding place, and poured iced tea in to fill the rest of the glass. The tea was almost the same color.

She grabbed both glasses, remembering that hers was in her right hand. She glanced around the small kitchen. Yes, she was going to miss this place, the welcome mat at the sink and the yellow curtains with little white daisies. She still remembered the day she found those curtains at a garage sale down the street. How could she be expected to leave this place without some sort of help?

When she came back into the living room, Maggie had discovered one of the figurines she had left half wrapped on the window bench

"I remember these," she said, handling the statue and gently turning it just as she had taught her to do, just like Kathleen's grandmother had taught her.

She had forgotten that she had even shown them to Maggie. But now seeing one in her hands, the memory came back as though it were yesterday. She was such a beautiful little girl, so curious and cautious. And now she was a beautiful young woman, still curious and oh, so very cautious.

"You're not getting rid of them, are you?"

"Actually, I've had them in storage. I was just getting them out to take a look and…and well, decide just what to do with them." It was partly the truth. She couldn't be expected to get rid of all her things, move from her nice little apartment *and* tell the truth. That was just too much to expect.

She watched as Maggie carefully returned the figurine to the window bench. She took the glass of tea Kathleen handed her from her left hand. Yes, her left hand had Maggie's tea. She couldn't mix them up now.

Maggie sipped her drink and continued to glance around the room. Kathleen gulped hers. She wasn't sure she wanted Maggie examining any more of her things, stirring up more memories. The past belonged in the past. Wasn't that what Reverend Everett always said? He said so many things. Sometimes it was just too hard to remember them all. She was almost finished with her tea. Perhaps she would need more.

"What did you need to talk about that couldn't wait until Thursday?" she asked Maggie.

"Thursday?"

"Thanksgiving. You didn't forget, did you?"

Another flinch.

"Oh, jeez, mom. I'm not sure I'll be able to make it."

"But you must. I've already bought the turkey. It's in the frig. Practically fills up the entire damn thing." Oh, Jesus, she shouldn't cuss. She needed to watch her language or Reverend Everett would be upset. "I'm thinking we'll have dinner at five o'clock, but you can come earlier, if you like."

She remembered that she still needed to buy cranberries and that bread stuff. Where did she leave her list? She started searching the tabletops.

"Mom, what are you doing?"

"Oh, nothing, sweetie. I just remembered a few things for

Thursday. I wanted to write them—oh, here it is." She found the list on the lamp stand, sat down and jotted *cranberries* and *bread stuff* at the bottom. "Do you know what that bread stuff is actually called that you use to make the stuffing?"

"What?"

"The bread. You know those small pieces of dry bread that you use to make stuffing." Maggie stared at her like she didn't know what she was talking about. "Oh, never mind. I'm sure I'll figure it out."

Of course, Maggie probably didn't know. She was never much of a cook, either. She remembered the girl trying to bake sugar cookies one Christmas and ending up with rock-hard, burnt Santas. Then she refused to be consoled when one of the guys from Lucky Eddie's suggested they paint them and use them for coasters. Poor girl. She never had much of a sense of humor. She was always so sensitive and took too many things to heart.

When she finally looked up from the list, Maggie was staring at her, again. Uh-oh. Now she looked pissed.

"What else should we have for our Thanksgiving dinner?" Kathleen asked.

"Mom, I didn't come here today to talk about Thanksgiving."

"Okay, so what did you come here to talk about?"

"I need to ask you some questions about Reverend Everett."

"What kind of questions?" she asked. Father had warned them about family members wanting to turn them against him.

"Just some general stuff about the church."

"Well, I have an appointment I need to get to," she lied, glancing at her wrist only to find no watch. "Gee, Mag-pie, I wish you would have called. Why don't we talk about all this on Thursday."

She walked to the door, hoping to lead Maggie out, but

when she turned back, Maggie stood in the same spot, clear across the room. Now Maggie frowned at her. No, not a frown. It was that worried, angry look. No, not anger. Well, yes, anger but also sadness. She had the saddest brown eyes sometimes. Just like her father, just like Thomas. Yes, she knew that look. And yes, Kathleen knew exactly what her daughter was thinking even before Maggie said it.

"I don't believe this. You're drunk."

CHAPTER 53

M aggie knew as soon as her mother called her "Mag-pie."
It had been her father's nickname for her. One her mother had
adopted, but only when she was drunk. Instead of a nickname,
it had become a signal, a warning, a grate on her nerves like
fingernails on a chalkboard.

She stared at her mother, but the woman didn't flinch. Her
hand stayed firmly planted on the front doorknob. God! She
had forgotten how good her mother was at this game. And how
god-awful she was, because she let the emotion rule and carry
her away—the emotion of a twelve-year-old. Suddenly, she
found herself pacing the short length of her mother's living
room.

"How could I have been so stupid to believe you?" Maggie said, annoyed that her lower lip was quivering. A quick
glance showed no change in her mother's face. That perfected

combination of puzzlement and innocence, as if she had no clue what Maggie was talking about.

"I have an appointment, Mag-pie…and lots of packing to do." Even her voice had not shifted, not even a notch. There was still that sugary cheerfulness that came with the alcohol.

"How could I have believed you?" Maggie tried to ward off the anger. Why did this always feel so personal? Why did it seem like a betrayal? "I thought you stopped."

"Well, of course, I stopped. I stopped packing to talk to you." But she stayed by the door, hand still planted—maybe she hoped if Maggie didn't leave, she could simply escape. She watched Maggie pace from one end of the room to the other.

"It was the tea," Maggie said, slapping her forehead like a child finally getting an answer to a quiz. She snatched up her mother's glass and took a whiff. "Of course."

"Just a little something to take the edge off." Kathleen O'Dell waved it away, a familiar gesture that reminded Maggie of some form of alcoholics' absolution.

"To take the edge off? For what? What did you need to take the edge off of? So you could get through one goddamn visit with your own daughter?"

"A surprise visit. You really should have called first, Mag-pie. And please don't swear." Even that tone, that Pollyanna tone, grated on Maggie's nerves. "Why are you here?" her mother asked. "Are you checking up on me?"

Maggie tried to slow down, tried to focus. Yes, why had she come? She rubbed a hand across her face, again annoyed that there was a bit of a tremor in her fingers. Why did she have so little control over her reaction, over her body's response? It was as if the hurt little girl inside of her came to the surface to deal with this, because the adult woman had not yet found a sufficient way.

"Maggie, why are you here?"

Now her mother had come back into the room, suddenly anxious for an answer.

"I needed to…" She needed to remember the investigation. She was a professional. She needed answers. Answers her mother could provide. She needed to focus. "I was worried about you."

It was her mother's turn to stare. Suddenly, Maggie wanted to smile. Yes, she did know a thing or two about playing games, about the power of denial or in her mother's world, the power of pretend. Her mother wanted to pretend one drink to take the edge off was not a fall off the wagon? Well Maggie could pretend she was simply worried about her, afraid for her safety, instead of looking for answers about Everett. That was what brought her here, wasn't it? The investigation and trying to solve it. Of course it was.

"Worried?" her mother finally said, as if it had taken this long for her to formulate a definition for the word itself. "Why in the world would you be worried about me?"

"There are some things about Reverend Everett that I don't think you know."

"Really?"

Maggie saw suspicion slipping in past the bewilderment. Careful. She didn't want her to get defensive. "Reverend Everett is not who he seems to be."

"How do you know? You've never met him."

"No, but I did some research and—"

"Ah, research?" her mother interrupted. "Like a background check?"

"Yes," Maggie said, keeping her voice calm and steady now. The professional kicked back into gear.

"The FBI has always hated him. They want to destroy him."

"I don't want to destroy him."

"I didn't mean you."

"Mom, I am the FBI. Please, just listen to me for a minute."

But her mother was fidgeting with the living room blinds, wandering from one window to the next, shutting each and taking her time. "I've talked to others who have told—"

"Others who have left the church." Another interruption, but still with that annoying distracted cheerfulness.

"Yes."

"Ex-members."

"Yes."

"Well, you simply can't believe a word they say. Surely, you must know that." This time she looked at Maggie, and there was something in her eyes, an impatience Maggie didn't recognize. "But you'd rather believe them, wouldn't you?"

Maggie stared at her again. Her mother's mind was already made up. Nothing Maggie could say would change what she believed or didn't believe. No surprise there. What exactly was it that she had expected to find out? Why had she come? It wasn't likely her mother had any damning information about Everett. To warn her mother, perhaps? Why did she believe her mother would suddenly listen to anything Maggie had to say or to advise? This was ridiculous. She shouldn't have come.

"I shouldn't have come," she said out loud, and turned to leave.

"Yes, you'd rather believe them, strangers you've never met before." Her mother's tone was no longer cheerful, a cruel sarcasm edging in. This, Maggie recognized. This, she remembered. "Not like you would ever believe me. Your own mother."

"I didn't mean to suggest that," Maggie said calmly, facing her mother and trying to ignore the change, not only in her mother's tone but even in her gestures—nervous swipes of fingers through her hair. Her eyes darted around the room, looking for a tumbler or bottle and finding the tea glass. She grabbed it and emptied it in one gulp, satisfied and not realizing it had been Maggie's glass by mistake.

"You never believed in me."

Maggie continued to stare at her. How could the insertion of one little word like "in" make such a world of difference? "I've never said that."

But her mother didn't seem to hear her. She was going back around the room, opening the window blinds that she had just shut, one after the other. "It was always him. Always him."

She was ranting, and Maggie knew it was too late to have any semblance of a conversation with her now. But she had no idea who she meant by "him." This was a new rant. One she didn't recognize.

"Maybe I should go," Maggie said, but made no attempt to leave. She only wanted to get her mother's attention. But her mother was no longer listening. No longer paying attention. This was a mistake.

"It was always him." This time her mother stopped in front of her, facing her with accusation. "You loved him so much, you have nothing left for any of the rest of us. Not for me. Not for Greg. Probably not even for your cowboy."

"Okay now, that's enough." Maggie wouldn't put up with this. It was ridiculous. The woman didn't know what she was even saying.

"He was no saint, you know."

"Who are you talking about?"

"Your father."

Maggie's stomach took a plunge.

"Your precious father," her mother added as if she needed clarification. "You always loved him more. So much love for him that there was never enough left for the rest of us. You buried it all with him."

"That's not true."

"And he was no saint, you know."

"Don't you dare," Maggie said, immediately disappointed to find the quiver return to her lower lip.

"Dare to tell the truth?" Her mother managed a cruel smile.

Why was she doing this?

"I need to leave." Maggie turned toward the door.

"He was out fucking his girlfriend the night of the fire."

It was like a knife had been thrust into her back, stopping her in her tracks, making her turn to face her mother again.

"I had to call her house," she continued, "when the fire department's dispatcher called looking for him. Everyone thought he was up sleeping in our bed, but he was in her bed. Her bed, fucking her."

"Stop it," Maggie said, but it came out as a whisper, because all the air had suddenly been sucked out of her.

"I never told you. I never told anyone. How could I after he went out that night, ran into that burning building and died a fucking hero."

"You're making this up."

"He got her pregnant. She has a son. His son. The son I never could give him."

"Why are you doing this? Why are you making this up?" Maggie said, trying to keep the twelve-year-old hurt little girl from surfacing, though in her head, her voice sounded exactly like a child's. "You're lying."

"I thought I was protecting you. Yes, I lied then. But not now. Why would I lie now?"

"To hurt me."

"To hurt you?" Her mother rolled her eyes, the sarcasm having overpowered any other emotion or response. "I've been trying to protect you from the truth for years."

"Protect me?" Now the anger began to unleash itself. "You call moving me halfway across the country protecting me? You call bringing home strange men to fondle me, protecting me?"

"I did the best I could." The eyes were darting around the room again, and Maggie knew she had said what she wanted to say and was now looking to retreat, searching to escape.

"You lost a husband that night. But I lost both my parents."

"That's ridiculous."

"I lost both my father *and* my mother. And what did I get in their place? A drunken invalid to take care of. A drunken slut instead of a mother."

The slap came so suddenly, Maggie didn't have time to react. She wiped at the sting and was more unnerved by the tears already dampening her cheek.

"Oh, Jesus! Maggie." Her mother reached for her and Maggie pulled away. "I'm sorry. I didn't mean—"

"No, don't." Maggie raised a hand in warning. She stood straight, avoided her mother's eyes. "Don't apologize," she said, allowing one more swipe at the tears. "This was the perfect response from you. I wouldn't have expected anything less."

Then she turned and left, making it to her car, managing to drive through the blur before stopping at the entrance to I-95. She pulled off on the side, killed the headlights and switched on the car's flashers, shoved the emergency brake into place, left the engine running and the radio blaring while she let the sobs pour out of her. While she gave in and let those damn leaky compartments burst wide open.

CHAPTER 54

Gwen needed to slow down, but she gulped the remainder of her wine, anyway. She could feel Tully watching her from across the small round table with a polite look of concern while he fumbled with his spaghetti and meatballs.

He had chosen a lovely Italian restaurant with crisp white tablecloths, candles in every window and an array of wait staff that treated them with a kind and friendly manner, then screamed at each other in Italian as soon as they got behind the swinging kitchen door.

She had barely touched her fettuccine Alfredo with fresh cream sauce and portobello mushrooms. It smelled wonderful; however, right now the wine and its anesthetizing effect was all she wanted. She needed something to wipe away the feel of that pencil stabbing into her throat and the desire to kick herself for being so stupid. She was beginning to understand why Maggie resorted to Scotch so often. Maggie had a much longer and more grisly list of images to wipe out of her memory bank.

"I'm sorry," she finally said. "You probably should have left me in my hotel room. I'm afraid I'm not very good company tonight."

"Actually, I'm used to women not talking to me at the dinner table."

It wasn't at all what she expected him to say, and she found herself laughing. He smiled, and it only then occurred to her how awful this afternoon must have been for him, too.

"Thanks," she said. "I really needed to laugh."

"Glad I could help."

"I certainly messed up this trip. We didn't get anything."

"I wouldn't say that. Pratt thought that Father Joseph sent you. He said it. That's more than we knew before, and it may be all we need to connect him and the others to Reverend Joseph Everett. It will be a wasted trip, though, if you don't eat something."

He smiled at her again, and she wondered if he wanted to forget about this afternoon as much as she did. He was still looking at her as if expecting an answer.

"If you'd like, we could go somewhere else, if this isn't quite what you had in mind," he offered.

"Oh, no, this is fine. It smells wonderful. I'm just waiting for my appetite."

She hadn't told him she helped herself to a glass of champagne while she changed for dinner. The hotel had mistakenly sent up a newlywed basket to her room. When she called down to the front desk, the clerk was so embarrassed, he insisted she keep and enjoy it, that they would send another to the intended couple. Well, she wouldn't be able to enjoy all of it. The basket included massage oils and an assortment of condoms. She'd have to settle for the champagne and chocolates.

She watched Tully wrestle with his spaghetti, mutilating it into small pieces instead of wrapping it around his fork. It was painful to watch.

"Mind if I show you how to do that?" she asked.

He looked up, saw what she meant and immediately turned red. Before he could answer, she slid her chair over, so that she was sitting next to his right arm. Without making a big deal or fuss, she gently put her hand over his, barely getting her fingers around his large hand in order to show him how to hold his fork.

"The secret," she said, while reaching across his lap and taking his other hand, "is in the spoon." She nodded for him to pick up his spoon in his left hand. "You pull just a little spaghetti with your fork to release it from the pile, and then you wrap it, slowly in a smooth gentle motion, against the bowl of the spoon."

She could feel his breath in her hair and could smell the subtle scent of his aftershave. His hands complied with her every command, and it surprised her how good they felt against her own palms. When the task was complete, she let go, sat back into her chair and scooted to her side of the table, all the while avoiding his eyes.

"Mission accomplished." She pointed to the perfectly wound spaghetti still on his fork. "You're a quick learner."

He hesitated, then brought it to his mouth. He tried the process again while he chewed, lifting his fork to show her when he managed it on his own. This time their eyes met and neither of them looked away until one of the wait staff interrupted, offering to refill their wineglasses, which Gwen accepted. She was sure it was probably a good idea to also anesthetize the unfamiliar arousal she was suddenly feeling.

With this glass of wine, she did manage to eat some of her fettuccine and even clean up her half of a cannoli dessert. Through coffee and during a long cab ride back to the hotel, she found herself telling Tully about her practice and the old brownstone she was restoring, while he told her about Emma and the trials and tribulations of raising a fifteen-year-old girl. She hadn't realized he had custody of his daughter. Somehow his being a devoted single father only completed the annoying image she already had of him as the perfect Boy Scout.

At her hotel door, she invited him in for a glass of her complimentary champagne, sure the Boy Scout wouldn't accept and that she was safe. The Boy Scout accepted. Before she poured the champagne, she turned to him, needing to say what she had avoided saying all evening.

"I need to thank you," she said, meeting his eyes and holding him there, so he couldn't joke his way out of this. "You saved my life today, Tully."

"I couldn't have done it without your help. You have really good instincts, Doc." He smiled at her, obviously still uncomfortable with taking any of the credit. Okay, so he was going to make this difficult.

"Could you just let me thank you?"

"Okay."

She came to him, stood on tiptoe and still had to tug on his tie to bring him down to her height so she could kiss his cheek. As she did this, she noticed that his eyes were now serious. Before she pulled back, his mouth caught hers in a gentle but passionate kiss that was no longer about gratitude.

She rocked back on her feet, feeling a bit out of breath and staring up at him.

"That was unexpected," she said, surprised that she was feeling light-headed. It had to be all the wine.

"I'm sorry," he said, restoring her image of the Boy Scout. "I shouldn't have—"

"No, you don't need to apologize. Actually, it was…it was quite nice."

"Nice?" He looked wounded, and she smiled though his eyes were still serious. "I think I can do better than nice."

In two steps he was kissing her again, only this time it

wasn't long before his mouth refused to be confined to her lips. Gwen leaned against the back of the sofa and her fingers slid across its texture, looking for something to grab hold of while Tully continued to convince her that he could, indeed, do better than nice.

CHAPTER 55

Ben Garrison didn't get back to the Ritz-Carlton until late. He found the employee door at the back alley and took the freight elevator up to the fourteenth floor. This morning he had argued with the desk clerk about getting moved to a different floor. No matter how anyone looked at it, the fourteenth floor was still the thirteenth floor. Surely there had to be another corner suite available. But now, it looked like it wouldn't matter. His luck was back. Nothing could go wrong. After these photos hit the newsstands, he would be king of the fucking world again.

As soon as he got back to his room he threw his duffel bag on the bed and stripped out of his clothes, bagged them in one of the plastic hotel laundry bags and tossed the bag next to the other trash he'd dump in the morning. He set his boots in the whirlpool tub to clean later and slipped on the plush terrycloth robe that the wonderful housekeeping staff had left fresh and clean on the back of the bathroom door.

He had packed his developing tank and enough chemicals to develop the film. He could make a contact sheet of the exposures he wanted to sell. That way he wouldn't have to take them to a local twenty-four-hour photo shop and have some pimply faced kid freaking out by what he saw.

While he pulled out everything he'd need, he called down to room service. He ordered their roast duck with raspberry chocolate cheesecake and the most expensive bottle of Sangiovese on their wine list. Then he dialed his own number to retrieve his messages. After the *National Enquirer* had hit the stands, he expected some calls from news editors he hadn't heard from in years, suddenly pretending to be his best buddies again.

He was right. There were fifteen messages. His damn machine could take only eighteen. He grabbed the notepad with the hotel's embossed logo and began going through the list. He could hardly contain the smile and finally laughed out loud at the two messages from Curtis, the first wanting to know why he hadn't brought the exclusive to him and the second telling him he'd beat anyone's price for whatever else Ben had. Oh, yes, life was good again. It was very good.

One of the messages was from his old pal, Detective Julia Racine—he had been hoping to hear from her. Unlike the other messages, Racine didn't waste her breath sweet-talking or befriending him. Instead, she threatened to arrest him and charge him with obstruction of a police investigation. Jesus! She could turn him on just with her voice, especially when she talked dirty. Hearing her call him a "fucker" gave him an incredible hard-on. He played the message again, just to enjoy the sensation. Then he decided to save it for future use, rather than erase it.

He flipped through his little black book, and it occurred to him that he might be able to make it up to Detective Racine.

As much as he enjoyed her calling him a fucker, he wouldn't mind cashing in on one of the quid pro quos she was so famous for. From the tone of her voice, the poor woman probably hadn't been laid for some time, be it male or female. And he had to admit, tonight had sorta put him in the mood. He was quite certain he could come up with a proposition that might be as interesting to Racine as it was to him.

Finally, he found the phone number he was looking for and started dialing Britt Harwood's number at the *Boston Globe*. It was late, but he'd go ahead and leave a message. Hell, might as well give the hometown boy a first shot at this exclusive. He smiled, thinking of Harwood's face when he showed him the contact sheet of a dozen good little Christian boys mauling and ripping the clothes off women in the middle of Boston Common.

CHAPTER 56

Tully still couldn't believe it. If it hadn't been for cellular technology, he'd be back at the hotel with Gwen, perhaps even making their way through that gift basket of champagne and condoms. How close had they come to making a huge mistake? Yet, he'd give anything to be back there with her instead of standing under a moonlit sky, up to his ankles in mud, listening to a chain-smoking detective mangle the English language as they waited for the medical examiner.

At first, he'd wanted to strangle Morrelli for the interruption, even if there really had just been a murder similar to the one at the FDR Memorial. He caught himself wondering if Morrelli had done it on purpose, which he knew was crazy. After all, how could Morrelli have known what he was interrupting? Hell, Tully hadn't known what was going to happen. Fact was, he still couldn't believe he had even kissed her, let alone... What was he thinking? Maybe it was for the better that they had been interrupted. Otherwise...otherwise, it could have been...hell, otherwise, it would have been pretty incredible.

"Here's maybe the marks you talkin' about?" Detective Kubat shined the flashlight on an area six feet from the body.

Tully bent down and examined the circular indentations. One was clearly stamped in the mud. A possible second one looked rubbed out. They did look like the marks at the FDR Memorial. What the hell did they mean?

"Did someone get a photo of these?"

"Hey, Marshall," Kubat yelled. "Get your ass over here and shoot a couple of Polaroids of this here."

"What about her clothes?"

"Folded all nice like and piled up over there." He swung the flashlight to highlight the spot, though the clothes had already been bagged and taken by the mobile crime unit. "Weird thing, though, they'd been all ripped up and ripped pretty good."

Tully stood and looked around. They appeared to be in a fairly secluded area of the park. On one side were trees, on another a brick wall, and yet the girl's body was sitting against a tree and staring out at a clearing with a wooden bench and lamppost. In fact, it looked like she was staring right at the bench, posing for some admirer sitting there.

"What about ropes or cords? Anything?"

"Nope, nothin'. But get a load of this.

He led Tully closer to the body. A police spotlight lit up the area around her, its stark light transforming her into a white-faced puppet. She was bruised much worse than the Brier girl, a black eye and bruising from what looked like a left hook to the jaw. Her head tilted to one side, revealing three or four tracks of ligature marks. Without saying anything more, Kubat bent down and snapped off the spotlight. At first, Tully couldn't figure out what he was doing and then he saw. The girl's neck lit up, the track marks glowing in the dark.

"What the hell?"

"Pretty fuckin' weird, huh?" Kubat said, and snapped the spotlight back on. "Anything like that with your victim?"

"There was some sort of glittery stuff found on her neck. I guess I didn't realize it glowed in the dark."

"Oh, hey. Here's Doc Samuel," Detective Kubat said, waving to the tall, distinguished-looking woman in a trench coat and black rubber ankle boots. She looked like the only one who'd come prepared. "Doc, this here's that FBI guy, J.R. Scully."

"Actually, it's R.J. Tully."

"Really? You sure?" Kubat looked at him as if it were possible Tully could have gotten his own name wrong. "I was thinking it was like that *X-Files* lady. Ain't her name Scully?"

"I wouldn't know."

"Yeah, I'm sure it's gotta be Scully."

"Agent Tully," Dr. Samuel said, ignoring Detective Kubat and holding out her hand. "I've been told you might know a thing or two about this killer."

"Maybe. It looks like the same guy."

"So the victim's ID might be in her throat?"

"Yeah, sorry, Doc," Kubat said. "If that's the case, it sure would speed up things on our end."

"As long as we can do this without compromising any evidence," the medical examiner told him with a stern tone that sounded more like a schoolteacher's. "You mind putting out your cigarette, Detective?"

"Oh, yeah, sure thing, Doc." He stabbed it against a tree, pinched the end off with his fingers and tucked the unused portion behind his ear.

Dr. Samuel found a dry rock big enough to set her case on. She began pulling out latex gloves, forceps and plastic bags. She handed Tully a pair of gloves.

"You mind? I may need another pair of hands."

He took the gloves and tried to ignore the knot forming at the pit of his stomach. He hated this part and missed the days when he could stay in his office and do his own style of analysis from photos and digital scans.

Suddenly, he found himself wondering why the hell he hadn't shut off his cellular phone. He had honestly considered it after that spaghetti-twirling lesson, but then was embarrassed that he had even considered it. He probably would have turned off the damn phone if he hadn't been worried about Emma and her trip to Cleveland. But she had called to say she'd arrived safe and sound at her mother's early that afternoon, so why was he still worried about her?

Dr. Samuel was ready. He followed her instructions, being careful where to kneel and keeping out of the spotlight. He tried to not think about the girl's eyes staring at him or the smell of decomposing flesh. Flies were already buzzing, despite the night being chilly. Tully couldn't help thinking they were the insect world's version of vultures. The damn things could sense blood and set up shop in a matter of hours, sometimes minutes.

Kubat stood to the side. He handed Tully his flashlight. "Might need that to see inside her mouth."

The medical examiner used the forceps to tug gently at the duct tape, peeling it off easily and bagging it. She had to use her gloved fingers to pry open the mouth, then she nodded for Tully to shine the flashlight while she picked up the forceps again. Tully pointed the light.

Something moved inside.

"Wait a minute," he said. "Did something just move?"

The medical examiner leaned in for a closer look, tilting her head while he positioned the light. Then suddenly she jerked back.

"Oh, dear, God!" she said, scrambling to her feet. "Get a couple of bags, Detective."

Tully stayed where he was, stunned and motionless, still holding the flashlight in position and listening to Kubat and Dr. Samuel. They scurried around, trying to find something, anything to capture the huge cockroaches that started pouring out of the dead woman's mouth.

CHAPTER 57

Maggie knew she should get up and go to sleep in her bed for a change, but to do so would disturb Harvey's huge snoring head, which was nestled in her lap. So she stayed put. The old La-Z-Boy recliner had become a sort of sanctuary. It sat in her sunroom, facing the floor-to-ceiling windows that looked out over her backyard, though there wasn't much to see in the dark. The moonlight created dancing shadows and skeletal arms waving at her, but thankfully no wisps of fog ghosts tonight.

She wished she could erase from her mind the visit to her mother's, like rinsing out a bad taste from her mouth, but the Scotch wasn't cooperating. It wouldn't stop the memories. It couldn't fill that goddamn hollow feeling. And for some reason, she kept hearing that voice, over and over again in her head.

Your father was no saint.

Why in the world had her mother made up such a lie? Why did she want to hurt her?

Memories kept replaying in her head, some in slow motion, some in short, quick flashes, others in painful stings. Her mother had been with so many men, so many losers, bastards. Why then would she insist on putting Maggie's father in that same category? What kind of cruel joke was she trying to play? Was this something Everett had planted? Something he had convinced her mother to do? Whatever the reason, it managed to bring the walls—those carefully constructed barriers—crashing down, and now the flood of memories wouldn't stop.

Maggie sipped her Scotch, holding it in her mouth and then letting it slide down her throat as she closed her eyes and relished the slow burn. She waited for its heat to warm her and to erase that tension in the back of her neck. She waited for it to fill that hollow gap deep inside her, though she knew it would need to travel to her heart to accomplish that feat. Tonight for some reason the pleasant buzz had simply made her feel a bit light-headed, restless and...and admit it, damn it. Restless and alone. Alone with all those goddamn memories invading her mind and shattering her soul piece by piece.

How could her mother try to take away, to tarnish, the one thing from her childhood that Maggie still held so dear—her father's love? How *could* she? Why would she even try? Yes, perhaps she was slow to love and trust, quick to suspect, but that had nothing to do with her father, and everything to do with a mother who had abandoned her for Jack Daniel's. Maggie had done the only thing a child knew how to do. She had survived, making herself strong. If that meant keeping others at arm's length, then so be it. It was necessary. It was one of the few things in her life she had control over. If people who cared about her didn't get that, then maybe it was their problem and not hers.

She reached for the bottle of Scotch, then paused when its neck clinked against the lip of the glass, waiting to make sure her movement and the noise hadn't disturbed Harvey. An ear twitched, but his head stayed solidly in her lap.

Maggie remembered her mother telling her after her father's death that he would always be with her. That he would watch over her.

Bullshit! Why even say that?

And yet, she knew she should have found some comfort in the thought that her father was still with them somehow, perhaps watching. But even as a child she remembered wondering that, if her mother truly believed that, why then had she acted the way she had? Why had she brought strange men home with her night after night? That is, until she moved her recreation to hotel rooms. Maggie wasn't sure what had been worse, listening through the paper-thin walls of their apartment to some stranger fucking her drunk mother or being twelve and spending the nights home all alone.

That which does not destroy us, makes us stronger.

So now she was this tough FBI agent who battled evil on a regular basis. Then why the hell was it still so difficult to deal with her childhood? Why were those memories of her mother's drunken bouts and suicide attempts still able to demolish her and leave her feeling vulnerable? Leave her feeling like the only way she could examine those memories was through the bottom of a Scotch glass? Why did visions of that twelve-year-old little girl tossing handfuls of dirt onto her father's shiny casket remind her of how hollow she felt inside?

She thought she had risen above her past long ago. Why did it keep seeping into her present? Why could her mother's words, her lies, crumble away that solid barrier she had created?

Goddamn it!

Somewhere deep inside, Maggie knew something was broken. She hadn't ever admitted it to anyone, but she knew. She could feel it. There was a hole, a wound that still bled, an emptiness that could still chill her, stop her in her tracks and send her reaching, searching for more bricks to build up the wall around it. If she could not heal the wound, perhaps she could at least seal it and keep it off-limits from anyone else, maybe even herself.

She knew about the syndromes, the psychology, the inevitable scars from growing up with an alcoholic parent. How a child could be left feeling there was no one to trust. Happiness was as allusive as the fleeting moment of the parent making promises one minute and then breaking them within hours. The child learns not to trust today, because tomorrow his or her world could be turned upside down again. And then there were the lies. Jesus! All the lies. This was just another one. Of course it was.

She sipped her Scotch and watched the moonlight bring shadows to life in her backyard, while the memories, the voices kept coming.

Like mother, like daughter.

No. She was not like her mother. She wasn't like her at all.

Her cellular phone suddenly began chirping inside her jacket pocket. Only now did she remember she had unplugged her regular phone, in case her mother felt some need to call. Maggie stretched to grab the jacket off a nearby stand without disturbing Harvey, whose eyes were open but whose head was still claiming her lap.

"Maggie O'Dell."

"Maggie, it's Julia Racine. Sorry to call so late."

She closed her eyes and took a deep breath. Racine was the last person Maggie wanted to talk to right now.

"I need to talk to you," she said, her voice uncommonly humbled. "Do you have a few minutes? I didn't wake you, did I?"

"No, it's okay." She petted Harvey, who closed his eyes

again. "I haven't made it to bed yet, partly because my dog's oversize head has taken up residence in my lap."

"Lucky guy."

"Jesus! Racine."

"Sorry."

"If that's what this conversation—"

"No, it's not. Really, I'm sorry." Racine hesitated, as if there was something more on the subject she wanted to add before going on. Then she said, "I'm in deep shit with the chief. Senator Brier wants my ass kicked off the force because of those photos Garrison managed to get in the *Enquirer*."

"I'm sure things will cool down as soon as we figure out who is responsible for his daughter's death."

"I wish it was that easy," Racine said, only this time there was something different about her voice. Not anger, not frustration. Maybe a bit of fear. "Chief Henderson is seriously pissed. I may lose my badge."

Maggie didn't know what to say. As much as she disliked Racine and questioned her competency, she knew this was harsh.

"To make matters worse, that asshole Garrison called me." The anger returned. "He said he has some photos to show me that might help the case."

"Why would he suddenly want to help?"

Silence. Maggie knew it. There had to be something in it for Garrison. But what?

"He wants something from me," Racine admitted, going from fear to anger to embarrassment.

"He wants something like what? Sorry, Racine, but you're not getting off that easy. What does he want?"

"He wants photos."

"What photos could he possibly want from you?"

"No, he wants to take photos *of* me." Racine let the anger slip out.

"Oh, Jesus!" Maggie couldn't believe it. No wonder Racine

sounded like an emotional wreck. "And why would he think that's possible?"

"Cut the crap, O'Dell. You know why he thinks it's possible."

So the rumors were true. The stories about Racine exchanging favors weren't just crude locker-room talk.

"Does he realize we could already have him arrested for obstructing a police investigation?"

"I told him."

"And?"

"He laughed."

"Let's do it, then."

"Are you kidding?"

"No. I'll talk to Cunningham. You talk to Henderson. Let's bring him in."

"I'm in enough trouble, O'Dell. If Garrison is bluffing—"

"If Garrison's as arrogant as I think he is, and he does have something, then we'll just convince him it's in his best interests to share that information."

"And just how do we convince him?"

"I'm gonna give Cunningham a call. You talk to Henderson and call me back. Let's bring this asshole in."

Maggie hung up the phone, put the Scotch aside and felt a renewed energy. Gently she nudged Harvey awake. Suddenly, she found herself grateful for bastards like Garrison.

CHAPTER 58

WEDNESDAY
November 27
Washington, D.C.

Ben Garrison pretended to keep his cool while he sat and waited in the middle of the twelfth precinct, handcuffed to a fucking chair. Officers shoved their way around him, ignoring him. A stoned, toothless hooker kept smiling at him from across the room. She even winked at him once, uncrossed her legs and gave him a Sharon Stone view of her merchandise. He wasn't impressed.

His wrists itched under the too-tight handcuffs. The chair's wobbly legs drove him nuts, and he shoved it back against the wall, drawing scowls from the two bastards who brought him in. He still couldn't believe Racine would do this. Who would have thought she had it in her? Oddly, it only made him want to fuck her all the more.

He returned from Boston to find two of the District's finest waiting for him at his apartment. At first, he thought Mrs.

Fowler was having him evicted, especially if she smelled the fumigator crap he had left for the cockroaches to enjoy. And if the little bastards had escaped into the rest of the building, the poor old woman probably would have a coronary. But, no, it wasn't Mrs. Fowler. It was Racine. What a surprise. The little cunt had a game plan all of her own. And part of it, obviously, was to make him wait.

Well, he refused to let her ruin his lucky streak, especially after he had just spent the morning blowing away Britt Harwood with yet another Garrison exclusive. Ben smiled. Not much Racine could do about the photos that would be in this evening's *Boston Globe.*

Hell, he had done what he wanted with the prints, so, no, he didn't mind sharing them with Racine. He had planned to, anyway. She couldn't blame a guy for wanting a little treat in return.

"They're ready for you, Garrison," one of the thick-necked Neanderthals in blue said as he undid one handcuff to release Ben from the chair, then quickly snapped it onto his wrist again. When Ben stood, the guy grabbed his elbow and led him down the hall.

The room was small, with no windows and several pockmarks in the bare walls, some small enough to be bullet holes, a couple of large ones that looked like someone had tried to put a fist or head through the plaster. The room smelled like burnt toast and sweaty gym socks. The officer sat him down in one of the chairs that surrounded the table. Then he did his little weaving trick again with the handcuffs and the steel folding chair.

Ben wanted to point out that if he really wanted, he could fold up the chair and simply take it with him, maybe even knocking some heads with it on his way out. But now probably wasn't a good time to be a smart-ass, so he sat quietly, expecting to be in for another wait.

Surprisingly, Racine came in within minutes, stopping to

consult the Neanderthal at the door before she even acknowledged Ben's presence. She was followed in by an attractive dark-haired woman in an official-looking navy suit.
He thought he recognized her. Surely, he'd remember. What
a treat! Two police babes.

Racine looked pretty good, too. If she wanted to look
butch, she would need to try harder. Although he had to admit
her spiky blond hair looked like she had just gotten out of the
shower, and she had no fashion sense. Today she had on blue
jeans and a sweater that he wished was tighter. But with no
jacket—thank goodness—it was still a rush seeing her in the
leather shoulder holster with the butt of her Glock tucked
nicely under her left breast. Yes, indeed, he could already feel
the effect. Poor Racine. She probably thought hauling him in
here would be some sort of punishment.

The Neanderthal brought in Ben's duffel bag and set it on
the table. Then he left, closing the door behind him. Racine
pulled out a chair and put up one foot, trying to look tough.
The other woman leaned against the wall, crossed her arms
and began examining Ben.

"So, Garrison, glad we could finally arrange that little
meeting you wanted," Racine said. "This is Special Agent
Maggie O'Dell with the FBI. Thought maybe you wouldn't
mind if we made this a threesome."

"Sorry, Racine. If this is your idea of intimidation then
you're gonna be really disappointed when I tell you you're
giving me an incredible hard-on."

She didn't blush, not even slightly. Maybe Detective
Racine was tougher than Officer Racine.

"This case is a federal investigation, Garrison. It could
mean—"

"Cut the crap, Racine," he stopped her, glancing at O'Dell,
who stayed put, looking official while she continued to lean
against the wall. He knew who the real power broker was, so

when he spoke again, he addressed O'Dell. "I know you just want the photos. I always intended to hand them over."

"Really?" O'Dell said.

"Yeah, really. I have no idea what Racine misunderstood. Probably all that sexual tension from not knowing who or what to fuck this week."

"Oh, I think you'll certainly feel fucked, Garrison, when we're through with you," Racine said without so much as a blink, playing out her role as the bad cop.

O'Dell, also, remained cool and calm. "You have the photos with you?" she asked, nodding at the duffel bag.

"Sure. And I'm more than willing to show them to you." He lifted his hands and clanked the handcuffs against the steel chair. "Hell, I'll give them to you. As soon as all the charges are dropped, of course."

"Charges?" Racine glanced at O'Dell, then back at him. "Did the boys give you the impression you were under arrest? I'm sure you must have misunderstood, Garrison."

He wanted to tell her to go fuck herself, but instead he smiled and held up his hands again for her to remove the cuffs.

O'Dell reached over and knocked on the door, bringing in the thick-necked cop to unlock the handcuffs. Then he left again, without a word to either woman.

Ben rubbed his wrists, taking his time before he pulled over the bag and began digging through his equipment. He didn't want them messing with his stuff. He set his camera, lens and collapsible tripod out on the table. Then he removed a couple of T-shirts, a pair of sweatpants and a towel to get the manila envelopes at the bottom. He opened one and spilled its contents on the table: negatives, contact sheet and the prints Harwood's people had developed and given him copies of. He laid five eight-by-tens on the table, putting them in chronological order for the full effect.

"Jesus!" Racine said. "Where and when was this?"

"Yesterday. Late afternoon. Boston."

From one of the other envelopes, he pulled out several prints from the Brier girl's crime scene along with about a dozen from Everett's rally in the District. One showed Everett with a young blond-haired girl and Ginny Brier, alongside two of the same boys in the Boston photos. He slid them across the table.

"Pretty easy to recognize some of these good Christian boys," Ben told them. "When I was at the District rally, Saturday night, I heard them talking about some kind of initiation they were planning in Boston Common on Tuesday. I played my hunch that it might be something interesting."

"Funny how you didn't mention that to me. You didn't even mention that you had been at that rally," Racine said.

"Didn't seem important at the time."

"Even though you knew you had photos of the dead girl attending the rally?"

"I took lots of photos over the weekend. Maybe I didn't know exactly what or who I had shot."

"Just like you didn't know that you hadn't turned over all the film you shot at the crime scene?"

He smiled again and shrugged.

"Was Everett in Boston?" O'Dell asked as she picked up each photo, carefully scrutinized it, then moved on to the next.

"No sign of him, but I heard them talking like maybe he was."

He pointed to Brandon in several of the Boston photos and in the District one. "This one seemed to be in charge. They were all drunk. You can see in one of the photos that they had beer bottles and were spraying the women."

"I don't believe this," Racine said. "Where were the cops?"

"It was a Tuesday afternoon. Who knows? I didn't see any around."

"And you just watched?" O'Dell was staring at him now as if she was trying to figure him out.

"No, I took pictures. It's my job. It's what I do."

"They were attacking these girls, and you just stood around and took pictures?"

"When I'm behind the lens, I'm not there as a participant. I'm there to record and capture what's going on."

"How could you do nothing?" O'Dell wasn't going to give it up. He could hear the anger in her voice.

"You don't get it. If I had put down my camera, you wouldn't have these fucking photos so you can now go out and charge these motherfuckers."

"If you had put down your camera and tried to stop them, maybe we wouldn't need any photos. Maybe those girls wouldn't have had to go through this."

"Oh, right. Like this is my fault. Let me tell you, it takes a lot more work and planning to make news happen, Ms. FBI Agent. I record the images. I capture the emotions. I'm not a part of what happens. I'm a part of the instruments. I'm fucking invisible when I'm behind the camera. Look, you've got your photos. I'm outta here."

He grabbed his duffel bag, stuffed his camera and lens inside and started to leave, expecting one of them to stop him. Instead, they were both busy examining the photos. Racine was already jotting down notes.

Fuck them! If they didn't get it, he didn't need to explain it. He left, a bit disappointed that even the Neanderthal wasn't around for him to shove or at least flip off. Guess Racine won this round.

CHAPTER 59

"**D**o you believe this?" Racine said, standing over the pictures and shaking her head as if she was truly having a tough time believing it. "You think this is what happens to them?"

Without any more of an explanation, Maggie knew Racine was talking about the murdered women: Ginny Brier, the transient they had found under the viaduct and the floater in Raleigh. And now, after talking to Tully, they could add this poor woman whom the Boston PD had just identified as a stockbroker named Maria Leonetti to their list.

"Is it possible?" Racine continued when Maggie didn't answer. "Could it be some savage initiation? Some rite of passage for Everett's young male members?"

"I don't know," Maggie finally said. "I almost hope not."

"It would sure answer a lot of questions. Like why they weren't killed right away. You know. Some crazy game they play with them. And it makes sense that it would coincide with the rallies."

"But there was no rally in Boston," Maggie reminded her.

The two women fell silent again, standing side by side, staring at the photos scattered across the table, neither touching them.

"Why do you say you almost hope not?" Racine broke the silence.

"What?"

"You said you almost hope it's not the way the murders happened."

"Because I hate to believe one man can incite a group of boys to do something like this. That one man could convince a group of boys to rape, brutalize and possibly murder women simply on command."

"Wouldn't be the first time in history. Men can be such bastards," Racine said, letting some anger slip through.

Maggie glanced at her. Perhaps her anger came from personal experience. Perhaps it came from spending several years on the sexual assault unit. Whatever the reason, it seemed a bit personal, and not something Maggie wanted to know.

"It means Everett is much more dangerous than we ever thought," Maggie said, then added in almost a whisper, "Eve was right."

"Who's Eve?"

"An ex-member I talked to. Cunningham and Senator Brier were able to set up the meeting. I thought she was being silly for being so paranoid."

"So what do we do now?"

Maggie finally began to sort through the pile of stuff Garrison had left behind when he'd emptied the duffel bag. He had been in such a hurry to leave that he had taken only his camera and a lens. She pushed aside the strange metal contraption, a smelly T-shirt and sweatpants and reached for the manila envelope. She opened it and spilled its contents—

more photos—onto the table alongside the Boston ones. These all looked like shots from Ginny Brier's crime scene. They had to be from the roll of film he had kept for himself—leftover prints from what he had sold to the *Enquirer.*

"I still can't believe I was so stupid," Racine said as soon as she saw what the prints were. "Chief Henderson is so pissed."

"You made a mistake. It happens to all of us," Maggie told her without accusation. She felt Racine staring at her.

"Why are you being so understanding? I thought you were still pissed at me, too."

"I'm pissed with Garrison. Not you," Maggie said without looking over at Racine. Instead, she sorted through the photos of Ginny Brier. Something about the close-ups bothered her. What was it?

"I meant the DeLong case."

Maggie stopped at a close-cropped shot of Ginny Brier's face, but she could feel Racine's eyes on her. So the DeLong case was still bothering her, too.

"You were pretty upset with me." Racine wouldn't let it go. Maybe she was feeling she needed some absolution. "I made a mistake and some evidence got leaked. Is that why you're still so pissed at me?"

This time Maggie glanced at her. "It almost cost us the conviction." She went back to the shot of Ginny Brier's face, the eyes staring directly out at her. Something was different about this photo, about her eyes. What the hell was it?

"But it didn't cost us the conviction," Racine insisted. "It all worked out." She wasn't finished. "Sometimes I wonder..." she hesitated. "Sometimes I wonder if that's really why you got so pissed at me."

Now Maggie looked at her, meeting her eyes and waiting for Racine to get whatever it was she needed off her chest, although she had a pretty good idea what it was. "What exactly are you talking about?"

"Are you still pissed at me because I made a mistake and leaked evidence? Or are you still pissed at me because I made a pass at you?"

"Both were unprofessional," Maggie said without hesitation and without any emotion. "I have little patience for colleagues who are unprofessional." She went back to the photos, but she could feel the detective still watching, still waiting. "That's it, Racine. There really isn't anything more to it. Now, can we get on with this case?" She handed her the photo. "What's different about this one?"

Racine shifted her stance, but Maggie could tell the woman wasn't quite comfortable about moving on. "Different how?" she asked.

"I'm not sure," Maggie said, rubbing at her own eyes and feeling the effects of too much Scotch from the night before. "Maybe I need to see the other crime scene photos. Do we have those handy?"

But Racine didn't make an attempt to search. "Do you still think I'm unprofessional? I mean with this case?"

Maggie stopped and turned to face the detective. They were eye level, almost the same height. The normally cocky detective waited for an answer with one hand on her hip and the other tapping the photo on the table's surface. She held Maggie's eyes in that same tough stare she probably thought she had perfected, but there was something—a slight vulnerability in her eyes as they blinked, darted to one side then quickly returned, as if it took a conscious and silent reminder not to flinch.

"I haven't had any complaints," Maggie finally said. Then she relinquished a smile and added, "Yet."

Racine rolled her eyes, but Maggie could see the relief.

"Tell me what you know about Ben Garrison," Maggie said, hoping to get back to work, despite the nagging sensation she had about Ginny Brier's dead eyes, staring out from Garrison's illicit photos.

"You mean other than that he's an arrogant, lying bastard?"

"It sounds like you worked with him before."

"Years ago, he sometimes moonlighted for second shift as a crime scene photographer when I was with Vice," Racine said. "He's always been an arrogant bastard, even before he became a big-shot photojournalist."

"Any famous shots I may have seen?"

"Oh, sure. I'm sure you've seen that god-awful one of Princess Diana. The blurred one, shot through the shattered windshield? Garrison just happened to be in France. And one of his Oklahoma City bombing ones made the cover of *Time*. The dead man staring up out of the pile of rubble. You don't even see the body unless you look at the photo closely, and then there's those eyes, staring right out at you."

"Sounds like he has a fascination with photographing death," Maggie said, picking up another photo of Ginny Brier and studying those horrified eyes. "Do you know anything about his personal life?"

Racine shot her a suspicious look with enough distaste that Maggie knew it was the wrong thing to ask. But Racine didn't let it stop her. "He's hit on me plenty of times, but no, I don't know him outside of crime scenes and what I've heard."

"And what have you heard?"

"I don't think he's ever been married. He grew up around here, maybe someplace in Virginia. Oh, and someone said his mom just died recently."

"What do you mean, someone said. How did they know?"

"Not sure." The detective squinted as if trying to remember. "Wait a minute, I think it was Wenhoff. When we were waiting for you at the FDR scene, right after Garrison left. I don't know how Wenhoff knew. Maybe somehow through the medical examiner's office. I just remember he made the comment that it was hard to believe someone like Garrison even had a mother. Why? You think that means something? You think that's why he's suddenly so reckless and anxious to be famous again?"

"I have no idea." But Maggie couldn't help thinking about her own mother. What kind of danger was she in just by being a part of Everett's group? And was there any way Maggie could convince her she *was* in danger? "Are you close to your mother, Racine?"

The detective looked at her as though it were a trick question, and only then did Maggie realize it wasn't a fair question, certainly not a professional one. "Sorry. I didn't mean to be personal," she said before Racine could answer. "Mine's just been on my mind lately."

"No, I don't mind," Racine said, appearing relaxed and casual with the subject even when she added, "My mom died when I was a girl."

"Racine, I'm sorry. I didn't know."

"It's okay. The bad part is, I have few memories of her, you know?" She was flipping through the crime scene photos, and Maggie wondered if perhaps Racine wasn't as comfortable with the topic as she pretended. She seemed to need to have her hands occupied, her eyes busy somewhere else. But still, she continued, "My dad tells me stuff about her all the time. I guess I look just like her when she was my age. Guess I need to be the one to remember the stories, because he's starting to forget them."

Maggie waited. It felt like Racine wasn't finished, and when she glanced up, Maggie knew she was right. Racine added, "He's starting to forget a lot of stuff lately."

"Alzheimer's?"

"Early symptoms, but yeah."

She looked away again, but not before Maggie caught a glimpse of vulnerability in the tough, wise-cracking detective's eyes. Then she began sorting through Garrison's stuff as if looking for something and asked, "What do we do about Everett? Everett and his little gang of boys?"

"Are the photos enough for an arrest warrant?"

"For this Brandon kid, I'd say definitely. We have these photos and an eyewitness that puts him with Ginny Brier in the hours before her murder."

"If we can get a DNA sample, I bet we've got a match to the semen."

"We'll need to have the warrant served at the compound," Racine said. "We might not have any idea what we're walking into out there."

"Call Cunningham. He'll know what to do. It'll probably require an HRT unit." As soon as she said it, Maggie thought of Delaney. "Hopefully this won't get messy. How long do you think it'll take to get a warrant?"

"For the possible murder suspect of a senator's daughter?" Racine smiled. "I think we should have one before the end of the day."

"I need to make a quick trip down to Richmond, but I'll be back."

"Ganza said he needed to talk to you. He left a message earlier."

"Any idea what about?" But Maggie was already headed for the door.

"Not sure. Something about an old police report and a possible DNA sample?"

Maggie shook her head. She didn't have time. Besides, maybe it was a different case. "I'll call him from the road."

"Wait a minute." Racine stopped her. "Where are you going in such a hurry?"

"To try to talk some sense into a very stubborn woman."

CHAPTER 60

Gwen slid into the window seat while Tully shoved their bags into the overhead compartment. During the cab ride to Logan International Airport, they had managed to fill the awkward silences with niceties about the weather and some details about the crime scene. So far they had avoided talking about last night and what Nick Morrelli's phone call had interrupted. She caught herself thinking that it might be best if they pretended it had never happened. Then she realized how stupid that probably was for a psychologist to even consider. Okay, so she wasn't good at practicing what she preached.

He took the seat next to her, fumbling with his seat belt and watching the other passengers file onto the plane. It looked like it wouldn't be a full flight. With no one to occupy the aisle seat there would be more opportunity for them to talk. Oh, wonderful!

Tully mentioned that he hadn't gotten back to the hotel until almost sunrise. Maybe he would want to sleep. She wasn't ready to talk about what had happened between them last night.

She knew it wasn't unusual for two people who had just gone through a crisis to be drawn together in a way they ordinarily would never consider. And yesterday's attempt on her life could certainly be considered a crisis. Of course that was exactly what had happened.

The flight attendants began the preflight procedure, and Tully watched as though he was captivated and had never flown before, an obvious giveaway that he, too, was uncomfortable. Now Gwen wished she had bought a paperback at the airport bookstore. At this rate, the sixty-minute flight would be excruciatingly long.

Once they were in the air, Tully brought his briefcase out from under the seat. With it in his lap, he suddenly seemed more comfortable, a sort of this-is-strictly-business security blanket.

"I talked to O'Dell," he said while he flipped through a mess of papers, shoving pens, a day-planner and a clump of paper clips out of the way.

Gwen immediately wondered if he actually used the day-planner. Then she caught herself wondering what Maggie would think when she found out about last night, and about Gwen breaking her own golden rule of not getting involved with a man she worked with. But nothing had happened. They hadn't had time to get...involved.

Tully brought out some copies of crime scene photos and was pointing out similarities. "O'Dell said that photographer, the one who sold the crime scene photos to the *Enquirer,* has photos of Reverend Everett's boys mauling women in Boston Common yesterday."

"You're kidding. Yesterday?" Now he had her attention. "How did he just happen to be in Boston?"

"Supposedly, he overheard something about an initiation rite when he was shooting photos at the District's prayer rally. O'Dell said last night's victim is one of the women, and that it should be easy to identify the young men, too. Several of the boys show up in photos with Everett at the prayer rally, so there's our connection."

"This is starting to sound too easy. If Everett's boys are involved in the murders, why would Everett allow them to be photographed?"

"Maybe he didn't know they were."

"How did Maggie manage to get these photos from Garrison?"

Tully shook his head, and Gwen could see a slight smile. "Not sure, and I don't even want to know."

Gwen laughed. "So I gather you already know my good friend quite well."

"Let me just say that sometimes she's a little more willing than I am to skip over procedure."

"You're a by-the-book kind of guy?"

"Yeah, I try to be. Something wrong with that?"

"I didn't say there was."

He looked over at her as if he expected more of an explanation, then he said, "It sounded like you wanted to attach a *but* to that."

"No, not at all. I was just wondering how last night played into your rules-and-procedure book."

He actually turned a slight shade of red and quickly looked away. Gwen followed his lead and looked in the other direction, out the window. Oh, smooth move, Patterson, she scolded herself. Who would ever guess she had a doctorate in psychology.

"I suppose we should talk about last night," he finally said.

"We don't need to talk about it," she found herself saying, all the while thinking that yes, they did. What was wrong with her? "I just don't want it to get in the way of us working together."

God, how pathetic. Where did she come up with this stuff? She should stop and yet she found herself continuing. "It was simply the crisis."

He was looking at her, waiting. She didn't think she had to explain it to him, but obviously she would. "A crisis can often make people act in a way they might not normally act."

"We weren't in the middle of a crisis then."

"No, of course not. It doesn't have to be during the crisis. It's the effect of the crisis."

He went back to his computer and punched at a couple of keys to close a file he had just opened. Without looking up at her, he said, "Sounds like you'd rather we pretend it didn't happen."

She glanced at him, looking for some sign of what he wanted. But with the computer screen to distract him, he kept his eyes ahead, now watching the flight attendant's serving cart coming down the aisle as if he couldn't wait for his beverage and package of pretzels.

"Look, Tully, I have to admit—" She stopped herself, something only now occurring to her. "Should I be calling you R.J.? And what does R.J. stand for?"

He grimaced. Another wrong thing to say. Oh, she was definitely good at this.

"All my friends call me Tully."

She waited, then realized that was all she was getting. So much for intimacy. Last night had been about sex and nothing more. Why did that suddenly surprise her? Wasn't that all it had been to her? Thank God for Morrelli's interruption.

"What were you going to admit?" he asked, looking over at her. "You started to say that you had to admit something?"

"Just that I had to admit I wasn't quite sure what to call you. That's all," she said, while some inner voice told her what a good liar she was.

But how could she admit that last night had been surprising and incredible and then say, So let's forget it, okay? She had managed to keep her life uncomplicated for years now. Seemed a shame to throw all that away for one surprisingly pleasant encounter.

"So we chalk it up to the crisis of the moment," Tully said with a casual shrug, not able to hide just a hint of…a hint of what? Disappointment? Sarcasm?

"Yes. I think it's best that we do that," she told him.

She imagined Freud would have a perfect word for what she was doing, for what she was telling herself, for how she was handling this situation. Although she couldn't quite imagine Freud actually saying the word "bullshit" out loud.

CHAPTER 61

This time Maggie remembered to exit I-95 before she reached the turnpike. She ended up on Jefferson Davis Highway, and as she crossed the James River she realized she would probably need to do some backtracking to get to her mother's. Two trips in two days—she should be able to do this without a hitch. After all, she had spent her adolescent years here until she left for good to go to the University of Virginia in Charlottesville. Yet this city had never felt like home. At that point in her life, no place on earth would have felt like home. No place, that is, without her father.

After his death, Maggie had never understood why her mother insisted they move from Green Bay to Richmond. Why wouldn't they want to stay in their home surrounded by people who knew and loved them, comforted by the memories? Unless, of course, there had been an affair and gossip, rumors… No, it had to be a lie. She wouldn't allow the thought, wouldn't dignify it with… Except *why* had they moved? Had her mother ever given her a reason?

Kathleen O'Dell had plopped them down in the middle of a strange and unfamiliar place, a place she had never visited nor even heard of before. And her mother's only explanation… What? What had it been? Something about a fresh start, a new beginning. Right. A fresh start after every failed suicide attempt. So many of them Maggie had stopped counting.

But here she was again, trying to rescue her mother once more.

She pulled up in front of her mother's apartment building, driving around the huge white paneled truck that took up five prime parking spaces. Several men were loading the truck with furniture while a small gray-haired man propped open the apartment building's security door. So much for security.

It wasn't until Maggie walked up the front sidewalk and past the truck that she recognized the flowered love seat the men were shoving into the back. Immediately, she glanced up at her mother's second-floor apartment and noticed all the curtains gone from the windows. The stab of panic caught her off guard.

"Excuse me." She stopped the small gray-haired man who seemed to be supervising the move. "I recognize some of these items. What's going on?"

"Mrs. O'Dell is selling out."

"You mean moving out?"

"Well, I'm sure she's moving someplace else, but no, I meant selling out."

The confusion must have shown on her face, because he went on to explain, "I'm Frank Bartle." He dug into his jacket pocket and handed her a business card. "Al and Frank's Antiques and Secondhand Treasures. We're down on Kirby. If you see something here you like, we'll have it ready to sell next week."

"But I don't understand why she would sell everything. I guess I should go up and ask her myself, rather than bother you."

"'Fraid you won't be able to do that."

"I promise I won't get in your men's way." She smiled and started for the door.

"No, I just meant that she's not there."

Now Maggie felt a clammy chill. "Where is she?"

"Don't know. I was gonna buy a few of her antiques. You know some trinkets, a few figurines and things like that. She gave me a call early this morning and asked if I wanted the whole lot."

Maggie leaned against the doorjamb. "Where did she go?"

"Don't know."

"But she must have left you a forwarding address."

"Nope."

"What about payment?"

"I came over this morning. Gave her an estimate and then a check. She gave me a key. Said to hand it in to the landlady when we're through."

How could all this happen in less than twenty-four hours? And what had happened to make her mother do this? Or had she planned it and just didn't tell Maggie? Yesterday there had been quite a few boxes packed and stacked. But why make a production of Thanksgiving dinner if she hadn't planned on being here? What the hell was going on?

"I have a receipt, if you don't believe me." Frank Bartle was digging in his jacket pocket again.

"No, that's fine." She stopped him with a wave of her hand. "I believe you. It's just very strange. I saw her yesterday."

"Sorry, but that's all I know," he said, but his attention wandered to one of the moving men who was coming out the apartment building. "Be careful with that one, Emile. Put it someplace safe, okay?"

On the side of the carton the man carried Maggie could see scrawled in black marker the single word, Figurines. Her grandmother's figurines, the one prize possession her mother owned. Suddenly, Maggie felt sick to her stomach. Wherever her mother had gone, she didn't intend on coming back.

CHAPTER 62

Ben Garrison kicked the unlocked door open. He wanted to strangle Mrs. Fowler. How dare she come into his apartment without letting him know. In the past, the old lady had usually been good about locking up after herself and her string of handymen, almost compulsive about it, in fact. Maybe she had developed a few loose screws in her old age.

He set down his duffel bag on the kitchen counter and out of the corner of his eye he could see them. Quietly, slowly, he picked up the closest thing he could find, pulled back his arm and flung the old tennis shoe at the moving row of black skittering up his living room wall.

Shit! He was sick of these things. Would he ever be rid of them? Is that why Mrs. Fowler let herself in? Maybe the simple solution would be to move to a new apartment. He could certainly afford it now that his lucky streak had returned.

He'd need to wait and decide. Right now he barely had enough time to take a quick shower, repack his bags, load up on more film and head to the airport.

He dumped his duffel bag onto the counter, sifting through the contents, tossing empty film canisters and doing a quick inventory. It still pissed him off that he had left all the Boston negatives with Racine. But he couldn't afford to have her trip him up. Not now. Not when he was on a roll.

As he sorted through everything he realized he must have left his collapsible tripod at the police station. Damn it! How could he have been so careless? It happened every time he got a little too cocky. Now he wondered what else he may have left behind. The T-shirts and sweatpants he could do without, but the tripod he couldn't. He'd need to stop and pick up another. No way would he go back to the police station.

He checked his phone messages, jotting down the names of editors and phone numbers he had never heard of or from before. Suddenly everyone wanted a Garrison exclusive. In no time, he'd be back to shooting whatever he wanted, although it would be difficult to beat the rush of adrenaline this little project was producing. Maybe he could find a gallery that would display his outtakes. Those, after all, were the true rush, his true genuine works of art.

There were five hangups on his answering machine, definite hangups with a pause and then a click. Probably Everett's little warriors checking up on him. But why the hangups and no more clever messages? Were they running out of intimidation ammunition?

Poor Everett. He'd finally get what he deserved, what he had coming to him. Perhaps Racine and that FBI chick would be smart enough to put the puzzle pieces together. Hopefully, that wouldn't happen before Cleveland. Ben needed this one last trip, one last rally.

He headed for the bathroom, peeling off his clothes and leaving a trail, not caring whether the cockroaches took up residence in his old worn jeans. Maybe he'd burn them when he got back. Yeah, he'd wrap them all up in a plastic bag, so he could watch the fucking roaches squirm while he set the jeans on fire. He wondered if cockroaches made any kind of noise. Did they scream?

When he stepped into the bathroom, he immediately noticed that the smudged glass door to his shower was closed. He never left it closed. The trapped fog and steam ended up producing a crop of mildew, so he always left it open. He couldn't see through the milky glass, but surely there would be a shadow or silhouette if someone was hiding inside. Maybe Mrs. Fowler's handyman had been screwing around with the plumbing. That had to be it.

He pulled a towel from the rack and shook it out, making sure it was cockroach-free. He opened the shower door and reached in to turn on the water. One glance inside the tub made him jerk backward hard and fast, tangling his feet and sending him crashing to the bathroom floor. He scrambled to his feet, grabbed the shower door and slammed it shut, but not before he took one last look to make sure he wasn't imagining things.

They had gone too fucking far this time.

Coiled inside his bathtub was a snake that looked big enough to swallow him whole.

CHAPTER 63

The Compound

Kathleen O'Dell sat on the floor next to Reverend Everett in his high-backed chair as they waited for the meeting hall to fill. Stephen sat on his other side with Emily. Stephen nor Emily had said much to her since they picked her up. Not a word of explanation the entire trip to the compound, just short, almost curt nonanswers to her questions. Kathleen wasn't sure if it was anger or urgency. She hadn't been able to read either one of them. Now as they sat, she stole a glance at Reverend Everett. He didn't seem angry, either, but earlier there had been something in his voice and in his mannerisms. Kathleen wondered if it was panic.

No, of course not. She was being paranoid. There was no reason to panic. And yet, his morning phone call sounded just frantic enough to set her on edge. All morning, as she waited for Frank from Al and Frank's and then for Stephen and

Emily, she kept wishing she hadn't finished that entire bottle from the back of her cupboard.

Reverend Everett hadn't given much of an explanation as to why they had to leave so soon. When they arrived at the compound, they found the others scurrying around, preparing for another stretch of prayer rallies, the first being in Cleveland, the following night. That was all it was—preparation. But then, why did Reverend Everett call this emergency meeting? Why did Emily's face look pinched with panic?

Kathleen wasn't even supposed to be here. She wasn't supposed to be going to the Cleveland rally. It had been Reverend Everett's recommendation that she spend the holiday with Maggie. Except that she hadn't had the chance to tell him about Maggie. Now it was best she didn't mention it at all. Because now, it seemed as if everything had changed. Something terrible had happened. Something terrible enough to make Emily speechless. Something terrible enough that prevented Stephen from meeting Kathleen's eyes.

Kathleen felt like she was in a fog, where nothing seemed to be quite clear. She still couldn't believe all her things were gone, her apartment, her cheerful yellow curtains and her grandmother's figurines. Perhaps that's why her head had been throbbing all day. It was just too much to expect a person to handle in one day. Surely Reverend Everett understood that. Perhaps by the time they reached Cleveland, he would change his mind. Yes, she was certain he would be able to calm down and realize that everything would be just fine.

As he stood, the room grew silent, despite the nervous tension that spread through the crowd as they sat crossed-legged on the floor and waited.

"My children," he began, "before those of us who are going on our mission to Ohio leave, I'm afraid we have some disturbing news. I've warned many times that we have traitors who wish to hurt us. Those who hate us because we choose to live free. Now I must tell you that one of those among us has betrayed us, has become a traitor. Has exposed us to those mongrel media hounds. And you know how the media can lie."

He waited for the appropriate response, nodding at the few hisses that grew when he encouraged them. Kathleen looked around, hoping there would be no snake tonight. She wasn't sure her nerves could handle that.

"I'm afraid this matter is much too personal and painful for me, and so I'm asking Stephen to take over from here." Reverend Everett sat back down and looked to Stephen, who seemed surprised and perhaps a bit embarrassed by the request. Evidently, this part was unplanned. Poor timid Stephen. Kathleen knew he hated having attention drawn to him. She could see the discomfort taking over his entire face.

He stood, slowly, reluctantly. "It's true." His voice cracked, and he cleared his throat. "We have a traitor among us."

He glanced back at Reverend Everett and the reverend waved a hand at him to proceed, indicating that Stephen knew the drill. Yes, Kathleen looked around at the crowd, now silent and waiting. They all knew the drill. The traitor must be brought forward. Must be taught a lesson. But she was so exhausted tonight that all she wanted was for it to be over.

"The traitor has exposed valuable information to the FBI and the *Boston Globe*," Stephen continued. "Information that has them talking to ex-members. Information that could tarnish the church's reputation and distract from our mission. This is why the rally in Ohio is even more important now. We cannot be intimidated."

He looked to Reverend Everett as if for approval. Then Stephen's voice grew stronger, deeper. "But traitors must be punished. I ask the guilty person to stand. You know who you are." Another glance back at Reverend Everett. "Stand before us and take your punishment."

They all remained silent. No one dared to look around for

fear that they might be the one. No one stirred or dared to shift. Then Stephen turned and pointed his finger.

"Stand up right now and face your punishment," he said.

Kathleen thought she heard a hint of a quiver as he pointed his finger in her direction. No. There had to be a mistake. She looked to Reverend Everett, but he kept his eyes straight ahead. He was the only one who wasn't staring at her.

"Kathleen, come face your punishment for betraying us all." Stephen now managed an angry, stern tone.

"But there must be a mistake," she said, getting to her feet. "I haven't—"

"Silence!" Stephen yelled. "Arms at your sides, stand up straight, eyes forward." When her only response was to stare at him, he grabbed her arms and shoved her to the front of the room where several others, including Emily, had gathered. "Your selfishness could have destroyed us," he screamed into her face. Then he looked to the others to take their turn.

"You betrayed us," shouted an old woman Kathleen had never met.

"How could you?" Emily screamed into her face.

"You should be ashamed," came another.

"Traitor!"

"What makes you think you're special?"

"Ungrateful bitch!"

"What makes you think you're better than the rest of us?"

"Shame!"

One after another, they circled her, hurling insults, screaming at her, poking and shoving.

"How dare you."

"Traitor!"

Kathleen's eyes were already blurred and stinging with tears by the time the first one spit at her. Then came another and another. She attempted to wipe her face, only to have Stephen slap down her arms.

"You know the rules. Arms at your sides," he yelled, only

it wasn't Stephen anymore. Those were not Stephen's eyes. It was some creature, some ugly entity who had taken over his body.

She stood, closing her eyes to the spittle and trying to shut her mind to the angry words, absorbing the blows and shoves that reminded her to stand up straight. It went on forever until her eyes burned and her ears were ringing, her feet hurt and the bruises were visible. Then suddenly, they stopped. Suddenly, it got quiet again. Everyone filed out in an orderly fashion, as if they had come for dinner and were now finished. And Kathleen found herself alone, standing in the empty meeting hall.

She was afraid to move, afraid her knees would collapse. The silence inside the hall surrounded her, and she listened to sounds outside—ordinary sounds of preparation for the impending trip. It was as if nothing had happened. As if her biggest fear had not just been played out for everyone to witness; her fear of being humiliated in front of those she thought respected her. What was worse was that they went about their punishment as if it was nothing unusual. As if it wasn't out of the ordinary for her to have her soul ripped out in front of them.

That's when she saw the young man, standing in the shadows, next to the back exit. When he realized he had been discovered, he came to her, slowly, head down, one hand in his pocket, the other holding out a towel to her.

A towel. She wanted to laugh. What she really needed was a bottle, a fucking bottle of anything…Jack Daniel's, Absolut… Hell, rubbing alcohol would do the job. But she took the towel and began gently wiping her face and then her arms, working her way over her body, trying to not think about the black-and-blue marks, trying to pretend… How the hell could she pretend? No, she could do it. She had done it before. She'd be okay. She just needed to steady herself. Was the room spinning? Or was it her imagination?

He was helping her sit. He was saying something to her, taking the towel and leaving. Was he gone? Did he decide she was a lost cause? Had he left her, just like the rest of them? But suddenly, he was back at her side. Two of him this time, handing her the towel. A fresh one, but this one damp.

She dabbed her forehead, the back of her neck, and then pulled up her sleeves and dabbed at the insides of her wrists. Already she was feeling better. This time when she looked up she found only one of him. And thank God, the room…it finally sat still. The young man seemed preoccupied. He was staring at her wrists. Or rather, he was staring at the hideous horizontal scars she had uncovered when she pulled up the sleeves of her knit cardigan.

"Believe me," she said to him, "I'll know how to do it right the next time."

CHAPTER 64

Justin wanted to tell the woman that he understood, that he had thought about offing himself so many times he had the methods categorized. But he had never known someone older, someone who reminded him of his mother—and she *did* remind him an awful lot of his mother—who had actually tried it.

"Ma'am, are you okay now?" he asked. "Because I really should be helping load and haul stuff."

"I'll be fine." She smiled at him and pushed down the sleeves. "My name's Kathleen. No need to call me ma'am. But then, I guess you should already know my name after tonight."

"I'm Justin," he said.

"Well, thanks for your help, Justin."

He nodded at her. "I know you didn't do anything wrong."

Then he turned and left out the back exit. He needed to get back to the kitchen. Back to packing boxes with cans of beans and soup and enough rice to gag a small nation. Maybe he was trying too hard to be helpful, but he knew he had fucked up big time in Boston. Since they returned, he was half expecting to end up with that boa constrictor around his neck. He knew how close he had come to being the one standing in front of the room. Maybe that's why he had to go back and help this woman, this Kathleen. That and because she reminded him of his mom. He hadn't realized until tonight that he actually missed his mom. And he missed Eric. Now he wondered if Eric was ever really coming back.

At first, he thought he wouldn't be allowed to go to Cleveland, to the next prayer rally. That would have been okay by him. In fact, he was thinking maybe he'd just leave the compound while the others were away. He was pretty sure he could find his way back into Shenandoah National Park. He had done it last time without really trying. But then Alice told him he was on the list, the fucking anointed list that got to go.

He found the old lady named Mavis and helped her load the steel cart full of cartons into the buses' storage compartments. Some of the compartments were already loaded with other boxes. Inside both buses, the overhead compartments looked filled beyond capacity. A woman from the laundry room instructed Justin to place all the boxes she had brought on another steel cart under the seats.

"They have to fit. Make them fit," she told him, and left.

These were labeled: Shirts, Undergarments, Towels. Why would they be needing all this crap for a two-night trip? He stuffed the last one under the driver's seat just as Alice came up the bus steps with an armful of blankets. He helped her find space for them, avoiding her eyes and any other contact. He hadn't been alone with her since his meeting with Father. It shouldn't matter, but he had a hard time looking at her. He couldn't believe how much of a phony she was, pretending to be all pure and good and stuff. To think she had tried to lecture him on his bad habits. Well, at least he wasn't a fucking whore.

Shit! He promised himself he wouldn't think that way, especially after seeing those poor girls yesterday, screaming and kicking. He still couldn't get those images out of his mind.

"You've been really quiet since you got back from Boston," Alice said, staring at him with that look of concern that he used to believe was genuine. Now he wasn't sure what to think. Nobody seemed to be what he thought they were. Including himself. "Are you okay?"

"Yeah, I'm fine. Just tired." He pretended to be inspecting all the boxes, making sure they were secured under the seats.

"Well, you should be able to get some sleep once we get on the road," she said, sounding sympathetic—but how did he know that was real?

When he still didn't look at her, she put her hand on his arm, stopping his bogus inspection.

"Justin? Did I do something to make you angry with me?"

"No, why?"

"Why won't you look at me?"

Shit! He had forgotten. She really could see inside his soul. He looked into her eyes just to prove to her that he could. It was a mistake. She could see something was wrong, and now he was the one responsible for the sadness looking back at him from her eyes.

"Please tell me," she said, "if I've done something wrong. I couldn't stand the thought of you being angry with me."

He used to think she was the only one who was being straight with him, the only person he could trust. Now he didn't know. Fuck! He was so tired, and he still felt sick to his stomach. He hadn't eaten anything since he had thrown up the Quarter Pounders and beer.

"I'm not angry at you," he finally said. "I told you, I'm just really tired." He could see he hadn't convinced her, but he squeezed past her, anyway. "I'll see you later." He escaped, walking away from the bus in quick, long strides, hoping to discourage her from following him.

As he walked past the administrative building, he could see the office staff. It looked like they were shredding papers and taking apart computer hard drives. Back behind the building, three women had started a small bonfire and were tossing into the flames what looked like file folders and stacks of papers. Far off in the trees, Justin could see a spotlight and the broad-shouldered silhouettes of some of Father's bodyguards. He couldn't tell what they were doing. It almost looked like they were laying cable. Something really weird was going on. This didn't look like the ordinary preparation for a road trip.

Justin stopped suddenly and stared. At the construction site, everything had been cleared away—no stacked lumber, no crates, no sawhorses. Even the old John Deere tractor was gone. He went over for a closer look. How the hell did they get rid of it all? How could they move all that crap in such a short time?

Then he saw the flashlight back behind the garbage dump. Two men were digging while one held a flashlight. Justin leaned against an old outhouse where he could hide in the shadows. He saw them bring up four strongboxes out of the ground. It took all three of them to carry one box all the way around the corner, taking slow, deliberate steps as they hauled it down the road to where the bus was parked.

As he watched, it only now occurred to Justin. They weren't going to all this trouble just to prepare for the prayer rally. He couldn't believe it had taken him this long to figure it out. They were doing it because they weren't coming back.

CHAPTER 65

On her way back from Richmond, Maggie's cellular phone began ringing.

"Hello?"

"O'Dell," Racine said with enough urgency to set Maggie on edge even more than she already was. "Where the hell are you?"

"I'm on I-95, heading back to the District."

"We're all meeting out at Quantico."

"Okay, then I'm only about ten minutes away."

"Good." Racine sounded relieved. "You didn't call Ganza."

"Damn! No, I forgot. Is he there?"

"He's here someplace. I'm not sure where."

Maggie could hear background noise. She knew Racine was pacing. A nervous habit Maggie quickly recognized.

"What is it, Racine? What's going on? Did you get the arrest warrant?"

"Actually, that's now multiple warrants, thanks to Ganza. There was some old police case Tully was checking out. It's one you found about Everett raping…or excuse me, allegedly raping that journalism student?"

"That was over twenty years ago. And the charges were dropped."

"Yeah, well, Rappahannock County has this thing about keeping evidence on file. I guess Ganza knows some boys out there in the sheriff's department and they managed to FedEx some samples to him."

"I can't believe he's wasting time on that old case. We can't get Everett on that case, no matter what he thinks he found. The charges were dropped, the case closed. Besides, the statute of limitations on rape—"

"The sample was old," Racine interrupted her, and continued as if not hearing her. "There was some degradation so he says he couldn't get an exact match. But there're enough hits that it's close."

"What are you talking about?"

"The sample Ganza took from the old case? The sample from Everett? The DNA matches the DNA sample of foreign skin found under Ginny Brier's fingernails. Remember you said most of the skin was her own, but that she managed to get a piece of him? Well, she got a piece of him, all right, and Ganza swears it's Everett."

Maggie slowed and pulled her car to the side of the interstate, eliciting a blare of horns behind her before she was safely stopped and out of the way. She couldn't believe this. It couldn't be Everett. Could it? "Wait a minute. What about the gang thing?"

"It's all starting to make sense, O'Dell. Maybe it's some sick initiation ritual. Who knows how it works. But this also explains why the semen found in the Brier girl doesn't match the DNA of the skin under the nails. One of Everett's boys may have had that duty, while Everett took care of the rest."

"I don't believe this," Maggie said, and felt a new sense of tension instead of relief. Why was there no relief in knowing Everett and his gang were behind the murders? What was still nagging at her? Why did this all seem so easy? She could see Everett orchestrating all of this, but somehow she couldn't see his getting his hands dirty or getting close enough to get under Ginny Brier's fingernails.

"Cunningham's kinda pissed you're not here yet. He's been looking for you." Then Racine's voice came almost in a whisper as she added, "Actually, he looks more worried than pissed. Where did you say you were?"

"Getting to exit 148 now."

"Good. An HRT unit and some agents are headed out to Everett's compound now. The Rappahannock County officials are meeting them out there. In fact, they might already be there."

"Oh, Jesus! They're on their way to the compound now?" The panic slipped. "Racine, my mom's a member of Everett's organization," Maggie said over the lump that suddenly obstructed her throat. "She may be out there at the compound."

CHAPTER 66

Quantico, Virginia

Tully stood over the table, sorting through a mess of photos, documents, police reports and computer printouts. Garrison's T-shirt and sweatpants were starting to smell. Why the hell did Racine bring this stuff out here? He tossed it beside the strange metal contraption set on the far corner of the table.

"Where is everyone?" O'Dell came rushing into the conference room, breathless, her hair tousled, her face flushed and her FBI windbreaker hanging off one shoulder.

He glanced at his watch. "Ganza went to get some dinner. Racine's around here somewhere. Cunningham's down in his office. He's been looking for you. Where the heck have you been? You look like hell."

"What about the HRT unit? Have they made it to the compound yet?"

"Haven't heard."

She went to the window and stared out at the darkness, as if hoping she could see the unit from there.

"They'll be careful," he said, and she glanced at him over her shoulder. "Why didn't you say anything sooner about your mom being a part of Everett's church?"

She came back from the window, stood on the opposite side of the table, in front of him. "Guess I didn't want to believe it myself. And then I thought I could just talk some sense into her. You know, warn her. Pretty stupid, huh?"

"Nah. I think we all like to believe we have some sort of powers of influence over family members. Like, of course they'd want our advice, our suggestions. Sometimes I think the only thing natural about families is that we happen to share some of the same DNA."

She managed a weak smile, and he was pleased that he could help. But then he realized it wasn't enough when she asked, "Is Gwen around?"

Of course, she'd want her best friend.

"No, I don't think Cunningham called her in. She was headed for her office when we got back from Boston. Maybe she's still there." He pretended not to care, but found himself wondering if Gwen was working late or home fixing some gourmet meal for herself in her cozy brownstone. Maybe spaghetti. He smiled, then caught himself, glanced at O'Dell to see if she noticed. She was looking over the mess. He was safe. Besides, Gwen wanted to forget it happened. And it probably was better that they do just that. He knew she was right.

He flipped through one of the many documents scattered over the table but wasn't taking any of it in. He should probably go home. Even if they brought in Everett and that kid, Brandon, there was nothing more they could do tonight. But he didn't want to go home. With Emma in Cleveland at her mom's, the house was too empty, too quiet. It would probably just give him time to think about Boston. That wasn't good—he was supposed be forgetting about Boston.

O'Dell started pacing, close to the table so she could review the messy pile. He watched her as her eyes darted over the crime scene photos, but instead of stopping, she kept pacing, looking at them with each sweep. Had she not been worried about her mother, she'd be straightening out the mess, organizing and sorting and putting things into her neat little piles, trying to create order out of everyone else's disorder. He wished she was doing just that. It unnerved him to see her like this.

Suddenly, she noticed something and stopped. She picked up two of the photos from Ginny Brier's crime scene and started looking from one to the other.

"What is it?"

"Not sure." And she set the photos down. The pacing began again.

"Do you have any idea what this stuff is and what it's doing here?" Tully pointed to the heap on the corner of the table. More than anything, he just wanted her attention. She was starting to spook him.

"Garrison left those things behind. Guess he was in a hurry this morning."

"And we're keeping them because…?"

She shrugged and this time stopped to pick up the lightweight contraption, turning it over in her hands. She fidgeted with it and accidently popped what was a security latch. The thing sprung open.

"It's a tripod," she said, setting it on the table.

Now Tully could see the small plate where a camera could be attached and the lever to tilt and swivel it around. Suddenly, he was beside her, staring at the tripod. He rushed around the table and started riffling through photos, plucking three, one from each crime scene out of the mess. Still not saying a word, he came back around to Maggie's side and placed the photos on the table next to the feet of the tripod. The photos were of the strange circular marks left in the dirt. In the photo from the FDR Memorial crime scene, there had been two, possibly three circular marks, spaced in such a way they could form a triangle.

"Is it possible?" he asked.

He had the tripod in his hands and was examining its feet and the length between them. Why hadn't he thought about it before? The tripod's feet would certainly leave similar marks in the dirt. While he turned the thing over, Maggie suddenly grabbed the two photos of Ginny Brier—the ones she had picked up earlier—and slapped them down on the table in front of Tully.

"Look at these two photos," she said. "Do you see anything different from one to the other?"

He set the tripod aside and picked up the photos to study them. They looked almost exactly the same, same pose, same angle. There was a flash mark at the bottom of one print where the photo ended just above Ginny Brier's hands, almost exactly where her wrists were. Tully wondered if perhaps it was some mark caused by the developing process, though he knew little about film or print processing.

"You mean this white mark at the bottom? This one has it, but the other doesn't."

"What do you think it is?"

"Not sure. Could just be a smudge from developing, couldn't it?"

"Doesn't it look more like the flash reflecting off of something?"

He looked again. "Yeah, I guess so. It's hard to tell. A reflection off of what, though?"

"How about handcuffs?"

He stared at the photo again, then remembered. "She wasn't wearing handcuffs when we found her."

"Exactly," she said, now excited as she grabbed two other

photos and slapped them down. "Now look at these two."
They were close-ups of the Brier girl's face, the dead eyes
wide open, staring directly at her audience. They, too, looked
the same.

"I'm not following, O'Dell."

"One is from the roll of film Garrison kept for himself. The
roll he used to sell shots to the *Enquirer.*"

"Okay. How can you tell? They look identical. Same angle,
same distance. Seems like he was trying really hard to dupli-
cate what he took for himself and what he took for us."

"Both photos are the same angle, same distance, same
shot, but taken at different times," O'Dell said, slowing down
her excitement, as if she was figuring out the puzzle as she
spoke.

"What are you talking about?"

"The eyes," she said. "Take a close look."

As she pointed to the corners of the eyes in each photo
Tully finally saw what she was talking about. In one photo
there were small clumps of the whitish-yellow eggs in the corners of her eyes. Tully wasn't an expert, but he knew blowflies
usually arrived within minutes to a few hours after death and
began laying their eggs immediately. Yet in the photo Garrison had kept for himself, the dead girl's eyes were completely
clear. There wasn't even the hint of infestation.

"That's impossible," he said, looking to O'Dell. "This
photo had to have been taken shortly after her death."

"Exactly."

Tully picked up the tripod again, now more certain than
ever that its feet had caused the strange indentations found at
the three crime scenes. "Which would mean he's on the scene
before the cops are. Just what the hell is Ben Garrison up to?"

"More important, how does he know about the murders before we do?"

"O'Dell, you're back," Cunningham interrupted. He carried a mug of coffee, sipping as he walked, as if he had no time or patience to do only one thing at a time.

"Any word if the agents arrived at the compound yet?" she asked him.

"Why don't you sit down," he told her, pointing to a chair.

Tully immediately felt his own muscles tense as he saw O'Dell's back straighten.

"It's another standoff, isn't it?" she wanted to know.

"Not exactly."

"Eve told me that Everett would never allow himself to be taken alive. He has them prepared for suicide drills. Just like those boys at the cabin." Her voice seemed calm, but Tully could see her right hand twisting the hem of her windbreaker into her fist. "He's refusing to give up, isn't he?"

"Actually..." Cunningham pulled off his eyeglasses and rubbed his eyes. Tully knew their boss wasn't the type to stall, but lately the man seemed a bit unpredictable. "Everett isn't there. He's gone. We think he might already be on his way to Ohio, maybe Colorado."

O'Dell looked relieved until Cunningham put a hand on her shoulder and said, "That's not all, Maggie. There were people still at the compound. Between the short time that the Hostage Rescue Team announced its presence and then actually gained access to the compound there must have been a panic. You're right about the suicide drill. HRT's not sure how many, but there are bodies."

CHAPTER 67

He closed his eyes and leaned his head back, but the nausea remained. How the hell could he have motion sickness? It was impossible. It had to be something else. Perhaps just the excitement, the anticipation for the inevitable climax.

The engines continued to rumble. He hated having them so close. He tried to let the sound relax him. He tried to concentrate on the next step, the last step. He just needed to keep steady. He was almost out of his homemade concoction. He couldn't afford to take any until it was absolutely necessary. He'd need to wait. He could do that. He could be patient. Patience was a virtue. His mother had written that somewhere in one of her journal entries. So much patience. So much wisdom.

Then he realized he didn't have the book. Damn it! How the hell could he have forgotten it?

CHAPTER 68

Kathleen O'Dell lay her head back against the seat and tried to let the rumbling of the bus lull the throbbing at her temples. She knew exactly what would get rid of the pain, but unfortunately, there hadn't been a drop of alcohol in sight. She had even raided the cafeteria's medicine cabinet, hoping to find some cough medicine. Instead, all she had found was a plastic bag full of red-and-white headache capsules. Now she wished she had taken several of them to stop this insistent banging in her head.

The girl named Alice sat quietly in the aisle seat beside her, but her eyes kept looking over at the young man who had helped Kathleen earlier in the cafeteria. Now she couldn't remember his name. Why did she have such a problem remembering names? Or was it just because too much was happening? Her eyes still stung. Her ears were still ringing with the memory of those insults, those verbal jabs. And, of course, the physical jabs—she could feel the bruises. She just wanted to forget. She just wanted to sleep, to pretend everything was okay. And maybe everything would be as soon as they got to Colorado.

She noticed Alice's glances getting longer, braver now that all the inside lights on the bus had been extinguished, except for the bright green floor tracking lights. "You like him, don't you?" she whispered to Alice.

"What?"

"The boy across the aisle that you keep looking at. Justin."

Even in the dim light, Kathleen could see Alice blush, the freckles even more pronounced.

"We're just friends," Alice said. "You know Father doesn't allow anything more. We must keep ourselves chaste and our bodies pure." It sounded like she was reading the words off a pamphlet.

"I think he's very nice." She ignored Alice's benediction and nodded her chin in his direction. "And quite handsome."

Another blush, but this time it came with a smile. "I think he's upset with me, but I don't know why."

"Did you ask him?"

"Yes."

"And what did he say?"

"He told me he was just tired. That everything was fine."

Kathleen leaned closer to the girl. "It's been my experience with men that they're just as confused as we are. If he says he's just tired, he may just be tired."

"Really? You think so?"

"Sure."

It seemed to bring the girl relief and she relaxed in her seat. "I was worried, because I really don't have very much experience with boys."

"Really? A pretty girl like you?"

"My parents were always very strict. They never even let me date."

"Where are your parents now?"

Alice got quiet, and Kathleen wished she hadn't pried.

"They died in a car accident two years ago. A month later, I went to one of Father's rallies. It was like he could see how lost and alone I was. I don't know what I would have done if I hadn't found the church. I have no other family." She was quiet for a while, then she looked at Kathleen. "Why did you join the church?"

Good question, she wanted to tell the girl. For the last twenty-four hours she had been asking herself that very same thing. She needed to remember all the good things she had found since joining, like self-respect and dignity. Things the alcohol had stolen from her. Yet, after tonight's humiliation... It was hard to think of anything except sleep.

"I'm sorry," Alice said. "You probably don't want to talk about stuff like that after tonight's meeting."

"No, it's okay." She wanted to tell the girl that she hadn't betrayed the church. That she hadn't told Maggie anything and she wasn't sure why Stephen thought she had. But she knew it wouldn't matter to Alice or probably any of the other members. Most of them were simply relieved they hadn't been the ones called up. "I suppose I was lost in a different sort of way," Kathleen finally said.

"You don't have any family, either, huh?"

"I have a daughter. A beautiful, smart, young woman."

"I bet she looks a lot like you. You're very pretty."

"Well, thank you, Alice. It's been a long time since someone has said that to me." Tonight she certainly didn't feel pretty.

"So why aren't you with your daughter?"

"We have a...well, a strained relationship. She's been angry with me for more years than I can remember."

"Angry? Why would she be angry with you?"

"Lots of reasons. But mostly because I'm not her father."

"What?"

She saw the confusion on Alice's face and smiled. "It's a long, boring story, I'm afraid." She patted Alice's hand. "Why don't you try to get some sleep?"

She rested her own head against the seat again, but now her mind was filled with thoughts about Maggie and thoughts about Thomas. Dear God, she hadn't thought of him in years. At least, not without getting angry all over again. Maggie still idolized the man. And Kathleen had promised herself years ago to never tell Maggie the truth about her father. So why had she? Why now after all these years?

She remembered the disbelief, the hurt on Maggie's face. The surprise when she slapped her. Those sad, brown eyes— they were the eyes of a twelve-year-old little girl who still loved her daddy so much. How in the world could she have tried to destroy that? And why would she want to? What was wrong with her? No wonder her own daughter didn't love her. Maybe she didn't deserve her love. But Thomas didn't, either.

Kathleen still remembered getting the phone call from the fire station in the middle of the night. The dispatcher had been calling in every available man to answer the three-alarm blaze. She had lied to the dispatcher and told her Thomas was upstairs, asleep. And then she had to call him. She hated that she knew exactly where he was. And she hated even more that she had to call him at that woman's apartment. But she had to. She had no choice but to call and give him the message, so that no one else would know the lie.

She had always imagined she had interrupted their love-making, their passionate sex-fests, which Thomas had told her she wasn't capable of. Maybe that was why she had spent the last twenty years trying to prove him wrong, sleeping with any man who wanted her, and unlike Thomas, there had been plenty of men who *had* wanted her. But back then, that particular day, she had vowed to herself that she wouldn't take it anymore, that she would take Maggie and leave. And then the son of a bitch had to go and get himself killed. Not only killed but made into a hero.

There had been many times she'd wondered what Maggie would think of her saintly, heroic father if she knew the truth. So many times in a drunken fit, she had come close to telling her. But somehow she had always managed to stop herself.

After Thomas's death, she had moved as far away as she could. It was part of the pact she had made with the devil, with the whore who claimed she was carrying Thomas's child. In order to keep Maggie from knowing the truth about her father, she had to also keep Maggie from knowing her half brother. At the time it seemed a small price to pay. It had seemed like the right thing to do. But now she wasn't sure.

The other day Maggie had been so angry, so unwilling to accept the truth about her father. Would she also not want to accept that she had a brother, a half brother who had been kept from her for all these years? Would she be too angry to believe?

The woman had even named the boy Patrick, after Thomas's brother who had been killed in Vietnam. Kathleen wondered if he looked like Thomas. He'd be a young man now—twenty-one years old, the same age Thomas was when they first met.

Kathleen felt a tap on her shoulder and looked up to find Reverend Everett standing in the aisle. He smiled at Alice, and then to Kathleen he said, "There are some things we need to discuss, Kathleen. Perhaps we can discuss them in my compartment."

She crawled over Alice and followed him to the small space at the back of the bus. Her knees were unsteady and her stomach tense. He hadn't said a word to her since her punishment ceremony. Was he still upset?

The compartment was small, with a bed that filled most of the area and a tiny bathroom in the corner next to a desk. She could hear the roar of the engines. He closed the door behind them, and Kathleen heard him turn the lock.

"I know how painful that was for you tonight, Kathleen," he said in such a soft, gentle voice that she immediately felt relieved. "I would have stepped in, but it would have looked as though I was playing favorites, and that would have only made it harder on you. I do care about you and that's why I'm willing to do this special favor for you."

He motioned for her to sit on the bed and make herself comfortable. Despite his soft and gentle voice, she saw a coldness in his eyes that she didn't recognize, that unnerved her. She sat, anyway, not wanting to make him upset, especially if he was willing to do some special favor for her. He had been so kind in the past.

"I'm very sorry," she offered, not knowing what explanation he hoped to receive. She knew he didn't like it when members made excuses, and no matter what she told him, he might misconstrue it as an excuse.

"Well, that's in the past. With my special graces, I'm sure you'll not betray us like that again."

"Of course," she said.

Then with that same cold look in his eyes, he began unzipping his pants while he said to her, "I'm doing this for your own good, Kathleen. Now you must take off all your clothes."

CHAPTER 69

Gwen found Maggie down in her office, curled in the overstuffed chair, her legs thrown over an arm, a stack of files resting on her chest, her eyes closed. Without saying a word, she let go of Harvey's leash and gave him a pat on the hind end, telling him it was okay to go to his master. He didn't hesitate and didn't ask for permission to put his huge paws up on the chair to reach Maggie's face and begin licking.

"Hey, you!" Maggie grabbed the dog's head and hugged him. He jumped back when the file folders opened and the contents started sliding down on top of him. "It's okay, big guy," Maggie reassured him, but she was already out of her comfortable position and on her feet by the time Gwen came over to help pick up crime scene photos and lab reports.

"Thanks for bringing him," Maggie said. She stopped and waited until Gwen met her eyes. "And thanks for coming."

"Actually I was glad you called." The truth was Gwen had been surprised, not by the call but by the request. Harvey may have started out as a good excuse, but Gwen had heard the vulnerability in Maggie's voice immediately, long before her friend quietly told her, "I need you here, Gwen. Can you please come?"

Gwen hadn't hesitated. She had left linguine in a colander in the sink, a pot of homemade Alfredo sauce probably now congealing on a cold stove. She was out the door and in her car, heading for Quantico by the time Maggie finished giving her what scant details were available. "So what's the plan?" she asked. "Or do you even know?"

"You mean since I don't get to participate?"

Gwen studied her friend's eyes. There was no anger. Good. "You know it's best that you don't. You do know that, right?"

"Sure." But Maggie was watching Harvey investigate the corners of her office, pretending to be distracted by his curiosity. "Cunningham says the government has an informant. Someone who just recently came forward. He works in Senator Brier's office and he's also a member of Everett's church. His name's Stephen Caldwell."

Gwen helped herself to a Diet Pepsi from the minifrig in the corner of Maggie's office. She looked up at Maggie. "No Scotch?" Maggie smiled at her and held out her hand, so Gwen grabbed another Pepsi. "This informant," she said, "how do we know he's not double-crossing us, too? How do we know that he can be trusted?"

"I'm not convinced that he can be. For one thing, it may have been Caldwell who used his high-level security clearance to gain access to those retired weapons, the ones found at the cabin. But Cunningham tells me it was Caldwell who arranged my secret meeting with Eve." She saw Gwen's question before she asked. "Eve is an ex-member. I talked to her when you and Tully were in Boston."

"Ah, yes. Boston." Gwen felt uncomfortable at the mere

mention of the trip, but Maggie didn't seem to notice. As far as Gwen knew, Maggie hadn't even heard about Eric Pratt's attempt on her life. No sense in bringing it up now. "If Caldwell has been stealing weapons and possibly leaking classified information to Everett, why is he suddenly willing to help the government?"

"Evidently, he's grown attached to Senator Brier and his family." Maggie wrestled a tennis shoe away from Harvey. "Ginny's murder shook up Caldwell's loyalties. He claims he's convinced Everett that they need to proceed to Cleveland, that Everett doesn't know about the arrest warrants, only about the negative media attention. Caldwell claims we can safely arrest Everett and Brandon in Cleveland at the prayer rally, in public with little resistance and no threat of Everett being able to stage a standoff. That Everett won't be expecting such a public arrest and will be taken completely by surprise."

"Wait a minute," Gwen interrupted. "If Everett didn't know about the warrants, then what about the dead bodies the FBI's Hostage Rescue Team found?"

"Cunningham said the unit announced themselves. Too many booby traps around the compound to sneak in. They think those left behind got scared, did the one thing they were prepared to do when the FBI came knocking at their door."

"Jesus! Are we sure they weren't in contact with Everett?"

"That we don't know for sure. But there wasn't a whole lot of time. It happened quickly."

"But what about Caldwell?"

"He was informed about the arrest warrants. He wasn't tipped off about the raid. It was meant to be a surprise. A surprise so no one would get hurt."

At this, Maggie avoided Gwen's eyes again. She noticed Harvey scooting under her desk and reached down, rescuing the tennis shoe's mate. She set the pair on the bookcase, out of his reach. The big dog sat and watched as if waiting for compensation. Gwen watched, too, quietly waiting for Maggie to continue. She knew the distraction was intentional. Maggie was doing an excellent job of giving her all the difficult details while sidestepping the subject of her mother. Even Gwen remembered the countless times Maggie had mentioned her mother's new friends, Emily and Stephen. This Stephen Caldwell had to be the same Stephen.

"And Caldwell's conflicted loyalties," Gwen finally said, "how do they affect your mother and her safety?"

"That I don't know. As far as we know, Caldwell is still with Everett. And so is my mother." She sat back down in the chair and Harvey went to her, laying his head in her lap as if this was an expected routine. Maggie absently petted him while leaning her head back into the soft cushion. "I tried to talk to her about Everett. We ended up…it was pretty awful."

Gwen knew to be quiet. Maggie had shared very little about her childhood, and what Gwen knew of Maggie and her mother's relationship came from hints, personal observations over the years and a few rare and accidental admissions from Maggie. She knew about the alcohol abuse and learned about the suicide attempts only after the fact, even though there had been several attempts within the time since Gwen and Maggie had become friends. But Maggie had kept her mother and their relationship off-limits, and whether it was right or wrong, Gwen had allowed it, hoping that one day Maggie would decide on her own to share that obvious struggle. Even tonight and under the present circumstances, Gwen expected little insight, little sharing. She leaned against the corner of Maggie's desk and waited, just in case.

"She always does and says such hurtful things," Maggie said quietly without moving her head from the back of the cushion, avoiding Gwen's eyes. "Not just to me but to herself. It's like she's been spending a lifetime trying to punish me."

"Why in the world would she want to punish you, Maggie?"

"For loving my father more than I love her."

"Maybe it's not you she's trying to punish."

Maggie looked up at her with watery eyes. "What do you mean?"

"Could be she's not trying to punish you at all. Did it ever occur to you that all these years she may have been trying to punish herself?"

CHAPTER 70

THURSDAY
November 28
Thanksgiving Day
Cleveland, Ohio

Kathleen looked out over Lake Erie and for the first time in years found herself homesick for Green Bay, Wisconsin. An unseasonably warm breeze ruffled her hair. She wished she could forget everything and leave it all behind her like one more black mark in her past. She wished she could take off her shoes, run down to the beach and spend the rest of the day, the rest of the week, the rest of her life walking with no destination, no intention other than to feel the sand between her toes.

"Cassie will begin to lead the prayer rally," Reverend Everett said from behind her.

She looked over her shoulder without moving from her place in front of the open patio door. Reverend Everett had checked into a ritzy hotel in order to shower, shave and have access to a telephone to finalize their arrangements. Earlier, when she used the bathroom, Kathleen had been amazed at the wonderful luxuries: perfumed soaps, a shoe-shine kit, a real razor with a real blade instead of the disposable kind, a shower cap and even a jar filled with Q-Tips.

Now, while Stephen and Emily took notes and concentrated on everything Reverend Everett was telling the three of them, Kathleen stood quietly, enjoying the sunshine and the breeze.

She felt like she needed to learn how to breathe again after last night's humiliating ritual and then the cramped bus ride. She hoped the fresh air and sunlight would help wipe away the feel of Everett's hot breath, the sounds of his grunts and groans while he thrust himself into her over and over again. When he was finished, he had pointed to her clothes, instructing her to get dressed with a coldness in his voice that she had never heard before. He had told her she needed this cleansing ritual in order for him to be able to trust her again.

Without a word, she had slipped her clothes on over her sticky flesh, the smell of his aftershave so pungent she wanted to gag. And as she left his compartment to return to her seat, she couldn't help thinking he had also cleansed her of every last remaining bit of her self-respect.

"The FBI will most likely be surrounding the park," Stephen said. "Father, you can't possibly think of showing up at the prayer rally."

"What time will the cargo plane be ready?"

"It's scheduled for a seven o'clock takeoff. We must be there early to board."

"How can we be certain the FBI won't be waiting at the airport?"

"Because I told them you would be at the rally. That you wouldn't expect an arrest in such a public arena. Even if they do suspect something, they might be waiting at the international airport. However, they won't even think to check a government relief-aid cargo jet leaving from Cuyahoga County Airport."

Reverend Everett rewarded Stephen with a smile. "Very good. You're a good man, Stephen. You will be justly rewarded when we get to South America. I promise you that."

The reverend sat down to finish the platter he had ordered from room service; a platter with several different cheeses, fresh fruits, shrimp cocktail and a loaf of French bread. He made no offer for the others to join him. Instead, Kathleen thought he looked as though he enjoyed having them watch him, and before he had even gotten started on this tray, he had called down to place a whole new order.

None of them had eaten since yesterday's lunch, and it was almost dinnertime. Was this yet another important lesson, another important sacrifice that they were supposed to willingly accept? She turned back to the tranquil view of the water. At the moment, it seemed to be the only thing that didn't threaten to rip away at her sanity.

"You honestly don't intend to go to the rally?" Stephen asked again.

"I suppose I can stay here until it's time to leave." He waved a hand as if making do with his current surroundings. "But the three of you will need to be my eyes and ears at the rally. You'll need to gather those on the list when the time comes. Cassie will keep the rally going so as to give the appearance that everything is as scheduled."

Kathleen turned at this, stunned by the realization. "You don't want Cassie to come with us?"

The woman had attended to Reverend Everett's every command and probably desire for as long as Kathleen could remember.

"She's a lovely woman, Kathleen, but I'm quite certain there are many beautiful dark-skinned women in South America who would probably give anything to be my personal assistant."

She turned back to the sunshine, wondering if it would have been any different had they been able to go to Colorado. If Reverend Everett would have been any different. Or had he always been this way, and she was the one who was changing, who was seeing things differently?

"Now, you all must go," he said while still chewing. He took a drink of wine as if to cleanse his palate. It was certainly not to be polite, because he took a bite out of a huge strawberry, the juice dripping down his chin, his mouth full again as he said, "Go now. The rally will be getting started soon. No one will be suspicious if my faithful counsel is there waiting for me."

Stephen and Emily didn't hesitate. They waited at the door for Kathleen.

"Oh, Kathleen." Reverend Everett stopped her. "Find Alice and send her up to my room. I have some things I need to discuss with her before the trip."

Kathleen stared at him for a minute. Did he honestly have something to discuss with the girl or did he have another of his cleansing rituals in mind? Did she dare say anything? Could she afford to make him angry with her again? Did she even care? She decided she would conveniently forget to tell Alice, but she nodded and followed Stephen and Emily out.

She slipped her hand into the pocket of her cardigan. She caressed the metal razor she had stolen from the bathroom. It gave her an odd sense of relief and calm to know it was there, a comfort as if it were an old friend. Yes, an old friend, this simple metal razor with the real metal blade.

This time she would finally get it right.

CHAPTER 71

"Come in," Everett yelled, not even bothering to check whom he was allowing to enter his hotel room. Could it possibly be any easier?

He smiled and rolled the room service tray into the room. Then he waited. The excitement, the anticipation was better than any homemade concoction the Zulu tribe could brew. After all, this was the moment he had been waiting for all along. And so he stood patiently and waited as if expecting a tip.

Finally Everett turned, his hand ready to wave him away, when his eyes swept across his face, then back. A quick double take.

"You? What the hell are you doing here?"

"Thought I might bring you a treat, a surprise before your last rally."

"I would think you'd be down wandering around, looking for another young girl. Looking for ways to destroy me."

"I can't take all the credit."

Everett shook his head, discounting him, unafraid as if he were one of his ordinary followers. "Go away," he told him. "Go and leave me alone. I'm tired of your shenanigans. You're lucky to have gotten away with only warnings."

"Right. Only warnings. Is that because you wouldn't dare hurt your own son? Is that the only reason I've been so lucky?"

Everett stared at him. But there was no surprise. Had he known all along? No. It was impossible. It was simply another one of his performances.

"How did you find out?" His voice was calm, steady.

Oh, Jesus! He did know. Did it make this more difficult? Or no, it would make it easier. The bastard knew. All these years and he knew.

"She told you before she died," Everett said, as if he had known all about it, as if her death was something he shared. He had no right and yet he continued, "I read about her death. I think it was in the *New York Times* or perhaps the *Daily News*. You know I did care about her. Did she tell you that, too?"

He wouldn't listen. It was lies. "No, she didn't tell me that. She managed to leave that part out of her journal." He needed to confine the anger, but the concoction had already begun to seep into his system, and Everett's words felt like hot, liquid lava scalding his brain, contaminating his memories. "But she did mention what you did to her. There are pages and pages about that. About what kind of a bastard you really are."

He felt his fingers twisting into fists. Yes, he'd let the anger fuel him. The anger and the precious words of his mother, that mantra he had memorized from her journal entries. Her words had empowered him throughout his mission. They wouldn't fail him now.

"I wondered when you would find out." Everett's voice still

sounded too calm, not a hint of fear. "I knew it was only a matter of time. I thought perhaps that was what all this was about—all those young girls. You were trying to get back at me, weren't you?"

"Yes."

"You wanted to hurt me." Everett smiled as he gave him a nod of confirmation, almost acceptance, as if it was exactly what he had expected from a son of his. "Maybe you even wanted to punish me?"

"Yes."

"Destroy my reputation."

"Destroy you."

The smile disappeared.

"There's only one thing left now," he said, picking up the tray from the room service cart. He held it out to Everett, and with his other hand lifted the insulated cover. The tray was empty except for one small red-and-white capsule, sitting on a perfectly folded cloth napkin.

CHAPTER 72

Justin looked for Father or even his henchmen. Already, the pavilion was jam-packed with giggling teenagers mixed in between the others, an odd assortment with little in common except that they all looked like lost souls. They were fucking pathetic, is what they were. Though he had to hand it to Father. There were plenty who looked like they would be ideal recruits and gullible donors.

He had spent the night on the bus trying to plot a strategy and the entire afternoon scoping out as much as he could see of Cleveland. Someone had told him that Edgewater Park was on the west side of Cleveland. There was a circular lot adjacent to the upper section of the park, overlooking the downtown area. Still, he had no idea where the hell he would go. All he knew was that he had to escape while the rally was going on. He'd need to find a way to duck out without Alice or Brandon noticing. Where he'd go seemed a small detail at the moment.

He dug his hands into both his jeans pockets and made sure the wads of bills hadn't disappeared. Then he pulled down the hem of his T-shirt to make sure the bulge couldn't be seen. He wasn't even sure how much he had taken.

While the men who were digging up the strongboxes hauled each box to the bus, Justin stole two fistfuls. He was in such a hurry, all he took time to do was open one of the boxes, reach in and grab and stuff his pockets. Later, he tried to pick out the mothballs and smooth the bills into a neat, folded wad. Then he helped the women at the bonfire, standing in the smoke so he would smell like burnt trash and not mothballs.

He couldn't help wondering what good the money would do if he had no fucking place to go. He saw Cassie walking to the stage. She waved to the crowd, and the sight of the long purple choir robe she wore got them clapping. Soon she'd have them singing, too. This might be a good time.

Justin looked down at the bike trail and the beach below. There was a statue near the pavilion and some playground equipment. There wasn't much cover, all the trees were back behind. But he'd already checked. There was a six-foot fence on the other side of the trees, a dead end.

Down by the beach he could see a fishing pier and about ten boat ramps, all empty this time of year. He wondered how hard it would be to take a boat without anyone noticing. Except on the bus ride to the park, he thought he had noticed a Coast Guard station not far from here. Shit! This wasn't going to be easy.

"Hey, Justin." Alice waved to him as she weaved her way through the crowd to join him.

Shit! It just got harder.

"I've been looking for you." She smiled.

Why did she have to be so fucking pretty? And damn, she

had on another tight sweater, this one blue, and he couldn't help noticing how fucking beautiful blue her eyes were.

"Why were you looking for me? Do you need something?" He needed to play out the role of complete asshole, or he'd never be able to pull this off.

The wounded look in those blue eyes just about ripped his heart out.

"No, I don't need anything. I just wanted to…you know, be with you. Is that okay?"

Shit! Double shit! He couldn't do this.

"Yeah, I guess," he said, and felt like he had just tossed away his entire plan.

"Hi, Alice, Justin." The woman named Kathleen squeezed through to get to them. Justin couldn't believe she remembered his name. She hadn't been in very good shape last night during their introductions. "I'm glad to see you kids together." She smiled at Alice, and Justin thought he saw Alice blush. Then suddenly, Kathleen looked sad, the smile replaced with almost a frown as she squeezed Alice's shoulder and said, "You kids take care of each other, okay? No matter what happens."

Then she left them, only she was headed in the wrong direction back toward the exit. Maybe she needed to use the rest room. Justin thought he had seen them back that way.

"She's really a nice woman. We talked about a lot of stuff last night," Alice said in her soft voice. "She helped me see a lot of things."

"What kinds of things?" he asked, but his eyes were scanning the surroundings again, looking, hoping for a miracle.

"Things like how much you mean to me and how I don't want to lose you."

He stopped and stared at her. She reached for his hand and intertwined her fingers with his.

"I care about you, Justin. Please just tell me what I can do to make things right with us again."

God, her hand felt good in his, like it belonged. Was she being straight with him, or was this another of Father's tricks? Before he could say anything Brandon appeared from out of nowhere.

"Alice," he said, scowling down at their hands with some kind of power that made Alice pull hers away. "Father wants to see you before the prayer rally. You need to come with me."

She looked up at Justin, apologetic, almost pained. He immediately wondered if Father had yet another lesson for her. Nah, there wasn't much time. Cassie already had the crowd all revved up.

He watched Brandon lead Alice away, taking some weird shortcut up through the trees. What the hell was Father doing up there, anyway? Probably some strange ritual he does to prepare.

He scanned the crowd again. How much time did he have before Brandon, Alice and Father came back down? Could they see him from up above? Shit! He was fucked.

Then, just as he turned, he recognized a tall blonde at the edge of the bike trail, waving at him. It took him a minute. He probably would have remembered who she was sooner if she was with her short, blond bookend. He smiled and waved, noticing that she was away from the stage and with an older woman who looked enough like her to be her mother. Maybe that meant they had come in a car.

He started toward them, feeling a surge of excitement again, starting to actually believe in miracles.

CHAPTER 73

Tully tried to blend into the crowd. It took him a minute to pick out the plainclothes agents from the Cleveland field office. They were scattered throughout the park. If Everett expected to find the place crawling with men in black, he wouldn't be able to pick them out. All of them were in place, and they were ready. Tully knew most of the agents, though he could hardly recognize them in their ordinary, everyday disguises. He had worked with this group on plenty of cases before his transfer to the District. In fact, it felt comfortable being back home.

He looked for Racine and spotted her close to the rest rooms at the back exit of the park. He had to admit, in her baseball cap, worn blue jeans, a borrowed Cleveland Indians T-shirt and her leather bomber jacket, she looked like one of the locals, checking out the pavilion's excitement. No one probably even noticed her mumbling into the cuff of her jacket or the bulge at the back of her waistband. Whatever O'Dell's misgivings about Racine, the detective was doing a hell of a job. Maybe it was simply the threat of suspension or possible demotion. Chief Henderson was still adamant about a discipline review board. Perhaps Racine was trying to make up for past mistakes. Whatever it was, Tully didn't care. The important thing was that she not screw this up.

The prayer rally had started without Reverend Everett, but according to Stephen Caldwell, the good reverend would be here anytime now. Although none of them had seen Everett or even Caldwell, for that matter. In the meantime, a beautiful black woman in a purple choir robe had the crowd stomping, clapping and singing at the top of their lungs. Tully could barely hear the other agents, checking in. He tapped his earpiece just to make sure it was functioning properly.

"Tully," he heard Racine whisper in his right ear. "Any sign of him?"

"No, not yet." He glanced around just to make certain no one noticed he was talking to himself. "But it's early. Any sign of Garrison?"

There was a buzz, then, "I thought I saw him when we first got here. Not sure if it was him, though."

"Keep an eye out for him. He can probably lead us to the action."

Just then, he noticed the kid, the tall redhead, going up the hill on the opposite side from him. He had a girl with him, a girl with long blond hair. Immediately, he was reminded of Emma.

"Here we go," he said into his cuff. "Southeast end of the pavilion, headed for the trees on the hill. I'm going up. I'll wait for backup."

He glanced over at Racine, who seemed distracted, looking in the opposite direction toward the rest rooms.

"Is everyone clear?" Tully whispered to all the agents but meant it for Racine.

Hers was the only voice he didn't hear check in. And now he couldn't see where she went. Damn it! What the hell was she up to? He didn't have time to rein her in. The kid, Brandon, was already leading his next victim up into the trees. Tully squeezed through the crowd, not taking his eyes off the pair. He remained so focused that he practically slammed into an attractive blond woman without stopping. It wasn't until she grabbed his elbow that he turned back.

"R.J. What in the world are you doing here?"

"Caroline?"

Then Tully saw Emma and his stomach began to knot.

"What are you doing in Cleveland?" his ex-wife demanded.

"I'm here on business," he said quietly, trying not to draw attention. Caroline's face already sprouted lines of anger. Yet, all Tully could think about was getting his daughter as far the hell away from this park as he could.

"I just can't believe you'd pull a stunt like this," Caroline was saying now, but she was looking at Emma instead of him. "So is this the reason you wanted to come here tonight, because you knew your father would be here?"

Tully looked at Emma, and her face went red. He could be dense sometimes, but evidently, he knew his daughter better than her mother did. He knew Emma was here because of the athletic-looking young man beside her. The young man whose eyes had been darting around everywhere as if he wanted to be anyplace but here.

"Please, Caroline," he tried again, taking her by the elbow to lead her away from the crowd.

"You two think this is funny?"

"No, not at all." He kept his voice as calm as he could while trying to yell over the noise. "Can we talk about this later?"

"Yeah, Mom, you're really embarrassing me."

Tully glanced around, looking to see if anyone was watching them. But everyone seemed fixated on the stage. His eyes scanned the area, and suddenly he could no longer see Brandon or the girl. Jesus! It was happening.

He couldn't use his mike or Caroline would really blow his cover. Instead, he turned back to Emma and the young man, meeting the boy's eyes and addressing him more than Emma. "Please, get out of this area now."

Then he left them, ignoring the new list of names Caroline called him in front of their daughter. He pushed through the crowd, whispering into his cuff to the others, letting them know what he was doing and trying to find out what the hell Racine was doing.

Again, she was the only one not to respond.

CHAPTER 74

Kathleen checked all the bathroom stalls. Good. The place was empty. She wished she could lock the door. But there was no lock on the inside. No chair to shove against the handle. Maybe it wouldn't matter. She could hear the rally had already begun. Hopefully, she wouldn't be interrupted.

She starting filling one of the sinks with lukewarm water. The water kept stopping. One of those conservation faucets. Damn it! At this rate, it would take forever. She punched the "on" faucet again and laid out paper towels on the counter. Silly, really. Why would she need paper towels?

She reached into her pocket and pulled out the razor blade she had confiscated from Reverend Everett's hotel bathroom, a real razor with a real metal blade. Her fingers shook as she tried to pop the blade out of the razor. It took several attempts.

Why couldn't she keep her fingers from shaking? This was ridiculous. It wasn't like it was her first time.

Finally!

She laid the blade carefully, almost reverently, on one of the paper towels. The stupid water had shut off again. Another punch. The sink would never fill at this rate. Maybe she didn't need it to. Maybe she didn't care whether it hurt or not. Maybe she just didn't care anymore about anything.

She glanced around the bathroom and stopped when she saw her reflection in the mirror, meeting her own eyes, almost afraid to look too closely. She didn't want to see the betrayal, the accusations, the guilt or even the failure. Because this time she had tried to make things work. She really had. She had stopped drinking. She thought she had found some sense of direction, some sense of self-respect. But she was wrong. She had even tried telling Maggie the truth, the painful truth that made her own daughter only hate her more. There was nothing left.

She picked up the razor between her thumb and index finger just as the bathroom door opened.

The young woman stopped when she saw Kathleen, letting the door slam shut behind her. She wore a baseball cap over short blond hair and a leather bomber jacket with blue jeans and old scuffed boots. She stood exactly where she stopped, staring at Kathleen and recognizing the object in her hand. But the woman didn't look surprised or alarmed. Instead, she smiled and said, "You're Kathleen O'Dell, aren't you?"

Kathleen's heart began pounding, but she didn't move. She tried to place the young woman. She wasn't a member of the church.

"I'm sorry," the woman said, stepping forward, then stopping abruptly when Kathleen shifted. "We've never met before." She kept her voice friendly and calm despite her eyes which kept darting to the razor blade in Kathleen's hand.

"I'm Julia Racine. I know your daughter, Maggie. I can see the resemblance." She smiled again. "She has your eyes."

Kathleen felt the panic twisting in her stomach. Damn it! Why couldn't they all just go away and leave her. She gripped the blade tighter, felt it against her wrist, the sharp edge promising such warm silence, promising to shut off the throbbing in her head and plug up the hollow place deep inside her.

"Is Maggie here?" she asked, glancing at the door, almost expecting her daughter to come barging in to rescue her once again. Always the savior, pulling her up out of the darkness, even when Kathleen wanted, needed, longed for the darkness.

"No. Maggie's not here. She's back in the District." The woman, this Julia, looked unsure of herself now. Like maybe she shouldn't have told a truth when a lie would have sufficed. "You know I never got a chance to know my mother," she said, changing the subject quickly, but with such a smooth, steady voice that Kathleen didn't mind. She wasn't stupid. She knew what the woman was doing. But she was better at it than most. Almost as if she had some experience with talking people down off ledges.

Is that what she was doing? Trying to talk her off this ledge? It only worked if the person wanted to be talked down. Kathleen glanced at her wrist and could see blood dripping where she had started to cut. She hadn't realized she had done that. She certainly hadn't felt it. It surprised her that it didn't hurt. Was that a good sign? That it didn't hurt? When she looked back up she saw the woman had noticed, too, and before Julia Racine could snap back to her professional calm, Kathleen caught a glimpse of something else in the woman's eyes. Something…maybe doubt, maybe fear. So she wasn't as cool and calm as she pretended.

"My mom," the woman continued, "died when I was a little girl. I remember things, you know, pieces of things, really. Like the scent of lavender. I guess it was her favorite perfume. Oh, and her humming. Sometimes I can hear her humming to me. But I never recognize the tune. It's soothing, though. Kinda like a lullaby."

She was rambling but still calm. It was distracting and Kathleen knew that was part of the game. It was a game, after all, wasn't it?

"You know, Maggie's really concerned about you, Kathleen."

She stared at her, but the blue eyes were strong, unflinching, no longer playing or maybe just very good at lying.

"She's so angry with me," Kathleen found herself saying without really meaning to.

"Just because we get angry with people we love, it doesn't mean we want them gone forever."

"She doesn't love me." She said this with almost a laugh, as if letting this Racine woman know that she could see through her lies.

"You are her *mother.* How could she not love you?"

"I've made it very easy. Believe me."

"Okay, so she's angry with you."

"It's more than that."

"Okay, sometimes she doesn't even like you very much. Right?"

Now Kathleen did laugh and nodded.

Julia Racine remained serious and said, "It doesn't mean she wants you gone forever."

When it looked like that sentimental stuff wouldn't work, the young woman smiled and added, "Look Mrs. O'Dell, I'm already in a shitload of trouble with your daughter. How 'bout giving me a break?"

CHAPTER 75

Tully almost stumbled over a jacket.

Jesus! He had already started.

Darkness had just begun to take over, and up here in the trees, it was hard to see. He waited. He tried to slow down his pulse. He needed to give his eyes a chance to adjust. The moon cast some light, but it also added an eerie blue tint to shadows.

Tully held his breath. He got down on his knees. He couldn't hear with all the noise from below. Did that mean anyone up here couldn't hear him, either? He couldn't take any chances. He heard the other agents checking in, whispering their positions into his ear, but he couldn't answer them. He had to ignore them. But they knew that, and they were still getting into position. It was so quiet. What if he was already too late?

He pulled out his gun and started crawling on hands and knees. That's when he saw them, only twenty feet away. He saw them on the ground, scuffling. He was on top. She was fighting, struggling.

But it looked like they were alone. Tully carefully looked around, examining the surroundings. There was no one else. No other young men, waiting or guarding the area. No Reverend Everett. Or did that come later? Did the good reverend wait until the struggle was over? And could Tully wait? Jesus! He was ripping her clothes. There was a slap, a whimper, more wrestling. Did he dare wait for Everett to show himself? Could he risk it?

He thought he heard a belt buckle, maybe a zipper. Another whimper. He thought of Emma. This girl wasn't much older. His eyes searched the trees. Movement on the right. One of the agents moving in. But no Everett.

Damn it!

He couldn't see any glowing clothesline. No handcuffs. Maybe all that stuff was Everett's job. If he interrupted now?

This time she cried out and Brandon slapped her again.

"Shut the fuck up and hold still," he hissed at her.

Without hesitation, Tully was on his feet. In just a few rushed steps he had the barrel of his Glock pressed at the base of Brandon's head even before the boy had a chance to flinch.

"No, you shut the fuck up, you bastard," Tully yelled into his ear, so he wouldn't miss a word. "Game's over."

CHAPTER 76

Washington, D.C.

Maggie drove down several unfamiliar streets but found the old building easily. It was an unsavory neighborhood where she'd probably need to worry about her little red Toyota. Three teenage boys watched her the entire time she parked her car and walked to the front door. It made her want to flash her holstered Smith & Wesson nestled under her jacket. Instead, she did the next best thing—she ignored them.

She wasn't sure why she was here, except that she was tired of waiting. She needed to do something, anything. She was just so tired of those old memories taunting her, making her feel guilty, that she was somehow responsible—once again—for her mother being in harm's way. She knew she wasn't responsible. Of course she knew that, but what she knew and what she felt were two entirely separate things.

The inside of the old building surprised Maggie. It was

clean, better than clean, with the scent of Murphy's Oil. As she climbed the wooden staircase, she noticed the walls had been freshly painted and the second-floor landing's carpet, though threadbare, showed not a spot of dirt. On the third level, however, she could smell something like a disinfectant, and the odor grew as she progressed down the hall. It seemed to be coming from number five, Ben Garrison's apartment.

She knocked and waited, though she didn't expect him to be here. He'd still be in Cleveland, only hopefully this time he hadn't gotten to the crime scene before everyone else. Tully and Racine had probably already arrested Everett and his accomplice, Brandon. They had DNA to prove Everett's guilt, eyewitnesses and photos to put Brandon with two of the victims minutes before their deaths. Case closed. So what was still nagging her? Maybe she simply hated that Garrison—that the "invisible cameraman"—had gotten away with screwing up crime scenes. Maybe she was curious about his apparent obsession with death, his voyeurism. Perhaps she simply needed to keep her mind preoccupied.

Maggie glanced down the hallway and knocked again. This time she heard scuffles on the staircase. A little gray-haired lady appeared on the landing, staring up at her through thick glasses.

"I think he's out of town," she told Maggie. But before Maggie could respond, she asked, "Are you from the health department? I don't have anything to do with those roaches. I want you to know, it was his doing."

Maggie's suit must have looked official. She didn't say a word, and yet the woman was scooting in front of her to unlock Garrison's door.

"I try to keep the place clean, but some of these tenants… Well, you just can't trust people these days." She opened the door and waved a hand at Maggie as she headed back to the staircase.

"Just close up when you're finished."

Maggie hesitated. What would it hurt to take a look?

The first thing to catch her eyes were the African death masks, three of them, on the wall over the cracked vinyl sofa. They had been carved from wood with paint-smeared tribal symbols across the forehead and cheeks and under the eyeholes. On the opposite wall were several black-and-white photographs, labeled portraits: Zulu, Three-Hill Tribe, Aborigine, Basuto, Andamanese. Garrison seemed obsessed with his subjects' eyes, sometimes cropping the forehead and chin in order to draw more focus to the eyes. A bottom photo, labeled: Tepchuane, showed what looked like the back of his subject's head, perhaps a defiant stance, a denial. One meaningful enough for Garrison to keep.

Maggie shook her head. She didn't have time to psychoanalyze Garrison, nor was she certain she would if she had the time. There was something odd about a man who could be so fascinated by ancient cultures and their people and yet stand back and watch young women be attacked in a public park. Or did Garrison consider everyone to be simply a photographic subject and nothing more?

At the police station, when she questioned him about the incident in Boston Common, he had said something strange about her having no idea what it took to stop or to make news happen. Yet, wasn't that exactly what he had been doing with Everett? His photos had broken the story about the church's members and their possible connection to the murder of the senator's daughter and the murder in Boston. But it went further than that. It was his photographs that caused Everett to initially even become a suspect. In a sense Garrison's photos had led them directly to Everett. He had made news happen.

Something skittered across the floor behind her. Maggie spun around. Three huge cockroaches escaped into a crack half their size under the kitchen counter.

Damn it!

She tried to settle her nerves. Cockroaches. Why did it not surprise her that Garrison would be surrounded by them?

But the landlady was correct in that Garrison's apartment did not match the spotless hall and the staircase, nor the rest of the aging but clean building. Discarded clothes trailed to the bedroom and bathroom. Crusty dishes and empty beer bottles littered the kitchen counter. Stacks of magazines and newspapers created leaning roach hotels in almost every corner. No, she shouldn't be surprised to see Garrison's roommates were cockroaches.

She wandered through the rooms, finding nothing interesting in his clutter. Although she wasn't sure what she expected to find. Suddenly, she stepped on a book that lay in the middle of the floor, as if someone had dropped it. The leather binding was clean and smooth. It was definitely not something he usually kept on the floor. On closer inspection she realized it was a journal, the pages filled with a lovely, slanted penmanship that sometimes took on a frantic urgency, easily visible by the dramatic changes in jagged lines and curves.

She picked it up and it opened to a page bookmarked with what looked to be an old unused airline ticket, the corners worn and creased. Destination was Uganda, Africa, though it certainly was long expired. The entry it marked was also dogeared, the only page with its gold-trim creased.

"Dear son," the entry began, "this is something I could never tell you. If you're reading it now, it's only after my death, and I apologize that this is the manner in which I have resorted to tell you. A coward's manner—it would certainly embarrass any Zulu tribe member. Please forgive me for that. But how could I possibly look into your sad and already angry eyes and tell you that your father had brutally raped me? Yes, that's right. Raped me. I was only nineteen. It was my first year in college. I had a brilliant career I was preparing for."

Maggie stopped and flipped to the beginning of the journal, looking for a name, a reference to the owner, and finding none. But she didn't need a name. She already knew whose journal it was. It certainly couldn't be a coincidence. But how had Garrison come across the book? Where in the world had he found it? Among Everett's personal belongings, perhaps? Would Everett have kept the journal of a woman he had raped more than twenty-five years ago? And how would he have gotten it?

She slipped the book into her jacket pocket. If Garrison had stolen it, he couldn't mind her borrowing it. She was ready to leave when she noticed a small room off the kitchen. It wouldn't have attracted her attention except that a faint red light glowed from inside. Of course, Garrison would have his own darkroom.

No. She was wrong, she realized as she opened the door. It wasn't just a darkroom. It was a gold mine.

Prints were strung on a clothesline that stretched the length of the small room. Chemicals had been left in the plastic trays, lining the inside of an oversize sink. Bottles and canisters and developing tanks filled the shelves. And there were prints everywhere, overlapping one another and covering every bit of space on the walls and counter.

There were more prints of tribes doing their ceremonial dances. Prints of Africans with hideous scars. Prints of strange mutant frogs with legs coming out of their heads.

And then she saw them—prints of dead women.

There must have been about a dozen prints. Women naked and braced against trees, eyes wide open with duct tape across their mouths and their wrists handcuffed. Maggie recognized Ginny Brier, the transient they had found under the viaduct, the floater pulled from the lake outside of Raleigh and Maria Leonetti. But there were others. At least a half dozen others. All in the same pose. All with their eyes wide open, looking directly at the camera.

Jesus! How long had this been going on? And how long had Garrison been following Everett and his boys?

Her hand reached for the light switch without looking to find it. She couldn't take her eyes away from the dead women's eyes. Surely there was a light other than the red safe-light. She found the set of switches and flipped one, causing the entire room to go black. But before she could flip the other one on, she stood paralyzed, staring in disbelief. The clothes-line that stretched across the room glowed in the dark.

She leaned against the counter. Her knees went weak. Her stomach plunged. The clothesline glowed in the dark. Of course, what a perfect invention for a darkroom. What a perfect weapon for a killer.

How could she have been so stupid! Garrison didn't just photograph the dead women. It wasn't dead eyes that interested him. The eyes are the windows to the soul. Why hadn't she thought of it before? Was Garrison trying to photograph the fleeting soul?

She flipped on the red light again and took a closer look at the photos, the track marks on the victims' necks. Over and over again, he must have brought them back to consciousness, posing them, waiting, patiently waiting for that one moment while he watched with his camera ready on a tripod nearby, waiting. Waiting over and over again to catch a glimpse, to photograph that moment when the soul left.

Garrison. It was Garrison and his obsession with that last moment of death.

Maggie heard the creak of floorboards in the living room. She grabbed for her gun. No cockroach was that fucking big. Was it the landlady? Maybe the real health inspector had arrived. It couldn't be Garrison. He was in Cleveland.

She inched her way to the darkroom's door, edging along the counter. Another creak, this time louder, closer, just on the other side of the door. She took aim, holding the gun with both hands and ignoring the slight tremor in her knees. Then in one quick motion she kicked open the darkroom door and rushed out, pointing her gun and yelling "Freeze!"

It was Garrison.

He stood in the middle of his apartment over the frightened landlady, holding a length of clothesline around her neck, yanking on it like a leash. The old lady was on her small bony knees, gasping for air, her glasses gone, her eyes glazed over as her skeletal arms flayed and struggled against him. He seemed unfazed by it all as he looked up at Maggie. It was as if he didn't even notice Maggie's gun pointed at his chest. Instead, he held out his free hand and demanded, "If she doesn't have it, then you must. Hand over my mother's journal."

CHAPTER 77

Tully had a bad feeling about this whole mess. Yes, they had caught a rapist, but had they caught a murderer? The kid, Brandon—the tough guy, the asshole who beat up and raped young girls—broke down into a sniveling crybaby when they arrested him for the murders of Ginny Brier and Maria Leonetti. But now, as he and several agents followed Stephen Caldwell into the hotel where Everett was supposedly staying, now Tully wasn't too sure anymore.

The desk clerk had given them a card key. No questions were asked when the badges came out. Caldwell claimed he didn't know why Everett hadn't shown up at the park. There was something in the polite black man's manner that told Tully he was lying through his teeth. It didn't help matters that Caldwell himself seemed in a rush to get somewhere when they finally found him outside the pavilion, gathering certain members together. No, Tully had a feeling this Caldwell, this stool-pigeon asshole, had his own agenda. Now he wondered if they were wasting time. If that was also Caldwell's agenda. Was the hotel a distraction? Was Everett on his way to some airfield?

The elevator opened at the fifteenth floor and Caldwell hesitated. Agents Rizzo and Markham gave him a shove, not even bothering to wait for Tully's instructions. They were pissed, too. None of them had to say a word to one another to know something was not quite right.

Caldwell hesitated again at the hotel room door, and Tully noticed the man's hand tremble as he missed the slot for the card key twice. Finally the door unlocked.

Rizzo and Markham had their weapons drawn but at their sides. Tully gave Caldwell another shove for the man to go in ahead of them. He could see the perspiration glistening on his forehead, but Caldwell opened the door and entered.

Caldwell came to an abrupt halt, and Tully could see he was just as surprised as the rest of them. In the center of the room, Reverend Everett sat in a chair, his wrists handcuffed, his mouth taped shut and his dead eyes staring directly at them. Tully didn't need a medical examiner for this one. He recognized the pinkish tint to the skin and would need only one guess. Cause of death would be cyanide poisoning.

CHAPTER 78

"Just let her go," Maggie said, not flinching, keeping the gun pointed directly at Garrison's head.

"You have the fucking book, don't you?" His eyes held hers while his hand tightened the noose around the old woman's neck. Maggie heard her sputter, and out of the corner of her eye she could see her bent and misshapen fingers clawing at the clothesline, clawing at her own neck.

"Yes, I have it." She wouldn't move, even to give him the book. "Let her go and I'll give it to you."

"Oh, right!" He laughed, but it was a nervous, angry laugh. "I let her go, you give me the book and we both just go our separate ways. What do you think! I'm some fucking idiot?"

"Of course not." A few more minutes and none of it would matter. The old woman was gasping, her fingers making a pathetic attempt. Maggie knew she could take him but it would need to be a head shot and there could be no missing. But then they'd never have all the answers.

"It makes sense now," she told him instead, hoping to distract him. "Everett's your father. That's why you wanted to destroy him."

"Not my father. Just a sperm donor," he said. Suddenly he yanked the woman up in front of him, as if only now realizing he needed a shield and taking away Maggie's clean head shot. "I can't do anything about biology, but I could make sure that fucker paid for what he did to my mother."

"And all those women," Maggie said calmly. "Why did they have to pay? Why did they have to die?"

"Oh, that." He laughed again and got a better twist on the clothesline. "It was a study, an experiment...an assignment. You might say for the greater good."

"Like father, like son?"

"What the hell are you talking about?"

"Everett stole lost souls. You wanted to capture them, too. Only on film."

"We are nothing alike," he insisted, a rash of red spreading across his face and betraying his calm. She had struck a nerve.

"You're more alike than you want to believe." Maggie watched closely as he listened, his fingers forgetting as he did so. "Even your DNA was close enough to throw us off. We thought Everett killed those girls."

He smiled, pleased by this. "I really did have everyone fooled, didn't I?"

"Yes," Maggie said, playing along. "You certainly did."

"And I have photos of his unfortunate demise. Just got back from Cleveland with the exclusive." He waved a free hand at the duffel bag on the counter that separated the kitchen from the living room.

He pulled the old woman with him, getting close to the bag. She was breathing more steadily now. Garrison seemed unaware of the loosened noose as he tried to find his precious film. "Haven't decided yet who I'll give the exclusive to. Looks like it might be a bigger story than I thought. Especially now. Now that you're here. Now that you've changed everything."

He didn't seem angry about this. No, he seemed resigned. Perhaps he was just as happy to be caught, so that he could finally share all his illicit photos, all those horrible images, and get the credit, receive the fame—no matter what the cost—just to stroke his overactive ego. It wasn't that unusual. Maggie had known of other serial killers who purposely got caught, just to show off their handiwork, just to make sure they didn't go unrecognized.

She found herself releasing the tension in her arm. She kept the gun pointed at him, but her trigger finger relaxed. Garrison's mind was preoccupied, his only concern on the film, on his fame.

"Three fucking rolls in living color," he said, reaching into the duffel bag as if to show her, dragging the old woman with him.

She expected to see black film canisters. The pistol was in his hand and he fired before she could duck. It ripped through her shoulder, knocking her into the wall. She tried to regain her balance. Instead, she felt her body sliding down the wall. She couldn't move her arm. Tried to raise her gun. The arm and the gun wouldn't move.

Garrison was pleased.

"Yes, looks like I'll be very famous, indeed," he said, smiling. Then he shoved the woman aside and at the same time raised the gun.

"No!" Maggie screamed at him.

In one smooth, easy movement he shot the old woman. Her small body slammed against the wall with a sickening snap of bones and flesh as her body crumpled into a heap.

Maggie tried to raise her own gun again. Damn it! She

couldn't feel her fingers. She couldn't even feel the gun. It was still gripped in her hand, but she couldn't feel it, couldn't move it. The bullet had paralyzed her arm from shoulder to fingers.

He came at her, his gun aimed at her chest. She needed to lift the goddamn gun. She needed to point, to squeeze, but her arm wasn't obeying. Just as she reached for her weapon with her left hand, Garrison was there, standing above her. His black boot kicked at her useless fingers, knocking the gun out and sending it skidding across the floor.

There was a stinging pain in the side of her neck, but still no feeling in her right arm. She could feel blood trickling down her sleeve and could see several spots on the floor. She still couldn't move the goddamn hand.

"Where's the book?" he said, standing over her. Then he saw it in her jacket pocket and pointed at it.

"You'll need to get it yourself," she told him. "I honestly can't move." She would make him get it. She still had one good hand. She could grab him, grab the gun.

But he didn't make a move toward her. In fact, he no longer seemed to care about the precious book. He glanced back at the old woman, then looked around his apartment as if assessing the damage, as if trying to decide what his next move should be.

"You keep it," he said, to Maggie's surprise, and he went back to the kitchen counter, rummaging through his duffel bag. "Just remember it goes with the photos," he told her as he took out several black canisters and set them on the counter. "This can't be anything less than a front-page exclusive—above the fold, continued inside."

Then he started bringing out the rest, and Maggie's stomach took a plunge. Out came the handcuffs, duct tape, more clothesline, a camera and another collapsible tripod. She tried her feet. What the hell was he doing? She steadied herself and eased herself up, using the wall as an anchor and her good arm to balance her. Garrison swung back around, gun pointed and ready, stopping her in half-stance.

"It's best you stay right where you are," he said, grabbing the handcuffs. "Back down." He pointed to the floor, and moved in front of her, waiting as she eased her body down the wall.

He snapped the handcuffs on, pinching the wrist of her already wounded hand. And still she could not feel it. He shoved her shoulders against the wall, as if straightening her posture, carefully posing her with restrained hands in her lap. It was all a part of the staged look. He was preparing her for her own death photo.

He took the extra length of clothesline and bound her feet, pulling her legs out in front of her, safely away from her hands. Then he dropped three of the film canisters into her jacket pocket, so that now she had the film in one pocket and the book, his mother's journal, in the other.

"They'll be sending backup here any minute, Garrison," she told him, trying desperately to remember if she had told anyone about stopping at his apartment. But she hadn't. Not even Gwen. The old woman was the only one who knew.

"Why would you need backup?" He wasn't even concerned, almost humored by the idea. "You said yourself, everyone is convinced that Everett is the murderer. He and his accomplice Brandon. Poor boy. His Achilles' heel is that he doesn't know how to fuck a woman."

Garrison was back at the counter. He spoke with no sense of panic, no sense of urgency. Instead, he put the gun down and began assembling the tripod with careful, deliberate movements. "This isn't exactly what I had in mind," he said almost absently as if talking to himself now. "But what better way to go out than with one last hurrah."

She needed to do something. He was setting the tripod up five feet directly in front of her, just as he had done with each of his victims.

"Yes, you really did have us all fooled," she told him, hoping to get the attention of his overworked ego while she scanned the surroundings. Her gun lay against the opposite wall, about ten feet away. Too far away. With her hands in front—well, one good hand—she could grab something, anything and use it as a weapon. Her eyes searched. A lamp to her left. In the messy pile of clothing, a belt with a buckle. On the coffee table, some kind of African pottery.

Garrison snapped a new roll of film into the camera. Not much time. Damn it! She needed to concentrate. Needed to think. Needed to ignore the throbbing in her shoulder and the blood that continued to trickle down her sleeve. The camera was loaded. He began attaching it to the tripod and then unwinding some sort of cable, plugging one end in to the camera. A trip-cable, a release cable—that's what it was—so he could snap the picture from several feet away. He didn't need to be behind the camera, he didn't need to even touch the camera. He could be strangling her into unconsciousness while he shot the picture.

She shifted her back closer to the wall. How long would it take to bend her knees? To shove against the wall and get to her feet? Even with them tied together, she could do it. But how long would it take?

He was checking the camera's sight, tilting the tripod's platform to adjust the camera's angle. Maggie tried to ignore his preparations, his ritual, trying not to be alarmed by his calculating calm, by his steady and intent hands. Instead, her mind raced. Her eyes darted. Her damn arm throbbed and so did her heart, filling her ears with the constant thump, threatening to dismantle her thought process.

"I'll go down in history for sure," Garrison mumbled, adjusting shutter speed, assessing, then twisting the camera's lens. Focusing, making another change. Readjusting the aperture. Checking again, preparing.

Maggie edged her knees up toward her chest, quietly,

slowly. Garrison was too involved to notice, at times his back to her, blocking her view of the camera. He seemed lost in his process. He was quickly becoming the invisible cameraman.

"No one has attempted this. A self-portrait along with a fleeting soul caught on film…all in the timing." His voice continued, his words becoming a sort of mantra of encouragement to himself. "And the angle," he said. "It's definitely the timing and the angle. Oh, yes, I'll be famous. That's for sure. Beyond my wildest dreams. Beyond my mother's dreams." He was caught up in the process, forgetting his victim, or rather reducing her to just another subject, waiting—hopelessly waiting to become a part of his bizarre process.

But Maggie wasn't waiting. She scooted her feet up, straining to be quiet, straining to pull them up as close as possible. Just a little more. Close enough. Yes, she could reach the clothesline. But not the knot. She shifted her weight and a pain shot through her arm, stopping her, almost bringing her to tears. Damn it!

She checked on Garrison. He was unwinding the cable, untangling it as he marched back to the counter. Jesus! He was almost ready. She tried for the knot again, her fingers reaching, her wrists scraping against the metal of the handcuffs. If she could get her feet free she might have some defense when he came at her, ready to strangle her. With the pain throbbing in her arm, she knew consciousness would be difficult to hang on to. She couldn't let him get that far. She couldn't let the clothesline even get around her neck, or else—or else she would be gone.

He stood at the counter, the air bulb of the release cable in one hand. Maggie watched him pick up the gun in his other hand. Her entire body froze. He wasn't going to use the clothesline. Was he actually considering the gun, instead?

He turned to face her. Her knees stayed at her chest. Her fingers stopped at the knot. It didn't matter that he noticed. It was too late. He was ready. And suddenly the rest of her body had become as paralyzed as her right arm. Even her mind came screeching to a halt.

Without a word he walked toward her, carefully dragging the cable. He stood directly in front of her, hovering over her, less than a foot away. He looked back at the camera, checking the angle. He readjusted the cable in his hand, positioning between his thumb and index finger the small plastic bulb—the gizmo that with one quick squeeze would click the photo.

He was ready.

"Just remember," he told her without taking his sight off the camera lens, "front-page exclusive."

Before she could move, before she could react, Garrison lifted the gun barrel to his right temple. Both hands squeezed, trigger and air bulb in morbid unison. Maggie closed her eyes to the spray of blood and brain matter, hitting her in the face, splatting against the wall. The sound of the camera's shutter got lost in the explosion of the gun. The smell of discharge filled the air.

When she opened her eyes, it was just in time to see Garrison's body thump to the floor in front of her. His eyes remained open. But they were already empty. Ben Garrison's own soul, Maggie decided, had left long before this, long before his death.

MONDAY
December 2
Washington, D.C.

Maggie waited outside the police chief's conference room. She leaned her head against the wall. Her neck still ached, even more than the shoulder she had in a sling. Tully sat quietly next to her, staring at the door as though willing it to open, ignoring the newspaper he had spread out on his lap. The front-page headline of the *Washington Times* spoke of yet another new and improved piece of airport security equipment. Somewhere below the fold was a sidebar story about a photojournalist's suicide.

Tully caught her glancing at the newspaper. "*Cleveland Plain Dealer* kept Everett's suicide below the fold, too," he said, as if reading his partner's mind. "Probably would have made top headlines if there had been photos to go along with the stories."

"Yes." Maggie nodded. "Too bad there were no available photos."

He gave her one of his looks, the raised brow and the unconvincing frown. "But there *were* photos."

"Unfortunately, they're considered evidence. We certainly can't release photos that are considered evidence, right? Aren't you always trying to get me to play by the rules?"

At this, he smiled. "So this evidence is being stored in a proper place?"

She simply nodded again, sitting back and adjusting her sling. It was her own personal attempt at justice—that Ben Garrison's horrifying images would not win him the notoriety he so longed for. A notoriety that he had become so obsessed with that he had even been willing to include himself as one of those horrifying images.

"Have you heard from Emma?" Maggie asked, a transparent attempt at getting Tully to put an end to the subject of evidence, of photos and film canisters that remained safely stashed in her file cabinet back at her Quantico office.

"She's staying an extra week with her mom," he answered, folding the newspaper and willingly abandoning the subject along with the newspaper next to a pile of outdated *Newsweek*s on the table beside him. "She invited Alice to stay with them. She wanted to invite Justin Pratt, too."

"Really? What did Caroline have to say about that?"

"I don't think Caroline would have cared. The house is huge, but I said no boys allowed." He smiled as if he was glad he had some say. "Didn't really matter, though. As soon as Justin heard about Eric, he wanted to be in Boston."

"So there are actually some happy endings to this, after all?"

As the words left her mouth, Maggie saw her mother coming down the hall. She was dressed in a conservative brown suit, wore heels and makeup and was drawing a few looks from police officers in the hall and doorways. Her mother looked good, in control, not at all like some lost soul, and yet Maggie felt her muscles tense and her stomach knot.

"Hello, Mrs. O'Dell," Tully said, standing. He offered her his chair and she sat next to Maggie with only a nod to her daughter and a quiet "thank you" to Tully.

"I think I'm gonna get some coffee," Tully said. "Can I get a cup for either of you?"

"Yes, please," Kathleen O'Dell said with a smile. "With cream."

He was waiting. "Maggie? How 'bout a Diet Pepsi?"

She glanced up at him and shook her head, but caught his eyes to show him she appreciated the gesture. He simply nodded and started down the hall.

"I'm not sure why you're here," Maggie said, looking straight ahead, following her mother's lead.

"I wanted to be here to put in a good word." Then as if she remembered something, she set her purse on her lap, opened it and removed an envelope. She hesitated, tapping it against her hand. She set the purse back down. More tapping. Then she handed the envelope to Maggie with only a glance.

"What's this?"

"For when you're ready," her mother said in a soft, gentle voice that made Maggie look over at her. "It's his name, address and phone number."

The knot in Maggie's stomach twisted even tighter. She looked away and laid the envelope in her lap. She wanted to hand it back and forget about it. And yet at the same time, she couldn't wait to open it. "What is his name?" she asked.

"Patrick." Her mother managed a smile. "After Thomas's brother. I think your father would have liked that."

The door opened, startling both women. Chief Henderson held it open while Julia Racine stepped out, her face immediately showing surprise at seeing Maggie and her mother. Today the detective wore a well-pressed navy suit and heels, her blond hair tamed and styled. She was even wearing lipstick.

"Agent O'Dell? Mrs. O'Dell?" Racine made an effort to hide her astonishment and be polite. Maggie couldn't help thinking the detective would have felt more comfortable asking what the hell the two of them were doing. But Racine was on her best behavior this morning. She had better be. Henderson wasn't taking any of these discipline hearings lightly.

"We'll hear from you first, Agent O'Dell," Henderson said, still holding the door, waiting.

Maggie could feel Racine watching, wondering whose side she would take. She stopped in front of her, met Racine's questioning eyes and said, "You mind keeping my mom distracted, just one more time?"

She waited for Racine's smile, then she walked past Chief Henderson and into the conference room.

'Somewhere out there is a monster and he's even more hideous than me'

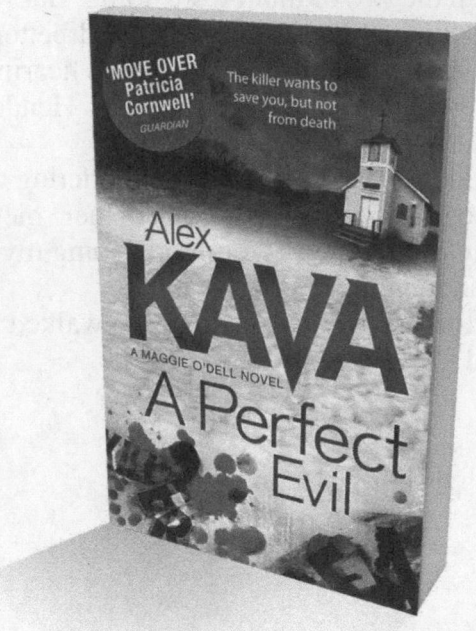

'MOVE OVER Patricia Cornwell'
GUARDIAN

The killer wants to save you, but not from death

Alex **KAVA**

A MAGGIE O'DELL NOVEL

A Perfect Evil

On 17th July convicted serial killer Ronald Jeffreys was executed for the murders of three innocent boys. Three months later, the body of another boy is found butchered in the same style.

Cold-blooded copy-cat or the real thing— there's a killer on the loose and someone will atone for his sins...

HARLEQUIN®MIRA®
www.mirabooks.co.uk

The line between good and evil can be crossed in a SPLIT SECOND

They called him the Collector—and now he's on
the loose again…

Criminal profiler Maggie O'Dell had been instrumental
in putting Albert Stucky, the notorious Collector, away, so
named for his ritual of collecting victims before disposing of
them in the most heinous ways possible. Since then, O'Dell
has lost her edge, tortured by the nightmares and
guilt for the ones she couldn't save.

But as the death toll increases, Maggie becomes the FBI's
best hope to hunt this man down. Only she can see into
this psychopath's twisted mind. And Albert Stucky
wouldn't have it any other way.

In the tomb-like silence of an abandoned quarry, someone is trying to hide their dirty little secrets...

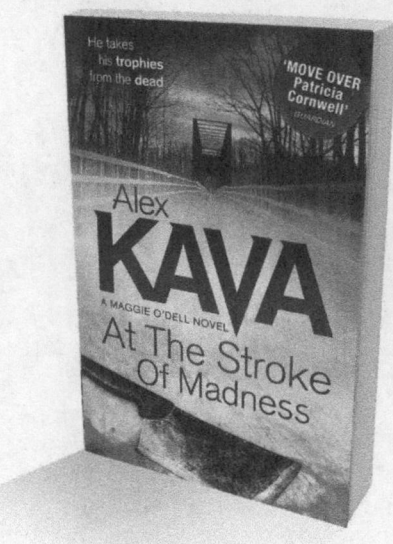

When Special Agent Maggie O'Dell receives a concerned phone call from Dr Gwen Patterson about a missing patient, she agrees to look into the woman's disappearance.

At first she dismisses Gwen's fears, but then a graveyard of bodies is discovered in rusted barrels buried in a rock quarry.

Is there a link between the missing patient and the horrifying murders?

HARLEQUIN® MIRA®
www.mirabooks.co.uk